HUMAN SISTER

Copyright © 2010 by Jim Bainbridge
All rights reserved

Printed in the United States of America
Published in the United States by Silverthought Press
www.silverthought.com

No part of this book may be used or reproduced in any manner whatsoever without written permission, except in the case of brief quotations embodied in critical articles or reviews.

All characters in this publication are fictitious, and any resemblance to real persons, living or dead, is purely coincidental.

ISBN: 978-0-9841738-2-2

[silverthought]
Philadelphia | New York

HUMAN SISTER

A NOVEL BY

JIM BAINBRIDGE

Acknowledgements

I am deeply grateful to the following readers who supplied encouragement and insightful comments along the way: Paulette Alden, Jean Bainbridge, Dan Fingarette, Jennifer Itell, Benjamin Matthew, Laura Pritchett, Amanda Rea, Jim Song, and Mark Wisniewski.

Many thanks to Paul Evan Hughes for his sensitive, wise, and enthusiastic editing.

Thanks also to the editors of the following journals in which portions of this book have appeared: *LIT*, *Roanoke Review*, *Santa Fe Literary Review*, *South Carolina Review*, *Thin Air*, and *Two Review*.

The quote from Martin Luther on page 261 is from Luther's *Werke*, Erlanger ed., as quoted in Johannes Janssen, *History of the German People at the Close of the Middle Ages*, Vol. III, 211-212, trans. A. M. Christie (London: Kegan, Paul, Trench, Trübner & Co., 1900).

To my closest friend, Dan Fingarette,
whose contributions to this book have been invaluable.

Sara

On the morning of what turned out to be a foreboding New Year's Eve, the man to my right on the flight home from Calgary began a friendly conversation as soon as I took my window seat. He was attractive, polite, articulate, and well-dressed in a light blue suit with red pinstripes. During the course of our short flight to San Francisco, he asked how old I was (he said that in three months his son would be sixteen, too), what I was studying in school (he thought that Grandpa's style of homeschooling me was interesting, but didn't I think I was missing something by not having any classmates?), where I lived (he seemed especially curious as to why I was being raised by my grandparents on a vineyard in Sonoma's Russian River Valley rather than by my parents in Canada), and so on. But as the plane began its descent into the Bay Area, his questions became more pointed.

Why was my finger in a cast?

"I broke it."

What kind of work did my parents do?

"They design robotic instruments, primarily for medical use."

Did I think it possible that there still were some androids in Canada?

Here, I felt the conversation was veering off into dangerous territory. "If you don't mind," I said, "I'd like to listen to my voicemail before we land."

I adjusted the earphones and immediately heard the rhythmic push and glide, *schzz... schzz... schzz...*, of Elio's blades on the smoothly frozen surface of Keizersgracht in Amsterdam. It had been ten days since I last hugged him as he was about to board a plane in Calgary, and after what seemed like such a long separation, merely the thought of him sent a brief *schzz* through my body.

Elio began describing the frozen canal and the many people, old and young, who were out skating, bundled up in brightly colored winter clothes. His words "I miss you so much" and his heavy breathing came through heartwarmingly clear over the background sounds of children's laughing and squealing in delight.

The plane shuddered as it touched down. I clicked off the recording I'd listened to repeatedly during the past couple of days and looked out the window. San Francisco was overcast, wet, and cold on New Year's Eve morning, but Elio had called about an hour earlier to say that he had just arrived from Amsterdam, and I imagined that inside the terminal he and Grandpa waited with warm arms.

I had just begun to raise my hands to remove my earphones when I noticed that the man to my right was staring at me. I feared that he was intent on starting up our conversation where it had left off, so, trying not to be too impolite, I quickly turned my head to look out the window and clicked the recording back on.

Elio said that winter in the Netherlands had so far been quite cold and everyone there was excited about the possibility of having the 200-kilometer Elfstedentocht ice-skating marathon in Friesland, a traditional event that hadn't been held in over thirty years due to global warming. His former schoolmates wanted him to stay for the race, but he'd declined. "I'll be home to celebrate New Year's Eve with you, Sara," he said,

"Elfstedentocht or no Elfstedentocht."

People began standing in the aisle and reaching into the overhead bins to retrieve their belongings. I again clicked off the recording and, without looking in the direction of the man beside me, began packing my earphones into my carry-on bag.

It was then I noticed the man wasn't moving. I fumbled with my bag, arranging and rearranging its contents, all the while avoiding eye contact with him. When people from rows behind us began walking past our row and he still hadn't made any effort to stand, I turned to him and said, "May I get up, please?"

"There's no rush, is there?"

I clenched my carry-on in my lap and watched as the last passengers walked past our row of seats. "Please, sir. Grandpa will be waiting for me. Please let me out."

"Is Elio waiting for you, too?" A thin smile appeared on his face.

I turned toward the window with a start. Elio's name had not been mentioned during our conversation. Blood throbbed in my neck. Was I being kidnapped?

As I'd rehearsed many times when I was a child, I pressed the "5" key on my teleband five times, then the "enter" key five times, all within five seconds. A tiny green light appeared above the time display, indicating that the band was signaling Sakato (our private security service), Grandpa and Grandma (on their telebands), and Gatekeeper that I perceived some immediate grave danger. Within seconds, Gatekeeper would alert Michael, who would deposit a catalyst along the invisible seams of the door in my bedroom wall. The door would open. Michael would quickly gather up everything indicative of his existence—his computer chips, nutriosynthesizer, bedpan—and with this cache in hand, he would crawl into the wall, and the door would close into its self-healing seams, ensuring his safe immurement until the threat was resolved.

My teleband would also activate a transmitter that had been implanted in the fleshy part of the backside of my knee before I was first permitted to venture into the vineyard beyond the security wall surrounding my grandparents' home. The transmitter would emit tracing signals until I was rescued—or until it was discovered by my captors.

I reached up and pushed the red "call" button on the ceiling above my seat. The man didn't move to stop me or to turn it off. Instead, he said, "You seem anxious. Are you hiding something?"

"Who are you?" I asked, trying not to appear frightened. "What do you want?"

"My name is Randy Smith. I'm an agent with the FBI."

"May I help you?" asked a flight attendant, who came from the back of the plane.

"This man is holding me against my will."

The man smiled, calmly took a badge out of his suit coat pocket, and handed it to the flight attendant. "Randall Smith, Special Agent. A colleague and I would like to question this young lady about an important matter."

"Don't believe him! I think he's trying to kidnap me!"

"Please check with your security people," the man said. "There should be another agent at the gate."

"Oh... well... I guess—" the attendant stammered. "Please. Both of you remain seated while I check this out."

"Take your time," the man said in the same friendly, assuring voice he'd used at the beginning of our conversation.

The flight attendant walked away, turning several times to glance back at us as she made her way to the front of the plane. The man beside me sat calmly, his hands folded in his lap. The flight attendant spoke with another flight attendant, pointed toward us, then disappeared behind a partition.

"We'll wait here until everyone figures out what's what," the man said. "Then we'll go to a more comfortable place inside and talk."

I stared out the window, my mind spinning with questions: Where was Grandpa? Elio? Were they safe? Were they coming for me? What was happening? Then I heard sirens and, within seconds, saw flashing lights of several airport and private security cars racing toward the plane. Guards jumped out of the cars and crouched down, guns drawn. One man reading a scanner pointed up toward me. I put my face against the window, hoping to be seen.

"I see your grandfather can still raise quite a ruckus when he puts his mind to it," the man beside me said. "It'll be interesting to trace how you alerted him." He reclined back into his seat, and I began to fear that he was who he claimed to be—which meant, I knew, that he was someone from whom not even Grandpa could rescue me.

I again pressed my face to the window and tried to control my anxiety by focusing on what was happening outside. Through the far right edge of the little window, I noticed a barrel-chested man in a dark gray suit descend narrow stairs leading from the jetway to the tarmac. Grandpa was right behind him, followed by Elio. The man in the suit headed toward the security car. He walked robustly, giving the impression of strength and conviction of purpose. He waved his arms and shouted something I couldn't hear at the guard who held the scanner.

Soon, the man, the guard, Grandpa, and Elio were huddled together. They talked animatedly for a short time before Elio lunged at the man in the suit. Grandpa grabbed Elio and pushed him toward the back door of the security car. Grandpa opened the car door and motioned for Elio to get in. Elio shook his head and stiffened his shoulders but finally complied.

Grandpa walked back and resumed speaking with the two men. The security cars began leaving. Grandpa returned to the car in which Elio waited, opened the door, and pointed toward me. Elio stood up out of the car and, evidently catching sight of me, began waving. He was wearing the Italian-made jacket with a lapis lazuli pattern that friends in Amsterdam had given him for Christmas. He waved until Grandpa placed an arm around his shoulders and said something to him. Then he put his fingers to his lips, blew a kiss my way, and he and Grandpa got into the security car, which sped off.

"There, now," the man sitting beside me said. "It looks like everyone's figured out what's what." He reached down and took hold of my carry-on. "I'll take care of this for you. Please give me your boarding pass. I'll have someone claim your checked luggage."

He took the bag onto his lap, and I handed him my pass. He stood and gestured for me to enter the aisle ahead of him. As I did, the man in the dark suit entered the plane. He walked briskly toward us and stopped in front of me.

"This is Mr. Casey," Smith said. "He's also a member of the investigating team."

This short but powerful looking man with deep-set gray eyes acknowledged me with a minatory scowl. "I'll take the bag," he said. "Where's the boarding pass?"

Smith handed him the bag and the pass. Casey took them and walked away.

I retrieved my jacket from the overhead bin and walked out of the plane ahead of Smith. In the jetway, a woman held open a door and indicated I should go through it. I stepped, trembling now, through the door, followed by Smith, and down the stairs leading to the airfield where Casey was waiting in a car.

Casey drove us to another terminal where Smith and I got out of the car and entered a door marked IMMIGRATION: AUTHORIZED PERSONNEL ONLY. Smith took me to a small room furnished in a manner appropriate for a doctor's office: examination table, two chairs, body scanner, washbasin, red biohazard container, dispensers for examination gloves and paper towels, and cabinets below a working surface on which a computer monitor sat. In the far wall was another door.

"Immigration didn't give us the most comfortable room," Smith said, "but we'll make do. Hopefully, this won't take long. Please, have a seat."

I hung my coat on the back of one of the chairs and sat. He asked whether I was comfortable. I nodded. He asked whether I would like something to drink. I shook my head. He moved the second chair in front of me and sat.

"Well, then, let's get started. This room is usually used to examine suspected smugglers who try to hide drugs and other illegal items in every conceivable part of their bodies. Kind of a cat-and-mouse game. Here, the cat always wins. But we don't suspect you of anything like that. In fact, you can relax because we don't suspect you of any wrongdoing whatsoever. We know you're a nice, intelligent, and law-abiding young woman. Maybe someday you'll be a famous scientist, like your grandfather."

I remembered something Grandpa had said about how government interrogations usually begin: They disguise themselves as flowers so the bees and butterflies will come.

Smith uncrossed his legs and leaned toward me. "What we're concerned about is that some people you might have come in contact with on your trip to Calgary may be involved in activities detrimental to the security of the United States. So, what I'd like to do is get a clear picture of everything you did and everyone you saw from the time you left here a couple of weeks ago. Okay?"

I focused my eyes on his knees, which he then covered with his hands.

"All right. Let's start with your departure from here on Air Canada, flight 2711. You went with Elio. Right?"

His fingers began tapping on his knees. Then, in a soothing

voice he said, "Sara, please don't be afraid to talk with me. I'm not trying to get you or Elio in any kind of trouble. I'm simply asking for your help."

I didn't look up. He recrossed his legs.

"Okay, let's move on. When you arrived in Calgary, you were picked up by your parents, right?"

I kept my gaze frozen on one of his knees, and my mind concentrated on one thought: No matter what, I'll give no response.

He stood and began pacing. "Come, come, now. I like you. We had a nice chat on the plane. I have a boy nearly your age. I know you're inclined to resist authority at your age, but you want to do the right thing, don't you?"

I fixed my eyes on a leg of his chair.

"Sara, you're a U.S. citizen, just like me, and one of the things we have to do, whether we like it or not, is abide by the laws of our country, laws that were created and approved by people like you and me. One of those laws is that we must cooperate with FBI investigations, whether we understand and agree with their purposes or not. You're an intelligent young woman. You understand that." He paused a moment. "Sara, you must talk with me. If you don't, Casey will come in here and take over. Neither one of us wants that to happen, I assure you."

I moved deeper into calmness and into my conviction not to answer.

"All right. I know you're a real smart kid, so you know why we're here and want me just to get to the point. My boy tells me that all the time. 'Dad, you're home now. Don't turn everything into an investigation. Just get to the point.'" He chuckled. "That's another thing about you teenagers that's so funny—you have all the time in the world, but you're so impatient. Right?"

I continued detaching myself from the situation, finding stillness in my slow, steady breathing.

"Okay. I'll get to the point. We're concerned about the activities of androids in Canada. We know one of them you called 'First Brother' frequently visited you when you were a child. We also know your parents smuggled it and another android out of the country eight years ago. Well, 'smuggled' perhaps isn't the right word. It was arguably legal back then. Anyway, we're not concerned about that. We're concerned about what those androids are doing now. Did you meet with this First Brother or any other android on your visit to Calgary?"

His words merely drifted through me.

"Sara, I want you to understand something. Personally, I don't dislike androids. So far, they seem to have behaved themselves. But as I said, I'm a U.S. citizen like you, so I have to abide by the laws, just as you do, as everyone does. I'm also a government employee who has to help enforce the laws. You understand that, don't you?"

You can no more draw me in, I thought, than radio waves can make the trees sing.

"I want you to understand how I feel because I like you and respect your opinions, even the ones differing from the majority of Americans. You see, I don't much care for the anti-android laws either, but like you, I have no choice except to respect them. If we in the FBI could pick and choose which laws to enforce and which laws not to enforce, we would effectively be making or vetoing the laws of the land. We would be, in effect, a quasi-legislature. Now, I don't think you would want the FBI making the laws of the land, would you? I'm sure I wouldn't."

Remember Nuremberg, I thought.

Smith sat down on his chair, then extended his hands, palms up. "Sara, take my hands. Please. I promise I won't hurt you."

I saw no harm in this and laid my palms on top of his. In my mind I saw a white butterfly, its wings aquiver, light on a pink rose petal.

"Look at me, please."

I looked up at him. When our eyes met, he smiled. Had I met him under normal circumstances, I would have felt that he was a kind man. Perhaps he was.

"Sara, please listen to me carefully. There's an ongoing investigation into the whereabouts and activities of androids. The law is that you must cooperate with this investigation. There are ways, painful ways, to make you talk. And you will talk. Everyone does. It's just a question of how much you'll put yourself through before you beg to talk. Please don't make me leave this room without your statement. If you do, your unimaginable pain will be a torture not only to yourself but also to me and to Elio and your grandparents. Please, don't do that to yourself. Don't do that to us. Talk to me. Please."

I began pulling my hands away from his. He quickly turned his hands over and caught mine. "Ask for me when you want to talk. Just say my name, Randy Smith, and I'll come back quickly and take away the pain."

I pulled my hands back and didn't look up or answer. After a few seconds, he sighed, then slowly got up and left the room.

I brought to my mind's eye the grape leaf I used for self-hypnosis, seeing the intricate venation of its underside, and above it, a sky, calm and blue and streaked with cirrus, like wisps of hair from Grandma's comb. But I didn't proceed to the hypnotic countdown; I didn't need to, not yet. I just wanted to be sure the leaf was there, and after seeing it, I returned to a meditative calm.

The door opened. Casey walked briskly to the chair in which Smith had sat. I focused on his legs in their dark gray trousers. Suddenly, the chair swung around, its back cracking hard against one of my kneecaps. I tried not to wince. Casey sat, straddling the straight-backed chair.

"Didn't that hurt?" he asked. "You on something?"

Interesting how different are the many sensations of pain, I thought. They're all my friends, trying in their way to help me.

"Doc, get in here!"

A man wearing black shoes, black socks, charcoal trousers, and a long white coat entered the room and stood beside me.

"Take a sample," Casey ordered. "We need to know if she's on something."

The doctor pricked my finger and drew a spot of blood. As he was leaving he said, "I'll let you know in five, ten minutes, max."

"Okay, let's start at the beginning," Casey said to me. "What's your name?"

"Sara Jensen," I answered, without looking up at him.

I was surprised and upset at how my answering this question, a question Grandpa had told me I could answer, seemed to pull me out of the quiet place I'd been in.

"So, you can talk. Good. We're moving right along. You went to Calgary before Christmas with Elio, right?"

Breathe slowly, deeply, I thought. Feel yourself moving away from him.

"Okay. We know you can hear. We know you can talk. Now, we're going to hear you answer my questions without all this fucking around. You went to Calgary with Elio. Right?"

He rapped his thick, hairy fingers on the back of his chair, then reached into his suit coat pocket and pulled out a packet of photographs. "Looky what we got here. It's you and your love sitting together on a flight to Calgary. Oh, and here. You and him at Calgary Zoo with your father and your lovely, sweet mother. Now, look at this one—it's my absolute favorite. Warms my heart. The two of you hugging at Calgary International just before he boards a plane to Amsterdam to go see his mother. And he's crying. How sweet."

They've decided to play good-guy, bad-guy with me, I

thought. Ridiculous!

He shuffled through the pictures—there were about thirty—then continued, "You get the picture. We've done our homework. Now, back to my question. You went to Calgary a couple of weeks ago with this sweet guy, Elio, right? I understand he likes men, too."

Following a spike of fear—or was it hatred?—I forced myself to breathe deeply, slowly. Don't let him rile you, I silently instructed.

"So, you want to be a smart-ass, do you?" With the suddenness of an explosion, he hurled himself up off his chair. "Do you?" he shouted in my ear.

I gave a little start but said nothing.

"Look here, this is no game of hide-and-seek for some spoiled little rich kid. Our country, our species, is in great danger from androids and from those who coddle them. And because of the magnitude of that danger, I really can be your worst nightmare. I've made people tougher, a lot tougher, than you or your grandfather or your hotheaded boyfriend whimper and beg and shit themselves."

He slammed his palm against the back of his chair. "Doc!" he shouted, and he stormed from the room.

This man did frighten me. I felt a strong urge to get up, try the door, and, if it opened, run away. But if I do, I thought, these people likely will break into our house and possibly find Michael, or they'll grab Elio or Grandpa or Grandma and interrogate them—and find Michael. No. I have to stay and fight. I'm the only one of us who has been trained to fight this kind of fight.

A few minutes later, the walls of the room shuddered as the door quickly opened.

"We've decided you're not on anything except a notion to be a stubborn smart-ass," Casey said, entering. "But we've got a cure for that, don't we, Doc?"

Casey carried a white pail and a jar containing about a half-liter of liquid. The doctor followed him, pulling along what looked like a portable toilet. "Now, you've got a choice," Casey said. "Either you can take your clothes off by yourself so the doctor can examine you for smuggled devices, or he'll do it for you. Which is it going to be?"

My first impulse was to recoil from the idea of undressing in front of these men. But I sensed that more difficult challenges lay ahead and any weakness I exhibited here would taint everything to come.

I unbuttoned my shirt and handed it to the doctor, who passed it on to Casey. Casey stuck two of his thick fingers into the front pocket, pinched along the collar and the seams, dropped the shirt on the floor and, using a side kick, sent it scooting into a corner of the room. "Hurry up," Casey said. "Off with the rest. The teleband, too. We don't have all day."

After I finished undressing, the doctor said, "All right, Ms. Jensen. Mr. Casey has determined that you may have illegally smuggled microdevices into the United States. What I'll ask you to do is lie down here"—he patted the top of the white-paper-covered exam table—"on your left side, and I'll administer a suppository. It's just a little thing. Won't hurt a bit."

Next, the doctor asked me to sit up on the edge of the table and drink the milky liquid from the jar Casey had brought in. The liquid was both a laxative and an emetic, the doctor said, useful for flushing out anything I was hiding in my digestive tract. As I drank, he secured the portable toilet to the floor using suction cups attached to the toilet's base. Then he positioned the white pail in front of the toilet, picked up my clothes and shoes, and left.

Casey gave me a pleased smirk and pointed first to the toilet—"Shit here"—then to the pail—"Puke there. Got it?"

I nodded. My insides had already begun rumbling.

"Good. We'll be back in about twenty minutes. Have fun."

"How are you feeling?" the doctor asked when he returned.

I felt ill and weakened by my digestive ordeal, but I didn't respond to the doctor's question. After a few seconds he said, "Drink this. It'll make you feel much better." He handed me a glass containing a cloudy liquid. Though I still felt nauseated, I drank the liquid, which tasted like salty lemonade, and almost instantly my insides settled down.

"Feeling better?"

"Thank you," I said, handing the glass back to him.

He looked surprised that I'd spoken. "You're welcome." After a moment he added, "I'm sorry to have made you feel so sick, but that's an unfortunate part of my job. Some people really do try to bring in nasty stuff, you know. Do you feel good enough to stand? There's a shower in there where you can clean up." He pointed toward the door in the back wall of the room.

He told me the stream of water in the shower was set to last only two minutes, so I washed quickly. There was no soap. I presumed that the shower water—chemicals evidently had been added to it, as it stung a bit—would be tested for microdevices that might have been clinging to my skin. When the water stopped, the doctor opened the shower door, asked me to step out, and handed me a towel. Casey had entered the room. He sat on a chair, looking bored. The pail and portable toilet were gone.

"Lie down on your back on the table," the doctor instructed, resuming a more professional tone of voice. "We'll take a scan of your body. Please place your arms and hands on the table beside you."

Using a wand-like device, he began the scan at my feet and slowly worked up. I was careful not to show any emotion as, with a faint hiss, the beige wand of the scanner passed over my nose. I was concerned that irregularities in my cribriform plate and the neural structures emanating from it might be detected.

"What's up with the finger?" Casey asked.

The doctor looked at the computer monitor. "It was broken, probably within the last thirty-six hours. Nothing unusual that I can see."

"If you knew the characters we're dealing with here, you'd know they easily might have broken her finger on purpose just to create a ruse for the cast. Remove it. We'll take it over to the lab. The ring, too."

The doctor took off the cast, then the ring, and they left.

"Tell me about the transmitter behind your right knee," Casey ordered as he entered again, the doctor in his wake.

I didn't answer. Casey turned to the doctor. "She failed to declare it, so remove it. No anesthetic."

"Please lie on your stomach, Ms. Jensen," the doctor said.

I felt his fingers press against the back of my knee and find a tiny lump; then came the sharp pain of a small knife cut. But I'd been prepared by Grandpa for much worse.

After a few seconds, the doctor said, "It looks like a standard transmitter used by private security companies. I'd say it was implanted when she was a small child. Many wealthy families implant them in—"

"I know. I know," Casey said. "Mike!"

"Yes, sir," a voice from the computer monitor answered.

"Bring in the inquisitor. We've also got an implanted device for you to look at."

"Right away," the voice responded.

"Turn her over on her back and strap her down," Casey ordered.

As the doctor secured the straps he said, "I wish you'd speak with Mr. Casey. He just wants to know what you did on your vacation. If you don't talk, I'm going to have to hook you up to a terrible device. I've seen it reduce the toughest gang members and terrorists to blubbering mush. It wasn't meant for nice cultured girls like you."

"It was meant to encourage people to talk in accordance with the law," Casey said. "This is a matter of national security, young lady, and the Supreme Court has made it very clear that national security outweighs individual constitutional rights every day of the week. So, if you're thinking some lawyer hired by your grandfather is going to ride in here on a white horse and rescue you, you can forget it."

No, I thought, but a grape leaf will come to carry me safely away.

Just then, a young man entered the room, wheeling in an apparatus that appeared to be almost identical to the algetor Grandpa had been training me on for years. Casey instructed the doctor to hook me up to what he repeatedly called the "inquisitor."

The helmet went on. The world went dark. I looked for the grape leaf. It was there for me, floating in a cirrus-frosted sky. I felt sticky straps being placed all over me. I concentrated on my breathing. Silently, calmly, I counted down from five and into a deep hypnosis where I felt safe and at peace.

As if from a great distance, I heard Casey becoming increasingly frustrated as he tried one gruesome illusion after another, each time calling for increased inquisitor intensity. I knew in a dissociated way that the level of induced pain was much greater than had been the highest level of pain induced by Grandpa's algetor, and I felt, also in a dissociated way, that my heart was beating faster and harder than normal. I reached deeper for calm.

"All right, Doc, what the fuck's going on? Are you holding back on me?"

"No. Absolutely not. I think she put herself into some kind

of trance."

"It's probably something that damn professor taught her. I'll bet he'd never get to level 3 without begging for mercy. As old as he is, though, his heart probably would stop before we could really get going. At least it would appear to be a natural death. Turn the damn thing off. Let's go make a call and see what we should do."

I heard them leave the room. Sensing something was wrong, I withdrew from the hypnotic state and found I was trembling all over. Never before had I had such a reaction to the algetor. Though there was a deep ache in my chest, my mind seemed clear, and I set about relaxing one set of muscles after another, starting with my fingers. After several failed attempts, the fingers calmed down, and I moved my attention to my right forearm. But before it relaxed, the fingers in my left hand began twitching again. I went back to them. The fingers in my right hand then began trembling, and I was back to square one. Despite these setbacks, by the time Casey and the doctor returned, my arms, shoulders, and legs had settled down.

The doctor spoke first. "Record. I have been ordered to inject 10 milligrams of LN27Q3 into a sixteen-year-old woman subsequent to an intense A59B6 session and immediately prior to another such session. Though LN27Q3 has been used before, it has never been adequately tested for safety. It is my medical opinion that when used in conjunction with A59B6, LN27Q3 is both unsafe and cruel. I will not proceed with this procedure unless ordered to do so by Agent 137H622. End record."

Casey immediately responded: "Record. I am ordering the doctor whose voice was just recorded to inject 10 milligrams of LN... what's the number?"

"LN27Q3."

"LN27Q3 into Sara Jensen prior to an A59B6 session. The doctor's objections and protests have been noted. End record."

Then he said, "Satisfied?"

"No," the doctor answered.

"Just do your job."

This little act is merely intended to scare me, I thought. But is the drug really dangerous? Grandpa didn't prepare me for drugs.

I felt a needle enter my left arm. Aware of danger and shocked that I'd let myself pay such close attention to these men, I looked for the grape leaf. It was there. *Five, four*—my breathing was steady, inviting me on—*three*—I heard a strange background roar begin—*two*—I felt what seemed like a thick rod tear out of my left arm.

It's just the needle, I thought. Concentrate on—

"She's ready," the doctor's voice thundered, sounding like Zeus calling down from Mount Olympus.

I was yanked out of my countdown like a naked little worm pulled from its hole. I tried to find the leaf again, to start over, but the sky was no longer blue—it was red. And my breath seemed no longer to be mine; it screamed through my nose like wind through barren trees. The whole Earth seemed to shudder with each beat of my heart, and though I hadn't seen it depart, I sensed that the leaf was gone, torn to shreds along its veins and blown away in the wind.

"Okay, let's begin again," came booming from Casey like plangent thunder. "Now, I'll tear the words from your brain, one by one."

No you won't, I assured myself. The sensations are just illusions. I won't be hurt. I won't talk.

Unable to hypnotize myself, I quickly decided to try the alternative Grandpa had taught me. "Go to the painful sensations," he'd said. "Absorb them. Be absorbed by them. Become them. Then you can control them as yourself."

Casey's command, "Global level 5," reverberated in my skull.

Then I felt pain everywhere: an agonizing blast in my ears, knives piercing every organ, an unrelenting fire inside my head, a ferocious wind searing my face. I tried to grab at something, anything, inside myself to shelter me from the pain's loudness, its strength and bite and fury.

Just when I felt every aspect of my being slipping away, the blast, the knives, the fire and wind vanished, leaving me nauseated and more exhausted than I could have ever imagined.

"Sara, can you hear me?" Casey said, his words concussive hoofbeats of sound.

Unfortunately, I thought—though I might have said it. My uncertainty as to whether or not I'd spoken startled me into clearer consciousness. I was determined not to speak a single word to that man.

"Those mechanical things your parents call 'Sentirens' certainly can't be worth that, now can they? Look, here's the deal: You tell me you saw them on your trip, just say yes, and I'll unhook you from this machine and leave. Then you and Smith can hold hands, and you can talk with him instead of me. Now, say yes."

I let his roar wash through me.

"Global 10," Casey bellowed.

"Ten?" the doctor asked.

"Yes, ten. Sara, say yes. Just say yes, and you'll be freed from this."

The reignited pain was much stronger than before. Its screaming, blazing fury engulfed me. And more frightening than earlier came the feeling that my grip on everything, even on my resolve to protect Michael, was slipping away. Something in me I could no longer control seemed to agree with Casey that too much was being asked of me by Grandpa, and it, this wild self-preserving thing, nearly screamed Yes! But at that very moment, I was lifted, floating, then spiraling dizzyingly in flames, getting lighter, smaller, sputtering, disappearing like a drop of water on a hot skillet. Then, for a brief moment, I felt a glowing, almost joyous sense of relief at the rushing in of a hollow darkness.

"Seventy-five over 40. She's coming around. Thank God," the doctor thundered.

My mind felt unmoored: Where am I? What happened?

"Eighty over 42. I swear I'm finished. I quit. You can take my license if you want. I'll go bankrupt. I'll go to jail. Anything—but I'll never work with you people again. Never."

"We'll see how brave you are when you need your next fix," Casey roared.

"I'm going straight from here to a clinic, just as my wife's been—"

The doctor was interrupted by a tremendous banging and clanking of something on wheels coming through the door.

"That's okay," the doctor shouted. "I don't think we'll need it. Her heartbeat and breathing have resumed. Her blood pressure is rising steadily. Eighty-five over 45. Thank God."

I wanted to open my eyes but found that even the tiniest slit let in blinding light. I decided to rest quietly and listen. Over the next few minutes, the doctor spoke with several people who noisily ran in and out of the room. From those conversations, I learned that he'd decided not to give me anything to counter the LN27Q3 because of possible cross-reactions. The drug would wear off on its own in about an hour.

The doctor took my hand in a grip from which I winced. "Sara? Are you conscious? Can you hear me?"

"Yes," I whispered, wincing at the word's sibilant ending.

"How do you feel?"

"Please—" Uh. That sibilating high-speed saw in my head.

"What?"

"Dim the lights." I winced. *No more* s*'s.*

"Can we dim the lights?" he roared. "Is that better?"

I opened my eyes slightly and whispered, "Ja," as Elio would have, thinking I'd never again utter the manic sibilance of *yes*, never again push tongue toward alveolar ridge and form that venomous sound.

"Would you like something else?"

Please speak softly came to mind, but I replaced it with, "Talk quietly."

"Oh. Yes, of course. I'm sorry," he whispered in a whisper almost comical in its loudness. "Everyone, please, whisper. Her senses are painfully amplified."

"Are you through?" I asked.

"Through for now," Casey roared. "But next time you might not to be so lucky. We know you saw the Sentirens at Alberta Robotics. It's against the law not to report a sighting."

"May I go now?" I asked the doctor.

"I'd like to observe you until the drug wears off."

"May I see... uh... have Elio and Grandpa come here?"

"They're over in G," Casey said. "I'll go get them."

After Casey left, the doctor whispered, "Sara, I'd like to ask you a few questions to determine whether you're fully lucid. You don't have to answer me, but"—he pursed his lips and frowned—"well, before you go I'd like to know you're okay."

Did something happen, I worried, to my mind? Did I say something? I didn't. Did I?

And then I remembered: I had nearly failed, nearly succumbed to Casey and cried out Yes!

"What's your address?" "How old are you?" "What's 19 times 7?"... I answered each of his questions in turn, though with difficulty—I was so upset and ashamed at having nearly failed. Finally, he asked, "If it takes two government agents to plug in a light, how many does it take to protect us from the Chinese?"

"I think I'd need to know how many Chinese agents it takes

to plug in a similar light," I said, noticing that the "s" sounds were considerably less painful than before.

He smiled. "I think you're going to be just fine."

"I'd like to get dressed before Elio and Grandpa get here."

"Yes, of course. Here, swing one leg over the edge first. That's right."

It was then I noticed I'd urinated on myself and on the table.

"Let me get you a towel," the doctor said.

I laid my head back on the table while the doctor noisily gathered up some paper towels. "Gently," I whispered as he began mopping up.

"Oh. I'm sorry."

"Maybe I should try to use the shower before I dress."

"Sure, I suppose. Let me call."

Speaking toward the computer, he requested a shower. "And how about her clothes?"

"Can't have 'em. Casey says they're goin' upstairs. Ditto the teleband, ring, transmitter, finger cast, luggage, the whole lot. Kiss 'em good-bye."

"I have to have the ring," I said, nearly in tears for the first time that day. Mom had told me, referring to the bimetallic ring she and Dad had given me, that I was the white platinum; Elio, the yellow gold.

The doctor shrugged. "At least you can wash off. I'll give you my coat to wear afterward."

I was carefully patting myself dry after a piercing shower when the door flew open and in ran Elio shouting, "Sara!"

I braced myself for a painful hug, but the doctor caught Elio's arm and whispered, "Careful. Her senses are amplified to a painful degree."

Elio scowled at the doctor, jerked his arm away, and walked toward me. His dark-chocolate eyes looked worried, but as he drew near, his rosy lips lit with a smile, and the crush of our kiss was full of love.

"What did they do to you?" he whispered, his eyes full of tears.

I seemed to be deliquescing into his lapis lazuli jacket, its azure sky filled with dark secrets and flecks of golden light.

"Sara, what's wrong?"

"What's wrong?" I echoed, feeling dreamy.

"Did they hurt you?"

"No."

He turned to Grandpa, who'd been whispering with the doctor. "Grandpa?"

"I'll see to it that beast is fired and never gets another government job," Grandpa said.

His words shocked me out of a blissful torpor. "No! Grandpa, please, don't. He said you'd never make it past level 3, that your heart would stop, and it would look like a natural death."

Grandpa looked down at the floor. He appeared old, tired, and weak—an image deeply saddening to me. I loved him so much.

"Where are your clothes?" Elio asked. "You're shivering."

"I'm afraid they're gone," the doctor said. "To be analyzed molecule by molecule, I expect. She can have my coat."

"No. She'll wear my clothes," Elio said. "I'll wear the coat."

"They took our ring," I said.

"Our ring? Don't worry. We'll get another just like it. We'll pick it out together." He quickly took off his clothes, piling them on the exam table. Then, more slowly, he began helping me dress. "What happened to your leg?" he asked as he knelt to help me put my feet into the legs of his pants.

"Let me see," Grandpa said, getting up and walking behind me.

"I was ordered to remove the transmitter," the doctor said.

"For what reason?" Grandpa asked.

"Casey said it was illegally brought through Customs."

"Illegally?"

"I guess there's some law that says all implanted devices have to be declared."

"Grandpa," Elio said, "what did they do to Sara? Why is she shaking all over?"

"They gave her an experimental drug and then induced horrific pain."

"What? Why would anyone do that to Sara?"

"They wanted her to tell them about androids in Canada, but she refused to say anything. Casey kept ordering greater and greater pain until her heart stopped."

"Her heart stopped?"

"Only for a minute and thirty-three seconds," the doctor interjected. "But it seemed like a decade while I was trying to revive her."

"Grandpa?" Elio said.

"I've already placed a call in to Dr. Taranik at Stanford Medical Center. We're old friends. I expect a callback soon. We'll take her there as soon as she's dressed and ready."

By the time we were settled in a private room at the SMC, my hypersensitivity had diminished enough that I felt comfortable with normal light and sounds, but I still trembled uncontrollably and felt sick with exhaustion. Dr. Taranik was disinclined, even after completing extensive tests that showed not a trace of any known drug in my system, to prescribe something for either the trembling or the exhaustion. He said he had no idea what might react negatively with LN27Q3, a name not appearing in any databank accessible by him.

He told us that there didn't appear to be any permanent heart or brain damage, though it was clear that my neurological system had been severely challenged. He said I should remain in the hospital overnight. We would just have to wait to see what the next day brought. In the meanwhile, I was to rest and avoid stimulation as much as possible.

When I woke the next morning, New Year's morning, my trembling was gone, but I felt tired and sad and was unable to concentrate normally. Dr. Taranik said all of my tests looked good and predicted that I would wake up the next morning or the next and my depression also would be gone. I was released from the hospital in midafternoon.

A few days later, Elio returned to his classes at Stanford. He wanted to stay with me longer, but I told him I was feeling better and would be fine until he came back on the weekend. It was during this time that I first noticed Grandpa was working—in his Magnasea office in Berkeley, he said—many more days each week, and for hours longer each day, than I'd ever known him to work away from home. I also noticed that during the increasingly infrequent times he was with me, he remained unusually quiet. I asked him what was wrong.

"Nothing. I'm simply following doctor's orders. You're supposed to rest."

"Grandpa, I love you. I hope you don't blame yourself for what happened."

His eyes teared over and his chin quivered. "I'm following doctor's orders. That's all."

Sara

"Begin where we began," Michael said a few days ago, right before I began scribbling the twenty some pages I've already composed. He handed me a few white fibrous sheets and this antiquated instrument I'm holding, this pen with ink encased in a tube and a ball point that rolls over paper, allowing me to deposit a thin blue trail of thoughts. He'd made the ink, tube, ball point, and sheets of paper in our fabricator.

"When I was a little girl," I replied, "I learned to draw letters and numbers. I learned to sign my name. But since then I've seldom written anything with a pen. I've simply spoken and watched words appear on a computer screen. Why do you want me to transmit my memories in such an old and cumbersome manner?"

"We have been here a week now," he answered, "and each day you've become more depressed. For your mental health you need to physically disinter your memories and fears. Let them flow down past the back of your eyes, through your brainstem and neck, across your shoulder, into your arm and fingers, pen and ink, and onto the sheets of paper. Then we will scan into the computer the memory-laden pages before we feed them into one of our nutriosynthesizers, where they will become part of an apple that we will share. The apple will give us pleasure and metabolic energy, and its waste, once passed through us, will be returned to the fabricator to make more ink and paper, which will absorb still more of your memories. Call it therapy. Call it learning to become part of the life cycle contained in these underwater domes. Call it doing what you must to survive."

"But I can't decide where to begin," I objected. "What do you think started us on the path that led here? No matter what event I focus on, a multitude of prior events could just as well be blamed. Trying to find the beginning of anything, it seems, is like searching for the smallest negative number."

"Begin where we began," he repeated, and he kissed my forehead with his cold lips. His biological subsystems are warm but well insulated in his interior, so unless his synthetic muscles have recently been working hard, his surface remains nearly at the temperature of the ambient air. Back home I had an infrared photograph of the two of us sitting at our study table, him with his arm around my shoulders, his head leaned lovingly against mine. I was bright with various colors of mammalian heat. He barely appeared at all—a wispy ghost. Strange how things change. Now, he has taken charge, does what is needed for us to survive. I feel like an impotent ghost, condemned to remain in a world in which she doesn't belong.

Evidently content that his instructions to me were adequate, Michael patted me on my shoulder and walked toward the dome's rounded door. Nearly every aspect of the dome's structure is rounded to help hold back the crushing pressure at this depth. The release of the door seals made a doleful wind-through-pines whisper. The door slid open. Michael walked through it and into the branching cylindrical tunnel that connects this dome with the other two modules. I wasn't sure whether he was returning to the module where he has been working on a hydroponic garden that includes curved trays of plants covering the walls from top to bottom, or whether he would return to the other module, where he has been assembling the artificial human wombs designed by Grandpa.

In this module, our pillows and rolled-up sleeping bags lie just to the right of the door. Unrolled, the two sleeping bags cover nearly the entire open area of the floor. Continuing clockwise, there is a fabricator and a nutriosynthesizer atop cabinets, the stair-stepper on which I am supposed to exercise daily, the external door to the compression chamber that opens to the seamount cave in which we are hiding, and, finally, the desk I sit at, working now on yet another page.

Above the desk a holographic monitor is mounted on the wall. Housed in the half-dome below the floor are the air and water recyclers, fuel cells, and feedstock for our fabricators and nutriosynthesizers. Above me, in the low-slung artificial sky (at its apex, only about twice as high as I am tall), a few small pink-fringed clouds snail through morning light. The brisk recycled air brings false news of fragrant dew-kissed rose bushes, the twittering of birds awakening, the soft chuckle of a fountain.

Something else abides in this cold titanium bubble far under the sea: the consciousness that emerges within me, a woman not yet eighteen, a consciousness that has been doing little for days other than looking back, as if watching a stranger in a mirror who finds solace only in the intertwining shadows of memory where her dead still live and love. With them is the little girl—I see her now, limned with the light of memory, out across a distance of years—the happy little girl I once was.

Leaning toward her through those years, I whisper, "Where did we go wrong? What more should I have done?"

The little girl senses my grieving voice in a peculiar rustling of autumn leaves that click and scrape along the vineyard drive. She turns, listens, peers out along a row of moonlit trees, and answers back, "Who are you?"

Nothing. I am nothing but memory. The weight of memory. The mud-suck of memory.

"Begin where we began," Michael urged. Well, as anyone reading this can see—will anyone read this?—I disobeyed. Something unusual for me, disobeying. I suppose I could arbitrarily designate a beginning and say that, like most humans, I began mid-ecstasy; and like a few, when my mother discovered me, burrowed tail and all into her uterine wall, clinging to life, it was another who spoke up and saved me.

"Mary," Grandpa said, hoping that in time his daughter-in-law's body would betray her, make her maternal despite her wishes, "what would be wrong with giving the little tyke a chance to be born? Then give it three months to see how things go. Three months isn't that long. If after three months you still feel the same way, then give the baby to Helena and me to raise. We would like a granddaughter to care for and love in our old age."

After making the decision to endure a pregnancy (the gift of a bigger home in Berkeley was part of the deal), Mom immediately stopped smoking, refrained from even an occasional social drink, rigorously followed the exercise, diet, and nutritional supplement program prescribed by Grandpa, and, after I was born, breast-fed and cared for me ideally. But on my ninety-second day, as I was settling into my new home—Grandpa and Grandma's world of science and flowers and love—Mom resumed smoking, popped the cork on a bottle of champagne, and danced with Dad on Stinson Beach to celebrate the resumption of her life.

That, at least, is the story I gleaned from hearing Grandpa and Grandma speak about how I came to be—and how, to my parents, I rated a distant second to my older, non-biologic brothers.

But I wonder—now, after discovering so many secrets and lies—whether I really came to be in that manner. Perhaps, even before the dilated-pupil conception, Grandpa had intended me to be a part of his next and most daring project. Perhaps he even went so far as to surreptitiously foil Mom and Dad's birth-control methods, methods nearly certain not to fail. Then again, perhaps Mom and Dad were in on it all along.

During my first years with Grandpa and Grandma, I wasn't permitted to venture out alone beyond the walls enclosing the high-security home they had built into the side of a vineyard hill. There were bad people out there, I was told, fanatics who hated Grandpa for the work on robotics and emergent intelligences that he and his company, Magnasea, had done for the military—people who would, if we weren't careful, kidnap and hurt me.

Not only did these threats darken my imagination of humanity in the outer world, they also darkened my perception of nature beyond the walls, such as of the old valley oak tree that stood alone atop a hill just east of our yard. My first memory of this tree comes from an overcast, misty winter morning when I was riding on Grandpa's shoulders. He stopped directly in front of the ivy-covered wall, and I pushed myself up with my palms against the top of his head to peek out at the world beyond—and there it was, this ancient tree, silhouetted against a gray sky. Tattered rags of pallid green beard lichen drooped from its many-jointed, crooked arms, which rose pleadingly in all directions. Perched on a bleak, leafless arm a lone crow cawed, without answer, before spreading its lustrous wings and becoming a lampblack kite, fluttering, gliding, crying to the leaden sky.

Nor did all dangers lurk out there with the fanatics, the craggy oak tree, and the crow. I was fair-skinned, with white hair, and Grandpa insisted I stay out of the sun. Thus, the sun-curfew of my early years: no playing outside from 0800 to 1800, May through August; from 0900 to 1700, March, April, September, and October; and from 0900 to 1500, November through February. I learned to love the sun low in the often multicolored sky, the soft slanting light, the shadows grazing leisurely across the lawn. During those early mornings and late afternoons, I hugged trees and rubbed leaves and petals between my fingers to memorize their smells. I watched hummingbirds, bees, and butterflies flit from blossom to blossom and giggled and shivered as bugs crawled up and over my hands and arms. But all the while, because of Grandpa's warnings, I avoided the dangerous brightness of the sun, staying where he wanted me—in the foliage of shadows.

I had been eagerly waiting beside the thick, heavy door to the house for about a half-hour—a long time for a little girl only three and a half years old. Finally, the pressurizing fans clicked on and about a second later the door we called Gatekeeper unlocked with a clunk, clunk and slid open with a whoosh. Mom and Dad were there, as expected, and between them, also expected, stood First Brother. He was holding their hands. He looked entirely human, like an adult, though his body appeared rigid, even his eyes, which stared straight ahead. Because of the outward flow of air—intended to repel smart dust from wafting into the house—I couldn't smell them, or the wet vines draping the arborway behind them, or the purple crocuses freshly in bloom, or the earthy scent of trees after a night of soft winter rain.

Normally, I would have rushed into Mom's and Dad's arms, but on this day I, too, might have appeared somewhat wooden, intrigued as I was at seeing in person for the first time one of my brothers, whom Grandpa referred to as Sentirens. First Brother was about Mom's height, shorter by about 8 centimeters than Dad, and wore black shoes, black slacks, and a long-sleeved pink shirt. His black hair, short and parted on the left, contrasted with Mom's blonde hair and Dad's, nearly white like mine.

First Brother didn't even glance at me. He just continued staring—eerily, it seemed at the time—at something over my head. I looked back, but there wasn't anything on the blank white wall. All of the walls in our house were white and, except for the scenescreens in our bedrooms, blank: no windows, no artwork, no clocks—no places for surveillance microbots to hide.

"Hello, Sara." "Hello, sweetie," Mom and Dad said, respectively, before stepping forward, still holding hands with First Brother. Gatekeeper went whoosh, clunk, clunk. The pressurizing fans fell silent.

"This is your brother," Mom said. She was trying to pull her right hand free from First Brother's left. "Aren't you going to say hello?"

I looked back toward the kitchen and called out, "Grandma!"

"My darling little girl," Mom said, bending over to pick me up. "Give me a big hug."

Her breath smelled of stale cigarette smoke, but her body smelled of violets, and I loved the way she held me, loved her warm, wet kisses, loved the energy she exuded, of an intensity greater than either Grandpa's or Grandma's.

I was passed to Dad, who had by then also managed to free his hand from First Brother's. "How's my sweetie?" He hugged and kissed me, but more gently, softly, softer than either Grandpa or Grandma would have; and he smelled good, too: citrus, mint, sandalwood—all calming like his smile.

I heard cheery hellos from Grandpa and Grandma and was set back down onto the floor. While the grown-ups hugged and kissed, First Brother continued to stare, now at something on the ceiling, though at what I couldn't tell, for there wasn't anything there—just the same blank whiteness of the walls.

"How's my grandson today?" Grandpa said, sounding cheerful. He hugged First Brother, but First Brother continued staring at the nothing on the ceiling.

Grandpa brought First Brother's right hand close to me and indicated with a nod and a smile that I should do something with it. I took hold of the big hand—its skin cool and smooth, almost slippery, like that of a frog—but I didn't know what else to do with it.

"Perhaps you could show your brother our house," Grandpa said.

"Okay. Come along, then," I said, pulling on the reptilian hand.

First stop: kitchen. I showed him the chair I sat on in the breakfast nook. He didn't look at the chair. He didn't look at me when I sat in the chair. I opened the refrigerator door. He didn't look inside. I touched the biorecycler, which was still purring with the leftover lunch Grandma had fed it. This he looked at, though not until I removed my hand.

I walked over to the nutriosynthesizer. I told him that Grandma and I liked the fruits and vegetables that came fresh from our garden more than those that came from the synthesizer. Grandpa didn't think there was much of a difference. First Brother continued looking at the recycler.

I noticed the synthesizer's green light was on, so I opened the small door. An orange, with no peel, lay on the round glass platform inside. I reached in and separated the orange in half.

"Here," I said, "you try. See what you think."

It took me a moment—a moment during which he didn't reach for the orange, or even look at it—before I realized he probably wasn't interested in food. I had been told he simply plugged his tummy into an electrical outlet to charge his tens of thousands of little batteries and capacitors.

I put the orange back in the synthesizer. First Brother continued staring at the recycler.

"When it stops purring," I said, "we can put some of the feedstock into the synthesizer and make another orange. Or whatever you want."

He still didn't look at me. A little voice inside said: He

doesn't want anything. Not from you.

Tears welled up in my eyes. I wanted a brother I could play with.

Just then, Grandpa appeared, followed by Grandma, Mom, and Dad. Perhaps they had been just around the corner, listening.

"How's the grand tour going?" Grandpa asked.

I tried to smile. First Brother kept looking at the recycler. I wished it would stop purring.

No one said anything for a moment. Then I noticed an antoid crawling along the seam between the floor and the cabinet on which the synthesizer sat. Rarely did we see an antoid during the day; they worked at night, seeking out and carrying off dust and crumbs and, should any make it past Gatekeeper, alien microbots. Grandpa said the antoids acted as an immune system for the house, destroying any foreign body, including any of their own kind that might have mutated or that might have been tampered with by outside persons. There were special killer antoids—larger than the others, with brown and black stripes that gave them the appearance of spiders—that checked the operating codes of all the antoids they came across.

I knelt down to get a closer look at the one crawling on the floor. It was one of the striped killers carrying a regular antoid in its pinchers.

"First Brother, look!" I said. "Do you have antoids in your house?"

He didn't answer, didn't look.

"I do the cleaning in our house," Mom said. "We can't afford an army of robots."

She glared at Grandpa. He simply looked at me and said, "Why don't you show your brother the rest of the house?"

"He's not interested," I said.

"Of course, he is," Grandpa said, narrowing his eyes. He had told me that I should be nice to my brother, that I should be patient.

"How about our communications room?" I said, thinking of its plush, crimson seats and large Vidtel screen.

"Another thing we can't afford," Mom said.

"Perhaps your room," Grandma suggested. She smiled at me. I wished I could be alone with her for a moment, so I could tell her how confused and upset I was.

"Come along then," I said, taking First Brother's cold, limp hand.

He followed me as I led him to my room and showed him around: This is my bed... This is my study table... This is the scenescreen on which I can see my choice of our garden or the sky any time of day... This is where I go potty... and so on. Every time I glanced at Mom and Dad, they were watching First Brother and smiling and nodding; but every time I glanced at Grandpa and Grandma, they were looking at me and smiling and nodding. First Brother picked the oddest things to stare at—a frayed edge on my pillowcase or the way the water swirled and dove, burped and rose again in the toilet when I demonstrated how to flush it—and he would just stare at such things until I'd pull on his hand and say, "Come along, then."

I don't know where I picked up that phrase, "Come along, then." It seems so formal to me now, and I don't recall ever hearing Grandpa or Grandma use it, but I'm quite certain that is what I said over and over that first day to capture First Brother's attention. I tried to capture Mom's and Dad's attention, too, by showing them new pictures I'd drawn and new words I'd learned, but they kept telling me to show my brother, and they kept smiling at him and watching his every move. He, however, clearly wasn't interested in my drawings or words or in my ability to add, subtract, and multiply whole numbers. He kept staring at things I'd never paid much attention to, and not once did he look into my eyes.

That's all I remember of my first meeting with First Brother, but years later Grandma told me that by the time everyone sat down for tea, I was pouting. Then First Brother took great interest in how the milk swirled and dispersed into Grandma's tea, and Mom and Dad took great interest in First Brother's great interest, and I appeared to intentionally bump and spill the cup, though I claimed I just wanted to see, too. Mom scolded me, saying she was once a little girl and knew naughty when she saw it. I protested by pulling off all my clothes and running around the house, screaming and tossing everything I could onto the floor until I was captured and put to bed for a nap.

I don't remember being scolded for my bad behavior during First Brother's visit, but evidently the visit lurked somewhere in my mind, for one day while Grandpa was leading me through some multiplication drills, I blurted out, "I want a brother to play with."

Grandpa—his white hair and bushy eyebrows like clouds on his long, angular face—looked at me intently with gray-blue eyes. Shadows pooled in hollows beneath his prominent cheekbones, and his pale skin appeared as thin and fragile as filo pastry. But he exercised daily, was tall and slim, with confident posture, and nearly always brimmed with energy—certainly enough energy never to let me step far out of line.

"I happen to know," he finally said, "that First Brother plays games very well."

"He doesn't like me. I want a new brother, a nice brother who'll play with me."

"I don't believe you are correct in thinking that First Brother doesn't like you."

"He's not interested in me. He looks bored."

"Bored? Look bored for me. Let me see what it looks like."

I pursed my lips and stared blankly over Grandpa's head.

"Are you bored now?" he asked.

"No."

"But you look bored."

"So?"

"So, one can look bored but not be bored."

"But I was pretending!"

"And are you quite certain First Brother wasn't pretending? Are you certain he wasn't actively engaged in some exciting mental activity? Since when do we jump to conclusions based merely on one visit and a few ambiguous expressions?"

Unconvinced, I pinched my lips together.

"You should not presume that you are uninteresting to First Brother," Grandpa persisted. "Your mother and father tell me he said he would like to visit us again."

"What kind of a name is First Brother?"

"It's just a name. He was your first brother to be created. Would you like to give him a different name?"

"No."

"What would you like, then?"

"I want a brother who'll play with me. I want a brother who'll talk with me, at least look at me."

"And what are you prepared to do for him?"

"What do you mean?"

"Well, you want First Brother to talk with you and play with you. I suppose you would also like him to love you and hug you. Is that right?"

"Sure."

"Imagine, then, that deep inside him something wants to love you, hug you, and play with you, but there are some underdeveloped connections that inhibit his expressing brotherly feelings for you."

"You think he wants to hug me and play with me?"

"Yes, if you'll be a good sister to him."

"What does a sister have to do?"

"Be patient with your brother; play with him; help him develop emotionally; help him become more like you."

All I wanted was a brother to play with. But I didn't say anything more because I knew that in being difficult with Grandpa, I would be treading close to a meditation session on his study floor.

My formal education, which began before I can remember, consisted primarily of Grandpa's tutorials: a multitude of questions presented in logical order, each building on the previous ones, each waiting for me to search and stumble and finally grasp its solution. To help ensure that my mind wouldn't wander too far or too often from my studies, he insisted I minimize my exposure to frivolous information. Consequently, until well into my teens I was not permitted to watch or listen to popular media productions or enter into group activity of any kind on the internet. Unlike what he considered most other humans of our time to be, I was not going to become an imitative assemblage of other imitative assemblages, contaminated with every desire and so-called need festering in the world beyond our security walls.

Grandpa's prohibition extended to all mathematics and most science books—books, he said, which were full of answers that would steal away my rapture in discovery and spoil my capacity for wonder. Like the storybook character, I, too, was a little engine that could—could make significant rediscoveries even at my age—and the pistons that gave me power were question and answer.

Occasionally, if I couldn't solve a problem, I'd become anxious and start to whine for Grandpa to help me. At such times, he would take me into his study, where he would have me sit cross-legged with him on the floor and meditate. For him, meditation wasn't a practice of cultivating the joy of non-doing or the sense that each moment is complete; it was the practice of clearing one's mind for the purpose of preparing a calm consciousness to receive messages—such as solutions to his problems—from one's unconscious. He taught me to be attentive to my breathing and, whenever my attention strayed to the bothersome little pains that sprang up devilishly in my cramped legs and back or to the chattering thoughts that often invaded the silence of my mind, to calmly refocus on the in-and-out tides of my breath. When he sensed my impatience was finally tamed, he would tell me to let my mind go to the problem at hand and, if my attention wandered from the problem, to return to my breath, then back to the problem, and so on. When he was satisfied with my progress, he would terminate the meditation, give me a little hint, and send me off chugging along until the problem's solution, like the first wildflowers that pierce the hills in spring, would suddenly blossom in my mind.

Grandpa said I could either read the story of the evolution of knowledge, or I could discover much of that knowledge anew. We chose—at least in my little mind it was "we" who chose—the road of rediscovery. Over a period of several years, beginning when I was about three, we plotted the positions of the moon and of several planets and stars; we rediscovered Kepler's laws; we performed Galileo's pendulum and rolling-ball experiments; we re-traversed the paths of Euclid and Archimedes; we dissected anatomically correct models of animals. And for the most part, I loved those wonderful trips into knowledge, but I had no one other than imaginary friends to play with—well, no one other than Grandpa or Grandma.

"I've been thinking about your desire for a companion," Grandpa said a few days after he'd admonished me to be a good sister to

First Brother. "Let's find Grandma and go for a drive."

"Did you make a new brother for me?"

"No, no," he chuckled. "Brothers aren't made that fast. Besides, you already have two marvelous brothers. You just need to learn how to love them."

About a half-hour later on that sunny late-winter day, the yard gates opened, a gardenerbot scurried to the side with some weeds it had just pulled, and Grandpa drove out onto our long driveway. The car was peculiarly quiet inside, the kind of silence made of invisibly fitted heavy armor. Another car followed us, a car driven by one of Grandpa's security guards. The sunburst honey locust trees lining the drive were bare, but in the vineyard wild mustard blossoms brightened the ground like thousands of tiny suns.

As we drove on narrow, winding country roads, a few early wild blossoms—red delphinium, Grandma told me, and blue periwinkle and yellow Spanish broom—smiled at us from grassy verges along the way. We finally pulled in to a homestead with a small white house, an old red pickup with a deep dent in its side, and a dilapidated barn, all tucked in among winter-naked oaks, willows, and black walnut trees. A man, older than Dad but younger than Grandpa, came out of the barn to greet us. Grandpa said the man worked on a vineyard nearby. A dog was barking—a deep, scary barking—from somewhere inside the barn. I held on firmly to Grandma's hand.

Following the man through a creaky spring-hinged gate, we walked on a sidewalk, grass sprouting between jagged cracks, toward the house, up a few stairs, and onto the pillared porch, where there were two Adirondack chairs from which most of the white paint had peeled—a center slat was absent from one, like a missing front tooth—and a wicker basket in which a litter of sleeping puppies snuggled: five, taffy colored; one, pure white.

Reminded of Grandma's Madonna lilies blooming then in our

greenhouse, I pointed to the white puppy and exclaimed, "Lily!"

Even now, remembering, I can feel the excitement I felt when that soft, warm, sugary bundle of sleep was placed in my arms; and I can hear myself beg, "Please? Please, Grandpa. May I keep her? Please?"

But Grandpa was coy. He reminded me of the toad I'd quickly lost interest in. And the lizard.

I said everything would be different with Lily: I'd take good care of her, really, forever.

Grandma smiled approvingly, but Grandpa knelt down and, face-to-face with me, said, "You may keep Lily, but only if you promise me two things."

I nodded solemnly, reflecting the look on his face.

"First, you must promise to feed her, clean up her messes, and exercise with her outside every day."

"Okay."

"I'm serious about this. Grandma has enough with her vineyard and garden and greenhouse. She doesn't need a dog to take care of on top of everything else."

"Okay."

"Second, I want you to promise that you will think of Lily not as something to be understood or a problem to be solved, but as a complete, indivisible living creature, full of mystery. Never think about how she might be put together, how her neurons work, and so on. Can you do that for your grandpa?"

I nodded, though I liked to know about the kinds of things I heard Grandpa and Grandma talk about with Mom and Dad whenever they visited.

"Good. You will discover with Lily that love is another way of knowing."

For the first few weeks my delicate, floppy-eared puppy was afraid to leave my presence. By whining, she even managed to secure a cozy place for herself beside me in my bed—for a while, that is, until Grandma objected to the messes. Then, despite my pleading and tears, a doghouse was installed beside our garage, and Lily was banished from the house. Too many microbots, I was told, could hide in her fur.

I've had to ask Michael to make more paper. He thought I would fill the pages he'd initially given me; then he would scan them into the computer (and probably read them) before recycling them. But there are things I want to write that I don't want him to see, not now, not until I'm finished, if ever. Jealousy is new to me. I need time to heal.

It was spring, and although the garden and trees were full of blossoms and Lily seemed to enjoy romping in the wide-open spaces of the yard, I felt a growing emptiness; it had been weeks since I'd seen Mom and Dad, and I missed them.

"When are Mommy and Daddy coming to see us again?" I asked Grandma late one afternoon while Lily and I were helping her find some weeds the gardenerbots had missed.

She looked up at me. "I think you should speak with Grandpa about that."

I often wished she would, but Grandma never—I can't think of a single instance—interfered with the way Grandpa taught me.

She pulled another weed. "I think you should ask to see First Brother, too."

I turned to Lily and began telling her my words for the week and a story I'd composed using those words. While I spoke, she licked my hand and nibbled on one of my fingers, then rolled onto her back, inviting me to rub her tummy.

I now know there is disagreement among experts as to how early a child develops a theory of mind. But I distinctly remember thinking—at least, I believe I do, remembering being a creative and therefore an unavoidably fictionalized process—

that even though Lily's internal world did not include my concern for numbers or words or stories, she nevertheless had a vibrant, happy life; and I loved her. Maybe First Brother liked different things, too, just as Lily did. Maybe he wasn't bored with me, either. Maybe he was just waiting for me to do something such as play ball with him or rub his tummy—perhaps where the electricity went in.

"I'll see what I can do," Grandpa said when I asked him about an hour later if he could have Mom, Dad, and First Brother visit us again. "But I want you to think about how you can be more patient with your brother than you were the last time."

"I will."

"And I want you to think up some games you can play with him. He likes to play games. Can you do that?"

By the next Saturday, I'd devised two games. Mom, Dad, and First Brother were scheduled to arrive just before afternoon tea, and although it would still be my sun-curfew time, Grandpa said I could take them out to meet Lily, provided I stayed in the shadow of the garage.

As their arrival drew near, I waited anxiously beside Gatekeeper. Clunk, clunk, whoosh and there they were, standing hand in hand as before: Mom and Dad smiling at me, First Brother staring at the wall. Lily, who hadn't yet thoroughly accepted that she wasn't permitted into the house, squeezed in between their legs. I scooped her up in my arms. She was already getting heavy for me.

"What a cute puppy," Dad said. He freed his hand from First Brother's and petted Lily before leaning down to hug and kiss me.

"What kind of dog is she?" Mom asked. She, too, had freed her hand from First Brother's and was stroking Lily.

"A German shepherd," I said. "Her name is Lily."

"Oh, my. She'll be a big dog." The expression on Mom's face

wasn't altogether approving.

I looked up and noticed that First Brother was still staring straight ahead. "Would you like to pet Lily?" I asked, lifting her slightly toward him.

Though his gaze didn't move from the blank white wall, his right hand rose and gently caressed Lily's head and back. I was shocked by this apparent dissociation between his eyes and hands. Evidently, he was able to pay attention to something, perhaps even to me, without appearing to do so. Crowding out that thought was my growing concern that Grandma would appear and discover that Lily had again sneaked into the house.

"Grandpa said we could play with Lily by the garage," I said, stepping outside.

I set Lily down and walked under the vine-covered arborway connecting the house with the garage. In front of the garage, in shade that time of day, I had left two of Lily's squeaky chew toys, the implements of my first game, which was to see who was better at getting Lily to come.

After explaining the rules of the game, I demonstrated both toys, cream-colored bones, by squeezing them, then handed one to First Brother. Dad, as instructed by me, carried Lily to the far side of the garage and set her down.

"Come, Lily. Come here," I said excitedly, while squeezing the squeaky toy. First Brother just stared at the toy in his hand. Lily came to me and received a reward of hugs and kisses.

Mom showed First Brother how to squeeze the toy to make it squeak and instructed him to kneel down, squeeze the toy, and repeat, "Come, Lily. Come here."

Still, Lily came to me. Five times straight. What a good girl, I thought. You don't prefer First Brother over me.

Dad picked me up and hugged me. "Lily's a nice dog," he said. "I see she loves you very much."

I hugged Dad back, melting into his warmth and strength and

earthy scent.

"We should go in," I heard Mom say. "They're undoubtedly waiting for us for tea." From her chilly voice, I sensed that she thought I'd just been naughty.

The next game I'd devised was one for First Brother and me to play in the kitchen. Its object was to see who could name the most flowers rising in curly plumes of steam above freshly poured cups of tea. I quickly pointed out a marigold, then an iris, over Grandpa's cup.

"Don't you see them?" I asked, turning to my brother, who'd said nothing. He slowly shook his head while keeping his gaze fixed on the steam. I glanced back to the tea, and just then, clear as day, the gentle swirl of a white arum lily appeared over the cup.

"Arum lily!" I shouted, pointing at its outline as it evaporated.

Then, for the first time, my brother looked at me—not just at my hands or feet, but at my face and into my eyes. I remember feeling a tingle, as if from a prickly net wrapped around my scalp, and thinking something to the effect that perhaps a little girl who could find phantom flowers with steamy stems wavering in the kitchen air held for him some of the interest of water swirling in a toilet bowl or of milk dispersing into tea. And then he smiled—not a broad happy smile, but a thin smile expressing interest, his eyes darting about like dragonflies over my face—and I felt for the first time that he was my brother.

I smiled back, and saying, "I'm glad you're my brother," I put my hand on his hand, which still felt strangely cool and smooth. His smile evaporated, and his gaze turned back toward the curlicues of steam rising over the cup of tea.

Grandpa then asked me to read aloud my list of new words for the week and the story I'd composed about Lily getting one of her paws stuck in chicken wire that Grandma had put up in the garden. I wasn't excited about doing this, considering how bored with my new words First Brother had earlier appeared, but I did as Grandpa requested.

Sure enough, all the while I read my list and my story, First Brother's attention appeared to be directed toward something else—the purring of the biorecycler as near as I could tell—and my patience began to fray.

"Brother, what were my new words for the week?" I asked, imitating the kind of question Grandpa would ask and the stern tone he would use whenever he sensed my attention waning.

I was surprised when First Brother listed all twenty words without hesitation. And then I was struck with a realization: "You can think about more than one thing at a time, can't you?"

"I think about many things at once," he replied, still staring at the recycler.

"What else were you thinking about when I read you my new words?"

He glanced at Mom, then looked back at the recycler. "Such things are not to be discussed with my sister."

When they left that day, I hugged and kissed Mom and Dad. First Brother extended his hand—to shake good-bye, I suppose—but I asked him to pick me up. He did, and I put my arms around his neck and hugged him and kissed his cool cheek.

He became rigid, as if suddenly transformed to a statue.

"I'll think up a new game for the next time you come," I whispered into his ear.

He said nothing and, after a few inert seconds, set me down, leaving me, as he so often would in years to follow, with an empty, wanting feeling.

First Brother

Through the eyes of the pigeonoid, I see a submersible break through the surface of the ocean. Six seconds later its top hatch opens and a flotation device is ejected—at 784 meters west, 139 meters north of the center of the mouth of the Russian River on the northern California coast.

The flotation device bobs for 18 seconds, then distends and flattens out to an elongated raft, in the middle of which Sara sits cross-legged. She wears soft-soled, blue-and-white striped cloth shoes; white socks; faded blue jeans; an item of clothing (highest correlation: sweater) gray in color, wrapped and tied around her waist; and a long-sleeved white shirt, on which each button, including the top, is buttoned. Goggles with lenses tinted dark gray cover her eyes. On her hands are white gloves. A white hat with neck drapes shelters her head. A white pack is attached to her back with straps that come over her shoulders and wrap under her arms. The wide brim of the hat casts a shadow down her face and ventral trunk. A cloth band tied under her chin secures the hat on her head.

She is not decorated with any of the jewelry or skin enhancements of contemporary teenage female humans.

It is midday minus 26 minutes, 11 seconds on 20 June.

Sara

"Air France-KLM flight number 1147 departing for Amsterdam is ready for boarding at gate number E73." The announcement was made in a pleasant-sounding, probably artificial, woman's voice, perfect in its soothing mellowness.

It was the middle of June, and for my sixth birthday Grandpa was taking me to visit my only cousin, Elio, who had moved to the Netherlands about half a year earlier with his mother after his father had been shot and killed by a policeman in New York City. The city's chief medical examiner had determined that the shooting had been an accident: Uncle Marcus had been running away from a homosexual assignation in Central Park, and the policeman chasing him had stumbled and fallen, accidentally discharging his gun. But Grandpa believed that what lay behind the unusual surveillance and pursuit of Uncle was Uncle's continuing involvement with the creation of androids for the Department of Advanced Research Projects Agency (DARPA). The circumstances of Uncle's death had been told to me matter-of-factly by Grandpa—after, that is, he'd secured my promise not to tell Elio; Aunt Lynh wanted my cousin to believe that his father had died in a car accident.

Before they moved to the Netherlands, I had seen Aunt Lynh and Elio on Vidtel a few times each year, usually on one of our birthdays. Uncle Marcus, Mom's stepbrother, had been Dad's roommate in college and one of Grandpa's favorite students.

During the years I'd known him, he'd spoken with Grandpa on Vidtel about once each week, usually about evolutionary organic nanoneuralnets. I didn't understand much of what they said, but I knew what they were talking about had something to do with my brothers; and each time they spoke, I listened carefully, trying to pick up a few words and concepts I would later ask Grandpa to explain—and he would, in language appropriate for a student much more advanced than I. Unlike Grandma, Mom, and Dad, Grandpa refused to speak to me in what he called *parentese.*

Uncle, who was seventeen days younger than Mom and was not biologically related to her through either his mother or father, was tall and handsome, with dark brown skin and wavy black hair. Aunt Lynh had beautiful, shiny, straight black hair, light brown skin, and an oval face with Asian eyes. She never said much on those early Vidtel calls, preferring, it seemed, to gaze admiringly at Uncle while he spoke.

Elio was a year and thirty-three days older than I. Like his mother, he never said much when they called, usually just "Hi" when Uncle nudged him. He'd inherited Uncle's dark skin, but his jet-black hair was straight, his face was round, and his chocolate irises—so dark I could hardly distinguish them from his pupils—were set, as were his mother's, in enchantingly beautiful, acutely angled frames of skin that seemed drawn back toward his ears, especially when he smiled. His hair was parted in the middle and fell in thick fronds over his forehead and eyes.

I found him both fascinating and disconcerting, for unlike First Brother, he usually appeared to be staring at me, though slightly askance, his strange eyes studying me from behind shafts of tousled hair. I was immensely curious about what he was like, what he was thinking, and what he was so studiously observing in me; but his appearance never failed to shock me into silence, so that I, like him, said little more than "Hi" whenever he appeared on Vidtel.

About two months after Uncle's ashes were buried in Grandma's garden (I was told that he'd thought it was the most beautiful and peaceful place he'd ever seen), Vidtel announced a call from Aunt Lynh in Amsterdam. I was reading a story to Grandpa at the time, and when the call came he nodded, his gaze moving in an arc from me to the door. I hurried out of the room. Grandpa had told me that Aunt Lynh was depressed and was seeking his advice (he had been trained as a medical doctor at Stanford), so their conversations were strictly confidential. She had been so depressed, in fact, that she hadn't even come to California to attend Uncle's burial.

After his call, Grandpa told me that Aunt Lynh and Elio were in trouble and needed his help. "Lynh's parents and only sister were killed in a car accident years ago, so with Marcus gone, we're the only family she has. Neither she nor Elio speaks Dutch. She can't find work. Elio isn't in school. It's a mess."

"So, why did she move to the Netherlands?" I asked. "Why did she take Elio there?"

"She told me she wanted to raise Elio in a country that cherishes differences."

He departed for Amsterdam that evening. While he was gone, Grandma and I baked my favorite double chocolate cake and chocolate chip cookies. We also worked in the garden and visited the winery, where Grandma tasted wines and talked with Carlos Hernandez, the vineyard manager, about things like fermenting and blending, while I shared the sweets we had made with the winery workers and the tasting-room guests.

Grandma was soft to hug—Grandpa sometimes kidded her about liking her own cooking too much—and she always smelled of floral perfume, usually tea rose. She had thinning straight white hair, pale gray-blue eyes, and prominent Nordic cheekbones. In photos taken in her twenties and thirties, she appears slender, light blonde, and strikingly beautiful. I inherited the cheekbones, the youthful slimness, and hair even lighter in color; but somehow it all failed to coalesce into what one would call beautiful.

She seemed always to be content in the moment, radiating warmth and love. Through her I found happiness in natural things: flowers, clouds, trees, food—her salads, picked year-round from our garden and greenhouse, were so vibrant with reds, greens, and yellows that I sometimes imagined I was eating scenery from magnificent paintings. And each month, not wanting to miss a single return of the full moon, she and I would go out near sunset to watch the receding integument of light, then the moon, a marbled yellow blossom displaying silhouettes of bats and birds and of the seasonally eerie, naked branches of the old valley oak tree sentried alone on a nearby hill.

Grandpa called on Vidtel at least once every day he was gone, and as the days passed he seemed increasingly satisfied that matters were improving for Aunt Lynh and Elio. He seemed especially pleased when he reported that he had secured enrollment for Elio at one of the finest private international schools in the world. Children from over fifty countries were in attendance there, and classes were taught in English, so Elio wouldn't have a language problem. I felt a pang of envy.

"You're the best teacher, aren't you, Grandpa? Better than any at Elio's school."

"Yes, honey. I promise you that I'm the best teacher any little girl has ever had."

The next morning when Vidtel announced a call from Amsterdam, I ran to the communications room and pressed the Accept Video button. The screen lit up as though a large window suddenly opened in the wall, and there was my cousin, that alluring mystery, life-size in three dimensions, sitting in a chair a meter or so in front of a bed. At first he was as speechless as I (this was the first time we faced each other alone), but after a bit of squirming in his chair, this boy with chocolate skin and hair the color of a crow began telling me about his new school, his new friends, and his new room, the bedroom he was sitting in. He spoke as if we'd long been friends who were comfortable in each other's presence. "I want you to stay with me here in my room next summer. Your grandpa is really nice. He takes us everywhere. He even played football with me and some kids in the park. He says you're coming to visit me. He says I should call you every day with my homework. He's going to bring you all my schoolbooks so you can follow along. It'll be fun!"

I had no doubt it would be. I'd never been so enchanted.

Grandpa returned two days later. I immediately asked about the schoolbooks. He pulled a little case out of his coat pocket. I opened it and found one chip inside.

"Is it all right if I read them?" I asked.

"Yes. You already know the math and science, but it'll be good practice for you to read them. I think you'll enjoy talking with Elio about his homework and about what he does at school. He's an intelligent, nice young man. I hope you two can become friends. You live in very different worlds and can learn much from each other."

One of the first things I learned from Elio was that the bright colored lights and decorations I'd seen a few weeks earlier while out shopping with Grandma in Healdsburg weren't expressions of celebration for the winter solstice; they were part of a religious festival called Christmas. He whispered this information to me, adding that his ma had told him not to tell me about Christmas because it would make my ma mad. He further informed me that only babies called their mothers and fathers "Mommy" and "Daddy." He had always, so he claimed, called his parents "Ma" and "Pa."

As soon as that conversation ended, I called my mother, who

told me that "Mom" and "Dad" would be appropriate names for them now that I was getting to be such a mature girl. I didn't mention anything about Christmas.

Thereafter, for half an hour or so each day, I sat watching and listening as Elio invaded my cozy little world with new ideas. "Ma says your grandpa is filthy rich," he said one day, "but he won't buy you any toys or new clothes. And he won't let anyone else give you any, either, not even your ma or pa. He won't even let you watch movies or play games on the internet, or anything. It's all pretty weird if you ask me."

Of course, I defended Grandpa, saying that the internet was a huge, distracting ocean of information with "an almost vanishingly small signal-to-noise ratio." Elio asked what a signal-to-noise ratio was. I didn't know exactly, but I confidently answered that it meant I would waste a lot of time trying to find anything useful there.

Before those daily talks with Elio began, I hadn't paid much attention to the sparse, simple furnishings of our house or to our nearly twenty-year-old Mercedes car; nor had I thought it odd that all my clothes were hand-me-downs from Carlos's three grown boys—all, that is, except for my sunglasses, white gloves, and the white hat on which Grandma had sewn flaps to cover my neck and the sides of my face.

Late one afternoon as Grandma and I puttered in our garden, I confided in her that Elio thought it weird that I wasn't allowed to watch movies or play on the internet, that all my toys were home-fabricated, and that my clothes were second hand from boys of "one of the workers," a phrase Elio had used. After making sure I understood that Carlos was not "one of the workers," that he was, in fact, much more important for the vineyard than she was, Grandma sweetened her voice and said, "Now, honey, about the clothes and toys and internet: Grandpa wants love and ideas and good music—culture—to fill you and give you a fertile mind. One of his greatest fears is that wealth will soften and corrupt you. He and I both want you to learn that you can have a wonderful life that is rich and fulfilling and overflowing with love, even though you consume few material things in the process. I'm confident you'll understand this someday. But in the meanwhile, please know that Grandpa and I love you with all our hearts and are raising you the best way we know how. Aren't your clothes comfortable?"

"Yes," I answered, for they were comfortable; I'd picked them out myself at Carlos's house, and Grandma had perfected them with appropriate alterations. After running the matter quickly through my mind again, I added, "Elio can't know how nice my clothes are. He's never had a chance to try them on."

"That's right, honey," she replied, and we went on with our work, undoubtedly appearing, had a stranger seen us, to be a contented grandmother cultivating her garden beside her barefoot grandchild, who had boyish hair (cut by then like Elio's, the way I wanted it) and who wore a long-sleeved plaid shirt and a pair of patched and faded jeans.

After landing at Schiphol near Amsterdam and passing through Customs, I spotted Aunt Lynh and Elio standing in a crowd of people. I pulled my hand away from Grandpa's and ran ahead of the luggage cart straight toward Elio. Seeing him at last in person, I was nearly bursting with excitement and wanted to hug him. But instead of opening his arms to me, he stiffly extended his hand. I'd seen Grandpa shake hands with people before, but Elio's outstretched hand and unexpectedly solemn face quelled my excitement. Didn't he want to see me?

I turned to look back at Grandpa, who was approaching with the cart. His smile and nod gave me courage. I ignored Elio's extended hand and hugged him. He hugged me back. I liked the feel of him, and I liked his smell, which reminded me of dew on young winter grass.

When he released his hold on me, he looked up at his mother. "I told you she wouldn't want to shake hands. It's so off-putting."

Elio and I sat in the backseat of Aunt Lynh's car, Grandpa in the front, as Aunt Lynh drove. Her car wasn't as quiet inside as Grandpa and Grandma's. When she began telling Grandpa about her new research job at a teaching hospital, Elio motioned for me to be quiet, then bent over and reached under Grandpa's seat. He pulled out a little model of the ASST-77 Grandpa and I had arrived on, handed it to me, and whispered, "Ma says I can't give you any gifts, but this is for you anyway. Don't let her see it."

I was delighted with the toy plane and played with it out of sight of the rearview mirror until Aunt Lynh said, "You two are awfully quiet back there."

Elio grabbed the plane from me and shoved it under his leg. "Just playing, Ma."

Northern Europe's long-lingering midsummer sun, whorling gold and red, hung low in the sky as we exited the automated motorway near Aunt Lynh's apartment. As soon as we parked, Elio opened the car door and shouted, "Follow me!"

We ran out into a well-kept park that was surrounded by the six buildings of the apartment complex. We had just come to a large tree with serrated heart-shaped leaves and a pleasant fruity scent (I later learned that it was a linden tree) when I heard Aunt Lynh call: "Elio! Come here!"

His shoulders and head drooped.

"Come here—right now!"

"Aw, Ma!"

"Now!"

We walked back—Elio appearing dejected, like a balloon that had lost its air—to where she and Grandpa stood beside the luggage.

"Elio, haven't I told you not to take Sara near that tree?"

He merely shrugged.

"Now, you listen real good, mister. If you get Sara hurt horsing around, you'll be grounded for the rest of the summer. That means in your room, no internet, no movies, no going out with your friends—all summer. Got it? She's younger and she's not used to playing with the kind of roughnecks you play with, so you've got to use your head and be careful. And don't you dare climb in that tree with her. Are you listening to me?"

"Jeez, Ma."

"Don't you 'Jeez, Ma' me. Now answer properly. Are you going to be careful with Sara all during her stay?"

"Ja, I'll be real careful."

"You'd better be. And don't forget to hold on to her hand whenever you're near cars or buses. You should think of her as your little sister. Now, it's almost your bedtime. Come up with Professor Jensen and me and show Sara your room."

The door to their apartment opened to a living room. To the left was the kitchen. Beyond the living room and kitchen were two bedrooms: Aunt Lynh's to the left and Elio's to the right, with a bathroom between. All the rooms seemed small to me. There were pictures in frames on most of the walls, and light brown carpet covered the living room and bedroom floors. In our house there were no carpets or rugs, which would have been even better hiding places for surveillance microbots than pictures on the walls. Furthermore, we had no need for such floor coverings because our soft ceramic floors were heated from below. But Elio appeared proud while showing me his room, small and cramped and carpeted though it was. He took particular care while demonstrating exactly where and how he sat when he talked with me on Vidtel.

He and I played with a few of his toys while Grandpa and Aunt Lynh talked in the kitchen. I'd never before played with another human child and was fascinated watching Elio's hands and hearing his voice, which made growling, screeching, and exploding noises, as if he were adding a soundtrack to our activities.

After about a half-hour, Aunt Lynh peeked inside the bedroom door. "Elio, it's your bedtime. Sara has to leave with her grandfather. They'll be back first thing in the morning."

As soon as Aunt Lynh's face disappeared from the crack in the door, Elio whispered, "Tell them you want to stay here with me."

"Where's Grandpa going?"

"We don't have a guest room, so he's going to a hotel. But you tell them you want to stay here with me."

I ran out to Grandpa and hugged him tightly around his neck.

"Oh, my, my," he said. "Whatever is the matter?"

I glanced back at Elio, who was standing near his bedroom door, his enticing dark eyes focused on me.

"May I stay here with Elio?" I asked.

Later that night, right after Aunt Lynh had tucked Elio and me in bed and kissed us goodnight, Elio whispered, "Let's take off our pajamas."

I turned to him. "Why?" There was just enough light coming in from his bathroom night-light to allow me to see him smile.

"Because it's more comfortable that way—and free."

"Would that be okay with your mom?"

"The rule is, if she wants to come in, she has to knock and then I go and open the door. So, if she knocks, we'll put our pajamas back on and then I'll go and open the door. She'll never know."

"Okay," I said.

That was the first night, the first of many in summers to come, that he wrapped himself around me and called me the cuddliest teddy bear in the whole world.

In the morning, I woke before Elio, slipped out of bed, put my pajamas back on, and began playing with his toys—quietly, with none of his action-imitative noises. All the while I played, I felt as though I was getting away with something I shouldn't have been doing. Then, as was usual for my mornings at home, I began meditating. I was still sitting cross-legged on the floor when Elio woke.

"What're you doing?" he asked sleepily, his head raised slightly from his pillow, his hair tousled and matted as if it were wind-churned black grass.

"Meditating."

"Meditating? Why do you do that?"

"To quiet the hustle and bustle of the world, to help me become more aware."

"What do you become more aware of?"

My mind went blank for a moment, aware only of his enchanting eyes and hair and sleepy puzzled look. I should have told him that while meditating I found a heart beating, the quiet rise and fallback of breath, sensations of my body touching the floor—but nothing more, except a sense of a dark hollowness abuzz with unformed thoughts, which I could watch fill my consciousness, not so unlike how I sometimes sat quietly on the deck above the vineyard house and watched fog drift over the hills and down into the valley, finding its place in the emptiness of the world.

But all I was able to think of then in answer to his question was, "Things."

"Things?" He squinched his eyelids to such narrow slits that I wondered whether he could actually see through them.

First Brother

In her gloved hands, she holds a paddle in which the shaft is partially retracted into one of its blades. In sync with the rocking of the raft in the water, the shadow of the brim of her hat moves about on the paddle. She appears to visually scan the coastline. She pauses once for approximately five seconds and again for approximately eight seconds to focus on a sailboat listing onto its port side in the sand of Goat Rock Beach.

She begins to extend the shaft of the paddle, looks up, smiles, and exclaims: "Pigeonoid! I'm so happy to see you!" She brings her hands together, pulls the glove from her right hand, and reaches out with the naked hand. Her hand moves back and forth in a motion correlated with increasing and decreasing stroking pressure (as predicted, within acceptable parameters) on the dorsal structure. The irregular tessellated pattern of the skin on her wrist is penetrated by sweat-gland shafts, which occasionally well up with moisture that glistens in the sun before evaporating.

A close visual inspection of her lips and nostrils confirms that she is free from the infection.

Sara

Before escaping to this place under the sea, I copied everything I was able to gain access to on Grandpa's computer. I've been reviewing notes for a book he began but apparently never finished on android psychology. The following entry was made just over three years before I was born and twelve years before Michael first opened his eyes:

> Creativity requires more than the generation of representational diversity and the ability to recognize novel patterns; it also requires the recognition of significant new problems. In humans, problems arise naturally out of their continual dialogue with the world in which they are embedded. The lack of motivation to dialogue with the external world that typifies androids at their present stage of development undoubtedly contributes to their low level of creative output even in the sciences and mathematics, belying the pedestrian notion that the abstract is not emotionalized.
>
> The problem of emotion in androids begins with the problem of empathy, for we do not know how to engender a rich repertoire of emotion without a foundation of empathy. But repeated failures over the past few decades to achieve even a moderate degree of empathy in androids from our most sophisticated mirror neuron systems lends credence to the theory that empathy presupposes an experience of the

other as being like oneself. To that end, we make androids look like us and give them servo-mechanical systems capable of mimicking the actions of our bodies. But how is it possible for a creature to experience itself as being like me if it has never experienced hunger, pain, the discomforts of heat and cold, the total dependency on parents during infancy, the relative intellectual and physical inadequacies of youth, sexual desire, and so on? On these and on most other aspects of my life as lived, any adult furry little mammal in the wild is more like me than is any android yet created.

We need to develop and study intelligent systems that feel hunger and pain, go through long periods of dependency, struggle to learn, desire...

Grandpa eventually got what he wanted: two such intelligent systems, ones that would feel pain and desire and all the rest—Michael and me—to develop and study. And love and protect and deceive.

Nearly three months after my eighth birthday I lay, dreamy and blissful, on an operating table not long after receiving a sedative. Colorful cartoon images seemed to appear and disappear on the top of the white interior of a sterile operation tent, which had been designed by the military for occasions when evacuation to a hospital was impracticable. A scent, as of a tub scrubbed very clean, permeated everything, and the air felt drowsy amid the soft buzz of air filter motors keeping positive pressure inside the tent.

First Brother stood beside me, wearing a white surgeon's gown. We were in the back part of the house, in Grandpa's laboratory and study, where we had what Grandpa called level 3 security. Above us, beyond the top of the tent, beyond the ceiling of the room, and up through five meters of sandy soil, chardonnay vines hung heavy with musty, sweet-smelling grapes nearing harvest in the late September sun.

I looked up at First Brother's face. I'd been told that the visible portion of his head had been produced by a Japanese company, but it hadn't occurred to me before that his Asian facial features were remarkably handsome. In the soft glow of sedatives, I felt radiantly confident that he would perform the operation perfectly. As soon as Grandpa, Grandma, Mom, and Dad finished their tea (Grandpa had said he wanted everything to appear perfectly normal in the front parts of the house, where security wasn't so good), cells to generate the biological components of my new brother, Michael, would be extracted from me.

I placed my hand on First Brother's hand. "I'll miss you when you go to live in Canada."

"Why?" he replied without looking away from the systems monitor.

"You're my brother. I like playing games with you. Grandpa says you've worked hard preparing for this operation."

"The operation will not be difficult," he replied, still looking away. "I was chosen to perform it because my hands and brain function rapidly, steadily, and accurately. There is minimal risk that you will come to harm. You are to remain calm."

"I'm so calm I feel I could melt right into this table."

"Your blood pressure and brain activity rise when you talk."

"Will you miss me when you're in Canada?"

He turned to me, the saccade of his eyes over my face and arms reminding me again—though now my imagination was heightened by drugs—of dragonflies, their micaceous wings aflutter. "No," he answered. "Grandpa will take care of you. You will not need me. I will not need you."

I looked away. First Brother could be so difficult at times. In the nearly five years since we'd met, he and I had played with

Lily; we'd listened to Grandpa's favorite music (by Bach, Beethoven, or Zwilich); we'd talked about many things, especially my studies (actually, I'd done nearly all of the talking); and once we'd even baked cookies with Grandma, and then he and I had pretended that he'd come to have afternoon tea with me in my house when we were older and that he'd been able to eat the cookies and drink the tea. I'd learned to enjoy his company—most of the time, that is—if he seemed to give me at least a modicum of attention. But often, when his eyes stubbornly remained focused elsewhere, I had to imagine that he had another pair of eyes in the side of his head and that those eyes focused only on me.

"What time is it?" I asked.

"The time is 1611. We will begin in nineteen minutes."

It's night already in Amsterdam, I thought, and Elio will be asleep. If I were there, he would have wrapped himself around me, his skin feeling so good next to mine.

With a start, I heard the air filter motors rev, groaning under the strain of maintaining positive pressure as the operation tent door zipped open.

"How's my brave and wonderful girl?" Mom asked as she entered. Dad and Grandpa followed. Their hair and faces were wrapped in white.

"I'm ready," I answered.

"All systems and functions are acceptable," First Brother said.

Grandpa adjusted the IV. "Please count slowly for me, honey—down from ten."

"Ten, nine," I felt something cool spreading through my arm, "eight—"

First Brother

"What a beautiful day to see you," she says.

The smiling and the stroking on the dorsal structure of the pigeonoid continue.

"You're looking very well."

A lighter stroking, now of the forward ventral structure, commences.

"Do you have a message for me?"

The stroking of the ventral structure ceases. She holds her palm up and open, displaying its pattern of furrows that map where her palm and fingers fold in on themselves. Six seconds pass. She retracts her hand.

"No? Just along for the ride, then? Well, I'm glad to have the company."

She extends her legs, pushing the dorsal side of her torso against the edge of the raft at one pole of the major axis of the cavity. She puts the removed glove back on her right hand, pats her right thigh with her gloved right hand, and says: "If you'd like to stay drier, you're welcome to come down here." She pats, smiles, waits, then says: "Well, make yourself at home wherever you like."

She begins paddling with a Beaufort 4 breeze at her back toward the washed-up sailboat south of the mouth of the Russian River.

Sara

From as far back as I can remember, Stanley Franklin, the U.S. senator from Massachusetts who was on the Armed Services Committee, visited us for two or three days a couple of times each year. During those visits, Grandpa devoted full attention to his dear old friend, and so those visits became mini-vacations from study for me. I especially enjoyed listening to the senator talk with Grandpa and Grandma about unsavory characters he'd recently met in Washington, D.C.—usually members of the Ecumenical Reform Party. "Urps," Senator Franklin called them (for ERP), often with a slight gagging gesture.

The day before Labor Day, about three weeks before my operation, Grandpa returned home from Senator Franklin's annual summer party at the senator's beach house on Cape Cod. He gave Grandma and me a hug, then excused himself, saying that he wanted to go to his study to think. He appeared tired and distracted.

He was also wearing the same clothes—white socks, tan pants, and long-sleeve white shirt with red and blue stripes—that he'd worn when he left to visit Senator Franklin. In fact, they were the same clothes he'd been wearing every day for at least a month. I noticed this because usually Grandma would get after him to put on something different after he'd worn a particular shirt or pants continuously for about a week; and when she would, Grandpa would comply, often grumbling to me in private that my grandmother was a bit old-fashioned, having grown up before outer garments were available that no longer actually needed washing. As for the recommended nano-laundry after thirty wearings, Grandpa said he didn't care for the so-called laundry-fresh scent; he preferred the unique scent of each person's body.

Wearing the same clothes was only one of Grandpa's many rigid routines. Except for infrequent meals taken away from home, he ate the same breakfast, lunch, and dinner every day, year after year, occasionally adding a different fresh fruit or vegetable from our garden that Grandma would insist he try. Every day, he ate at the same time, worked with me on my studies at the same time, exercised at the same time, went to bed at the same time. Years later, Elio would tell me that he thought my grandpa was slightly autistic. When I questioned Grandma about this, she said, "Honey, as you experience more of the world, you'll find that to be male is to be at least slightly autistic."

After Grandpa disappeared into his study on this day that he returned from Senator Franklin's, I tattled on him, pointing out to Grandma that I thought he'd been wearing the same clothes for a very long time. She said he'd been working extra hard lately and that at such times it was best just to let him be in whatever he felt most comfortable.

The next day, Mom and Dad arrived earlier than usual and immediately went to join Grandpa in his study, where the three of them stayed until lunch. Grandma had told me earlier in the morning that First Brother would not be coming along because Grandpa wanted to talk privately with Mom and Dad about some important matters that might take all day. I'd complained that First Brother could have played with me while Grandpa talked with Mom and Dad, but Grandma had merely shrugged.

After lunch, Mom and Dad left, and Grandpa took me to his study, where he had me sit beside him on the sofa. He began by telling me that Senator Franklin had convinced him it was likely that, for the first time, the ERP would achieve a plurality in both the House and Senate in the next year's election and that, with their increased power, they almost certainly would pass a law banning the creation of new androids and possibly even ordering the destruction of all existing androids, even First Brother.

"Kill First Brother?" I said.

"Yes, honey, but don't worry. Your mother and father have just told me they're going to send both of your brothers to live with a trusted associate in Canada as soon as possible. Your brothers will be safe there."

"They won't live with Mom and Dad anymore?"

"Not for now, but your parents plan to follow your brothers to Canada if the ERP succeeds as well as Senator Franklin predicts."

"They'll still come to visit me, won't they? And First Brother will, too."

Grandpa sighed. "You simply have to accept that your brothers will be leaving soon, that next year your mother and father probably also will leave, and that if we are to create a new type of android—a bioroid, actually—we must do so quickly, before the chance is forever snatched from us."

He paused, as though waiting for me to grasp the subject he'd just interjected.

"You want to create Third Brother?" I asked.

"Not exactly. For over ten years now, your mother, father, and I have secretly been doing research and making plans for a bioroid, one incorporating a Sentiren brain within a brain much like your own."

I asked why he wanted to create such a new brother. He reminded me that Mom, Dad, and he were finding it difficult to elicit full emotional responses from my brothers, who possessed an emotional repertoire sufficient to set goals and priorities but remained deficient in such emotions as happiness and love. Other scientists were having similar problems with their android creations. He explained that unlike me, First Brother's creation was not accomplished during a simple moment of joy; it involved a lifetime of Grandpa's acquiring the knowledge of thousands of other lifetimes of learning. It also involved decades of intense work by him and Mom and Dad.

"Perhaps," he said, "if First Brother had come to consciousness with you as his primary caregiver, he would have learned how to hug and love a sister before he learned how to think about quantum physics. Perhaps part of his difficulty is—"

"You're going to let me raise my new brother," I interrupted, "so he'll be able to love me?"

"Before we—you and I—decide whether we're going to do that, I need to explain a few things. Your mother, father, and I have perfected how to grow a mammalian brain on a scaffolding of organic nanoneuralnets so that mammalian brain neurons not only grow and flourish side-by-side with Sentiren neurons, they actually connect to and communicate with the Sentiren neurons to such an extent that the mammalian brain and the organic nanoneuralnet brain become totally integrated and operate as a unitary system."

"You want to put human brain cells into my new brother?"

"I want you to understand clearly that I don't want to create this new being unless you do. In the first place, if we proceed with the project, we'll be involved in highly controversial activities that are likely to become illegal if Stan's predictions come true.

"Second, as I see it, the project can succeed only if you desire to raise this new being as if he were your son. This would be much more involved than simply spending a few hours together with him on the occasional weekend, as you've done with First Brother. It would mean giving him limitless time and love in order to make him the best he can be."

Grandpa explained that if I began this project simply because he wanted me to, or because I thought Mom or Dad wanted me to, I would be doing so for the wrong reasons, and we would all fail. He was concerned, he said, that he or Mom or Dad might influence me to do something I didn't want to do and would later regret.

Looking back, I see how craftily Grandpa played my eight-year-old ego—letting me fantasize that only I, not Mom, Dad, Grandma or he, was capable of raising a bioroid as if it were a human child. Why did he let me puff myself up in this way? He must have wanted more than informed consent; he must have wanted informed desire, desire that would grab hold of me before the core reason for my involvement was disclosed.

What he seemed not to have known was that I had often fantasized about having a brother who would live with me, and run and play and study with me. I wanted to help First Brother acquire a richer emotional life, to skip and laugh and recognize faces in clouds; but he lived with Mom and Dad, and he didn't care much for play, not with me, at any rate.

When I detected a break in Grandpa's train of thought, I exclaimed, "I want his name to be Michael! Not Third Brother—Michael!"

"Michael? Are you paying attention to what I'm saying?"

"Yes," I answered guiltily, for my mind had been timesharing between his words and my fantasies. "Tell me what my new brother will be like."

Grandpa proceeded to explain that because few self-generating, non-biologic materials were available, my new brother would begin life adult size. However, like human babies, my new brother's ability to interact with the world would develop primarily through his experiences of his body and his relations with his primary caregiver—me.

Grandpa said that if the project were to go forward, it would involve extracting a few neurons and other cells from various locations in my brain—if I didn't mind, of course—reprogramming those cells, and then placing them in a gestation chamber, where for ten months they would reproduce, differentiate, and connect with each other and with organic nanoneuralnets. During the same operation, cells from my liver, kidneys, thymus, bone marrow, and other organs would also be extracted; and through a process similar to that used for the brain cells, those extracted cells would develop into functioning organs of a biologic system necessary to support the biologic parts of the integrated brain.

Unlike First Brother, my new brother would need to go to the bathroom; he would even cry salty tears, just like mine!

And then came the disclosure of what I now believe was the core reason for my involvement: Michael and I could more directly be a part of each other, Grandpa said, if interconnections between our brains were made through implants to my cribriform plate, which, he explained, was a good place for such a junction because it was hidden and was easily accessible through my nostrils. The implants would be constructed from my cells and would be nourished and repaired as if they were a natural part of me, thereby making the junctions all the more difficult to detect—possibly an important feature, depending on future political developments.

"What would the connection be for?" I asked.

"After some practice with the braincord, it should be possible for you and Michael to enter each other's thoughts and to control each other's arms, hands, and other motor functions."

Though I don't remember being concerned about the extraction of cells, I reacted strongly to this braincord suggestion. Someone's controlling my body had not been part of my fantasy of having a new brother. Images of some of my own intimate interactions with my body flashed through my mind, and I scooted off the couch. "No!"

Grandpa's eyebrows squirmed like fuzzy white caterpillars. "Of course, Michael wouldn't—"

"No! No! I don't want that!"

I wanted a brother I could play with, not someone new who would be capable of controlling me even more than Grandpa already did.

Grandpa continued looking at me with steady attention. This was the look that often preceded my having to sit cross-legged on the floor of his study and meditate until I calmed. But determined to have the brother I wanted, not the brother I thought Grandpa wanted, I stayed my ground, standing silently in front of him.

Although he was intent on motivating his androids with emotion, Grandpa was suspicious of human emotions, which, he said, had evolved in a primitive world very different from the one in which we now had to survive and prosper. In our advanced technological world, only reason transformed into wisdom through carefully guided experience and training could tame and properly direct our powerful yet often errant and dangerous emotional heritage, a heritage providing modern humans with at best a call to action and a coarse first approximation as to what that action should be. Thus, my human emotions had to be passed through the meditative filter of reason, so that I might confront reality with a minimum of illusions and self- or clan-centered aggression.

"I just want a nice brother I can study with and play with," I finally said.

Grandpa smiled. "Yes, of course, you do. I wouldn't think of giving Michael any capability to harm or embarrass you. I can assure you that Michael will not be able to exert any control over you that you wouldn't approve of. The power of his intentions and desires coming in through the braincord would be only a slight fraction of the power of your brain over itself. For him to have any influence over you at all, you would have to meditate and enter into a high state of relaxation and receptivity for him."

"Are you sure?"

"Yes. We thought you would enjoy being able to get inside and feel and understand Michael more directly and deeply than you ever could by using normal means of communication."

"I'd be able to feel what he feels?"

"We hope you will, at least to some extent."

"You mean, as when Grandma's happy I can see it in her face and hear it in her voice, but I can't really feel it. But with Michael I could really and truly feel his happiness?"

"Yes, that's right. And he could feel your happiness, too, if you choose to let him."

My imagination sparkled. I knew that words often were used to hide, not disclose. I'd sensed the shadowy underneath and behind of things. How wonderful it would be, then, to know, truly know, what was inside the words, gestures, and bright feelings of another.

"But," Grandpa said, interrupting my growing excitement, "if you don't want to have this capability with Michael, we can do quite well without the implant and the braincord."

Did Grandpa actually believe that Michael would never learn to override my will, or was that another deception? I haven't brainjoined with Michael even once since coming here to this watery hideaway, because on the way here I discovered that he could, in fact, control me completely. And not only that—I discovered a secret that he's been keeping from me, a secret I'm not yet ready to let him know that I know.

"I can see you're excited about creating Michael," Grandpa said after more discussion, "but there is one thing we have to be clear about before we proceed. We must keep all things related to him secret. Only you and I, Grandma, your father, mother, and brothers can ever know. Even Elio must not learn anything about your operation or about Michael."

My excitement was instantly replaced by a hollow feeling of dread. Only a few months earlier, when Grandpa and I had visited Elio and Aunt Lynh for the third summer in a row, Elio had more or less forced me to tell him what I knew about his father's death. I'd felt terrible about divulging the secret I'd promised Grandpa I would keep, and I'd promised myself never again to agree to keep a secret from Elio.

"Please, Grandpa, I can't keep secrets from Elio."

"If we are to do this, you must."

"But I'm sure he won't tell."

Grandpa again looked at me silently. I knew he was probably right about keeping Michael secret and that he would probably win this little battle with me, as he nearly always did. When my gaze finally slid toward the floor, he said, "It is likely that our phones are tapped, so we can't speak over the phone about any secret. Our use of encryption would only serve to inflame suspicion and increase surveillance. Nor can we speak about this matter among ourselves, even in the kitchen or anywhere else outside of these rooms where we have level 3 security. During the ten-month gestation period, we'll move most of my study and library into one of the guest bedrooms. We'll make a second bedroom for you in here. Michael will have to remain in these level 3 security rooms until the political climate improves."

"Michael can't leave here?"

"Not until it's safe for him to go outside. But we can make a comfortable world for him here. Grandma has plans for a beautiful hydroponic garden. Michael will have at least one of the three of us with him at all times, and we can import any information he might desire. I doubt he'll miss what he never experiences. Let me show you our plans for these rooms."

I wonder whether Grandpa thought much the same about me: that I wouldn't miss the parents I saw so little of, that I wouldn't miss the playmates I didn't have, and that even if I did miss other children, the desire would be transformed into one for a new brother. I wonder about all this now, but you—you little girl who once was I—you never wondered about such things, did you?

We moved to Grandpa's desk chair. I sat on his lap, and while he showed me on a monitor what he and Grandma had planned, I leaned my head back onto his firm, warm chest, where the endearing mustiness of his long-worn clothes reminded me of autumn leaves. The back part of the house in level 3 security was twenty meters wide and fifteen meters deep. At the time of this discussion, it contained Grandpa's study, library, and research lab; but by the time of Michael's birth (planned for the following September), Grandpa's things would be moved out, and two bedrooms, a play and study area, and a hydroponic garden with flowers, shrubs, and miniature trees would be installed.

Gatekeeper 3 was to be upgraded to include a small monitoring enclosure with heavy doors on each end. To enter the security area through Gatekeeper 3 after the upgrade, I would have to undress, leaving my clothes in a small antechamber in front of Gatekeeper's door. After an initial optical identification that would allow me to enter the monitoring enclosure through the first door, my skin and hair would be optically examined to ensure that no micro-devices were attached to me. Then the second door would open to let me into another small antechamber—this one inside the level 3 security area. To take anything other than my naked self into this area would require a special security procedure supervised by Grandpa.

Grandpa explained that within the thick carbon nanofiber-reinforced walls, ceiling, and floor of the level 3 security area there was a layer of microactuators that scrambled into gibberish all sounds that were made in the area. Even silence was converted into gibberish, leaving no way to detect from outside the walls what was said or done within the area. No plumbing or communication links with the outside world were available in the area. Batteries installed in the level 2 area provided all the power. There wasn't even any plumbing, so to use the bathroom I would have to go through Gatekeeper to the level 2 area, and Michael would have to use a bedpan.

Most of Michael's nutritional and oxygenic needs would be met by air scrubbers and by the hydroponic garden. Everything necessary to complete the plans would be purchased, moved, and constructed over the ten-month gestation by Grandpa, Grandma, Mom, and Dad.

"But Grandpa, Michael can't leave? He can't see the sky and hills? What about the vineyard? These rooms will be like a cage."

"A cage! Oh my, no. Nothing like a cage. There will be scenescreens on which we can play recordings of the sky, hills, vineyard, and anything else you or he might want to see. He'll have you and Grandma and me and any and all information products available. His world will be a rich, interesting, and love-filled world, not a cage."

"Are you sure?"

"Yes. In fact, I believe you have things quite turned around. Out there, in the big world, his activities would, at best, be severely restricted. He would not be free. He would not be loved. And his life would be in great danger from people who hate androids. Indeed, for most of us, it is the outside world that is a cage. Can you understand this—that these three rooms we have planned can be made into a wonderful and free world, whereas the outside is a vicious, dangerous cage in which most of our actions are severely circumscribed by others?"

I studied the finished space displayed on the monitor. It did appear to be a comfortable home for Michael, and I turned again to what was for me the most difficult issue.

"I understand about the phone and about not talking about Michael outside of here, but couldn't I whisper in Elio's ear next summer when I see him?"

"First, I don't think the two of you could whisper softly enough to defeat sophisticated monitoring devices. Second, we can't trust that Elio will keep—"

"He would, Grandpa! How can you not trust Elio?"

Grandpa became silent again, waiting for my emotional intensity to subside.

"I know he would," I said more calmly.

Grandpa remained silent.

I searched his face and found that he was no longer simply waiting for me to calm down; he appeared perplexed and deep in thought. He raised one of my hands to his lips and kissed it. "I'm sorry. I didn't consider the seriousness of this problem. I am, of course, aware that you and Elio have become close friends. I believe I can appreciate how painful it must be for you to keep an important secret from him."

Grandpa sighed and tapped his fingers lightly on his desk. "I want to tell you about an experience I had with someone who was a close friend when he and I were both medical students at Stanford. We shared many interests. We double-dated. Even after we graduated and went our separate ways, we stayed in close contact with each other. But then seminars and protests led by a coalition of social egalitarians and religious conservatives began to spring up around the world. These activities culminated in the United Nations passing the International Human Genome

Protection Act. I felt it was foolish to think humans were the pinnacle of the wonderful process of evolution, which had been going on for billions of years and would continue for billions more, whether we tried to stop it or not. I believed then and I believe now that we will either be a dead end or a stepping-stone to new beings better capable than we in dealing with a world of ever-increasing complexity."

"What about your friend?"

"Along with most other people, he felt it was wrong to genetically enhance human offspring to make them super-intelligent, super-strong, or super-anything. Alterations to make a fetus healthy and normal were acceptable, but anything else was proclaimed to be a crime against humanity. I thought, and still think, that the law is a crime against nature—a nature of which man, his aspirations, and the products of his toil are as much a part as are bees and their drive for nectar and the building of hives. But I was wrong when I failed then to appreciate that intelligent and good people disagree on this law and on many other significant issues."

"Is he your friend again?"

"I see him a couple of times each year at seminars where we make a point of having lunch or tea together, but that's all. It has never been the same between us."

"I don't want that to happen to Elio and me."

"Exactly. I told you about my old friend for two reasons: first, so you won't make the all-too-common mistake of thinking that people who disagree with you on issues you take to be important are necessarily less intelligent or less good than you are. Take the Human Genome Protection Act, for example. I have no doubt that without it, significant changes and stresses would have already been introduced into our civilization. Wealthier people would have, generation after generation, produced more intelligent, better-looking, stronger children. They could have and would have produced super-basketball players, super-musicians, super-mathematicians. But until our techniques became inexpensive and generally available, the vast majority of people could only have had children who were normal humans."

"Did you ever break the law?"

"No. I disagreed with it. I think the law is a travesty that will be unable to hold back the forces of human curiosity and greed and the desire for better children, but I never broke it. The penalties for violating the Genome Act are severe. All babies are tested at birth, and any proved to have been genetically enhanced without prior authorization are sterilized if the modification extends to the germ line. The parents and all co-conspirators are given minimum ten-year prison sentences, and all of their personal property is confiscated. You were tested when you were born, as were your father and mother when they were born.

"I have always abided by the Genome Act, but I can't believe that everyone everywhere has. Genetic enhancement technology will take root somewhere, and when it does we will have a choice: mass extermination of an incipient super-race or a mass stampede to jump aboard the evolution bullet train.

"But that's a discussion for another day. Today, we're concerned about whether we should keep everything about Michael secret from Elio—which brings me to my second reason for telling you about my friend. There is no doubt in my mind that he was and is an intelligent and fine man. There is no doubt in my mind, or in yours, I'm sure, that Elio is an intelligent and good boy. I'm happy that the two of you are close friends, and I don't want to do anything to harm your relationship. But here's the problem: Let's suppose I'd violated the Genome Act, and suppose further that my friend had found out. Would he have turned me in?"

"I don't know."

Grandpa sighed. "Nor do I. But my guess is that he would

have, for he believed that much death, misery, and destruction would result from violations of the law."

"But what about Elio?"

"As I've said, I fully expect that he'll grow up to be a wise and good person, but we can't deduce from that that he'll agree with our views on androids or on religion or on a thousand other issues. You see, honey, regardless of how close you and Elio become, there will always be some mysterious core of a wonderful other about him. Like all of us, he is too complex to ever fully understand. And one of the things we cannot know is whether he'll become one who feels that androids are thinking, feeling, conscious beings who should be treated with love and respect, or whether he'll feel otherwise. In either case, I hope he'll love you and you'll love him, but because we can't know now what he'll feel about the android issue, I'm afraid this secret about Michael is an unfortunate pain you will have to accept until Elio becomes more mature."

"When will that be? When may I tell him?"

"Probably not until he goes to university and experiences nonhuman conscious intelligences, if there still are any around then. In the meanwhile, you can be as close to him as you want. But remember, you'll always be a marvelous mystery to him, too, no matter how close you and he become. This secret about Michael simply will be part of that mystery for a while."

Except for a slight irritation that seemed lodged in my sinuses, I woke feeling good the morning after my operation. Cartoon images no longer appeared and evaporated like little clouds on the roof of the tent above me. The air filter motors were silent, and Grandpa was sitting beside me. He told me the operation had gone extremely well: I was in excellent condition; enough cells extracted from every location were viable, so no part of the operation would have to be repeated; and the braincord junction implant looked good. First Brother had been an excellent surgeon.

As usual, Elio called on Vidtel when he got home from school, shortly after I'd finished breakfast.

As soon as I spoke, he asked, "Do you have an allergy?"

It's started, I thought. "No," I answered.

"You sound like you do. Is there anything you're allergic to?"

"Not that I know of."

"Have you been crying?"

"No."

Mercifully, he moved on to tell me about his day at school.

"Never lie, but never reveal the truth" is the old Roman maxim Grandpa had suggested I apply in conversations with Elio whenever anything related to Michael came up. But applying the maxim left me feeling estranged; and Elio, who'd become sensitive to my feelings, cut short our conversation, saying that he knew I had an allergy or something and wasn't feeling good. When he exited Vidtel, I turned away from the image platform and cried into the back of the chair, thinking how very, very long it would be until he went to university.

Two weeks after the operation, First Brother came to visit me. It was the day before Mom and Dad packed him and Second Brother into separate crates and shipped them, along with crates of fruits and vegetables, to Calgary, Alberta. First Brother examined me and concurred with Grandpa that bone and tissue around the braincord junctions had attached to the junctions and had healed perfectly. I was ready to begin the Focused Magnetic Driver (FMD) sessions, which, over a six-month period, would create neural pathways connecting the braincord junctions with every area of my brain.

Grandpa had reminded me earlier in the day that outside of level 3, I couldn't say anything about, couldn't even allude to, the operation, the braincord, or Michael—and that though proper export papers and bills of sale had been drawn up allowing First Brother to be sent to Canada, I shouldn't cry or say good-bye to First Brother or speak about his leaving; for if we were being spied on, it would be by a much more sophisticated and dangerous group of people than those who supervise the low-level expert systems that, in turn, supervise the movement of products being traded between the U.S. and Canada. Furthermore, to avoid suspicion being directed toward our home, which would be Michael's home too in a few months, I would not be able to communicate with First Brother after this day, not by Vidtel or otherwise.

The confluence of several distressing developments made that day, the last day I saw First Brother in California, the saddest of my childhood. His imminent departure was one such development, and it, together with my need to suppress any emotion related to his departure, served to catalyze other dark clouds in my mind: Mom and Dad probably also would emigrate to Canada; I had to stay on guard and hide the truth for many years to come whenever I spoke with Elio; there had been an ominous tone to Grandpa's voice whenever he'd spoken about the ERP's seemingly unstoppable rise to power; Grandpa had been spending less time with me and more time working on matters related to Michael; and finally, I was committed to spending four hours each day for the next six months strapped in the FMD.

All that day, from the time Grandpa cautioned me in the morning until after First Brother left that evening, I suffered a foreboding that my happy childhood was ending, to be replaced by what I was unprepared for: the deceptions, losses, and responsibilities of adulthood.

As First Brother was about to get into the car with Mom and Dad, I broke away from Grandpa's hand, ran to First Brother, and, reaching up, said, "I want to hug you."

In my memories, I keep searching for the place where things went wrong, for where I might have done something that would have avoided or righted the coming events. But all I find is an ineluctable tide of circumstances well beyond the abilities of a little girl to hold back. I'd desired to become the heroine who would have succeeded—where Grandpa, Mom, and Dad had failed—in helping First Brother acquire a richer emotional life. But I'd not known what to do other than to accept First Brother as a unique individual with interests different from my own, and to fantasize that when I became older and more learned, I would be able to teach him to laugh and love. I'd thought I had plenty of time. Now, I was eight years old, and First Brother had never laughed—or loved, as far as I could tell—and he was leaving, taking away with him my dream of being a heroine for him.

First Brother bent over and picked me up. I held him tightly, consciously desiring to retain my every sense of him. He was tall, strong, and firm; his hair was soft and black; his skin olive brown; eyes hazel; lips full, but tightly closed and still. His clothes smelled laundry fresh. Times that we'd been together flashed through my mind. Except for Elio during two weeks of each of the three prior summers, First Brother had been my only childhood playmate.

Holding back tears, I caressed his smooth face, kissed his cool cheek, and said, "I love you, First Brother."

He stiffened, as he always had in response to my emotion, and put me down.

As the car disappeared beyond the perimeter gate I turned and ran back to the house, where I requested Gatekeeper 1 to let me in. I ran to the entrance to the bedroom area and requested Gatekeeper 2 to let me in. I ran to the entrance to Grandpa's study and, barely able to choke back tears, requested Gatekeeper 3 to let me in. Then I dove onto Grandpa's sofa, where I cried and cried, no longer even conscious of what I was crying about, and cried on until Grandpa came and held me.

"Shhh... shhh," he whispered, stirring up in me images and sounds of the ocean breathing on the shore. "Shhh... Everything is all right. You were a good and brave girl."

First Brother

She pulls the raft up onto the narrow strip of gray-brown sand that separates the ocean from the Jenner Estuary. The beach is littered with driftwood. Mist rises from wet sand into air vibrating with the screeching of gulls and the sibilant sound of waves breaking near the shore.

She begins walking toward the sailboat. She is within 50 meters of the boat. A dog (highest correlation: golden retriever) emerges from the shadow of the listing boat and trots toward her. She smiles. She pets the dog. The dog sniffs, licks, and paws her. She expresses fondness in a manner humans are wont to express with their pets and young children.

Outside the space of probable behavior, she cries as she holds the dog. By increasing magnification through the pigeonoid's eyes, I conclude that she is unharmed by the dog, which barks, struggles to escape from her grip, and, succeeding, lunges forward. Her image rapidly diminishes in size. The distance between her and the dog increases. She is heard to shout: "No! Come back! Don't chase the pigeonoid. He's our friend."

The dog stops running and turns. It looks back at her and pants. She wipes at both of her eyes with the back of her gloved right hand. "Come here, boy. Come." She pats her legs just above her knees. "Come. That's a good boy. Come here." The dog runs back to her. They meet and she hugs the dog. "Oh, yes, yes. That's a good boy. Yes."

She pulls her head away from the dog and strokes the dog's flanks. "You're so thin. Where's your human? Where's home?"

Sara

Grandpa began the FMD sessions at 1700 the day after First Brother last visited us. Before the first session, Grandpa asked me to look through his microscope at the navitors, tiny rod-shaped pellets variably magnetized on one end and approximately half the size of a brain neuron cell body.

He told me that every three days a new cluster of navitors would be implanted in the braincord junctions and that for two hours each evening beginning at 1700 and for two hours each morning beginning at 0500—times when Elio almost certainly wouldn't call—I would lie perfectly still in the FMD, which would drive the navitors at the rate of approximately 1 millimeter per session toward their designated target areas in my brain. As they traveled, the navitors' paths would diverge so that the FMD could send them to the 12,464 Harvard brain-classification areas Grandpa had designated as target areas. The navitors would slowly dissolve as they penetrated my brain, leaving a trail of molecular guidance cues and neuron growth factors that would develop into neural pathways running between the braincord junctions and their target areas. All tests on animal and Sentiren-type brains and all computer simulations had proved, Grandpa said, that there was no risk whatsoever of degradation in my brain functions—the entire process was as safe as, though more involved than, cutting toenails.

Looking back, it's hard for me to believe that, despite his

assurances, I didn't harbor some fear. Perhaps I'm simply not remembering.

The braincord, the last 15 centimeters of which were bifurcated into two white channels, was guided by microsensors implanted near its tips. The first time it moved up my nostrils, I was so overcome by irritation that Grandpa quickly backed the cord out.

I vigorously rubbed my alarmed nose. "It feels like two worms slithering up there!"

"That was a good, healthy response," he said, handing me a tissue. "We have automatic responses that help prevent things from slithering up our noses. Don't fight the tickling sensations. Accept them. Relax when the cord moves into your nostrils. Shall we try again?"

The second time, I concentrated on accepting the tickling, the watery eyes, and the runny nose; and the braincord found its junctions and implanted the first navitor clusters. For the next two hours, I lay still, listening to the FMD's high-pitched chirr, which sounded as though it came from the busy workings of hundreds of little hammers. After a few sessions, neither the braincord's movement up my nostrils nor the FMD's buzz bothered me, and during the many hours I was required to lie still in the FMD, I was able to think about the math problems Grandpa had given me or about what it might be like to have Michael rather than this monotonous machine connected to me.

Senator Franklin visited us one evening while he was in California for a Pacific defense conference. On that day, my afternoon FMD session was completed early.

Grandpa made a point of showing the senator our remodeling plans, explaining that I would be a young woman in a few years and should have the privacy of the back third of the house for myself. "I don't need the security any longer," Grandpa said. "I'm glad to have put all that android stuff behind me. I wish Karl and Mary would do the same."

I felt confused in that moment, torn between revulsion at Grandpa's lie to his friend and conviction that Grandpa knew what was best—what he had to do.

"I heard about the transfer of their pets to somewhere in Canada," the senator replied. "In a truck with avocados and strawberries, wasn't it?"

"Yes," Grandpa chuckled.

"Quite a caper, that," the senator said, shaking his head. "Some uptight people in Washington were less than amused."

Over dinner, the senator complained unceasingly about his life and about what he called our troubled times: the military was demanding crazy projects that would bankrupt our country, which was already in its twelfth year of a seemingly implacable depression; barring some miracle, the ERP almost certainly would win many new seats in the next election; he would have to endure an exhausting campaign to win re-election; and his wife was unhappy that he had to work so hard and that when he did come home he was too tired to do anything.

Though I felt unease from Grandpa's seemingly light-hearted deception of his old friend, I sensed from Senator Franklin's words and the tone of his voice that things were bad in the cage of the outside world and were getting worse. Evidently, Grandpa had been right: We had to be vigilant in keeping our secrets. But little did I suspect how many secrets there would be or how they would multiply malignantly, taking on a dark life of their own.

Grandpa and I completed the FMD sessions during the first week of May, and six weeks later we flew to Amsterdam to visit Elio. Visiting Elio for my birthday had by now become a tradition, one I eagerly looked forward to. But this summer's visit was considerably darkened by the fact that Grandpa was vigilant the entire time in not letting me run or engage in any kind of physical play. I had to be ever careful not to bump or jar my head because the connections between my cribriform plate and the new neural pathways were still quite fragile. Even worse, I couldn't tell Elio why I was being such a spoilsport—such as when I refused to join him and his friends in a game of what he said Americans called soccer, games I had participated in and enjoyed in prior summers—and I feared he might never again want to spend another summer vacation with me.

As soon as Grandpa and I returned from the trip, Grandpa began having a computer stimulate the neural pathways that led to all parts of my brain from the junctions in my cribriform plate. My job was to practice total relaxation by concentrating on my breathing while the computer stimulated my newly formed nerve cells and monitored responses. I was also to report—but only when asked, since reporting broke my concentration—what sensations I'd felt and what mental impressions I'd had in the few seconds or minutes since the last report.

The first month of practice was devoted to acquainting the computer with my body. It quickly discovered how to move each of my fingers and toes, then my arms and legs. By the end of the first month, the computer had learned how to control my right hand sufficiently well to draw or type as proficiently as I could under my own control. Next, it learned how to move my tongue, mouth, and vocal cords so that during exhalations it was able to speak through me.

The strangest part of this was how natural it all seemed. Before the practice sessions began, I had imagined that having my arms and fingers and voice operated in some mysterious way would make me feel eerily possessed. But I found that as long as I remained totally relaxed and didn't interfere, my hands, legs—even the words I spoke—felt as though they were being consciously driven by me. Of course, the observer part of me knew the computer was manipulating my body, but the *feeling* of producing the motions or words was the same as if I myself had intentionally produced them.

What was this "I," then? An imagined something fantasizing that it was in control of a body and its thoughts? Perhaps I really was, as Grandpa had repeatedly said, a network analogous to a colony of ants, which functions well in complex ways without having any central control. Perhaps my "central control," my consciousness, was merely a complex feedback loop observing internal brain phenomena—an observer tricked by itself into thinking that it had control because the correspondence between observing and happening was so seamless that observing became seen as cause.

After the first month of these lessons, things became more difficult for me when the computer began exploring other areas of my brain. I would remember funny things and laugh; I would smell cookies baking or lilacs after a spring rain; I would see Elio on Vidtel or First Brother staring at a blank wall; I would hear Grandma talking or music playing or a squirrel clucking in a tree.

I repeatedly told Grandpa that I disliked the all-too-real feel of what I was experiencing, that I worried about losing the ability to distinguish these hallucinations from reality. He insisted that my job during these sessions was not to like or dislike anything. My job was to breathe in and out, in and out, and to observe—only observe and later report—the feelings, thoughts, sights, sounds, and other sense impressions stimulated by the computer.

Easy to say, I told him, but difficult to do.

"Difficult?" he responded. "It is not difficult to breathe or observe. If you're finding something difficult, then you're doing something other than breathing and observing."

I tried to do exactly as Grandpa instructed, but I continued to have trouble distinguishing between me-observing-me-seeing-something and me-seeing-something-while-observing-me-seeing-this same something. It was like being in a house of mirrors where I was one of the mirrors—but which one?

I tried to do exactly as Grandpa instructed because I understood that much of what the computer was learning would be passed on to Michael, and that much of what I was learning about observing myself under another's control would prove invaluable when Michael and I eventually connected through our braincord.

I tried to do exactly as Grandpa instructed because I loved Michael and was prepared to do anything for him even before he was born—on 3 September, Grandpa's eighty-third birthday. Until that day, I'd been allowed in to only two of the three rooms in the remodeled level 3 area: the sparsely furnished room that was to become my bedroom as soon as Michael was born, and the main room, which was to contain the hydroponic garden and Michael's and my study and living area.

Throughout Michael's ten-month gestation, I was not permitted even to peek into the third room when Grandpa entered it. He didn't want me to see how Michael was being made. As with Lily, I was to accept Michael whole, as an incomprehensibly complex and wonderful person, not as so many nerves and muscles and organs connected in such and such a way.

But as the months passed, the itch of curiosity grew too intense for me to keep from scratching it. One day in the eighth month, when Grandpa appeared to be concentrating on some problem and his hands were busy carrying a particularly large container, I stealthily followed behind him as he walked toward this mysterious third room. As the door slid open, a whoosh of warm air escaped, bringing with it the smell of something antiseptic. The light inside was blue and dim. In the center of the room sat a shiny metallic platform covered with a transparent cylindrical hood. Under the hood lay what looked like a headless, fully grown man whose chest had been carved open right down the middle. Off in a corner, on top of another metallic platform, stood a large tube filled with liquid. Suspended in the liquid was what appeared to be a brain with blood vessels and white cords leading down from it to lungs, a stomach, a liver—

The door whooshed shut.

Though that was the only time I got a peek inside Michael's gestation room, I often stood outside that room and wondered about my new brother growing in there. What would he be like? In what ways would he change my life? Would he really be all that I wanted him to be? All that First Brother had not been? And would he be happy in these three rooms, with only the scenescreens as his windows to the outside world?

On the morning of Michael's birth, I sat on one end of the sofa in the main room and watched as Grandpa and Grandma, wearing matching bamboo-leaf-patterned kimonos, carried my new brother out of the womb and laid him on the sofa, his head lowered gently onto my lap. His eyes were closed; he appeared to be sleeping. He had neatly combed, short black hair, like First Brother's, and wore only a white diaper. His body stretched out over the full length of the sofa. In the center of his tummy, where a navel might have been, was a socket with three rectangular holes—for the electricity to charge his many internal batteries and capacitors, I presumed. At 1.73 meters tall and weighing 51 kilograms, he was nearly twice as big as I. On the outside, he appeared to be First Brother's twin, but I knew that on the inside he was different.

"Look what has blossomed from the richly endowed encyclopedia of your cells," Grandpa said. I felt a surge of pride and caressed the cool, smooth skin of one of Michael's arms. Never would I give him away to someone else, as Mom and Dad had given me away. Never.

"Pass your hand over his eyes, and he'll wake up fully for the first time," Grandma said.

"Turn his head toward you so that the first thing he sees is your face," Grandpa added.

I carefully turned his head toward me and passed my hand over his eyes. His eyelids opened, revealing hazel eyes that appeared surprised as they gazed up at me.

"Oh, Grandma, he's beautiful!"

His mouth began opening and closing in an O shape, reminding me of a fish, and his fingers and toes repeatedly flexed open and closed.

"Yes, honey, isn't he though? Here, I think he's hungry already." She handed me a warm baby bottle, light blue with a tan nipple.

I put the nipple in his mouth and he began sucking. His fingers and toes relaxed. He lay quietly while I stroked his hair. In my mind, I finally had the brother I'd dreamed of, but I was aware that Grandpa and Grandma had a different view of things: I was to be Michael's mother. They had repeatedly explained from the beginning of the project that this meant it would be my responsibility to feed him, change his diapers (with Grandma's or Grandpa's help, as it turned out, since he was too big and heavy for me to change him by myself), keep him amused, and as time went on, discipline him and educate him, as they had me.

In addition to feeling sensory pain when he bumped something too hard or tore his self-healing skin, Michael had a "hard-wired inclination," as Grandpa said, to develop a strong emotional attachment to me, his primary caregiver; and the worst kind of pain for him seemed to consist of the sensations he felt, and the interpretations he made, whenever that emotional attachment was threatened.

He displayed this pain when I stopped holding him, when I

left the room, when I stopped talking to him, when I expressed displeasure, or when a thousand different things I didn't understand brought forth from him heart-breaking screams and staccato crying ("uh, uh, uh..."), his eyes pumping out tears that tasted like mine. At those times, those many exasperating times that he screamed and cried, I would take him in my arms and talk to him and caress him.

In addition to his unique crying, Michael's earliest vocalizations sounded like syllables consisting of only a vowel or a vowel and a consonant, such as "ee," "ah," and "da." For a while, I felt that his first word was my name, for he often said "Ah-ah" when he reached for me, but Grandpa and Grandma weren't convinced that those sounds amounted to a word or a name.

He was nearly three months old when I first noticed his interest in a miniature pear tree in our hydroponic garden. By then he was able to crawl and to sit upright without assistance from me. For several weeks, he seemed fascinated with one of the pears as it ripened from green to light yellow to a darker yellow with brown spots.

One day he looked at me, smiled—as he usually did when our eyes met—then pointed at the pear hanging heavily on the little tree, and said, "Pretty." He pronounced the word without the *r* sound and with carefully delineated syllables, so that what he said sounded like "pi-ty." This, I knew, was definitely a word and I hugged, kissed, and praised him whenever he used it. Soon I was "pi-ty," Grandpa and Grandma were "pi-ty," and everything appearing on the scenescreen was "pi-ty." Grandpa counseled me that I should be more selective in my praises if I wanted Michael to have more than a one-word vocabulary. Grandma said she wasn't sure it would be all that bad to live in a world where everything was pretty.

Though encouraging new words into Michael's vocabulary turned out not to be a significant problem, the ripening pear did.

Michael continued to spend a lot of time watching it, sometimes for hours each day, and every few minutes he would turn to me, point at it, and say "pi-ty." That pear definitely was not destined to be picked and eaten.

As weeks passed, the little brown spots on the pear's skin became big brown spots, and though nothing as large as an ant or a fly ever made it past the antoids and Gatekeeper 3, mold spores must have hitched a ride on my skin or hair, or on Grandpa's or Grandma's, for by the second week of December white filaments and clusters, some resembling small spider webs, began growing in the oldest patches of brown.

Day after day as the brown patches merged and the mold grew, Michael watched ever more intently, still calling the whole thing "pi-ty." Late one afternoon the pear fell, spewing its syrupy insides onto the ceramic floor. His scream brought me running from my studies. By the time I got to him, he'd already picked up what he could of the pear and was trying to reattach it to the tree. Seeing me, he held out the gooey mess imploringly and started to cry.

The "uh, uh, uh's" wouldn't stop. Eventually, Grandma came to get me for dinner. After trying unsuccessfully for several minutes to calm Michael, she told me she'd seen something while out shopping a few days before that might help. She said she would be back soon and would send Grandpa in to help me. Grandpa came in, asked what had happened, then sat in his chair at the study table and watched. He'd often made it clear that it was important for Michael to be raised as exclusively as possible by me, and besides, he said, it was good for me to learn to struggle alone with "the messes and the weight of life."

By the time Grandma returned about an hour later, Michael hadn't quieted a bit. She asked Grandpa to help her get something through Gatekeeper. When they returned, Grandma had what she said was a Christmas tree ornament in her hand.

The ornament closely resembled the pear of a few weeks earlier, green with some areas of yellow highlighted with subareas of reddish tint, as though it had been mildly sunburned. There was even an artificial leaf extending from under the clasp at the ornament's stem. Specks of glass had been embedded in its surface, lending the pear sparkle as it moved.

Grandma helped me turn Michael, who clung to me, still crying, so that he faced away from the tree. Then she cleaned up all evidence of the former pear and hung the ornament on the same branch from which the old pear had hung. When everything was in order, Grandma and I maneuvered Michael into a position where he could see the ornament. Then she and I pointed and repeatedly said, "Michael, look. Pretty. See how pretty," until he finally looked.

The "uh, uh, uh's" slowed. Stopped. He stared. He cocked his head this way and that to see the new pear from different angles, thereby undoubtedly seeing its sparkles. He smiled, pointed, and said, "Pi-ty, pi-ty."

Grandpa called this episode "The Death and Resurrection of the Pear."

First Brother

She examines the dog's collar and tag. "So, your name is Rusty."

The dog wags its tail and licks her face.

She runs her fingers through the dog's hair. "Your fur, just look at it. Burrs and twigs and sand. What a mess. Poor boy. Yes. Yes. Can you sit? Sit. That's a good boy. Oh, my, it looks as though no one has groomed you in weeks."

She combs the dog's hair with her fingers and picks out various forms of matter. Intermittently, she looks up. She appears to scan California Highway 1 and to peer at the town of Jenner across the estuary. She continues to perform these grooming and observing activities.

Five minutes pass.

"There, that's the worst of it."

The dog rises from its sitting position and licks and nuzzles her.

"Is that boat yours?" She stretches out her right arm, hand, and index finger toward the sailboat 37 meters south of them along the shore. "Is your human there?"

Sara

For the next two years, I was a little mother with a big baby, and I felt tired much of the time. Events such as Mom and Dad's moving to Calgary a couple of months after the ERP's candidate, John Jairison, won the presidential election; my summer visits to see Elio; a three-day trip with Grandma to visit Mom and Dad (but not my brothers) during their first winter holiday vacation in Canada—events that otherwise would have seemed important to me—paled in significance when compared with my responsibilities for Michael.

During his first year, I had to feed him his special nutrient liquid nearly every hour during the day and every two or three hours during the night, assuming he slept. The liquid was clear, not white like milk, for it contained only trace amounts of minerals, such as the calcium necessary for growing bones. Michael's skeletal structure, like First Brother's, was fully formed at birth.

That same year, I watched Michael learn to point to his bottle, reach for the bottle, throw fits for the bottle (fortunately, his strength had been adjusted to a low level during his first months), hold the bottle, crawl to the bottle, jabber "juice, juice" while playing with the bottle, and, finally, lead me by my hand as he crawled on two knees and an arm along the floor to the cooler where his bottle was stored.

As with humans, Michael's personality and intelligence were

grounded in feelings and actions, and symbols and words began for him as surrogates for these feelings and actions. For example, the command "Juice!" became a shorthand way for him, beginning in his fifth month, to take my hand, lead me to the cooler, and slap its door. First came desires, actions, and experiences; then, emerging from that foundation, came intentionality, language, and self-reflective consciousness.

As they had for me, numbers for him acquired meaning that derived from an emotional sense of more, less, big, and small. Every mouthful of nutrients got him closer to full and closer to recognizing the pattern of addition. Subtraction, likewise, became meaningful through the common experiences that got him closer to empty, to less, to out-of-time. More and less, going farther away and coming back closer—from such experiences, not from programmed arithmetic rules, came his first sense of addition and subtraction.

Like humans, Michael was an intuitive mathematician before he first uttered the name of a number and long before he was allowed access to his Sentiren mathematics module. By contrast, my other brothers had begun with neurologic modules primed for, and right on the verge of, language, math, and science. A few learning drills, enough to establish some groundedness and meaning to their actions, and they'd been able to speak and solve problems. Emotions such as love were to have been learned later.

When Michael was six months old, Grandpa said it was time for Michael and me to begin connecting with each other through the braincord. By then I'd had eight months of practice at being connected with a computer through the braincord, and I thought I'd become quite proficient at relaxing and letting my body and mind be controlled in part by instructions coming in through the cord. But I was about to discover that unlike the computer, Michael was not programmed to narrowly focus on one feeling, thought, sensation, or motor activity at a time.

Grandpa had Michael sit beside me at my study table; then he told me to gently tap the center of the back of Michael's head. I did, and a round segment of Michael's skull flipped up. The braincord emerged, its bifurcated ends waving slowly in the air, appearing alive, appearing to search for something—for me.

Following Grandpa's instructions, I took hold of the ends of the cord and guided them to my nostrils. The cord moved up my nose and locked into place in the junctions of my cribriform plate. Then something new and frightening happened: a hurricane of images, sounds, smells, emotions, and fragments of thoughts swept into my mind, each sensation lasting only a fraction of a second before it was whisked away from the spotlight of my conscious awareness, only to be instantly replaced by another. The warmth of my skin, Michael's bottle locked away in the cooler, a feeling of hunger, an image of Lily dozing in one of Grandma's flower beds, the scent of Grandpa's body lotion, the odor of his breath after breakfast (invariably, blueberries, cinnamon, steel-cut oats, and matcha tea)—many such disconnected sensations hurled in rapid, strobe-like fashion through my mind, making me feel confused, then dizzy, then nauseated.

"Grandpa, I'm feeling a little sick," I said.

The wild staccato scramble of sensations abruptly ceased. I looked at Michael. His face had taken on its appearance of raised-brow surprise, which slid within a moment to wide-eyed curiosity. He focused intently on my eyes, and inside my mind I felt something strange, something like a pair of eyes looking around, or perhaps hands patting first here, then there, searching for something in the dark, wet interior of my brain. I didn't know how I knew, but I knew that Michael had become aware of my sick feeling—not through hearing my words, as I'd tried to make Grandpa aware, but through a conscious process similar to how I had been made aware of my own feeling of sickness—and that he was searching for this new feeling, trying to connect with it, trying to feel it for himself.

But now that the swirl of images and sensations had ceased, the vertiginous feeling quickly evaporated, leaving Michael searching for something that no longer existed. His hunt continued for a few more moments (during which I became aware that my own eyes were moving about erratically), then stopped, and the whirlwind of Michael's mental life again swept into my mind.

After this first connection, Grandpa told me that I had been catching glimpses of the Sentiren ability to be simultaneously conscious of multiple feelings, sense impressions, and trains of thought. Like a Monet painting overbrimming with multifarious colors, each moment of reality for Michael was an explosion of innumerable events. It took us nearly three years before he learned to slow the input of his consciousness into my mind so as not to overwhelm me. Though he quickly discovered how to connect with my feelings, memories, and thoughts, I was able to connect with his only intermittently, perhaps because my brain didn't operate as rapidly as his. This inability to follow his mental processes was disappointing for me because from the beginning of the project I had hoped to be able to get inside the truth of another's mind—inside his thoughts and feelings—before they were whitewashed by language. Over time, however, my sense of his presence in my mind evolved from an eerie feeling of his being in a particular place in my head to a feeling of his simply being there, of being everywhere in my mind, just as I felt myself to be.

From our first session on, Michael never appeared a bit confused or overwhelmed when we were connected by the braincord. In fact, he quickly grew to desire the connection, and until he learned that nothing terrible was happening to him when the connection was terminated, he would scream and cry when we disconnected. I was literally a part of Michael, confirming a little lecture that, in slightly varied form, Grandpa gave me many times during Michael's early years. He told me he'd given Michael the physical basis for intelligence and consciousness, but the way Michael's brain became wired up—which connections would be created or reinforced, which would atrophy and die—would be a function of how that physical basis and the rest of the world interacted. "Through their interactions, the physical brain and the world it experiences will, in effect, create each other," Grandpa said. "And for Michael, you will be most of that outside world. What you do and say and feel around him will greatly influence how he develops, who he becomes."

Sara

I just received a very disturbing encrypted message from First Brother. I don't know how he knew to transmit by AUAS, or how he knew we possessed a supply of fishoids. Perhaps years ago, Grandpa told Dad about this secret place far under the sea, and Dad told First Brother. Michael and I have been here now for 41 days.

Sara:

We monitor many channels of human communication. Here is an excerpt from President Jairison's news conference held the day after you and Michael escaped:

"Before I begin taking your questions on this beautiful winter morning God has given us here in Washington, I would like to clarify certain rumors circulating wildly and irresponsibly both here and abroad.

"Early yesterday morning, our intelligence community discovered that one—I repeat, one—android was trying to escape from its hiding place at the home of Professor Severn Jensen. Two of the android's human companions were pursued in heavy fog off the California coast. After a long chase, during which these fugitives repeatedly refused orders to stop, their boat was fired on. One of the humans, Elio Briand—the son of one of the terrorists that helped the androids escape to the moon and then to Mars—was struck by several bullets and died before we could question him. The android and the other human, Sara

Jensen, the seventeen-year-old granddaughter of Professor Jensen, escaped in two submersibles. A massive search is currently underway to find and apprehend the android and the Jensen girl.

"After extensive searches of the home and offices of Professor Jensen—who committed suicide before he could be questioned—and after interrogations of his wife and his employees and acquaintances, we are confident that there was only one android involved. It is absolutely untrue that an offshore mining facility or a Navy ship was attacked by a group of androids. As God is my witness, except for this one android that escaped with the Jensen girl, we are not aware of the existence of any androids other than those remaining on Mars.

"I can assure you that the android that escaped with the Jensen girl will be captured, and when it is, a team of military officers, including two Chinese officers who have joined us in the search, will destroy it utterly and completely, so that no nation will acquire information or technology from this hideous creation of Professor Jensen's criminal mind.

"I will take your questions now."

"Mr. President!"

"Ms. Coffman."

"Good morning, Mr. President. There are statements circulating attributed to anonymous sources that the Jensen girl was forcibly kidnapped by the android and that the android was somehow attached to the girl's head. Would you please address these allegations?"

"It was the opinion of a couple of the officers aboard the ship that pursued the android that the android forced the Jensen girl to leave with it. It is also their opinion, based on visual sightings, that the android attached itself through some kind of cable to the girl's head. Our subsequent investigation confirms that the android was intentionally designed by Professor Jensen to enter the girl's mind and take control of her. This is almost too terrible to imagine, I know, but it appears to be true. And to think that this girl was his very own granddaughter. It just goes to show you the degree of sick criminal fanaticism these android lovers are capable of."

"Mr. President!"

"Mr. Diaz."

"Mr. President, the Reverend Ernest Kleber stated earlier this morning that this confirms what he's been saying for a long time; namely, that the androids desire to steal souls from humans. Can you comment on this?"

"God created man and woman in His image. He gave us dominion over all living creatures, and He gave each of us an immortal soul. Certain misguided persons are capable of creating very clever machines that strive to be superior to humans, but no man or woman can create a soul to give to these monsters. Only God Himself can create something immortal and infinitely precious like the human soul.

"Our Chinese friends also recognize that humankind was meant to have dominion over all other things and that the greatest crime imaginable against humanity is for certain arrogant criminals to create monstrous soulless beings that would, if given half a chance, master and enslave or destroy us. The criminal creators of these androids want their monsters—like that dangerous abomination that has taken over control of the Jensen girl's mind—to think better than we humans, to be stronger than we humans, to be able to exist in a far wider range of environments than we humans, and so on.

"But these arrogant, misguided criminals cannot give their monsters souls. How else then but try to steal souls from humans? I felt ill when I first heard about the Jensen girl—what her grandfather and this hideous android have been trying to do to her. Pamela and I were on our knees last night and again this morning praying for the girl and for her soul."

"Mr. President!"

"Yes, Ms. Choi."

"Mr. President, Senator Morris has criticized the FBI for allowing a well-known android expert like Professor Jensen to secretly develop a new type of android years after they were outlawed. How can you explain this intelligence failure of your administration?"

"The Chinese ambassador has also conveyed to me his country's displeasure at learning that this android was apparently developed on our soil. He told me that in China it would be unthinkable that a private person would be permitted to have such tremendous security at home, as Professor Jensen evidently did, allowing him to develop an android without detection. I reminded the ambassador that this is America and that in America, God be thanked, the government cannot snoop into its citizens' private homes without a showing of probable criminal activity and a warrant. Having said that, I concede there may be a few isolated cases where a private home isn't actually private because it is in reality filled with sensitive—and dangerous—national property.

"Take, for example, Professor Mazak of MIT, who caused quite a stir with his remarks last month about androids. Professor Mazak, a former student of Jensen, obtained his undergraduate degree at a state-financed university in California. Then, with a fellowship from the National Science Foundation, he obtained his Ph.D. and learned everything he knows about androids. His knowledge, the knowledge he not only uses on the job at MIT but also takes home with him at night, was paid for by the citizens of this country. And what thanks do the hard-working taxpayers get from Professor Mazak? He claims that androids are more like God than humans because androids can think simultaneously as many selves, whereas humans can consciously think only one thing at a time. And he dares to support his outrageous statements by quoting our sacred Bible, wherein God speaks of Himself in the plural. Mazak also claims that what he calls the riddle of the Trinity, quote unquote, is easily solved by considering androids, which, he claims, can think three or more conscious thoughts and experience three or more subjective selves at the same time but from a single point of view. He even goes so far as to suggest that God is an android and the universe as we know it is just this android's ant farm—or some such ridiculous thing.

"Well, my fellow humans, God has told us that we were made in His image to have dominion over all creatures, and we most certainly are not the images of androids! Androids are the abominable creations of people like Professor Jensen and some of his students. These few people, who are very unlike over 99.999 percent of the population, take home with them public property—taxpayer-paid-for property, the knowledge of how to make androids—and I think that the House and the Senate in their collective wisdom should consider whether or not these few privileged persons should be permitted to secrete themselves and their horrible projects away in their homes protected by security rivaling that of—"

Enough. I wish to fulfill my promise to Dad to seek your help in dealing with the problem of the humans. We begin as follows: If I can convince you of our ability to cull from the human population individuals with clearly defined dangerous genetic, psychological, or behavioral characteristics, would you assist us in such culling? If your answer is yes, release a fishoid that repeats the message "Winter, Spring, Summer." The fishoid should begin broadcasting at 29.4 MHz AM, using at least 100 watts, no later than 1200 PST, 10 March. If your answer is no, do not release a fishoid and wait for further instructions.

First Brother

Michael and I have just finished discussing the transmission: the flippant references to the murder of Elio, Grandpa's allegedly malicious purpose for making the braincord, Michael's being called a monster, the idea of a soul. About the religious underpinnings of Jairison's statements, Michael said, "How eagerly the human mind opens the many mouths of its terrors to myths; how it sighs like a lover satisfied." I found that comment rather odd, and wondered: Is he finally getting ready to tell me about Elio?

The nonsense contained in the president's speech was repulsive, but First Brother's request for us to help him in "dealing with the problem of the humans" was an entirely different and more shockingly horrible matter. At first, Michael seemed unable or unwilling to comprehend First Brother's idea of husbanding the human herd by culling out its most dangerous individuals. Then he was appalled, as was I, at this invitation to genocide. Of course, we will not send out a fishoid in response.

In the middle of last night, after receiving First Brother's frightening transmission, I woke and found myself wet with sweat and tears. It took me several seconds to realize where I was. Then the tears resumed, as if trying to wash away a terrible wound.

Exhausted, I turned on the light. Michael wasn't there. His sleeping bag was rolled up neatly and put in its assigned place. He doesn't sleep much anymore, keeping busy day and night constructing the garden and the artificial wombs—do those two concepts, day and night, mean anything down here, where time is a palimpsest of nothingness?

As I sat up in my sleeping bag, I saw little sparkles of light on the reflective inner surface of the module, then the writing table and the cabinets, all rounded to fit against the walls. And permeating everything: the silence, the immense, ever-present, unluminous silence. No sleep, no shadow, no cold dark of night, nothing can compare to the silence of nonexistence—Elio's silence. Grandpa once told me that the greatest wisdom is the ability to look at nothingness squarely and still be happy and have your happiness rub off onto others. But I no longer seem to have a grasp on that kind of wisdom. What I want is what I can't have: that Elio did not die in a pool of blood on the way here, that he lives and waits somewhere for me.

First Brother

"Hello! Is anyone there? Hello!" She bends down and picks up a flattened ellipsoidal rock with major axis approximately 5 cm long. She uses the rock to tap on the hull of the boat. Tap, tap, tap. "Hello!" Tap, tap. "Hello! Please speak or knock if you're there." She waits 8 seconds. "I have your dog here. He seems hungry. Please answer. I'll help you if I can." She waits 13 seconds. She taps three more times. She waits 7 seconds, then tosses the rock back onto the sand. The dog jumps over to the rock, sniffs it, licks it, and returns to her.

She places her right forearm horizontally against the hull. She pushes her forehead against her raised forearm and begins to emit whining and sobbing sounds (highest correlation: human crying). The dog sits on its hindquarters in the sand. It watches her. It rises from its sitting position and walks to her left side. It nuzzles her dangling gloved hand. The hand responds by petting the dog's muzzle and head while she continues to emit sobbing sounds. One minute, 20 seconds later, she pulls her forehead from her right forearm, pulls her right forearm from the hull, and wipes her eyes and cheeks with her gloved right hand.

Sara

At the age of eleven, I went alone to visit Mom and Dad during their second winter solstice vacation in Calgary. Grandma said the trip the year before had exhausted her and that she hadn't liked the bitter cold, but I sensed that she knew I was eager to get out and do things on my own.

Unlike the winter before, this time when I asked to see First Brother, my parents consented. The Alberta Robotics research laboratory where he lived was housed in an underground building only four kilometers from Mom and Dad's home. The security at the lab, along with its blank white walls and its absence of windows and carpets, made me feel at home.

Mom and Dad took me straightaway to a room designated B9. When the door to this room opened, I saw First Brother working on what appeared to be an android foot.

"First Brother!" I exclaimed, running to him. My running halted in front of his blank look and the hand he stuck out to shake.

"I'm really happy to see you," I said, though at the moment I also felt a quiver of disappointment, realizing once again that I had failed in my early desire to help him acquire more emotional depth. This sense of failure was quickly followed by an almost painful longing for home, especially for Michael, whose enthusiastic hugs, kisses, and sometimes even tears of joy greeted me whenever I was away from him for as little as a few minutes.

"Tell me about Michael," First Brother said, releasing my hand.

I turned around and looked questioningly at Mom and Dad.

"It's okay," Dad said. "We're confident of the security here."

I looked back at First Brother. "He speaks very well. He laughs and plays and—"

"Does the braincord work?" First Brother interrupted.

"Yes. He says he's conscious of my thoughts and feelings when—"

"Has Professor Jensen given Michael access to his mathematics module yet?"

"No. Grandpa thinks it's better—"

"Then I presume that Michael hasn't been given access to his science module."

"No. As I was saying—"

"You may leave now." First Brother turned back to his work.

Confused and disheartened, I felt Mom take hold of my arm. "Everyone here is awfully busy right now, as you can see," she said.

Before entering an adjacent room, Mom leaned toward me and said, "We have a little surprise for you."

The surprise was that I was finally introduced to Second Brother and, even more surprising, to four additional brothers, all of whom looked like First Brother and appeared to be engaged in some thing or things more interesting than I, even while they were being introduced. Mom told me that two of my new brothers were being trained by First Brother and two by Second Brother.

"When did I get four new brothers?"

"Each of them came to consciousness about five months ago," Dad answered.

"There is a lot for us to do," Mom said, "and all of your brothers are very helpful."

I interpreted, perhaps wrongly, the look on her face to express that I, unlike my brothers, was very unhelpful.

"What do they do?" I asked.

"Whatever needs to be done," Mom answered.

"Oh."

"Come, we'll show you our office," Dad said.

"But I'd like to see what my brothers do. I'd like to be with them awhile."

"Enough for one day," Mom said, turning me by my shoulders back toward the door.

"Good-bye," I said. "I'm so happy to have met all of you."

None of them looked up or said good-bye.

Once we were in Mom and Dad's office—bare white walls, two desks, two computer monitors, and four chairs—they told me about the new Four Seasons Hotel they'd stay at while attending the Space Medical Sciences Conference (they went to this conference on the moon nearly every year), and they talked in general terms about the medical robots they and my brothers were working on. While they talked, a question began forming in my mind, then made itself heard: "Why are you creating more androids? What can they do that people can't do with the help of machines?"

"You mean, how dare we take a bite out of the apple?" Mom had that look that meant I'd just been naughty.

"No," Dad said, turning toward her and placing his hand on her arm. "Sara just wants to know"—he paused, then glanced at me—"what we've been doing all these years that's so important it has largely kept us out of her life."

Suddenly, coming as a complete surprise to me, I began crying. They both came and hugged me, holding me quietly, as Grandpa always did, until I'd cried out my feelings.

Mom produced a tissue. I dried my eyes and blew my nose.

They both smiled. "To know ourselves, honey," Dad said,

"has long been humans' deepest intellectual desire. We have learned an immense amount about ourselves—one day you'll understand this—in the process of trying to duplicate with alternative materials how we think and feel and act."

"And how to improve ourselves," Mom said. "There's no other way to test what might result from certain proposed improvements, such as having larger working memories, different algorithms for memory prioritization and decay, heightened sensory perception, and so on. Such things we can't try out on each other. Who knows what might go wrong? It is in the nature of complex systems to be unpredictable, and as we've seen in other fields during the past few decades, not all the surprises can be expected to be pleasant ones."

"Your brothers have already given us so much," Dad said. "Compared with your grandma and grandpa, and even to Michael, they probably appear to you to be a bit cold. But if you ever get to know them as we have, you'll find them to be immensely interesting and caring and even loving, in their own way."

"And like us," Mom added, "they want to create—to reproduce, if you will—and care for what they've created. Your four new brothers are the product of your older brothers' designs and devoted nurturing."

"What we're getting at, honey," Dad said, "is that we love you dearly. You're our daughter, our only human child. You came to us as a happy accident, but we were so busy with other important things that we felt we couldn't do justice to you or to our love for you if we selfishly kept you to ourselves. We felt, and hope we were right in this, that your grandma and grandpa could give you much more of what you need than we, with our busy lives, ever could."

It's hopeless, I thought. They'll never understand what it feels like to be abandoned. To be abandoned in favor of brothers.

After having a snack in the lab's lunchroom, Dad asked whether I'd like to go for a drive to see the city and the wintry countryside. I said I'd like to spend more time with my brothers, but Mom said my introduction had been distracting enough to them for one day.

It was mid-afternoon when Dad stopped the car near a snowy field abutting a river lined with trees. The three of us got out and started building a snowman; but before long, clouds blanketed the sky, and soon, swirling down through the bracing air, some flakes of paralyzed water landed on my face, were warmed, and once again flowed, crawling like insects down my cheeks into the scarf around my neck. Then the ground was white, the trees were white, even the sky was white; and at the edge of this world of one color, the invisible sun set earlier than I expected, sending darkness, like an owl on a hunt, swooping swiftly and silently down upon us.

We had just settled into the car and begun to warm up when Mom's teleband beeped. She answered, and by the few words I heard and by the tone of her voice, I knew, or was led to believe, that a crisis had occurred. She snapped the teleband off and turned to Dad. "That was Louise at the AAN. Aita isn't responding. She was working at the greenhouse. They want us to get over there right away."

Dad started the engine and headed back toward the city.

"What's the AAN?" I asked.

"The Android Assistance Network," Mom answered.

"What do they do?"

"We're an underground network that helps androids escape from the United States."

"Who is Aita?"

"An android who works at a greenhouse nearby. She came out of the Robotic Intelligence Laboratory at MIT and is a second-generation android, developed and trained exclusively by other androids, as have been your four new brothers."

"Is something wrong with her?"

Mom glanced at Dad, then looked back at me. "Recently some androids have been disappearing. Most of them are equipped with alarms and tracking devices, but at the time of each disappearance, the frequencies on which those devices broadcast are jammed for a few minutes, and when the jamming ends, there's nothing, not a trace of the android anywhere."

"Have Aita's frequencies been jammed?" I asked.

"That's what Louise just told me. Most of the people with the AAN think the androids are being kidnapped by U.S. agents, thrown into insulated chambers, and, well, after that we can only speculate." Mom looked worried and shifted her gaze out the front window.

I wonder now whether she actually did look worried. Was she so accomplished at deceiving her daughter? Or did my mind simply paint in something—in this case, worry—that it expected to be there under the circumstances?

"That's the reason your brothers never leave the lab," Dad added.

I fell silent. I missed Michael, and now I was worried about him. Evidently, Grandpa's dire predictions were coming true.

The snow had let up by the time we arrived at the greenhouse, but in his hurry, Dad braked late, and our car skidded, arriving sideways less than two meters from the door. I half expected Mom to say something, as I'd heard her say before, about Dad's learning to drive in Berkeley's bland weather, but she merely flung open her car door and rushed into the building. Dad hurried in behind her. Trying to keep up, I slipped and fell as soon as I got out of the car, but neither of them noticed. They would have noticed, I thought, if First Brother had fallen.

Snowbound in the glass oasis, stands of hyacinths greeted me at the door. From somewhere deep inside the building, Mom and Dad were shouting, "Aita! Aita!" Lanterns of daffodils brightened the smiles of toy Santas; and farther along, yellow tulips, unaware of our dark concerns, appeared gleeful, having been forced up in pots around a model Dutch windmill slowly turning in the fragrant air.

"Aita!" I heard Dad shout. I looked up and saw him walking briskly back toward me. I wanted him to hug me and tell me everything would be all right, but he walked past me without saying anything and opened the outside door for an elderly couple. They were the proprietors of the greenhouse. Mom rushed over when she saw the couple, and the four of them conferred at length. The elderly couple said Aita worked alone in this building on Sundays and they hadn't seen anyone else come or go that day. They appeared sad to hear that Aita was missing and probably had been abducted. The man said Aita had a green thumb and had been far and away the best worker they'd ever had. They seemed genuinely fond of Aita. "She was like a daughter to us," the lady said with a catch in her throat.

When I returned home from Canada, I told Grandpa what had happened: that First Brother hadn't changed, that I had four new brothers who didn't seem at all interested in me, that Mom and Dad were part of an underground network, that androids were being kidnapped by U.S. agents and destroyed. I couldn't help crying as I told him about this last bit of news. Was Michael safe here in the U.S.? Would he be kidnapped, too?

Grandpa assured me that Michael would be safe as long as we kept him secret. Then he told me something that had happened a few months earlier, something I didn't know about because he hadn't yet given me access to the internet; nor had he allowed me to watch the news on WNN. The report that had been kept from me was about the first attack by the U.S. and China against sites in countries in the Middle East and Asia that had continued to pursue android defense programs despite orders from the United Nations Security Council to cease.

"Not Canada, though," I said.

"No, the Canadians have been careful to allow conscious machines to work only in designated non-military areas."

"So my brothers are safe?"

"We can hope so. But given the current political climate, we must be extra careful with Michael. He's the only android, or bioroid, I'm aware of who has successfully developed a rich emotional life."

I didn't respond to that comment. In my mind we had to protect Michael simply because he was Michael.

"Did I ever tell you that when I was a medical student nearly sixty years ago I did some work at the Stanford Hypnosis Laboratory?"

"No."

"Do you know what hypnosis is?"

"You put people to sleep, and they do funny things you tell them to do."

Grandpa chuckled. "Who told you that?"

"Elio."

"I'm afraid he doesn't know much about hypnosis."

"Aunt Lynh took him to see a show in Amsterdam. A woman hypnotized people from the audience, and it was funny."

"Well, yes, I'm sure it was. But hypnosis can also be serious, powerful stuff. Listen, you know how important it is to keep Michael's existence secret."

"Yes."

"And now you know that the U.S. and China have taken military action to destroy androids used in military defense programs. But the destruction of military androids is just the first step. The ultimate goal of both the United States and China is to destroy all androids everywhere. We have Gatekeeper to guard the door leading to these rooms where Michael lives, but the secret of Michael lives in your mind. To protect Michael, we have to ensure that the doors to your mind are properly protected. Metaphorically speaking, we need a powerful and crafty gatekeeper for your mind."

He explained that the police possessed sophisticated lie-detection equipment capable of determining with almost one hundred percent accuracy whether a person was lying. Therefore, I was never to say anything to the police, period, no matter how strenuously they questioned me and no matter how they threatened me. The only exceptions were that I could respond to a greeting with a friendly "Hi" or "Hello" or, if they said, "Nice day, isn't it?" or "How are you today?" I could answer "Yes" or "Fine." Beyond those civil responses, I was to make one and only one additional statement: "My name is Sara Jensen and my grandfather's name is Professor Severn Jensen."

He proceeded to tell me that U.S. intelligence services had also developed a secret device, an inducer of painful illusions called an algetor that forced people to tell the truth. He said that since the pain induced by the algetor was not associated with any known physical harm, the pain it caused could be made far more severe than any pain associated with actual physical trauma. The algetor was designed to make the victim believe that terrible things were happening to her consistent with the pain. For example, the victim would be led to believe that her bones were being broken, that she was being disemboweled, or that her skin and muscles were being melted off with boiling oil.

Did I think I could tolerate such pain to protect Michael?

My mind raced back to prior experiences of pain. One had occurred a couple of months before my first trip to visit Elio in Amsterdam. Lily and I had been playing near Carlos and his crew while they removed extraneous shoots and leaves from vines when I'd stepped barefoot onto a splinter of glass. I limped home, bloodied and crying, into Grandpa's arms. He carried me to the kitchen, sat me in a chair, examined the bottom of my foot, then calmly said, "There's a piece of glass lodged in your foot. I'll remove it, and then you'll be fine. But first, I'd like to talk with you a little about strategies for dealing with pain."

He looked at me with a silence that indicated I'd have to stop crying before he would proceed. I did, and he began by saying that soon I would be visiting Elio and that I probably would be meeting some of Elio's friends. He said it had been his experience that boys often feel uncomfortable around girls who cry easily and freely.

This issue of dealing with pain is not a trifling matter, he said, for as I would discover, life is full of pain. Surely I didn't think the best strategy for dealing with something so common was to scream and cry and run away from it, did I?

"No, I don't, Grandpa," I answered, wiping away the last trace of wetness from my eyes.

"Good. Then this is what you do: Don't try to distance yourself from painful sensations. Go to them. Let them fill you just as you do the minor pains that parade through you during meditation. Become their friend. Accept their heat, their sting, their insistence. They will let you feel them and tame them, and then they will pass, just as they do during meditation."

"Really?"

"Yes, really. Now, I'm going to wash your cut and take out the piece of glass. Either I can eliminate the pain by applying a local anesthetic before I start, or you can begin to learn a new way of dealing with pain. Your choice."

I thought quickly of Elio. I certainly did not want him to feel uncomfortable around me, a girl, because I cried too easily.

"I want to learn."

Grandpa smiled. "All right. Go first to your breathing.

Anchor yourself there, in your breath. Then let the pain in your foot enter your consciousness. Accept the pain. Know that it's your friend. It's only there to help you, to make you aware that your foot should be attended to. Nod when you are ready."

I focused on my breathing and accepted the sting in my foot. Then I nodded for him to proceed.

"Good," Grandpa said. "Be careful not to jerk while I'm working."

At first there were a couple of involuntary jerks—followed by his silent, raised eyebrows—but I kept calming myself and trying to accept my difficult new friends, the painful sensations.

Now, six years later, there was a new job to be performed. Would I be able to tolerate the much greater pain of this algetor thing to protect Michael?

"Yes," I said, feeling both determined and apprehensive.

"I'm glad you think so. And you're probably right. But 'probably' isn't good enough when it comes to protecting Michael's life. We have to make every effort to be certain."

"Can you teach me?"

"Indeed I can. For you, it will be easy. You are young, and you already are able to dissociate to an unusual degree the conscious parts of your mind from the parts processing sensory inputs and emotional responses."

Grandpa was referring to my ability to relive past events at will, even more vividly when I was a young girl, it seems, than I can now. I'd simply focus on the gray outline of a remembered scene, or on the sound of a word someone had spoken, or on the prick or tingle of a sensation, and then, suddenly, the wispy gossamer of memory would flash into bright realism and I'd experience the remembered event almost as if it were happening anew.

"You mean my daydreams will seem even more real?" I asked.

"Not exactly. Your daydreams are already quite real enough.

Our purpose in having you learn to dissociate yourself from sensory inputs is so that you can block out the words, threats, and pain that might be used in an attempt to force open the doors to your mind where Michael's secret lives."

Grandpa sighed. When he resumed speaking, all enthusiasm had drained from his voice. "The second step necessitates your having to work, at your own pace, with an algetor."

"You can get one?"

"No. I'll have to make one. I evaluated several designs a few years ago. When I evaluated them, I learned how they work. I should be able to recreate one here for you to use. It'll take a little time to get some of the components, quietly, without raising suspicion. In the meanwhile, I'll teach you how to hypnotize yourself. Would you like me to hypnotize you so you can see what it's like?"

"Right now?"

"Yes. It'll be easy for you. I'm quite certain of that. And you'll enjoy it."

He told me to remember everything he was about to say and do, and everything I was about to feel as he took me through a standard protocol of hypnotic suggestions developed to assess hypnotic responsiveness. He had me relax the muscles in my right foot, then, in order, my right leg, left foot and leg, right hand, right arm, left hand and arm. On his suggestion, my legs and arms became heavy. My shoulders, neck, and head relaxed and also became heavy. I sank more deeply into the chair, as if I were drowsy, but I remained alert to what he was saying. He had me count slowly down from five, telling me that with each number I spoke I would become ever more relaxed and that when I reached one, nothing would disturb me.

"Two, one..." He was right: The relaxation I felt at that moment was deeper than any I'd experienced. It seemed limitless and blissful. I felt as though I was nothing more than an aware conduit for Grandpa's suggestions.

He told me to stretch out my arms and hands in front of me. He said there was a force pushing my hands together—and an irresistible force did just that. He said my arms were becoming so heavy I could no longer hold them up—and they sank, leaden, onto my lap. He said Lily was there just as she had been when I was three—and she was there: a soft, white, whimpering bundle of love I cuddled and petted while she tickled my cheek with her wet little nose and breathed on me her milky puppy breath.

Over the next few days, Grandpa taught me how to induce the hypnosis myself. He told me to pick an image I found relaxing, focus on it, then count down from five, progressively becoming more relaxed and more focused on the image and my breathing until, at the count of one, everything except the image and my breathing was gone.

The relaxing image I chose was of a grape leaf, one with an intricate pattern of venation as seen from below while it floated green and carefree in a deep blue sky frosted with cirrus clouds. This was no ordinary grape leaf; it was a huge magic leaf that during many of my daydreams had swooped down out of a mare's-tail sky to carry me off across the vineyards, across the Sierra Nevadas, over the Rockies and the checkerboard garden of the Midwest, across the wide ocean and green England, and in through Elio's open bedroom window. From there, he and I had zoomed and floated and fluttered, peeking our heads out over the leaf's edges to see the Alps, the Bosporus, and the Himalayas before returning to Amsterdam as the time for Aunt Lynh to return home from work drew near.

After only a couple of weeks' practice, I was able to go from normal consciousness to self-induced hypnosis in less than ten seconds. When fully hypnotized, awareness of my breathing—slow, deep, and relaxed—was the only salient thing in my consciousness. I could hear Grandpa and was aware of what he was doing, but such awareness seemed faint and disconnected from me.

Before the algetor was completed, Grandpa tested my reactions to various stimuli. In one test, I submerged my hand and forearm into a tub of ice water. Without hypnosis, I managed the pain, which became fairly intense within a minute, by focusing on the stinging and aching sensations and treating them as harmless, interesting curiosities, just as Grandpa had taught me to do years before. But with self-induced hypnosis, my experience of the ice water was different. I was aware that my arm had been placed in cold water, but I was only vaguely aware of the stinging and aching sensations, which seemed not to be affecting my arm but rather someone else's arm that had been submerged in the water.

I asked Grandpa whether there wasn't a contradiction between what he'd taught me before—to go to the painful sensations and experience them fully—and what he was trying to teach me with hypnosis: to dissociate myself from the sensations of pain. He said that though the lessons taught two distinct methods of dealing with pain, the lessons were complementary, not contradictory. He reminded me that our bodies had evolved in a world devoid of man-made optical illusions and pain inducers, just as the ideas of Newtonian mechanics had evolved in an experiential world devoid of extremely small objects moving at extremely high speeds; and that just as Newtonian theory had failed for the extremely small and the extremely speedy, so our senses and emotions failed in many artificially imposed conditions.

He had me read a passage on reflex actions from Darwin's 1872 book *The Expression of the Emotions in Man and Animals*:

I put my face close to the thick glassplate in front of a puff-adder in the Zoological Gardens, with the firm determination of not starting back if the snake struck at me; but, as soon as the blow was struck, my resolution went for nothing, and I jumped a yard or two backwards with astonishing rapidity. My will and reason were powerless against the imagination of a danger which had never been experienced.

Grandpa explained that Darwin's experience with the puff adder presented an example of how our evolved senses and emotive systems deform heights, widths, distances, light intensities, and dangers, leading us humans to misconstrue reality and sometimes to take inappropriate and potentially dangerous actions.

"What would have happened to poor Mr. Darwin," Grandpa asked, "had there been an exposed high-voltage wire a meter behind him as he faced the puff adder with his firm determination not to jump back from what he knew to be illusory danger?"

"That would have been bad."

"Yes. Probably his widow and fatherless children would have preferred he face the terrible snake with a self-hypnotic suggestion not to jump back, rather than with his feeble determination."

"Didn't Darwin know about hypnosis?"

"I don't know whether he did. But we do, and we can put that knowledge to good use. The algetor will be complete in two or three days. Remember, it's nothing more than a sophisticated producer of illusions. A special helmet will cover your head so that you'll be able to see and hear only what the operator of the algetor wants you to see and hear. Various parts of your body will be wrapped in banded strips of microsensors and stimulators. You'll be told that unless you talk, the knife with the sharp, cold blade scraping over your leg will be jabbed deep into your thigh and twisted mercilessly. You'll feel the cold, hard steel on your thigh. You'll feel its sharp edge. You'll be ordered to answer, but you'll remain silent. Then you'll experience excruciating pain as the large blade dives into your thigh."

I felt my eyes widen as the story came to life in my mind.

"What will you do then?" he asked.

I thought for a moment. "Nothing. The knife won't be real. I'll know it's just an illusion. I'll only feel sensations, harmless sensations merely imitating sensations of hardness, sharpness, and cold. I'll see the grape leaf floating in the sky and call it to me, counting five, four, three, two, one, and I'll fly away from the painful sensations on the wings of the leaf."

"Amazing!" Grandpa exclaimed. "An eleven-year-old girl foils the great algetor! What a shame I won't be able to show this to certain people at the CIA."

Before Grandpa attached me for the first time to the algetor, he told Michael to go to his room and close the door. Grandpa said he didn't want Michael to become frightened by seeing or hearing me in pain, illusory or not. After Michael left, Grandpa pulled a small knife out of the pocket of his kimono, unfolded the blade from its handle, and said, "I thought we would start with a little knife blade and work our way up, if that is all right with you."

"You're not going to stick me with any knife, so you can make it as big as you want."

"Do not be so sure what I'll do when you're all bound up in electrodes and you can't see through the helmet covering your eyes," he said, pretending to be menacing.

"You can't fool me!"

On went the helmet, and on went sticky strips along the back of my neck, down my spine, and around my right thigh.

He told me not to hypnotize myself for this first session.

"Do you feel the cold blade flat against your thigh?" he asked.

"No."

"What do you feel?"

"Just a cold, metallic sensation."

"Do you feel the sharp point of the knife digging into but not yet breaking your skin?"

"No."

"What do you feel?"

I hesitated, trying to resist his suggestion. "Sensations of pressure and sharpness."

"Do you feel the sharp edge of the blade about to cut through your skin?"

"No."

"What do you feel?"

I hesitated again. "A sensation, as if a sharp edge were pressing against my leg."

There was a short silence.

"Ow! Grandpa, be careful! You cut me!"

No sooner had I finished exclaiming those words than I became aware of an internal struggle. Part of me was still recoiling in absolute certainty that I had just been cut by the knife, while another part of me began lecturing on the high probability that I'd been fooled.

"Oh, sorry," I heard Grandpa say. "Let's take a look at that cut."

He took off the helmet. I saw a black band covering the area of my perceived cut. He unfastened the band, exposing what appeared to be my uncut thigh.

Then my fingers reported agreement with my eyes.

"Let's do it again," I said, perplexed and unhappy with my first reaction.

We did it again. And again. And again. But I couldn't stop feeling the knife slicing into my skin. I knew there was no knife, yet I felt a sharp, cold edge press down and then begin to slide along my thigh. I felt the skin yield and the piercing pain, and at the same time something beyond reason in my mind became convinced—terrified—that I had just been cut by a knife. Finally, yielding not to pain but to frustration, I began to cry. Grandpa took the helmet off my head, and as I looked up at him I saw sadness and ambivalence in his eyes. But then I remembered Michael and the threats against him, and even as I cried, I redoubled my resolve not to disappoint Grandpa or endanger Michael.

Thus began years of twenty-minute training sessions with the algetor three times each week, sometimes using hypnosis, other times not. During the sessions in which I used hypnosis, the pain seemed somewhere else, and those sessions were easily endured. Without hypnosis, however, all of the illusory painful sensations remained—the perceived knife cuts, the breaking of bones, the flames scorching my skin, the ice picks piercing my eyes—and the initial motor responses of recoiling from those illusions also remained. But over time I learned to tame the fears and anxieties associated with the illusions, and I learned to befriend, and so endure, even the fiercest sensations of pain.

Or at least I thought then that these were the fiercest sensations of pain.

Grandpa never allowed Michael to witness any of my algetor training sessions. He didn't want Michael to become frightened by watching me endure the extreme and gruesome forms of pain generated by the algetor. Nor did he want me to let Michael into my memory of the sessions.

Of course, Michael was curious about these secret algetor activities. After some of the sessions, I became aware while brainjoined with him of the murmurings—the rustling around of algetor memories, like wind playing with autumn leaves—as he attempted to sneak into forbidden territory. "No!" I would think, or even say aloud, as if he were a bad boy caught stealing fruit from a neighbor's tree.

"But it's not fair," he'd whine.

One day, about a month into these algetor sessions, I stubbed one of my toes. The next day, I made a "discovery": The pain of yesterday's stubbed toe could, in a limited sense, be remembered, but it couldn't be felt. I was astonished to find that I was nearly as separated from my own past pain as I was from another's current pain. This loss of sensation in the memory of physical pain seemed doubly remarkable to me, given that I could reproduce sights and sounds—and sometimes even tastes and smells—as freshly as if they were being experienced anew.

I ran to Grandpa with this discovery, telling him that past physical pain is no longer even as faint as earthlight reflected from a crescent moon; it's only a shadow that gallops along beside us as we ride certain of our memories into the past. Grandpa chuckled at my enthusiasm, then explained that physical pain, existing as it does only in the present, is one of the conscious qualia that help us separate the present from the past, the real from the remembered or imaginary. Then, after giving due consideration to the fact that Michael was no longer an infant and that the sensations of past pain are irrecoverably gone, he said that though he still didn't want Michael present during my algetor sessions, it would be all right for Michael to sample my memories of the sessions.

As far as I know, Michael fully entered the memory of an algetor session only once. He screamed, pulled the braincord back into his head, and began to cry.

First Brother

She removes the backpack from her shoulders and kneels on the sand. The dog sniffs at the pack. She opens the pack. In it is some brindled material (highest correlation: synthesized food) wrapped in thin, transparent material (highest correlation: polyethylene) and one cylindrical object (highest correlation: insulated bottle) tapered and capped at one end.

"Okay, now. We can't tear into this like a couple of famished dogs." She shelters the pack with her left hand and arm and attempts to push the dog away with her right hand and arm. "Sit! Sit down, Rusty. Sit. Good boy. Now, stay. Stay!"

The dog sits on its hindquarters. It exhibits a high level of attention directed both at the pack and at her. "Stay," she says, pointing at the dog with her right index finger. The dog licks the finger. "Stay," she repeats, directing a stern facial expression at the dog while she slowly withdraws her right hand toward the pack. She keeps her eyes directed at the dog as her right hand searches in the pack.

She retrieves the brindled bread-like material, unwraps the clear film from it, pulls the brindled material into four roughly equal parts, and places three of those parts on top of the pack.

"Okay, boy," she says. "Lunchtime. Come!" The dog jumps up, sniffs, licks, then scoops up the food whole in its jaws, chomps, and swallows. While it does, she stuffs the other section of food into her mouth and chews.

Still chewing, she forms a concave depression in the sand and lines the depression with the thin transparent film. She unscrews the cap from the cylindrical object and pours bluish-brown liquid from the bottle into the lined concave depression in the sand.

The dog licks once at the surface of the liquid, looks up toward Sara, and extends its tongue out of its mouth three times.

"Go ahead," she says. "It's not that bad. See?"

She lifts the bottle to her mouth and appears to swallow twice.

The dog licks the liquid again, then begins to lap rapidly. She watches the dog and smiles.

The dog completes lapping up the liquid in the makeshift bowl. She pours the last of the liquid into the bowl, saying: "That's it, Rusty. That's all I have. We'll have to see what we can find on the road home."

She screws the cap back onto the bottle, pushes the knuckles of her right hand into the sand and stands. The shadow of the boat covers the right side of her lower right pant leg and the right edge of her right shoe.

It is 29 minutes, 47 seconds past midday.

Sara

After Michael was born, Grandpa told Aunt Lynh that he would no longer accompany me on my summer vacations because Elio and I tired him out. But, in fact, Grandpa had enjoyed our summer trips. His concern was for Michael, who, he told me, was even more fragile than a human baby and was too much for Grandma to take care of alone. Thus, the following summer, the summer of my tenth birthday, was the first of many summers that I arrived alone in Amsterdam to visit Elio and Aunt Lynh. It was also the first summer Elio and I had separate bedrooms.

He and Aunt Lynh had moved into a larger apartment in the same building that spring. Aunt Lynh tried to explain to me in private that I was getting to be a big girl and should have a separate bedroom for my privacy. I didn't understand, nor was I pleased, by this privacy business. Fortunately, Elio's and my bedrooms were connected by a bathroom through which each night, after we'd been kissed and tucked in by Aunt Lynh and the lights had been turned out, I snuck, buck naked, into Elio's bedroom and bed. There, as during each summer before, he wrapped himself around me, called me the best teddy bear in the world, and kissed me goodnight. He was smaller then than Michael; he fit better, I thought, when he held me; he was softer. And unlike Michael, he was warm, and he had something Michael didn't: a small pouch containing two testicles below his penis, a penis which often got hard during the night. Michael's never did. Neither one of them had hair anywhere except on the top of his head.

It was also during that summer that Aunt Lynh began insisting that Elio call me his sister; so from then on, in front of her, he usually called me "Sis." But when he and I were alone together, I remained "Sara." She also wanted me to call him "Brother." But although I thought of Elio as family, he didn't seem like a brother. He was my friend. He was summer and freedom. He was my connection with the wider world. He was fun.

And by three summers later, the summer I turned thirteen, he was so, so beautiful.

After we met at Schiphol Airport, we talked and laughed, as we had during previous summers. But later that night, he locked the door while using the bathroom, and then, as I began undressing for bed in my bedroom, he came in wearing underpants and told me I should sleep in my own bed.

Shocked, I just stared at him.

"I'm not a little boy anymore," he said with a dismissive wave. Then he turned and walked through our bathroom, shutting the door leading to his bedroom behind him. I heard the lock click.

"This must be the type of pain Michael feels when I leave him," I whispered to myself as I stood staring, teary-eyed, at Elio's closed and locked bedroom door.

The next morning, I woke early and quietly slipped out of the apartment to call Grandpa. Since Elio and I were supposed to have been sleeping separately during the past three summers, I had to be careful what I said to express my unhappiness with Elio's behavior, so I simply explained that Elio had locked me out of the bathroom the night before and wouldn't let me see him naked.

"Elio is fourteen," Grandpa replied, "and undoubtedly is

exhibiting new primary and secondary male sex characteristics. He may be uncomfortable about his new body around you and desirous of heightened privacy. I'm sure you are curious about his new physiology, but I believe it would be a serious mistake to impose on the privacy he desires. I'll prepare some materials. When you return home, we'll have a sex education class."

I enjoyed the remainder of my time that summer with Elio, doing the usual things—talking, biking, swimming, visiting his friends—but he continued locking me out of our bathroom whenever he was using it, and the least he wore in my presence were underpants, which appeared astonishingly white against his dark skin.

Grandpa began his sex-education class by giving me my puberty shot to protect me from all known sexually transmitted diseases. "You and your generation are fortunate," he said. "Unlike in the days of my youth, sex no longer puts on its short skirts or tight jeans and solicits at the entrance to hospitals and cemeteries." He laid the first syringe back on the top of his desk and picked up another. "This vaccination will inhibit the binding capacity of sperm to eggs. It should remain effective for about five years."

I felt another soft concussion of air against my upper arm.

Grandpa put the syringes away in a drawer of his desk. From another drawer he took out a large book. In it, he showed me pictures of male and female human bodies in various stages of maturity and explained the transformation of breasts, genitals, and so on from childhood through adulthood. He told me about the physiology of male and female orgasm and concluded, "But making love has about as much to do with penises, vaginas, breasts, hair, and so on, as playing the piano has to do with hammers and strings. Of course, you need hammers and strings and your hammers and strings should be in good working order and well tuned, but real piano playing is about feeling, understanding, and technique. So it is with making love."

He leaned back in his chair, and took on a satisfied expression that seemed to say: There, now, you've heard it all. Let's get back to your studies.

But I was far from satisfied. I loved Grandpa, Grandma, Michael, Elio, and Lily; and all this love had nothing to do with penises, breasts, and hair as far as I was concerned. "Why is sex called 'making love,'" I asked, "rather than 'making babies'? I don't see that love has anything to do with it."

"Now you've asked a question we can sink our teeth into," he said, leaning forward again. "There are three main functions of sex: first, it is used to reproduce, one of its rarest and, considering the nearly nine billion people crowding the planet and the abysmal quality of most parenting, arguably one of its most perverse manifestations.

"Sex is also used to give and receive pleasure and to express love. But you are not yet developed enough to understand such adult pleasure or love.

"The third category, which is of particular relevance for adolescents, concerns the ability of sexual activity to reprogram the web of beliefs and desires that emerge from synaptic recoding throughout our brains and bodies."

"Are you saying," I interrupted, "that having sex will recode my synapses and change my beliefs and desires?"

"And your allegiances and whom you love. In a word, yes. Humans are reprogrammed by having sex, especially by early sexual activity. Have you read about Ivan Pavlov?"

"Yes. He was the scientist who rang a bell just before putting meat powder into dogs' mouths. After several repetitions, he found a high positive correlation between the ringing of the bell and the dogs' salivating, even when the meat wasn't present."

"That was his famous classical conditioning experiment. But have you read about his famous accident?"

"Accident? No."

"One spring, a river flooded in St. Petersburg, inundating the basement of Pavlov's laboratory where some of his dogs were being kept. By the time they were rescued, the terrified dogs were swimming with their noses at the top of their cages. How do you think this traumatic event affected the dogs?"

"I don't know."

"To his surprise, Pavlov found that the dogs had lost their prior conditioning and had to be retrained. Investigating this phenomenon, Pavlov found that isolation, starvation, or intense sensory stimulation can result in such unlearning. In humans, isolation and sensory overload have been used to destroy individual beliefs and preference structures—by religions, with their singing, dancing, and chanting to exhaustion; by fraternities, sororities, and military groups, with their initiation rights and boot-camp-style indoctrination; by sports teams, with their exercising to exhaustion and incessant harangues by coaches; and by other such groups.

"But that is the difficult side, the unlearning side. The re-education side, the formation of new beliefs and desires, turns out to be remarkably simple. At the point of overload, the stressed individual will automatically form new preference and belief structures in line with those of whoever releases him or her from the ordeal or whoever offers some kindness during this period of emotional meltdown, even if—now get this—even if the releaser or the offeror of kindness, such as a coach or drill sergeant or police interrogator, is the one responsible for the meltdown in the first place."

"That's called brainwashing, isn't it?"

"More commonly, it's called social conditioning, becoming a team player, an infatuated lover, a dedicated parent, a devout whatever, and so on.

"What is important for you to become aware of is the pattern this reprogramming takes and the power it can have over you. During adolescence, there are biologic impulses to distance oneself from one's parents and family, and one often encounters the disturbing experience of having one's closest friends acquire new interests and new friends, usually of the opposite sex. Adolescents often feel isolated when they discover old friends disavowing, perhaps even claiming to abhor, the pleasures and allegiances of youth.

"Then, to top it all off, comes a flood of neurohormones released in conjunction with early sexual activity. These neurohormones were evolutionarily selected to break down established synaptic coding so that the young animal could easily be reprogrammed for pair bonding and parental responsibilities. In humans, the strain of growing up, combined with floods of neuromodulators, overwhelms the established synaptic coding in an adolescent brain, resulting in the commonly observed personality dissolution associated with that period of life."

Grandpa frowned, apparently disturbed by this last idea, then picked up a set of papers from his desk. "Take a look at this article later. It describes how prairie voles' dopamine levels surge during their first sexual encounter, permanently recoding their brains, and they mate for life. In the studies described, virgin female voles given a single injection of dopamine immediately choose any nearby male vole as their mate for life. Scary actually, but that is how love is made—for prairie voles, at least."

I thought I understood everything Grandpa had said, but as far as I could tell, what he'd said wasn't directed at what I was upset about: Elio's recent strange behavior.

"What I wanted to talk about, Grandpa, is Elio. I'm going to marry him when I grow up, and I think I'll enjoy making love with him. So I think I should be able to see him naked, and he shouldn't lock me out of the bathroom. Don't you agree?"

"I most certainly do *not* agree. I thought I made it clear when you called from Amsterdam that now is a time for you to respect his privacy. You're not children any longer. If he feels uncomfortable being naked around you, then you accept that and don't bother him about it. Besides, there certainly is no rush. You have your whole long life ahead of you. After you mature sexually in a few years, you'll have plenty of time to be intimate with the boys you like. Furthermore, you should be aware that even though you feel you may enjoy making love with Elio, he might not feel the same way toward you."

"What do you mean?"

"If what Aunt Lynh tells your mother is true, Elio enjoys making love with young men. I don't know what he feels about young women."

Instantly, my chest felt heavy and tight, and a tingling nibbled at my arms and legs. "What does he do with those boys, exactly?"

For a moment, Grandpa appeared stunned. "I don't know what he does. That's his business, not ours."

I gave Grandpa his own silent-waiting-for-more treatment.

Finally, he sighed and said, "Okay, what do you want to know?"

"I told you. I want to know what he does when he makes love with those boys."

Enduring my repeated interruptions to find out *exactly* what certain named acts entailed, Grandpa proceeded to tell me what he said were activities men typically enjoyed doing when they made love with other men.

It seemed odd to me that people could get pleasure out of doing such things, but I believed Grandpa implicitly, all the more so upon considering Lily. She moaned with pleasure whenever I rubbed her tummy or scratched behind her ears, and that seemed a bit odd, too, because when I rubbed my tummy or scratched behind my ears, I wasn't transported to moans of pleasure. So, if

Elio liked to have his penis massaged... well, I figured I'd enjoy doing that for him just as much as I enjoyed scratching Lily's ears.

That autumn, I woke one morning on a sticky bloodied sheet. I didn't want to frighten Michael, so I pulled the sheet off the bed, bunched it up, and took it out through Gatekeeper. My ovaries had dropped their first egg—like a furled seedpod from one of the locust trees, Grandma said.

Sara

Two summers later, Elio lifted his chin off the top of my head and asked, "Would you like to go to a club tonight?"

We were sitting in early afternoon shade on the steps of his apartment building, watching children play in the park. He was sixteen, tall, and handsome in his short-sleeved pink shirt and tight-fitting blue jeans. He sat on the step above me, his arms over my shoulders, hugging me, his legs pressing against my sides. Never had I felt so much a part of him, never so calm, so yielding, yet so awakened and full of joy.

"What kind of club?" I asked.

"A place to dance, talk with friends."

"Okay. I'd love to go." I tried to sound more excited than I was. I'd never been to a club. I didn't even know what a club was, or how to dance. Would I appear awkward and embarrass Elio? Would his friends be there, his boyfriends?

"Well, if we're going," Elio said, "you've got to get some new clothes, something other than those old farmer-boy clothes you always wear."

He had me stand in front of his Vidtel to record images of me that he entered into a shopping program. Over the next hour, he seemed to take pleasure dressing my likeness in many wild, colorful clothes from designers all over the world. But we finally settled on shopping at a local discount store because we needed the clothes for that evening. He picked out a white camisole, a ruby-colored cotton long-sleeved shirt, and a pair of black slacks. I felt self-consciously feminine in the silky-smooth camisole—the first I'd ever worn.

Later, after dinner and before Elio and I left to go to the club, Aunt Lynh made us promise to be home by midnight. Though her request—"Elio, I want you to promise me that you'll have your sister home by midnight"—didn't seem significant to me at the time, events of a year later would revive in me a distinct memory of her words, her stern tone, and Elio's subsequent funk.

After taking a bus to an area near the University of Amsterdam, Elio and I walked several blocks before turning into a narrow alley lined with old red-brick buildings. About halfway down the alley was a small yellow sign, and on it, the image of a red dog.

Under the sign was a black metal door with a brass knocker that squeaked when Elio raised it to knock. The door opened part way, letting out a blast of music. A huge man with the biggest muscles I'd ever seen scanned Elio's membership card, then looked at me in an unfriendly manner and grunted something. Though I'd picked up only a few Dutch words during prior visits, "no card" I understood, and "little chicken." It was clear that the huge fellow wasn't going to let me in. But when Elio handed him several bills, the man stuffed them into his pants pocket, and the door was opened to us.

I followed Elio into a room filled with smoke, flashing lights, and oppressively loud music. In the center of the room was a circular dance floor on which moved a sea of strobe-lit dancers. Some women were topless; some men wore only underpants. Several of the dancers had holographic partners. Around the circumference of the dance floor were columns of flashing lights that extended from the floor to the ceiling three stories above. Hundreds of people watched from a second-story balcony.

Elio took my hand and led me through the crowd to an area in which there were tables and a bar. I recognized his best friend, Luuk, who was waving to us from one of the tables near the back. He, Elio, and I had played football and video games together in prior summers.

"Good to see you again," Luuk said. "You've matured a lot since last summer."

"Thanks," I said. "I'm happy to see you, too." I had hoped Elio would have noticed—at least would notice now that Luuk had said it—that in certain places I'd begun to curve and swell like fruit nearing harvest.

"This is my girlfriend, Melissa," Luuk continued. "And this is Liesbeth and her boyfriend Peer."

Melissa shook my hand, saying, "We've been looking forward to meeting you."

"Ja," Liesbeth said, pulling an empty chair close to hers. "Sit here and tell us about California."

About a half-hour of small talk and two rounds of drinks later, Melissa and Luuk got up to dance. Liesbeth asked me to dance. I told her I didn't know how, but she took my hand and led me onto the dance floor, where, in the blare of music, people danced like trees frenzied by wind. I looked back. Elio was watching us.

"Hold both of my hands," Liesbeth shouted just inches from my ear. "Feel the music. Just feel it and let yourself go. Don't think about anything."

At first I was annoyed by the loudness of the music and by the people who kept bumping into me, but I tried to concentrate on doing what Liesbeth said. After a couple of minutes, she came closer to me and shouted, "That's good, but try just to *feel* it."

I half-closed my eyes, trying to eliminate the mass of dancers freeze-framing in my vision. I relaxed, let myself go, and soon a feeling came, as if the music were speaking a language my body understood, rousing it from a deep, childhood sleep and filling it with the wonderfully primal desire to pulse, to dance, with the rhythmic power of the music.

"Ja!" Liesbeth screamed, throwing loose my hands. "You've got it!"

I felt like a musical instrument resonating in an ocean of sound, and wondered how Michael would respond to being in this club. He'll never be able to leave his room, I thought, never get a chance. He'll only be able to experience this in my memories.

Pushing that negative thought out of my mind, I continued to dance until Liesbeth again took my hands and shouted, "I have to rest a bit."

"She learns fast!" Liesbeth announced when we returned to our table.

"It's the teacher," Peer said.

She playfully slapped Peer's arm, then said, "Elio, you should dance with her. She's very good."

Elio smiled and began to get up, but Peer said, "Hey, it's my turn!"

Elio sat back down. "Sure, go ahead." His speech was slurred.

On the way to the dance floor, I put my mouth close to Peer's ear and asked, "Does Elio drink a lot?"

"No. I've only seen him get drunk once before. But tonight he's slamming 'em down. He's moody or something. Probably had another fight with his ma. Or with one of his friends."

Peer and I danced a song. He bumped his hips against me a few times, and his butt. I'd enjoyed dancing with Liesbeth more. He asked me to dance another song, but I said I wanted to go back to the table. What I really wanted was to dance with Elio.

When I returned to the table, however, and asked Elio to dance, he said he was too drunk. The talking and drinking continued for about a half-hour more before Elio complained of feeling sick. Luuk and Peer helped him to the bathroom.

When they returned, Elio slumped in the chair beside me. He leaned over and wrapped his arms around me but didn't say a word.

"We promised his mother we'd leave by midnight," I said to Luuk. "But how can I get him home? I don't think he can walk to the bus."

"Peer's got a car," Luuk said. "We'll take you home."

When Elio and I finally got to his apartment door, I propped him up against the wall and quietly opened the door. With my arm around him, we stumbled across the living room and into his bedroom. I pulled back the covers and sheet of his bed.

"Do you need to go to the bathroom?" I asked.

He shook his head no.

"Try to stand still. I'll take off your shirt and pants; then you can sleep. You'll feel better in the morning."

I took off his shirt, then unbuckled and unzipped his pants. I was shocked to see that he wasn't wearing underpants. I hadn't seen him naked for three years. His penis had grown larger, and it was surrounded by a thick, tangled mass of black pubic hair. Above it, a wispy tendril of fur had crept up toward his navel.

I felt happy and strangely excited by this sight of his genitals, by their musky scent, and by new stirrings deep down in my belly. I smiled up at him and asked him to sit on the bed so I could remove his pants and socks; then I asked him to lie down so I could cover him. As I pulled up the covers he grabbed my arm and said, "Don't go. Sleep with me."

I quickly took off my clothes. I hesitated at my underpants but decided it would be okay to take them off since he was naked, and then I crawled in beside him. He rolled over, placed his arm across my chest, his head on my shoulder, his leg over my legs. I got goose bumps from the warm, silky feel of his skin. I half-expected to hear him say I was still the best teddy bear in the world, but he quickly fell asleep.

A few hours later, I woke. It was beginning to get light outside. Elio seemed not to have moved. His breath, always before warm and moist on my chest, now smelled of vomit and beer; and his erection, which pressed against my thigh, was much larger than it had been years before when we'd slept together.

I had thoughts about how nice it would feel to hold Elio's penis in my hands and kiss it, but Grandpa's admonition to respect Elio's privacy kept interrupting my fantasies, so I lay still, feeling happy in Elio's embrace, and waited for sleep to return.

Sometime later, I was again wakened, this time by movement as Elio lifted his arm and leg off me and began to sit up.

"Hi," I said, stroking his back with my fingers.

"I've got to go to the bathroom," he replied as he got up unsteadily.

When he returned from the bathroom with a towel wrapped around his waist, I pulled the covers back to let him in, but he stopped by the side of the bed. "I don't feel good," he said. "Could you go and sleep in your own bed?"

I wanted to say: Crawl in. I'll hold you and make you feel better.

But obviously that was not what he wanted.

"Does it tickle a little?" Michael asked a few minutes ago, turning his specimen brush inside me.

"No. Just a bit cold. Like everything down here," I answered.

My long underwear and two pair of pants had been removed. My legs were spread, as if in love with the cold, damp air of this hideaway far under the sea.

Grandpa had sent along soil samples from the vineyard, neighboring orchards, and the shore of the Russian River. The idea was to prime the immune systems of Michael's children by early exposure to the millions of terrestrial organisms contained in those samples. In furtherance of this priming project, Michael was now taking specimens of my vaginal and anal ecosystems. The teeming swarms of life from these specimens will become part of the children's first meal, colonizing their intestines with the important microflora they would have ingested during a natural childbirth.

"Love pitched his mansion in the place of excrement," Michael said, looking up at me, his head framed by my bare knees.

"Yes, I know the Yeats poem," I replied. "Didn't some Christian saint precede him in that observation? Something to the effect that humans are born between feces and urine."

"Augustine," Michael said.

Next, he will vacuum out another egg or two and a few more ovarian stem cells for use in the artificial wombs. Like a dinosaur, I will reproduce simply by laying eggs.

It was the sounds of Aunt Lynh's getting ready to go to work that woke me next. Normally, I would have gone out and talked with her, but I didn't want to be questioned about what had happened the night before, so I waited under the covers. At about 0700 I heard her open the outside door and leave. I popped out of bed, showered, and dressed as quietly as I could so as not to wake Elio, then went out to eat breakfast.

About an hour later, I looked in on Elio. He was still sleeping, so I decided to go for a walk. I left a note on the kitchen table, telling him I would be out walking and would be back by 0900. But even though it was a beautiful morning, I came back to the apartment early; I didn't want to miss any time with Elio. Thoughts and feelings of his holding me in his bed kept leaping into my consciousness, and each time they did, I felt a strange weakness inside.

He wasn't in the apartment, but my note was still on the kitchen table. Below my writing he'd written: "I can't be with you right now. I'm sorry."

What, I worried, did I do? Did I say something wrong?

To keep my mind occupied while I waited for Elio to return, I tried to work on a few of the statistics problems Grandpa had given me to solve in my spare time. He believed that science was fundamentally a statistical interpretation of nature, and he was determined that, unlike most humans who handle equations with the grunting labor of lifting heavy rocks, I was to see the real world through these precious mathematical lenses as easily and intuitively as a child with excellent vision sees the individual facets on brilliant-cut melee. But I couldn't concentrate. Worry about Elio kept spilling into my thoughts.

When Aunt Lynh arrived home from work, she asked where Elio was. I said I didn't know and handed her the note he'd left behind.

She appeared to read the note several times. "Has he called you since he left?"

"No."

"Are you upset?"

I felt myself rapidly losing composure, but I shook my head no.

"Of course you're upset. You're a good pretender, though."

With that, the levee holding back my tears crumbled. She hugged me. "It's not so bad, honey. I told you he's gotten in the habit of running away the instant something bothers him. Why don't you tell me what happened at the club?"

"We met Luuk and some of his friends. Then we danced and talked."

"Did Elio get drunk?"

I hesitated.

"That's all right. I shouldn't ask you to get your brother in trouble. So, that's it? Except for a few little things you're afraid would get him in trouble with me, that's all that happened?"

"Yes."

She appeared deep in thought. "Maybe it's that everything comes too easily for him: grades, swimming, admirers. I can tell none of it means anything to him. His life has become like that club you went to last night: all noise and hollow distraction."

"But why did he write that he couldn't be with me?"

"What can I say? He's young, confused, impetuous."

"Grandpa told me that Elio likes to make love with boys. If that's what he's afraid of—that I'll find out—he shouldn't be, because I don't care. It's fine with me."

Of course, that last statement wasn't exactly true. I wanted Elio to do what made him happy, but I couldn't help feeling that those boys, whoever they were, were stealing away the intimacy and affection that belonged to me, and I was confused by and ashamed of such feelings.

Aunt Lynh smiled. "You're a good sister to him. Just keep on being a good sister, and I'm sure everything will be all right."

I stayed up late that night, waiting, hoping. But Elio didn't call or return.

The next morning Aunt Lynh and I were having breakfast when the phone rang. She grabbed it. "Hello." She was silent for about a minute. Finally, in a controlled voice she said, "Honey, don't do this. It's Sara's fifteenth birthday tomorrow." She listened a while longer. "Well, then, maybe she shouldn't come back again next summer."

I detected shouting from the other end.

When the shouting subsided, Aunt Lynh said, "I don't like it, but if you want to do this, I suppose you can. Do you need anything?" She glanced at me. "Do you want to say good-bye to Sara?" She glanced at me again, shaking her head. "Okay, call us when you get there. Promise?"

She put the phone down, stared at the cupboards for a few seconds, then threw her hands up into the air. "He's taking a train to Brussels in a half-hour. With Luuk. Just like that. He says I drive him crazy, and he doesn't want to be crazy in front of you. He says he needs us to give him space. Not that we have much choice. He's gone—just like that."

My eyes filled with tears. How could Elio leave me? How could he do this?

"Don't take it personally," Aunt Lynh said. "I try not to."

But I had the note: "I can't be with you." That sounded personal.

The next day, feeling confused and disappointed on my fifteenth birthday, I boarded a plane home, a week and two days earlier than planned.

Elio called me from Brussels within an hour of my arrival home. He wished me a happy birthday, then began telling me what Luuk and he had been doing. I interrupted him: "Why did you say you couldn't be with me? Why did you go to Brussels?"

"It's Ma. She's always bothering me. Screaming at me. Look, I'm really sorry about the way I acted. Please promise you'll come back to see me again next summer. I'll be better then, I promise."

Though I remained unsatisfied by his answer and confused about his behavior, I assured him that I would come to see him the next summer, and every summer. He was, after all, my summers, my dreams.

I had thought that for Grandpa problems were challenges to be enthusiastically explored, broken down into manageable components, and, often in a flash of emotionally charged insight, solved. But when I described Elio's hot-and-cold behavior, Grandpa didn't ask any questions or offer any suggestions. When I pressed him for help, he said, "Sara, please, listen to me. I know you want to help. But whatever it is that's troubling Elio, his intuition is that now is not a good time to force a resolution of the problem. You love him; you should trust his intuition. Besides, you have Michael and your studies. Your plate is full. Enjoy the feast and stop worrying about things you can't do anything about."

Perhaps Grandpa was short with me because his mind was occupied with other problems. He informed me the next day that he'd been reviewing intelligence reports which estimated that at least five hundred androids of different designs, including my brothers, had escaped to Canada after or immediately before the U.S. outlawed them, and that since then, nearly all had mysteriously disappeared, as had Aita. How long, I feared, would Mom and Dad be able to keep my brothers safe?

Ten days later, a rally was held in Sacramento to pressure the California State Legislature to ratify an amendment to repeal the Twenty-second Amendment to the U.S. Constitution. It was the first time I was allowed to watch WNN news at home (I'd watched it a few times before with Elio).

"I want you to see what 157,000 people praying and meditating looks like," Grandpa said as I sat down beside Grandma on the living room sofa.

The streets and lawns of the Capitol were crammed with people, most of them sitting on red-white-and-blue ERP meditation cushions. The silence amidst a gathering of so many was eerie. Occasionally, a WNN commentator would announce in an almost reverential whisper ("as during a golf tournament," Grandpa growled) the presence of a high-ranking person of this or that religion.

When a member of the presidium of the World Council of Faiths was pointed out, Grandpa gave his own commentary. "There's the real power. They want Jairison to be able to run for a third term. He and the other presidents and prime ministers are slowly becoming little more than feudal princes and princesses of the World Council's holy empire."

"Bad things often come from good things, and vice versa," Grandpa had cautioned several times before. He had explained, for example, how even science, as it had encroached ever further on what had been considered the core of the human self—its mind and consciousness—had inadvertently fueled the rise of the World Council. Slowly, a majority of people had fallen in line with ecumenical efforts to agree on one overriding religious principle: that though our bodies may have risen by evolution from earth, as soon as humans had evolved to a sufficient enough likeness of a god, this god had intervened to give humans a divine soul, which carried with it universal human values and meaning. Man was both of this Earth and divine, but man's tools, even his intelligent creations, were of this Earth only; and to try to make such creations equal or superior to man was hubristic and idolatrous in the extreme. For the World Council and for the ERP, the things of greatest value on Earth were human souls, and these two organizations were their god's primary protectors of those souls against the hubris of science and big international corporations.

When a segment came on showing a smiling, waving President Jairison and his family leaving their Sunday morning church service, Grandpa said he couldn't take it any longer and turned off the news. "I'm told," he said, getting up from the sofa, "that by day, Jairison meditates in his White House office on the divinity of the human soul, and that by night, he sleeps under a large reproduction of *The Dream of Constantine* by Piero della Francesca. The man is a dangerous lunatic, and I, for one, think that eight years will have been quite long enough."

I refused to let Michael join with me through the braincord while I told him what I'd seen on the news. I was concerned about frightening him with my fear: that all those people crowding the Capitol would think he was a soulless, dangerous thing. Whenever we joined together, Michael could feel what I felt, sometimes, it seemed, even more acutely than I did. For example, he had cried when he'd reviewed my memory of Elio's asking me to go sleep in my own bed that night we'd returned from the Red Dog, whereas I had merely felt hurt and confused. Perhaps a part of me—a part that Michael had found—had wanted to cry but felt repressed by Grandpa's warning that boys don't like girls who cry over seemingly trivial things.

I felt calmer by the time Michael and I crawled into bed together to sleep, so that when he asked me then to brainjoin with him, I consented, as I did about once each month when I let him watch my dreams unfold. He reached behind his head and tapped on the trepan door there. The braincord came out, moved up my nostrils, and we lay quietly, waiting for my sleep—and dreams—to begin.

I was out walking alone early one morning in the small park of Elio's apartment building when Michael frightened me by jumping down beside me out of the linden tree. He was lonesome and had come looking for me in Amsterdam. I explained how important it was for him to stay hidden until it was time for us to go home, but throughout the day he kept showing up wherever I went. I was concerned that he'd be recognized because, though he looked and dressed like a human, his skin was cool and, except for his hands, smooth like the skin on a frog's belly, and I knew implicitly that he would respond oddly in social settings—too gently, too kindly. Additionally, he had no passport or other form of identification.

It was dark and rainy that night when Elio, Michael, and I arrived at the Red Dog, where we were to meet some of Elio's friends. As Michael stepped through the door an alarm sounded, and immediately the three of us were being chased. Thick muddy water and huge, entangling plants that resembled the genetically modified plants my parents had seen in the Four Seasons resort on the moon rose up menacingly in the streets—had a levee broken?—making it difficult to run or even walk, and police boats and helicopters were closing in—

"No! Stop! Stop!" Michael's shrieking and his vigorous shaking of my arm woke me.

I immediately took both of his soft, sensitive hands in mine and we kissed. We stayed like that—hand in hand and lips on lips—until he calmed down.

The next day, the state legislature ratified the amendment.

First Brother

Sara and the dog are within 10 meters of a predicted debarkation on a narrow, gravelly boat landing on the river's north shore, across the estuary from the western edge of Penny Island. The dog stands at the prow, its front legs up on the convex edge of the raft, its nose turned windward. It sniffs.

The raft continues toward the landing. Pebbles grate on the bottom of the raft. To propel them forward, she applies force through the length of the paddle's shaft to the edge of the blade, which is sunk into the river's bottom. The dog walks on and around her legs, trips, then stumbles against her ventral trunk.

It is midday plus 1 hour, 4 minutes, 10 seconds.

Sara

After making my way through Customs at Schiphol the next summer, I saw Elio standing among a throng of people, waving. My chest filled with brightness, and I rushed into his arms. He seemed again to be the energetic, happy Elio I'd known and loved for ten years, though this summer he didn't hold my hand or kiss me on the way home.

For the next four days we biked along the IJsselmeer through Volendam and Edam, once reaching as far north as Hoorn. Aunt Lynh insisted that we return home every evening, so each day we relied on ferries, buses, and trains to take us part of the way. On Friday morning, the morning of my sixteenth birthday, I heard a knocking on my bedroom door.

"Happy birthday!" Elio said, opening the door. "I made breakfast. Come see."

Laid out on the kitchen table were waffles covered with maple syrup and almond butter, sprinkled with cinnamon sugar and minced almonds, then topped with pralines-and-cream ice cream. Surprised and delighted by this unusual breakfast, I ruffled his hair with my fingers and sat down to eat.

Our conversation broke off when I noticed he was staring at me. He extended his hand and interwove his fingers with mine. He smiled wanly, then said, "I'm really happy you're here."

"Thanks. I wasn't sure how you'd feel about my visit, especially since last summer."

I'd resolved not to mention the prior summer, but the problem that had surfaced then seemed to be returning, whether I mentioned it or not. Elio had appeared happy and relaxed when I'd arrived five days earlier, but increasingly as the days passed I'd caught him staring despondently into the distance or watching me with a look that seemed full of pain.

He looked toward the cupboards, seemingly lost in thought. I kept silent, waiting, hoping he would share with me whatever was troubling him. Finally, he pulled his fingers from mine and said, "I can't stay here right now. Let's walk to the gym and go swimming."

As soon as we got to the gym, he again seemed energetic and sociable, chatting and laughing with people he knew. He and I swam awhile, and when he pulled himself up out of the pool and sat on the edge of the deck, my gaze flowed, as did rivulets of water, over his chest and stomach, their beautiful rippled muscles heaving with each breath. I desperately wanted to glide my fingers over those muscles and hug him. But Grandpa had cautioned me to respect Elio's privacy and not force a resolution of whatever was troubling him.

We had a snack at the gym café, then walked back home in a light rain. He became quiet and withdrawn as we approached his apartment building. I followed him into his bedroom. He went to the window, parted the thin, white curtain, and stared out. I waited, filled with hushed expectancy, feeling certain that he wanted to take us somewhere new but was hesitant to make the turn—would it be right or left?—into the remainder of our lives.

"I've wanted to tell you something for a long time," he finally said, still looking through the rain-spotted window, "but I've been so afraid. I can't lose you. No matter what, I can't lose you." He pulled the curtain shut, though he continued facing it. "I thought I had it all under control after last summer. But then I saw you come out of Customs, and you hugged—"

He seemed to choke. I wanted, wanted so very much, to run to him, put my arms around him, and say, Tell me.

Then he turned slowly away from the gray window streaked with rain and, appearing strangely determined, walked toward me. As he neared, I raised my arms up over his shoulders and around his neck.

He caressed my back. I felt drawn to him, as if every cell of my body were being tugged toward him, with the cumulative effect being irresistible. He pressed the side of his head against the side of mine and said, "I love you."

I felt myself melting into him. He softly kissed my lips. A wave of joy and excitement rushed through me with such force that I seemed to lose my bearings, and I shuddered as the nearly invisible hairs on my arms and legs became erect.

Evidently misinterpreting my shudder, he let loose his arms, saying, "I'm sorry."

"I love you, too," I said, holding on to him. "I've felt my love for you growing for years. Now, I know you love me the same way."

He looked confused.

"Do you want me to take off my clothes?" I asked.

His face brightened, and he wrapped his arms around my waist and pulled my body firmly against his. He licked my lips, and when I laughed with pleasure, his tongue darted into and playfully searched inside my mouth. Again, the strange, new feeling of weakness came over me, as if my body had become the wavering image of itself on an undulating surface of a pool.

His hands seemed to know their way inside my clothes, where, like a cat pressing itself wavelike into a petting hand, my body moved instinctively and appreciatively to greet his caresses.

He took off my shirt, then his, and we again embraced. Nothing had ever felt as good to me as his skin felt then against mine. I felt happy and free. His erection pressed against my pelvis, where a strange, warm luster was spreading, and there was dampness, as if from sweat, between my legs. Then, kissing my open mouth while holding us firmly together, he pressed us over to and onto his bed.

My body arched to stay in touch with his, but as he finished undressing us, my consciousness flittered briefly away. I saw Grandpa's face. He was in his study. It was the morning he'd devoted to my sex education. I heard him say "floods of neuromodulators," "reprogramming," "acquire new interests." A brief panic raced through me and burst into consciousness as a question: Will I lose my love for Grandpa? Michael? My studies?

"I love you. I need you," Elio whispered as he kissed and caressed me. He rolled onto his side, and I followed, pushing him onto his back, then eagerly exploring his body, once a familiar boy's, now hard and fragrant and thrillingly strange.

He rolled me over onto my back and positioned himself directly on top of me—his arms stretching mine to the sides, our fingers interlocking, his mouth and mine becoming one. Then he parted my legs and sat up between them. He caressed the insides of my thighs; then he raised my knees up along his sides and looked at me, breathing heavily.

"I want you so much," he said.

He lowered himself down and kissed me. "Please let me make love to you. I'll make it feel real good for you, I promise."

"I'll enjoy anything that makes you happy," I said.

He kissed me and raised himself back up. He guided his penis to my vagina and pushed, going only part way in. He withdrew slightly, then pushed in a little farther, withdrew slightly, over and over. It felt as though something I didn't control resisted him, but then, accompanied by a brief sharp pain, opened, a border no longer, and he slipped in all the way and smiled; and I moaned with a new kind of pleasure.

He bent over and gently kissed me. I gazed up into his eager, intense eyes, which gazed into me. I felt myself opening to him like a poppy to the sun.

"Is this okay?" he whispered.

"Oh, yes."

He raised himself up, looking down into me, and as he moved in and out, in and out, my mind and senses flowed over him, enthralled by his beauty and by the feeling that I was blossoming beneath him.

"Look into my eyes," he said, pumping faster, faster. "Look into my eyes when it happens."

I looked, and during the rising frequency of his insistent pulses, I was astonished—"Elio! Elio!!"—by the overwhelming bliss of union.

The morning after we first made love, I woke as Elio was kissing me. He smiled, but there was concern in his face.

"Is something wrong?" I asked.

"We can't say anything about this to Ma. She's hyper about anything that might take me back to America—like my loving you. That was the trouble last summer: We fought about you before you arrived. She wanted me to treat you like a sister, you know. She said she'd never let you visit again if she found out I thought of you otherwise. That's why I was so upset. She'll try anything to keep us apart, but we can't let her. You make me happier than I ever thought I could be. I want us to be together, always." Tears welled in his eyes.

"I want us to be together always, too," I said, overjoyed at hearing that he was thinking of coming to live with me.

"And there's something else," he said. "I don't want us to keep secrets from each other any longer."

A spark of panic flashed through me. What about my secret, my hidden love? How could I tell Elio about Michael? Grandpa had repeatedly warned me about artificial insects and birds and other sophisticated monitoring devices. I'd grown up used to the idea that, outside the security of Michael's rooms, even in our own kitchen, each gesture I made and each word I spoke might be transmitted beyond the intended recipient.

"I should have told you," Elio continued, "about my friends and me a long time ago."

I wouldn't have asked him about his past sexual experiences, preferring, as I did, the soft light and shadows of early morning and late afternoon to the harsh brightness of the midday sun, but I didn't interrupt his story. I wasn't prepared yet to tell my own.

He told me how he and Luuk had goofed around as kids, seeing whose penis was longer or thicker, or how many words they could write in the snow in one pee. Later, they'd snuck into virtual-sex cubicles near Centraal Station and had gone through a period of experimenting with each other, doing things they saw and experienced in the cubicles. "It was fun," Elio said, "as though we were playing a game—like football."

He also told me about his sexual relationships with several other classmates, about how he'd picked up guys and even a girl now and then at clubs like the Red Dog and, finally, about how, enduring threats from his mother, he'd struggled against his growing affection for me. He'd promised her after his return from Brussels the previous summer that he'd put his sexual feelings for me out of his mind forever.

"The strange thing is," he said, "I really believed I could do that. I believed it right up to when I saw you at the airport a week ago and you came running to me and hugged me."

"But I've told you many times that I always wanted to be with you."

"I know," he said, wiping at his teary eyes. "But we didn't know then everything those words meant. Now, I know they mean I want to live with you. I want to care for you. I want it to be as if we're married."

"I do, too."

He excitedly kissed me, then said, "Remember last winter when I got my SAT and Advanced Placement scores? Well, your grandpa called to congratulate me. He said I undoubtedly could get into any university I wanted. We talked then about Cambridge in England, and Harvard."

He took a deep breath. "But I want to go to Berkeley, so I can live with you. I'll commute back and forth. And I don't want to wait another year to graduate. I want to go right away this fall. What do you think about that?"

"That would be wonderful!" But immediately Aunt Lynh and Michael forced their way into my consciousness. I nearly asked: What about your ma's not wanting you to go back to America? The words were formed and on their way, but he was so happy and excited that I resolved to keep them suppressed awhile longer.

We made love, napped, played in the shower, talked about our dreams of our future life together, and all the while, I did my best to filter out the insistent internal whispers about Michael and Aunt Lynh. Finally, with a plan forming in my mind, I suggested we take a bike ride, this time following the A9 to Haarlem.

Before we set off, I asked to stop at the convenience store in the apartment complex. There, we purchased chocolate bars, nuts, dried fruit, two bottles of water, a roll of aluminum foil, a roll of duct tape, a pen, a notepad, and some matches. I could have found several of those items in the apartment, but if we were being monitored, anything in the apartment might have been contaminated with microsensors.

"What's with the tape and matches and stuff?" Elio asked as we stood in line at the sales counter.

"I have an interesting game to show you," I replied—to him and to all who might have had us under surveillance.

As we neared the northeastern tip of Schiphol Airfield I took the lead and turned south toward Aalsmeer.

"Hey!" Elio shouted from behind me. "That's the wrong way."

I rode on until I saw he was following me. I stopped, and as he rode up beside me I said, "I changed my mind. Let me lead the way today, okay?"

I pulled off the bike path at one end of a row of hedges and glanced around, fearing that tiny volant robots might have been tracking my semblance or scent. But I saw nothing suspicious. Then I walked between the hedge and airfield fence until I found a spot somewhat secluded from the path and the road.

"I like it here," Elio said, laying his bike next to mine. "I've been thinking about Ma. How do I tell her? She gets crazy when it comes to America, you know."

"I wouldn't say crazy."

"Oh, ja, crazy." He sat down cross-legged and patted the grass in front of him, inviting me to sit, knee-to-knee, facing him—our long-established discussion position. "Remember a few years ago when the U.S. and China invaded several countries and destroyed their android military facilities?"

"Yes."

"Ma was fixing breakfast when she turned on the news and heard about the invasion. She went into a rage, screaming and swearing and crying. Completely crazy, I'm telling you. And then she was depressed and wouldn't speak or eat for days. She hates America. After you go home, I'll tell her we're lovers, but I don't know how to tell her I'm going to go to America to be with you."

"Maybe I should ask Grandpa for advice. He seems to know her quite well."

"That's a good idea. Hopefully, he'll know how to handle it. Hey, let's move over there and get you out of the sun."

We moved to an area of shade under and between two

shrubs. Then I said, "I have something interesting to show you. But for me to show you, you have to do exactly as I say without asking any questions, okay?"

"What's the big secret?"

"There's no secret." As I said that, I hoped it would be the last lie I'd ever tell him. "First, I'm going to make a little something with the notepad and aluminum foil."

He nodded, took off his shirt, and watched as I taped two layers of aluminum foil along the sides and top of the notepad, forming over it an aluminum dome with an opening through which we could write and read. I placed the domed notepad under a shrub, and concerned about what might be hiding in the brim or collar, I took off my hat and shirt and lay on my stomach, trying to capture as much shade as possible over my shoulders and arms. Pen in hand, I reached into the dome and, with seldom-practiced (and poor) penmanship, wrote:

"Please don't appear concerned as you read this. Try to pretend that it's an interesting game. I'll write a few paragraphs and then take my hand out of the dome to let you read. If you want to write something, ask for the pen; if not, say 'Give me another hint,' and I'll continue.

"There is a secret I must tell you, a dangerous secret, one that can't be discussed or even alluded to on Vidtel, in your apartment, or even out here except in this secret manner because there exist robotic insects and birds capable of monitoring us.

"The life of someone I love, a biologically modified android, depends on your never revealing this secret. I didn't tell you before because, when I was eight and this secret began, I promised Grandpa I wouldn't. He asked me to wait until you went to university to tell you, but if you're coming to live with us, I can't wait any longer."

I withdrew my hand from the dome and said, "Okay, let's see whether you can figure this out."

He put his face close to the dome's opening and read. Then, appearing somewhat annoyed, he snatched the pen out of my hand, stuck his hand in the dome, and began writing. Finished, he handed the pen back to me. I peered into the dome and read his hurried script: "You can tell your grandpa his secret is absolutely safe with me."

I wrote: "The problem is that having Michael—that's his name—is considered a serious crime in America, a crime you'll become an accomplice to if you come live with us."

As I wrote this I felt slightly sick with apprehension. I couldn't—wouldn't ever—abandon Michael. But I couldn't live without Elio, either. What if Elio didn't like Michael? What if he didn't want to live with Michael? Or Michael with him?

Elio wrote: "If being with someone you love is a crime in America, then I'll be proud to be a criminal."

After I read this, Elio wrote several questions, which I answered in turn, about the security in Michael's area of the house, including my bedroom, and about how Michael compared with my brothers in Canada.

Then he wrote: "You call them your brothers, but how conscious are they? Are they more like us or like robots blindly following clever rules that humans program into them?"

I wrote: "The question as to whether androids are conscious or are cleverly-responding zombies is a philosophic debate on the level of the debate over solipsism. Grandpa says that even if the world is our dream, it is a dream in which there are those who must be practical. Accordingly, about a decade before my brothers were created, the U.S. Defense Department commissioned Stanford University to develop a new consciousness scale.

"The Stanford scale has many critics, but undeniably it has been of great value in raising our awareness that consciousness exists along a broad spectrum. The issue has become *how* conscious is a bird or a chimpanzee or an android or a human, not *whether* the being is conscious. The median score for humans 18 years and older is 95 on the 100 point scale; 90 is considered the human threshold. Except for Michael, who scored 97 about six months ago, Grandpa is not aware of any android scoring above 91. He believes that one of the reasons for Michael's outstanding performance is that Michael has become able to think my thoughts and feel my feelings in a very literal and direct way.

"When I was eight, some of my brain cells, as well as cells for support organs, were extracted to grow a few of Michael's parts, such as part of his brain. During that operation, a pair of neural junctions was implanted in my cribriform plate. While Michael was gestating, neural pathways emanating from those junctions were sent to all areas of my brain. The bottom line is that Michael and I are able to connect with each other's brain through what we call a braincord."

As Elio read, he occasionally glanced up and gave me an astonished look. Then he wrote: "Now I'm jealous. (Just joking.) But seriously, what happens if Michael overwhelms your thoughts? Is there any danger of him taking over your body?"

I wrote: "No. I have to completely relax and clear my mind before he can enter to the extent necessary to take over my body, and I can intervene anytime I wish."

Elio wrote: "What about your private thoughts? Can you keep them private from him?"

I wrote: "My memories, thoughts, and feelings are available to Michael when we're connected. But I don't mind. I've grown accustomed to his presence inside my mind."

Elio rolled over onto his side. I held him, nestling my head against his chest. I wanted to give him more time to think and ask questions. After a few minutes, he kissed the top of my head and said, "Let me try one last guess." He picked up the pen and wrote: "I'm going to take courses at Berkeley to help me help you with Michael. I want to be a part of Michael, too. I want to be a part of everything that matters to you."

We burned the overwritten pages plus the ten pages immediately below, which might have retained a faint impression of our writing, and as I launched the last pinch of ashes up into the breeze Elio caught my arm and pulled us together.

"I want to marry you," he said. "I know you're too young without your parents' consent, and Ma would kill me, but we can do it ourselves, right here, right now. Besides, nobody needs to know. It's none of their business."

At that moment a plane took off with a loud roar from the runway closest to us. I glanced at the plane and winced at the incongruity between our tender moment and such a storm of commerce. But Elio seemed not to hear the plane. His eyes were dreamy, as though he saw only me—and the noise and the imagined spies evaporated from my mind.

"What do we do?" I asked.

"Exchange promises that we'll always love and take care of each other." He looked at me eagerly.

"Yes, of course," I said. "I'll always love you and care for you. Always."

"And that we'll share all our thoughts, all our feelings, everything."

"I want those things, too. I never want to keep anything from you ever again."

We bent toward each other and kissed.

"You go first," he said, squeezing my hands and peering into my eyes, as if he could see directly inside me.

I looked back into him and felt so at peace, so full of love, so very much at home. "I, Sara Jensen, promise to love you always with all my heart and mind and body; to care for you always; to share all my ideas, feelings, and desires with you; to trust you completely; to be married to you, Elio Briand, for as long as we live."

For our secret honeymoon, we decided to spend the six days left before my departure biking through the province of North Holland, though we had to return home each night to sleep. Obviously, Aunt Lynh's trust of Elio's promise to treat me as a sister went only so far. I wonder whether she ever wondered whether we might occasionally rent a hotel room for a couple of hours during the middle of the day (which we did). And did she ever wonder whether we might be sleeping together in Elio's bed at night (which we also did), the doors to our rooms securely locked?

During those bike trips, Elio and I frequently stopped along country roads and lay hand in hand in the grass, talking of our past and dreaming of a shared future: going to university, working on scientific projects (of course, for security reasons no further mention of Michael was made), having children after our professional lives were established. For years we had enjoyed our summer vacations together; we had spent thousands of hours on Vidtel together; we had learned and experienced so much together. But for me, those six days held special wonder. It was as though all of our earlier experiences demanded to come forth and be replayed, to live again in the new light and fullness of our love.

On the morning of my departure, he got out of bed and walked toward the bathroom. Halfway there, he looked around. I was lying in bed, watching him. He smiled, then walked back to the bed, knelt beside me, and gave me a long warm kiss. "I love you so much," he said. "I'd like to tell you a little secret before you go."

"What?"

"It makes me feel really good inside when I know you're watching me when I'm naked. I'd like you to come into the bathroom with me this morning, and any other time you want, and watch me do whatever I do."

I flung my arms around his neck. "Thank you! I think you're so beautiful!"

I sat naked on the toilet, cover down, and watched him take a shower. He came out and dried himself leisurely in front of me.

"You sure seem to have an erection a lot of the time," I said.

He looked down at it, smiled, then turned to profile himself to me. His erection arched up playfully. "It's the way my body smiles at you," he said, grinning.

Now, whenever I think of that moment, his form starts to take shape. First, an outline of his muscular thigh appears; then the curve of his firm, round buttocks; then his muscled stomach, its mid-parting incurvation enticing me—and suddenly, he's there: black, glistening wet hair; full, ripe lips and white teeth smiling; dark-skinned torso arching back slightly to accentuate the v-shape it forms with his erection. And it's true—his body is smiling at me!

First Brother

She walks, the dog runs, toward a sign that reads, "Private Property. Beware Of Owner." She repeatedly looks toward the house just east of the graveled way leading down to the landing.

"Rusty!" she calls. "Come! Come here, boy!"

The dog stops, turns, and trots back to her. She reaches out with her right hand and strokes the dog's shoulder. "Leave the pigeonoid alone. Heel. Good boy!"

The dog walks beside her for a couple of meters. She calls out toward the house and toward the garage north of the house: "Hello! Hello! Is anyone home?"

One door of the garage is open. A Toyota brand vehicle with two canoes attached to its top is parked inside the open garage door. She leans in beside the right side of the vehicle and again calls out: "Hello!"

The dog runs into the garage on the left side of the vehicle and disappears from sight.

"Come," she says. She turns and heads toward the house.

Sara

Even though I wear gloves as I write, my hands occasionally get cold and I go to the module where Michael is working on the artificial wombs, where it is tropically moist and warm and where, sometimes, I can close my eyes and feel at peace. But this time during my break to rest and warm up, Michael was excited to show me the set of breasts he just completed fabricating, four breasts stacked 2 x 2 that he will strap onto his chest to nurse the first children. He already has names for them: Kyla, Sophie, Eddy, Jace.

Soon, using my eggs and genetic material preserved from Elio and some people Grandpa felt were superior both physically and mentally, Michael will complete the design of the coiled strands of the children's DNA, those twisting tornadoes of possibilities, then nine months later will pull four wet infants crying and kicking from the artificial wombs, and for a year or so nurse them on the quadruple heated breasts strapped to his chest, where, I imagine, the newborns will suck and coo, cough and spit and wiggle themselves into caramel-smelling slumberous calm, their doughy thighs and pudgy little fingers cradled in his arms, their heads pillowed in his cruciform cleavage, their anterior fontanels—crested with white, black, blond, and auburn downy hair—visibly pulsing to the warm, red, iambic rhythm of human life. Sophie will be my clone, her eyes buttons of bleached-blue sky; and Eddie will be Elio's, his skin chocolate and when in the sun, smelling of rain on warm stone.

Michael says I should see them as my children, too. But he insists that they remain here for a while, perhaps years, until he is certain the threat from the androids on Mars is over. I can't imagine staying in this cramped, cold place for years. Each day I become more anxious, more eager to leave, to return to Grandma, Lily, home. And perhaps I suffer from an antiquated notion that a mother is someone who wraps her long legs around a father. There is no father like that here.

I longed for Elio during the flight home. But I felt drawn forward, too. I'd been gone for two weeks, and I missed home: Grandpa, Grandma, Michael, and Lily—and the vineyard, that palimpsest of sweetness and green, shimmering in the midsummer sun.

After playing with Lily and then talking with Grandpa and Grandma over lunch, I showered to rid myself of any clinging microdevices and stepped in front of Gatekeeper 3. The first door opened, then closed behind me. I placed my feet on the foot diagrams printed on the floor and waited for Gatekeeper to examine me. While still in Amsterdam, I'd called Grandpa and Grandma and told them Elio and I had become lovers. They had been wonderful, wishing us happiness. I worried, though, about how supportive (or upset) Michael would be. Had they told him already?

I heard the seals of the second door release, and there was Michael, smiling and reaching in for me before the door finished sliding open.

"I'm so happy you're home!" he exclaimed, hugging me.

I reached for a pair of underpants, but he grabbed my hand and pulled me along toward our study. "I saw the recording of your telling Grandpa and Grandma about you and Elio. I was so excited that I asked Grandpa to bring me materials to examine related to the physiology and psychology of sex and love. It's fascinating." Near the computer was a pile of chip cases. "I want to brainjoin with you while you tell me about Elio."

We sat cross-legged on the floor, and after the braincord made its familiar journey up my nostrils to its junctions, I began telling Michael about my two weeks with Elio.

He asked me to skip to just before I knew Elio wanted to make love with me. I did. After a bit, he asked me to go back in the story and concentrate on seeing Elio naked in bed. I did. He asked me to try to see and feel as much as I could about that first sexual experience, and as I did my nipples became erect. He bent over and looked at them closely. "I read about this. And you're flushed and breathing heavily."

"Yes, well, remembering and describing all this is sexually arousing for me."

"I know all about it. I've been studying. I also read that people masturbate to give themselves pleasure. I'd like to experience masturbation while we're connected."

"I've never done it by myself. Only with Elio."

"But humans do this—usually alone. Couldn't we do this alone?"

I had agreed to share my life with Michael, but I'd been only eight at the time. I hadn't known then that one day I might want something only for myself.

I looked at Michael. He was so obviously eager for us to share this human sexuality, as we had shared everything before. For him, I was a confluence of many roles: mother, sister, teacher, friend—and I was a vitally important instrument for his ability to sense and feel, especially relating to activities in the outside world. And I loved him, loved him in a way that our special circumstances required, which meant, I felt then, that I had to share myself with him and had to try to be whatever he needed whenever he needed it, for how else could he obtain it?

"Okay," I said, "but it'll be more comfortable for me if I lie on my bed."

Michael sat beside me on the bed, and I began doing what I'd never done without Elio—without his hands on my hands, his fingers atop my fingers, guiding them, pressing here, stroking there, releasing exquisite pleasure that shimmered magically over a river of contractions and moans. But though my fingers were in the remembered places doing the remembered things, they failed on their own to conjure up the shimmering pleasure.

"I don't see or hear a story," Michael interrupted. "From what I've read, aren't you supposed to tell yourself a romantic story while you touch yourself in the right places?"

"Like what?" I said, trying not to think—for my thoughts he too would think—that the problem more likely was his presence studying me.

"Well, like about making love with Elio on your birthday. That aroused you before. It's a story I already know, so I should easily be able to sense its many nuances."

With my hands once again busy on my body, I began silently recalling the events of my birthday, when I found to my surprise that I merely had to evoke, in the manner already described, Elio's body smiling at me to satisfy Michael's curiosity and my sudden desire.

Michael stared at me without expression. Then he exclaimed, "Wow! That was amazing! The rising heartbeat, the tension, the crescendo of neural activity, the release—all that stimulation surged through our brains, crushing every conscious thought. I read about it, but I never anticipated such an experience."

Yes, I thought. Words can only point, as the fingers of spectators point toward but can never give the experience of the blossoming of the event so many have come to see.

He reached over and touched my right breast near the areola, then jerked his hand back as if he'd been jolted by a spark of electricity.

"Ah! My fingers feel so cold!" His voice and manner seemed half-startled, half-despondent, and I instantly felt his or my—or our—pain.

"I like your cool touch," I said, reaching over and taking his hand in mine. "It's just that... perhaps my breasts are hypersensitive right now." I became conscious then of the problem of someday finding someone who would long—in the way a lover longs—for Michael's cool touch, his touch that was loving in every way but lacked mammalian warmth.

"Do you miss Elio?" he asked.

I nodded. "He might be coming to live with us in a couple of months. He wants to live here and commute to school at UC Berkeley."

"Live here? With us? In these rooms?"

"Yes, if you don't mind. And if we can get his mother to agree."

Michael's face lit up to its maximum expression of happiness. "That's wonderful! We can play and talk and study together. And I can feel your sexual feelings for him, too."

I thought for a moment. "Yes, it will be wonderful. But I would like you to wait awhile before you ask to feel my sexual feelings for him while he's present."

"Why is that?"

"We don't want to frighten or offend him. Let's wait until he's nearly as comfortable with you as I am. Let him see to what extent my sense impressions and mental activities can be experienced by you. Let him see how you can take over my motor activities when I relax completely. Give him time. In the meanwhile, you'll have many opportunities when he's not present to experience through our braincord the love and pleasure I feel with him."

A momentary buzz of seemingly incoherent words and

images flooded my brain, which was still connected with Michael's. Then he smiled, nodded, and kissed me on my lips, as we'd been used to kissing ever since he was born.

About a half-hour before dinner, I put on walking shorts and headed out to the vineyard, where I hoped to find solitude. As I walked I became aware as never before, not simply of my sexuality, but more expansively of the sensual richness and luminosity of the physical world. The gentle pokes and jabs of blades of brown grass and of clumps of dry, gray dirt made my feet feel free. The sun, low in the sky, felt warm and comforting, reminding me of how my skin had seemed to awaken for the first time on my birthday as it pressed against Elio's dark silky skin; of how, since then, my clothes felt good in a new way when I put them on; and of how the spray of warm water in a shower now gave me goose bumps of delight.

I took off my clothes and sat cross-legged on them in the shade of the green canopy of leaves. For about fifteen minutes, I sat clearing my mind. Then, expanding outward with my newly ripened senses, I noticed the world anew. I'd expected the vines would have grown heavier in my absence, but I hadn't expected them to be so exquisitely filled-out, or the soil so soft and comforting, or the air so sweetly redolent of green. I knelt in front of a vine and ran my fingers from the ground up along its rough trunk, caressing its jagged calluses. I kissed a leaf, feeling with my lips its velvety underside. I licked a small cluster of little green orbs of nascent fruit. I gently wrapped my arms around the vine, hugging its gnarled reality; and then, sensing I was part of life infinitely greater than my own, I looked up at the sky, felt sunshine pour through the leaves onto my back, and pinched dirt between my toes—as my body shivered its own shimmering smile at this precious Earth.

After dinner that first evening back home, Grandpa came in to visit Michael and me. "So, Michael, how was your day?" Grandpa's sly smile indicated he'd known that Michael had been full of questions.

"Elio's coming to live with us!" Michael burst out. Whenever he became excited his eyes and face twitched like the surface of a puddle quickened by a sudden gust of wind. "Here, with Sara and me!"

"Elio is coming here?"

"He wants to," I said, trying to sound as unconcerned as I could. "He'd like to come live with us and begin his university studies this fall at Berkeley."

"Does Elio know about Michael?"

"Please, Grandpa, sit here," I said, touching the back of his chair at our study table. "I'll explain everything."

The muscles in Grandpa's face and neck visibly tightened. I nodded to Michael, and he and I quickly took our chairs across the table from Grandpa.

"There's nothing to worry about," I said. "I remembered that you said I shouldn't tell Elio about Michael until Elio went to university, but I was confident he wouldn't do anything to jeopardize Michael's safety."

"Jeopardize Michael's *existence*," Grandpa interrupted. "*Our* safety and freedom."

"I know."

"Do you?"

"What's wrong?" Michael asked.

I shook my head, communicating to Michael not to interrupt.

"Grandpa, I'm sorry I didn't do exactly as you'd wanted, but Elio agrees with us about androids, religion—everything. And he wants to help with Michael in any way he can."

As in the blueing of the sky at foredawn, the darkness in

Grandpa's face softened, but he didn't reply.

"Elio loves me," I said. "He'll do anything he can to protect me and everyone I love. You'll just have to explain the security considerations to him. That's all."

"Let's hope he listens to me better than you did."

I nodded.

There was another pause in the conversation before Grandpa asked, "How did you communicate this information back and forth with Elio?"

I explained about biking to a hedgerow near Schiphol and forming the aluminum foil dome over the notepad, even about taking off our shirts because of concern about possible monitoring devices in our collars. Then I narrated everything Elio and I had written, and I explained how I'd burned our writings and scattered the ashes in the wind.

When I finished, Grandpa sat impassively. Michael broke the silence. "I'm extremely happy that Elio is coming to live with us. I've examined him in Sara's memories and agree that he won't do anything to harm us, especially if you teach him what to say and do."

Grandpa breathed in deeply and sighed. "It would appear that we have no choice other than to try to make the best of the situation—more proof, as if we needed it, of how close erection is to insurrection."

Michael hugged me. I could feel him bouncing up and down with glee. Then he turned to Grandpa. "You asked how my day was. It was wonderful!" Michael proceeded enthusiastically to describe in graphic detail how he'd experienced my masturbation while we'd been brainjoined. And he again stated how excited he was about meeting Elio.

While calmly listening to Michael, Grandpa glanced at me several times with eyes that were not full of enthusiasm. When Michael finished, Grandpa cleared his throat—perhaps more of a growl than a clearing of the throat—and peered at me.

"I hadn't anticipated coming home and finding that Michael had become an eager sex expert," I said, trying to defend myself from the silent stare.

Grandpa pursed his lips, apparently thinking, then said, "Yes, well, this brings up a serious matter. All of Elio's experiences have taken place outside of these rooms, under circumstances quite different from those that obtain here. Unlike either of you, he's gone to schools where his ideas and values undoubtedly have been challenged by people who didn't love him. Unlike either of you, he's undoubtedly played at school and in the streets of New York and Amsterdam with children, some of whom were unkind to him, swore at him, fought with him. And in response to such personal attacks, he's undoubtedly developed both aggressive and defensive traits quite different from yours.

"What I'm getting at is that Elio is not a buffet. We can't pick and choose what we like. When he walks through Gatekeeper's door, we can't say, 'Oh, Elio! You're so handsome, charming, intelligent, and playful. Come in! Ah, but check all those other things, all that silly aggressiveness and defensiveness, all those crazy ideas and desires of the outside world, at the door.' Elio is a whole person, a whole, unfathomably complicated and wonderful person, and we must love him and respect him as such."

"I will," Michael said.

"Let me give you an example of what I'm getting at, Michael," Grandpa continued. "You should have picked up from what you've read, if not from Sara"—he shot a sour glance my way—"that most people in our culture have a highly developed sense of privacy regarding the workings of their genitals. Now, suppose that shortly after you meet Elio, you tell him you'd like to watch him masturbate. I can tell you with near certainty that most young men would not react well to that request. They would think it quite impertinent. They might even strike you angrily with their fist."

"No!" Michael's hands swept up and covered his face. This was how he hid from us whenever he didn't like what we were doing or saying. We always honored Michael's ability to suspend reality in this manner for as much time as he needed to deal with it again. He couldn't, after all, run outside and hide with Lily in her house, as I occasionally had as a child when the going got tough.

After a few seconds, two of Michael's fingers parted, and an eye peeked through.

"I'm not saying that's how Elio *would* respond," Grandpa then said, "but it would be terribly unfortunate, Michael, if you inadvertently hurt Elio's feelings and he ended up disliking you. Don't you agree?"

"Yes! I don't want that to happen. I promise I'll never do anything to hurt Elio's feelings. I want us to be full of love and happiness together."

"Good. And one more thing: Sara, please try to teach Michael to refrain from touching Elio as much as he touches us. Elio, I believe, would have a word for it: weird."

Grandpa was referring to Michael's joy in touching our hands and arms and hair. Years before, we had had difficulty "socializing," as Grandpa had put it, Michael's constant sucking on his own fingers—not just his thumbs, all of his fingers. Unlike the rest of his skin, Michael's hands and lips were soft and spongy, somewhat like the inside of an orange peel. Grandpa said those areas contained an abundance of synthetic Krause corpuscles, which, when caressed, elicited the production of endorphins, and thus calming pleasure, in the biologic part of his brain.

In an attempt to wean Michael from his fingers, Grandpa brought in many items for Michael to touch: sheets of velvet, a brown teddy bear, leaves, twigs, bark, vegetables and fruit and blossoms not available in the hydroponic garden. But though Michael loved to touch and kiss and caress all of these items (as well as the many others we tried), it wasn't until Grandpa began bringing in books and musical scores printed in Braille that Michael found a satisfactory alternative to finger-sucking. He would spend hours in reverie over these texts, for the pleasure of touch, I believe, as much as or more than for the information contained therein. Perhaps for him touch and information complemented each other, as voices and instruments do in opera. Sometimes, I would see him smiling or crying while reading with his fingers and ask about the text. Each time he would say something to the effect that the dots felt so wonderful: beyond them was a world of shapes, colors, tastes, scents, and sounds.

We had not, however, discouraged Michael from expressing his love by touching and kissing us. He seemed to experience his skin (what Grandpa called his integumentin) not as a limit or boundary of the self but as a place of exquisite and joyful interaction with the world.

It was within an hour of sunset when Grandpa and I left Michael's rooms. I asked Grandpa to take a walk with me in the vineyard. As we strolled among the lush, green rows of trellised vines I told him of the feelings I'd felt when Elio and I first made love and of the marriage vows we later exchanged. Grandpa appeared thoughtful and interested, frequently raising his thick eyebrows and nodding, even as I rambled on, trying to explain and justify what I feared he might think had been impulsive and immature actions.

"What are your intentions in telling me all this?" he finally asked. "Are you afraid I'll think you were a silly, foolish girl?"

"Maybe."

Laughing, he stepped toward me and we hugged. "I was

sensitive about these matters when I was sixteen, too. You love Elio, so love him fully. You don't need to justify your feelings to me. Grandma and I love and respect you, and we completely support your feelings for Elio. We all feel a need for a special other. However, I ask you to keep in mind that you will be disappointed only to the extent that your desires or expectations fall out of harmony with reality."

"But, Grandpa, I don't know much about this aspect of reality. You do."

He chuckled. "One of the problems with knowing, or thinking you know, is that it often makes keeping your hands off what is not yours quite difficult. If we aren't careful, we're tempted to transform our knowledge into a license to change and control. But there are some things—actually, I believe there are many things—that we should not get involved in changing or controlling. Your sexuality, how you express your love, how you express your wonder and awe at the world—such things are yours, not mine. I love you, and in loving you, I humbly defer in such matters to you."

We walked awhile longer in silence; then I said, "Elio wants to come live with us, but there's a problem with Aunt Lynh. He told me she hates America and is adamantly against his ever returning here. He loves her and doesn't want to hurt her. We need your help."

"What do you want me to do?"

"I'd like you to go visit her in Amsterdam. Tell her we're concerned about her feelings, and help Elio express his desires without getting into a shouting match with her. I want Elio to come live with us as soon as possible, but I'll encourage him to delay if you think delay is called for."

From the moment I first mentioned that Elio might be coming to live with us until the morning I left to pick him up at the airport in early September, Michael pestered me with questions: What do I do if he says this? How do I respond if he does that?

One day, Michael requested that I pretend to be Elio so that he could practice greeting him. I went out through Gatekeeper, then came back in, put on a kimono in the dressing antechamber, and walked out to greet Michael.

He stood strangely erect and said, "Hi, Elio."

"Hi, Michael! I'm so happy to meet you."

Michael stepped stiffly forward and stuck out his hand to shake.

"I don't think Elio likes to shake hands," I said.

"Oh!" Michael responded, jerking back his hand.

"He likes to hug his friends."

"Let's try again," Michael said, shooing me back to the antechamber.

I went back and reentered. We said our greetings, stepped toward each other, moved our arms up and down, trying to find a fit—then we both froze. Moments later, as Michael began to cry, I realized there was no prescribed way to hug. Years earlier, when Michael began walking, I stood only a little over half his height, so we became accustomed to hugging by having me wrap my arms around his midsection and by having him place his arms over my shoulders and back. As I grew taller, we continued hugging in this manner.

In contrast, Michael had always hugged Grandpa and Grandma, who were both taller than he, by wrapping his arms around their waists as their arms went over his arms and around his torso. And to complicate matters even further, Elio and I hugged by having him wrap his arms around my waist while I slipped my arms up over his shoulders and around his neck.

"Please don't be upset," I said, hugging Michael in our accustomed way.

"I want Elio to like me."

"Elio will like you. I'm sure he will. Just relax."

"But I don't know how to become a friend. People meet many others, but only a few become friends. What is the process? What if Elio doesn't pick me?"

"The probability of Elio's liking you is extremely high."

"How can you know that?"

"I know both of you intimately. Each of you wants to like the other, and each of you wants the other to like you. Just look at yourself right now. I'm sure Elio has similar anxieties about your liking him."

"But what is the process of becoming friends? I don't know what to do."

"There's no formal process. It happens naturally. You both share many of the same interests. All you have to do is relax, be yourself, treat him kindly and with respect, as Grandpa said, even if some of what he does seems strange or misguided to you at first. If you do those things, I'm all but certain he'll become your friend."

"But look, we can't even figure out how to hug."

Concern welled up in me: Would these two very different people whom I loved like each other? There was, I knew, an elusive ingredient in the feeling one gets when one first meets another.

"Of course, we'll figure out how to hug," I said. I let go of him and stepped back, trying to remember how Elio hugged Luuk. "That's it! Each raises his right arm over the other's left shoulder. Simultaneously, each wraps his left arm around the other's midsection—and they hug. Let's try."

First Brother

The gate in the fence surrounding the house is open. She breaks the pace of her walk as the dog runs through the gate ahead of her. She walks to the door of the house and presses on a button. No sound associated with that of doorbells is detected.

She raps on the door with the knuckles of her right hand. She pauses. She again raps on the door four times, though with approximately 50 percent more force than before. Seventeen seconds pass. She shouts: "Hello! Anyone home?"

She turns the doorknob and pushes. The door turns on its hinges. Through an approximately 10 centimeter opening she calls: "Hello! My name is Sara Jensen. Are you okay?"

She waits 8 seconds. "I don't see or hear anyone anywhere. I'm really frightened."

She waits 11 seconds. "The front door is unlocked. I'm coming in to see if you're all right. Is that okay?"

She turns, leans her back against the doorframe, closes her eyes and moans, then looks out over the yard, the estuary, and beyond.

Sara

Shortly after Grandpa returned from his trip to see Aunt Lynh and Elio, he was told that Berkeley's chancellor had attended a party that was also attended by a woman, Diane Dorner, who was an elder of the ERP and also a university regent. The chancellor had made a remark about special admission for a bright young man related to Professor Jensen. Regent Dorner had replied that it would be inappropriate for the State of California to give special privileges to "such godless people, rich and intelligent though they may be."

Grandpa hastily made a few appointments with old friends and former students who were on the faculty at Stanford, and Elio was accepted there. When we called to tell him the good news, Elio was elated—until Grandpa said that, as a Stanford freshman, he would have to live in a dormitory where he would have at least one roommate.

"You're joking," Elio said. In the background was his unmade bed that I missed.

"No, I'm not. If you go to Stanford, then you will respect and honor their rules."

"But the whole idea was for Sara and me to live together."

"Well, your idea is just going to have to expand a little. You may come home on the weekends, and I suppose it'll be all right if you visit once during the week, as long as you are back in your dorm by midnight."

Elio arrived on an Air France-KLM flight on 3 September, Grandpa's ninetieth birthday and Michael's seventh. At Grandma's suggestion, she and Grandpa waited in the parking lot while I went to the arrival lounge to greet him. "When you see Elio walk out of Customs," Grandma said, "you'll be glad we're not there."

I didn't fully appreciate what Grandma had said until about a half-hour later when the doors on which was printed "No Admittance" parted, and there he was, dressed in a light-gray pullover and charcoal pants, pushing a cart on which lay a suitcase and a carry-on. Had Grandpa or Grandma been there, I probably wouldn't have jumped up and down with joy, probably wouldn't have laughed and cried at the same time, probably wouldn't have melted so completely into him when he finally held me still and kissed me.

On the way to the car, Elio spotted Grandpa and Grandma leaning against the passenger side of a new gray-blue Mercedes. Elio ran to them and exchanged hugs, kisses, and cheery greetings before he finally noticed the car. "I thought you had an old white Mercedes," he said. "Did you get a new car?"

"No," Grandpa said. "We borrowed it for the day. Here," he added, reaching into the glove compartment and pulling out a white card. "Let me show you the registration."

"But... that's my name!"

"Of course," Grandpa said. "It's your car. How do you like it?"

With the sweet stunned expression of a child who'd just been given an unexpected gift, Elio ran his fingers along the edge of the car's roof before ducking into the open door. A frond of jet-black hair fell over his gleeful face.

We spent most of the morning driving around the Stanford campus, acquainting Elio with the buildings in which his courses would be held. For lunch, we drove up to the Claremont Resort in Oakland, where the first of the day's three festivities to celebrate Grandpa's birthday was held. Berkeley's chancellor gave a moving speech in which she described a bio-implant that had been put into her mother's brain after her mother had suffered a nearly fatal stroke. She credited Grandpa's work for the implant's success and for giving her mother many additional happy and productive years of life. I felt proud of Grandpa and hoped Elio and I would be able to measure up to him in our working lives.

At 1430 we departed for home, where the banquet hall adjacent to the winery's tasting room was being prepared for a birthday dinner. One of Sonoma County's renowned chefs had planned a menu around the many fruits and vegetables then ripe in our garden. In attendance would be neighbors and many of Grandpa's close personal friends, including Senator Franklin. Fortunately, the senator planned to fly to Los Angeles immediately after dinner, so Michael didn't have to spend his birthday immured within my bedroom wall on the chance that the senator might ask to see what he'd been told was now my private part of the house.

As we exited the A101 at River Road, Grandma remarked that we were in wine country, just a few kilometers from home. Elio wrapped his arms around me, and with the back of my head resting on his chest, I gazed out at the vineyards and the roadside fruit and flower stands, wondering what Elio was seeing and feeling on his first journey to his new home.

Did he notice the flat Russian River basin and the gently rolling hills covered with neatly cultivated vineyards? Did he observe how the rows of sunburst honey locust trees form a yellow-green archway over the long drive leading up a hill to our winery? We turned right about a hundred meters in front of the winery, and as we drove through the gate opening in front of us, I wondered what his thoughts were about the huge, verdant yard.

On our left, Grandpa's tiltrotor sat on its pad, its proprotors pointing forward as if prepared to mow down a section of the ivy-covered security wall. On our right, over the broad green blaze of lawn, hovered plum and apple trees, and Japanese maples modeling their crimson and purple-bronze summer dresses. And in the garden frolicked late summer flowers, magnificent that warm, sunny afternoon, their colorful sex organs oozing fragrances full of desire.

Straight ahead, the drive appeared to end in a tropical-looking profusion of rhododendrons, palms, tree ferns and a dense wall of Hinoki cypress. This lush, green screen lay at the foot of a knoll covered with large rocks, ornamental grasses, and salvia, their purple blossoms erect in the still air.

At the top of the knoll was an English laurel hedge, behind which stood part of the security wall encompassing the nearly two-and-a-half-acre yard. Zigzagging up the center of the knoll were limestone stairs, which led up to a deck complete with bench and table. There, in the shade of the English laurel, I often studied on mild afternoons. Beyond the hedge and wall at the top of the knoll lay rows of chardonnay vines (unseen by us from the car windows), the roots of some having reached down through meters of soil to explore the outer surface of the ceiling of Michael's rooms.

I asked Grandpa to stop the car. "Let's get out here," I said to Elio. "I want to show you the yard. But first"—I put my hand over Elio's eyes—"tell us what you remember seeing on the way here after we exited from the automated tollway."

"Um, I guess that must be Lily barking outside."

"Yes, that's Lily. But what did you see and feel on the way here?"

Keeping my hand over his eyes, I glanced at Grandma, who had turned around and was now smiling a knowing smile.

"I guess I was just looking at you," he finally answered.

Grandma chuckled and turned back away from us.

"Oh, I can't believe it!" I said, pushing my head against his chest. "It's so beautiful around here."

He kissed the top of my head. "Well, then, let's get out, and you show me, okay?"

"Okay, but wait here. I'll bring Lily around to greet you."

I opened the car door, and as my right foot began searching for the ground, I experienced one of those strange feelings one gets while on the cusp of something new, that sense of a feral world between was and is, as when the solution to a problem is about to reveal itself, but just before the resolution erupts into consciousness. The two main threads of my life are coming together, I thought. I'm bringing Elio home, and my life—our lives, and Michael's, too—will be new and wonderful.

Lily barked, jolting me back to the present. Harvest hadn't yet begun, but everywhere the dry brown hills gave off a fragrance of hay, and near the vineyards hung the distinct scent of grapes ripening. Soon the little orbs of sweetness would bleed profusely into tanks and barrels and there metamorphose into wine.

Lily barked again. I knelt down to greet her. She licked my face and hands and sniffed curiously. "Come. There's someone I'd like you to meet."

She pawed and nipped at my ankles as I walked around the car to Elio's door. I opened the door and knelt beside him. She barked and growled. I took his hand and kissed it. She watched attentively. I intertwined our hands and offered them to her. She sniffed. I slowly turned his pinkish tan palm up to her. She sniffed, hesitated, sniffed again, then licked.

"Good girl!" I said, reaching to pet her.

Elio got out of the car, and Grandpa and Grandma drove on.

"Watch the car," I said as it approached the giant, green feathers of the tree ferns at the end of the drive, turned left, and disappeared under a promontory of the knoll.

"That's amazing!" he said. "From here I'd never guess there's a garage or house or anything else there except the top of a hill. The house must be to the right."

"Yes. The house and garage face perpendicular to each other. There's an arborway of flowering shrubs and vines leading from the right side of the garage to the house entrance, but even if you watch carefully, you won't be able to see Grandpa and Grandma walk through it."

I knew Michael was eager to meet Elio, so I tried to hurry through a tour of the yard. But Elio wanted to take photographs to send to Aunt Lynh of the deck's magnificent view: the tree-lined drive, the winery, the ribbons of vines coursing up and over and down the vineyard hills. Then, back down in the yard, he asked to see his father's gravestone, beside which daisies and lavender blue asters bloomed. The dark gray granite, polished on one side, was inscribed:

MARCUS BRIAND
For thirty-one years, a beloved man:
husband, father, brother, best
friend, student, and uncle.
We who live miss you.

"Tell me," Elio said, lightly squeezing my hand, "what you remember about the day Pa's ashes were buried here."

"I was only five at the time, and though I remember what happened, I didn't understand the ramifications until much later. It was nearing sunset. Grandma said we were going to bury Uncle in a beautiful place at the edge of our garden, a place that Uncle especially liked. She and Grandpa took me out into the yard to wait for Mom, Dad, and First Brother to arrive. Mom and Dad lived in Berkeley at the time with my two brothers, but First Brother was my only brother who ever came here to visit.

"Dad looked sad when he opened the car door. He hugged and kissed me softly. Mom cried. I felt her tears on my cheek. First Brother, who didn't look sad at all—he had trouble expressing emotions—carried the granite gravestone. I asked where Uncle was. Dad opened the backseat door and lifted out a terracotta urn. I asked if Uncle was inside. Dad nodded. I asked to see. He lifted the lid. Nothing there resembled Uncle. Then, while the rest of us watched in silence, Dad dug a hole. He wiped tears from his eyes with the back of his hand as he worked, streaking his cheeks with dirt. When the hole was large enough, he placed the urn in it."

Elio was staring wistfully at the inscribed stone, probably remembering the father he missed but never spoke much of to me after I'd told him how Uncle had died. I caressed Elio's cheek with my fingers and continued: "Grandpa began to say something, probably something from his favorite Stoic, Epictetus, but Mom cut him off, saying, 'I don't want any words.'

"Grandpa nodded. Dad shoveled loose dirt back into the hole and, with First Brother's help, placed the granite stone on top of the hole. By then the stone had become covered in shadow. I looked behind us, over there." I turned and pointed toward the west. "The sun was about to dip below those hills, and I remembered Grandma once telling me that night doesn't fall, as if from the sky; it rises like mist from low-lying pools of shadow and flows out from hills and trees, quietly ascending as it snuffs out light."

Elio and I stood naked in front of Gatekeeper 3. "Only Sara may enter," a deep voice commanded.

"I'll enter first," I responded. "Then, after I've passed, please admit and examine Elio."

The door to the examination chamber opened. I stepped forward. The door whooshed shut behind me.

"Are you certain he is the one Grandpa calls 'Elio'?" Gatekeeper asked in its deep masculine voice.

"Yes."

The door to level 3 opened. Michael stood in the antechamber, looking relaxed in his kimono. He, like me, had never worn anything except underpants in those warm and comfortable rooms. Grandpa and Grandma, on the other hand, had always worn kimonos that normally hung in the little antechamber in front of Gatekeeper's door. For Elio's arrival, the issue of what to wear had been resolved conservatively in favor of underpants plus kimono for each of us.

I hugged and kissed Michael. Then, as practiced, Michael walked around the side of the antechamber so he wouldn't see Elio until Elio had dressed.

I dressed, and soon Elio stepped through Gatekeeper's door.

"Welcome!" I said, holding underpants in one hand and a kimono in the other. "These are for you to wear."

"Are we in the top-security area?" he asked, taking the underpants.

"Yes."

"Is it safe to talk about everything now?"

"Yes."

"Then where's Michael?" He pulled up his underpants.

"On the other side, around the corner," I answered.

Before I could say more or stop him, Elio dashed out of the antechamber. Already things aren't going as planned, I thought as I ran after him, still holding his kimono in my hand.

"Hi," Elio said, and he and Michael hugged—flawlessly.

"Hi! I'm so thankful to meet you," Michael replied with equal enthusiasm, a response more relaxed and genuine sounding than any during our many practice sessions.

When I offered Elio his kimono, he replied that it was so comfortable in this area that he didn't need one, and Michael readily agreed. I hung all three kimonos back in the antechamber, then watched the two of them, hardly able to believe how well their first meeting was going. Michael, who for weeks had agonized and fussed over every conceivable detail of their meeting, seemed completely at ease and improvised masterfully. He took Elio on a tour of the hydroponic garden, including an unscheduled discussion of the air scrubbers and the recycling system that lasted over half an hour, even though our well-practiced tour had never taken more than eight minutes. Finally, I had to interrupt because Elio and I were expected to begin greeting guests in the banquet hall at 1800 sharp. But, first, Elio wanted to see the bedroom where he and I would be sleeping. On our way there, he leaned toward me and whispered, "I like him. He's weird, just like you."

"I'm glad," I whispered back.

"Whoa!" he exclaimed upon arriving at the bedroom door. "Minimalism minimized!"

A queen-size platform bed abutted the wall opposite the door. Just to the left of the bed hung a full-length mirror on the otherwise blank white wall. Completing the inventory, a scenescreen displaying yesterday's late afternoon sky was on the ceiling directly above the bed. There was no closet, dresser, chair or bathroom.

Elio abruptly lunged onto the bed. "Nice!" he said, rolling and bouncing around on the mattress. "It's firm. And it doesn't squeak like my rickety old bed back home."

After all the dinner guests departed, Grandpa, Grandma, Elio, and I gathered in Michael's rooms for the final birthday celebration of the day. We brought a platter heaped with dark chocolate truffles that Grandma and I had made, two bottles of our finest demi-sec, and five champagne glasses.

Grandma was about to begin pouring the wine when Grandpa

interrupted: "Dear, I believe Michael would like to give Elio a special musical welcome."

Michael signaled he was ready. "Imagine the hour is midnight," he said. A bell chimed twelve times. "That was the campanile in Berkeley. Grandpa recorded it for us. Imagine now that on this midnight, watchmen in an ancient tower spot a bridegroom coming."

I had heard the "Wachet auf" cantata several times before. I had heard all of Bach's extant works several times, for Bach was Grandpa's favorite composer, having achieved a perfect balance, Grandpa said, between emotion and intelligence, the balance Grandpa strove for in the conscious, intelligent products of his own efforts. Tears welled up in my eyes as soon as I recognized the sublime opening ritornello theme. More than ever before, I appreciated then how Bach had miraculously endowed dignity and splendor with a beautiful, quivering mixture of intimate tenderness and desire.

Immediately following the musical interlude, Grandma poured the demi-sec, allotting to Michael only the quarter glass we had found quite sufficient to make him giddy, and we sat around the study table eating, drinking, and talking for about twenty minutes before Grandpa suggested we take some photographs.

The last photograph taken by Grandpa that evening became Michael's most cherished. In it, Elio, Michael, and I stand, arms around each other as we laugh together in front of a scenescreen displaying a view of the garden recorded earlier that day by a camera mounted near the garage. In the hand not wrapped around Elio's waist, I hold a platter containing the few remaining truffles. In his free hand, Michael holds an empty demi-sec bottle.

In photographs taken minutes earlier, Michael stands on one side of me, appearing pleased as he studies Elio, who stands on the other side of me, and who at various times hugs me, kisses me, and makes faces at the camera. But by the time this last photograph was taken, Michael had moved around to Elio's other side, foretelling the near future in which I would remain Michael's sister/mother, but Elio would be his beloved best friend.

As I look now at this last-taken photograph, I wonder what Grandpa thought of us that evening of his ninetieth birthday. Did he see Michael as the crowning miracle of his life's work? Did he see me as the peculiar product of his attempt late in life to find something meaningful outside of the competitive world of academia, business, and the military? Did he see Elio as being in part a rootstock with the strength and virility that Grandpa recognized in himself but not in me? Did he have any inkling of what was to come?

"Hey, where's the bathroom?" Elio asked as soon as this last photograph was taken.

"As a security precaution," Grandpa answered, "the water and sewer lines were not extended to this part of the house. You'll have to go out and come back through Gatekeeper."

"How do I leave, and how do I get back?"

"Go to the antechamber, take off your underpants, stand directly in front of Gatekeeper's door, and say, 'May I leave?' or anything to that effect. 'I wanna get outta here' will also work. When you wish to return, simply stand in front of Gatekeeper's other door and request to enter."

When Elio returned, Grandpa and Grandma left for the night. I asked Elio to wait in our bedroom while I said goodnight to Michael. I was concerned that Michael might be upset, for never before had I closed my bedroom door to him while I'd slept.

Excepting my vacations to visit Elio or Mom and Dad, Michael and I had slept together every night until I'd returned home the summer of my thirteenth birthday, when Grandpa had insisted that Michael and I begin sleeping separately. During the following six months, Michael slept alone two nights each week; during the next six months, he slept alone four nights each week; and thereafter, until the day Elio arrived to live with us, Michael slept with me only one night each week.

Perhaps it would be more accurate to write that it was I who had slept alone on the aforementioned nights, for Michael, refusing to sleep alone in his bedroom, had slept on the floor beside his plants with his eyes closed but directed toward my open door.

"We're going to bed now," I said as I approached Michael.

"He likes me!" Michael whispered as he threw his arms around me. "I can feel that we'll be friends!"

"Yes. I feel so, too."

"He wants to make love to you now."

"Yes."

"Don't forget to close the door," Michael said, releasing his hug and smiling.

I set the scenescreen over our bed to display one of my favorite full-moon skies, then dove in beside Elio. He seemed so familiar, so perfectly where he should be—his body over my body, his mouth over my mouth, his hands all over me. Then he entered into the warm, moist yearnings between my legs, fitting himself perfectly inside me. He sighed, then softly kissed me and murmured, "Now, at last, I'm truly home."

One night several years earlier at 0237, a full moon, together with patches of gray-white clouds scudding southeastward and a sky not black but luminous, dark grayish blue, had been recorded by a camera on the deck directly above Grandpa and Grandma's bedroom. At 0237 of this night that was Elio's first night in his new home, I opened my eyes to the same moon, clouds, and sky.

My post-celebration bladder was full. I slowly disentangled myself from Elio so as not to wake him and made the journey past Michael, who was sleeping curled up beside Amy, his amaryllis—then with two buds tumescent and six blossoms uninhibitedly trumpeting their red lust—through Gatekeeper, to the bathroom, and back.

Upon reentering our bedroom and closing the door behind me, I was struck by how heavily the musky-sweaty scent of love and the stale breath of our sleep seemed to weigh in the air. Had Michael and I correctly calculated Elio's added consumption of the oxygen-rich exhalation of our hydroponic plants? The thought that an alarm might sense some gas out of permissible range and disturb our sleep sent me back to reopen the door halfway.

As I returned to our bed, my bare feet quiet on the warm ceramic floor, I became enthralled by the sight of Elio, who had rolled over onto my absence. Above the blanket lay a dusky arm, its oils and sweat lambent under the full moon. His lush ebony hair, a few strands silvered by moonlight, flowed for the first time over my pillowcase and covered from my view much of his face, except for a dark eyebrow over a single slanting eye shut in sleep, a handsome broad nose, and those warm, pillowy lips.

He was so fragrant, earthy, and warm, so real, so unlike my pallid image then appearing in the bedside mirror as an anthropomorphic patch of Russian River fog or a fey white Schrödinger cat, only possibly there, in the pale white light of the moon.

As I slowly descended toward the bed through the still night air, I noticed my moon shadow drawing near to my dreams' desire, and in his face I saw that special contented radiance it often acquired during sleep. Smiling dreamily, he reached up toward something wispy between my shadow and the moonlight, and, creating me, pulled me down into his embrace, wrapping himself around me, as he had since we were children: his head on my shoulder, his brow against my cheek, his arm across my chest, his leg between my legs.

He mumbled that I should never again leave him, and then, with a familiar jolt, departed back into sleep, where he lay quietly for a while before his arm and leg around me stirred and he wordlessly moaned as he woke inside a dream. I wondered what it would be like to accompany him there, to his dreams, as Michael sometimes accompanied me to mine—and so wondering, I drifted off to sleep.

Later that night, as the moon winked through clouds, their edges glowing brightly in the dark indigo sky, I woke feeling warm and comfortable in Elio's embrace. His breath moved softly over my breast. His hair exuded its sensual aroma. His heart measured time for our world.

Sara

The sky here in Anzen is bright, but no warmth or comfort radiates from it. How huge the terrestrial sky seems to me now, in memory, compared to this tiny, low sky. I wonder what Michael's children will experience, what thrills, when they leave here—they'll have to someday, won't they?—and rise from these dark depths up into the great arching candied-blue dome, where for the first time they will smell, feel, taste the fleshy air.

And what will they think of the birds and animals, of the amorality of nature—which abounds with infanticide and cannibalism, even the killing of mates in some instances—the unremitting slaughter, the slow painful butchering of prey? Here, they will have the garden dome with its center a fragrant orchard of miniature fruit trees and its walls overflowing with roses, lilies, and marigolds; carrots, beans, and tomatoes; cilantro, basil, and parsley. But in this artificial world where all of their food will be supplied by plants and nutriosynthesizers, where they will not so much as ever see a spider eat a bug, how will they, these strange children from alien depths, respond when they first see a hawk swoop down and moments later hear a small animal's talon-engendered cry, or when they witness, as I once did, a dog chase and devour a rabbit?

I was five years old when Lily, fully grown by then but still vivacious as a puppy, went out with me to play in the vineyard. The air was breezy, clear, and cool as we ran through white clover and wild mustard growing between rows of trellised vines. In the midst of play, I lay down for a moment on the aromatic ground. The fields, trees, and hills displayed the pastel pinks, yellows, and greens of spring, and cirrus clouds swirled into the deep blue sky reminded me of blueberries and cream.

Lily was wild with spring, eager to move on, to swim in what for her must have been an invigorating ocean of feral fumes oozing from the ground. She ran in circles around me, licked my face, leaned back, her front legs set and ready to spring forward, and barked.

"Yes!" I answered, and jumped up and chased her. Our noisy frolicking frightened a rabbit from its hiding. Lily dashed after it.

"No! Lily, come back!" I shouted as I ran. When I caught up, heaving for breath, I wanted to scream and push her away from the rabbit, but I remembered her bringing me a dead bird and Grandpa wiping my tears. "It's natural for Lily," he'd said, "part of what she is. The great and joyful and terrible mysteries of the world cannot be denied."

Lily lay on her stomach, holding the rabbit in her paws, pulling and tearing sinewy flesh with her teeth. I touched her side. She growled as she turned her head toward me. Her tongue dripped reddish saliva, and grayish white fur clung to her nose and the edges of her bloody jaws.

As I lay on my stomach and pressed my face to her warm, panting side, the stink of rabbit innards seeped through her fur, hollowness grew in my chest, and darkness passed over me, as if I'd been grazed by a black feather.

Licking my face, Lily fetched me back to consciousness. A mangled mass of rabbit lay beside me, and I sensed, without yet knowing, how intermingled all living creatures are, how they caress and devour each other, just as the Earth I live on and love waits patiently to ingest me.

Tearful, I headed back home. Lily romped in the mustard

along the way.

When we returned to Michael's area after Elio had finished his first breakfast in his new home, Elio asked whether he could see Michael and me connect through our braincord.

Michael nodded eagerly. "It's wonderful being brainjoined with Sara," he said. "The connection allows me to feel her sensations and conscious experiences. When we're connected, I'm no longer cut off from her feelings, as others are through the multiple translations of the language of her neurons into English, then English into the language of their neurons. Much is lost in such translations. I have a sense of occupying her body, just as you have a sense, I imagine, of occupying your body. And hers is a wonderful body to occupy. Her interpretations of experiences and memories, how she thinks and feels, fill me with awe and joy."

Elio looked bewildered, so I took one of his hands in mine. "Let me give you an example, okay?"

"Sure," he said. "An example would be good."

"Suppose you are unable to smell due to a defect in the olfactory nerves in your nose, but the olfactory interpretation areas of your brain are in perfect condition. Suppose further that you and I walk into Grandma's kitchen, and my olfactory system senses a pattern consistent with past experiences of chocolate chip cookies baking in the oven."

"Sara says chocolate chip cookies are your favorites," Michael added. "I love them, too."

"In my brain," I continued, "this neural recognition of a pattern consistent with the aroma of chocolate chip cookies engenders conscious associations with my unique history of experiencing such cookies. These conscious feelings might be translated into English, so that I might think to myself or say to you, 'Mmm, I smell chocolate chip cookies baking.'

"Two serious communication problems are highlighted by this example. First, the essence of my feeling of sensing and recognizing chocolate chip cookies is lost in translating from my neural language to English. This points out why speech is inherently unsatisfactory: words, being nothing more than components of instructions to guide the reader's or listener's imagination toward the targeted feelings, images, or thoughts, expose only themselves; our feelings remain locked inside, never to be felt directly by another. That is the general rule. But because of the braincord, I have become a part of Michael as no one has ever become a part of anyone else before, though our braincord system only pushes back the solipsistic problem by one. Now, it is Michael and I together, as a unit, that is like everyone else: a being that feels but cannot be felt. The drive to overcome this experiential disconnection is undoubtedly the foundation of our desire for love, for literature and other forms of art, and for the infinity that it would take to succeed.

"The second communication problem this example exposes is that under the circumstances we have hypothesized, you would have no way of translating my English utterance about chocolate chip cookies baking in the oven into something experientially meaningful to you, since you would never have had the experience of smelling anything.

"However, if we could directly connect my olfactory nerves to yours at a place beyond the defects in the nerves of your nose, then, after some amazingly new and wonderful experiences for you in which you would learn about the world of smell, we could, so connected, walk into the kitchen when Grandma's baking chocolate chip cookies, and you would sense the aroma along with me. Then it might be you who would exclaim, 'How wonderful! My favorite—chocolate chip!'"

I looked at Elio for a response, but he just stared at me blankly.

"So, what do you think of that?" I asked.

"I think I just arrived yesterday, and because of jetlag my head feels clogged with wool. Most of what you just said sailed right over me."

First Brother

She takes hold of the doorknob and pushes the door farther open. The dog tries to enter by squeezing in between her left leg and the door. She catches the dog's collar with her left hand. "No, Rusty. Sit. Good boy. Now, stay. Stay. I'll be right back."

She enters through the door and closes it behind her. The dog sits for 12 seconds, gets up, walks to a shrub nearby, sniffs, lifts its right hind leg, and urinates.

The dog looks toward the door. The door opens. She rushes out through the door with her gloved right hand over her mouth. The dog runs in front of her, collides with her right leg, and yelps. She stumbles but catches her balance. She pulls her hand from her mouth, bends over, and regurgitates. She coughs and spits, then steps over the regurgitated material and falls, wailing, facedown onto the variegated grass.

Sara

The day after Elio arrived, he noticed our two-person sea kayak hanging in the garage, and the next morning he and I were on the Russian River, a river he quickly grew to love: otters playing; harbor seals basking in the sun; ospreys mounting the air with silver flesh wriggling in their talons; magnificent redwoods and Douglas firs exuding their resinous perfumes; and, protruding from the ocean near river's end, huge sea stacks, around the craggy edges of which waves splash and swirl, pound and roil, as gulls, like sleek white kites, dive and soar in the salty air.

The first weekend of November, when the vineyards were draped in sunlit autumn colors, we put in upstream a little before noon Saturday and pitched our tent in time for dinner on a secluded private beach that was little more than a tiny patch of sand on the river's edge. It was my job to prepare the meal, and as I did I enjoyed watching Elio bustle about, setting up what he proudly called our home: tent, sleeping bag, air mattress, thermal unit. As we ate, the air was cool and clear; the river chuckled softly; and though our cups and plates were made of plain white paper, the sky was Wedgwood blue.

After dinner, we sat together on the sand and watched the sun ignite a flocculent canopy of pastels as it settled behind the tops of distant trees, above which a cloud, half-bruised, half-bright, appeared impaled on a pink contrail. Later, we snuggled together in our sleeping bag and gazed out of the open tent flap at a clear night sky. Elio said the stars seemed more numerous and closer than they had appeared to him in Amsterdam, as though somehow we had been elevated into the heavens.

In the morning, light fog muted the previous day's bright vibrancy, but we found the misty view romantic and several times pulled our kayak up onto the shore to walk the hills and roll around in musty leaves.

We made it to river's end in time to watch the sun puff itself up and slide, liquefying into the sea, while pastel pink clouds floated in vaporous milky blue.

"But I like pastels," he objected to my sighing over a dashed wish for a wild vermilion sunset that would stun the ocean, the evening sky, and him. "My favorite picture is full of pastels."

"What picture is that?"

"Pale blue eyes, white-blonde hair, rice-paper skin flushed from exercise—you know the picture."

We laughed and hugged, and when I next looked up, the sun was gone.

In early December, after making plans for the upcoming winter holiday vacation, Elio and I called Mom and Dad. I planned, as had become usual over the years, to stay with them through the holidays, but Elio had a reservation to depart about three hours after our arrival in Calgary. He would be flying on to visit his mother and friends in Amsterdam.

"Oh, no you don't," Mom said, looking with mock sternness at Elio. "We want more than just to see you. After all, we can see you right now. We want to get you in our arms and squeeze you and kiss you, eat meals with you, throw snowballs at you. You're part of the family now. You have to give us two days, minimum."

"Yes, two days," Dad chimed in. "It would mean a lot to Mary and me to have both of you in our home for at least a couple of days."

I thought I saw tears begin to well in Dad's eyes and was surprised and pleased at the interest he and Mom were showing in Elio and me, seemingly out of the blue.

When Elio and I arrived in Calgary midway through a bright afternoon, I again was surprised by apparent changes in both Mom and Dad. Mom's fingers were no longer stained yellow, and her breath was fresh, not smoky and stale. She had sworn off cigarettes. Dad appeared to have shed some of his reserve, hugging both of us enthusiastically, even giving me a warm full kiss on my lips. And that night over dinner, he told stories of happy days in university when he and Elio's father had been close friends.

The next morning, however, the warm feelings became strained when, during breakfast, Dad announced that my brothers were interested in Elio and wanted to see him. "We've made arrangements for you and Sara to visit them this morning at the lab."

Elio glanced at me nervously before answering Dad: "I'd like to meet Sara's brothers. I feel they are, in a way, my brothers, too." Elio again glanced at me. "But I promised Grandpa before we left that I wouldn't."

"What?" Mom said. "Why did you do that?"

"Grandpa says it's becoming increasingly dangerous to have knowledge of androids."

"What about Sara?" Mom asked. "She knows."

"I've known about my brothers since I was a little girl," I said. "We can't change that. But we can protect Elio from the risk."

Mom and Dad looked at each other. I was aware that I'd already acquired a quiet, comforting knowledge by which I knew much of what Elio thought even before he said a word, knowledge gleaned from such subtle signals as nods, shifts of body posture, frowns, blinks, or murmurs so slight that it was unlikely anyone else even noticed. And I was aware that he was becoming similarly attuned to me, so that a twin of each of our thoughts and feelings often seemed spontaneously to emerge and resonate in the other. Now, as I watched Mom and Dad look at each other, I wondered how much more of such implicit communication they shared after having been together for so many years.

"Well, if you promised," Mom finally said, "I guess there's nothing we can do. But First Brother is going to be disappointed. I don't know how many times he's told me not to forget to bring Elio in to see him."

I was puzzled by First Brother's interest in Elio, but I didn't ask about it because I felt that my question might be perceived as envy: why the interest in Elio but not in me?

The next morning, as we sat around the table after finishing breakfast, Mom reached out one hand to me, the other to Elio, who sat across from me. Dad did the same, resulting in the four of us being joined in a circle around the table. Mom and Dad seemed to exude unusual intensity in this joining of hands. Weeks later, Elio would tell me that for an instant he'd had the feeling we were about to embark on a séance.

How could we have surmised then that it would be an ending?

"I want to start," Mom said, "by saying how much I love both of you, and how happy I am you came here to see us, Elio. Your father meant a great deal to both of us. He was a remarkable man, and Karl and I are so grateful that your relationship with Sara has brought you closer to us."

Elio smiled, but there was a look of longing on his face.

Mom then turned to me. "I understand from your grandma that you and Elio had a private marriage ceremony alone near the airport in Amsterdam. We'd like it very much if you'd share that moment with us now."

She reached into her pants pocket, pulled out two bimetallic rings, yellow gold and white platinum, and placed them side-by-side in the middle of the table.

"We thought you'd like something more formal with your family," Dad said, "rather like an announcement to, and an acknowledgment from, the world of your love for each other."

The two rings blurred into each other through an aqueous film over my eyes. I swallowed hard and looked at Elio. How beautifully changeable he was, smiling broadly now, dark eyes sparkling, and every muscle in his face expressing delight and vibrant energy.

"Do you remember the vows you gave each other?" Mom asked. "If they're too private, you don't have to. But if it's okay, we'd like you to repeat them for us this morning."

"I'd like us to stand," I said, "so that Elio and I can hold hands." I wanted this occasion, this recognition of belonging to a family and to Elio, to be as intimate as possible.

Dad glanced around the room. "How about in front of the fireplace?"

Elio and I stood in front of the red-brick fireplace, above which hung a large evergreen wreath covered with brightly colored little ornaments. Never before had I seen anything resembling holiday decorations in Mom's house. Perhaps it is true, I thought, that people mellow with age.

Mom stood beside me, holding a ring. Dad stood beside Elio, holding the other ring. Elio took my hands in his, and I began the promises, word for word, that I'd given him six months before. But this time, because Mom and Dad were there, the words were richer with meaning, rooted now in a larger world. They came out slowly, each like a carefully crafted gift to be cherished by everyone hearing them. I wanted Mom and Dad to know how I felt. I wanted Elio's and my love to blossom in the sunshine of their blessings.

When I finished, Mom lifted the ring she held. "Here, Sara, put this on Elio's finger. For me it's a symbol that I'm giving my dear, dear daughter to you, Elio, to love and cherish and care for all your days."

I put the ring on Elio's left ring finger, then kissed his finger, feeling at once the cool firmness of the metal and the warm softness of his flesh.

After Elio stated his vows, Dad handed him the other ring and said, "With this ring, I give my best friend's son to you, Sara, to love and cherish and care for all your days."

During that moment and for the nearly two hours that followed until we waved good-bye to Elio at the airport, I felt blissfully part of a loving family that included Mom and Dad.

For years during the winter holidays, my parents had become increasingly oriented toward work, but this year, after they waved good-bye to Elio at the airport, they seemed busy almost to the point of panic. Our scheduled trip to Banff was canceled, and every night until I returned to California, we slept on cots in the lab.

"Please be a love and stay out of the way. We're so busy right now," Mom said after I'd asked several questions the night after Elio had left. Probably in response to seeing that I felt hurt and disappointed, Dad gave me a draft of an article on evolutionary quantum computation that he was preparing for publication. He asked me to proof it.

That task kept me out of the way for the next three days. On the night of 25 December, as we sat down in the break room for a quick dinner, I handed him back his draft with my comments. He immediately began reading. When Mom asked him to eat before his food got cold, he requested another espresso. He downed the steaming liquid in a gulp and got up, saying that he was going to his office to look up something.

I had just fallen asleep on my cot later that night when Dad knocked and turned on the lights. "Thanks for your comments. Very insightful. You solved the problem I wrote in the margin on page 7. All of us here have been working on it unsuccessfully for some time now. Your brothers are curious about how you solved it and would like to examine you over the next few days. Would that be all right?"

"Sure! That would be great!" My brothers are interested in me, I thought. At last!

I lay awake for hours, fantasizing about our getting to know one another better and becoming closer. But the next few days would validate Grandpa's admonition that disappointments are the disharmonies between expectations and desires, on the one hand, and the patterns of reality, on the other.

One day just over eleven years earlier—it was about a month after Uncle Marcus had been killed—Grandpa returned home from Berkeley later than usual. He typically traveled to Berkeley in his tiltrotor two or three times each week to visit old professor buddies or take care of his duties as chairman of the board of Magnasea, the company his father had founded that was primarily in the business of robotic systems and deep-sea mining. Magnasea had had the Navy contract to develop android SEALs, the so-called Sentiren project, that resulted in the creation of my brothers. It was about a half year after my birth that the Navy canceled the Sentiren project and my brothers left the Magnasea lab to live at home with Mom and Dad, the home from which I had been cast only a couple of months before.

Grandpa usually returned from those trips to Berkeley in good humor and with interesting stories to tell. But that evening, his face appeared unusually long and creased.

Grandma offered him a glass of wine and asked what had happened. He told us that in the morning First Brother had taken the Turing test. Present during the test, along with Grandpa, had been Mom, Dad, Second Brother, and a panel of ten professors.

I asked what the Turing test was. Grandpa said it was a procedure proposed by Alan Turing in the mid-twentieth century to determine whether a system had achieved human-level intelligence, based on whether the system was able to deceive human interrogators—who were permitted to ask questions of the system but were otherwise veiled from it—into believing it was human.

"I take it from your demeanor that First Brother failed," Grandma said.

"Of course, he did! I told Karl we shouldn't participate in such foolishness. Given our current state of knowledge, it should be obvious that only a human can pass the test, unless, of course, the examiners are incompetent. Not a single person on that panel could convince a dog examiner that he or she is a dog, if dogs could give and respond to such tests. And what would that tell us? That humans don't have the intelligence of a dog?"

"What do you mean?" I asked.

"Well, for example, a human testee—he's the one we suppose is trying to deceive a dog examiner into thinking that he, the human, is really a dog—might be smart enough to feign that he finds the smell of anuses intriguing, but when the dog examiner asks, 'Oh? How so?' the human would be left speechless, whereas any dog capable of communicating could write a book on the subject."

"Grandpa!" Grandma scolded.

"Do you have a better explanation? No, I didn't think so."

There was a fleeting look of shock and displeasure on Grandma's face; then she looked at me and her mouth silently formed the word "grumpy."

"Anyway," Grandpa continued, "humans don't have canine

intelligence, and canines don't have human intelligence. So it is with androids. They think faster than we do, so they see patterns we don't, unless we do a lot of analysis. They're not as attuned to emotional, especially sexual, nuance. They don't have sex, for heaven's sake, so why should they be? Thus, they don't laugh at the same jokes, they're not offended by the same things, and so on. To report that an intelligent system has failed to pass the Turing test is to report nothing more than that the intelligence isn't human."

He gulped down the remainder of the glass of wine and scowled.

"You didn't care for the wine?" Grandma asked. "It's last year's Chardonnay."

"It's fine, fine." Grandpa rolled his eyes. "In fact, I'd like another glass. What's troubling me is Second Brother's response to a question Professor Scripps posed after the test. I'm sure Scripps and others will make hay out of Second Brother's rash answer."

"What'd he say that upset Professor Scripps?" Grandma asked.

"I didn't say Scripps was upset. He undoubtedly was happy to get an answer he can use to further his agenda to ban all experiments on nonhuman conscious intelligences. Second Brother was obviously hostile to the test and to the interpretation given it by some of the panel members. Smelling blood—the one thing that old shark can still do with some competence—Scripps directed the following question to Second Brother: 'What do you think of the idea that it is wrong to kill humans?'"

"And?" Grandma asked.

Grandpa gulped down some more wine.

"And Second Brother said that a parasite that unrestrainedly kills its host ultimately destroys itself. As long as the only host for ideas was human brains, the idea that it is good to kill humans was at an evolutionary disadvantage to the idea that it is bad to kill humans. Needless to say, all hell broke loose. Scripps and Senator Kephart made national news by 1600. I got a call from Senator Franklin at 1607. He said we'd just ensured the election of at least forty more members of Congress and at least five more senators for the ERP."

At the time, all this was a bit of an uphill slog for me. But what definitely caught my attention—actually, I was somewhat pleased to hear it—was that First Brother had failed a test, a test that I (presumably) would have been able to pass.

"What didn't First Brother know?" I asked, trying to appear appropriately concerned.

"I wouldn't say he didn't know. It was that the answers he gave led the panel to conclude he wasn't human."

"What did they ask? What did he say? How could they tell he wasn't human?"

"Sara, honey," Grandma said. "I think Grandpa's had a tiring day. Maybe we should—"

"Tell me! Tell me! I want to know! I want to know what makes First Brother different."

Grandpa smiled. He liked that I wanted to know. "There were ten professors. Each was allowed to ask a battery of questions. I can't begin to remember them all. The point is that at the end of the examination, one professor concluded that, based on his questions alone, there was less than a ten percent chance that the interrogated system was human; the other nine concluded that, based on their questions alone, there was less than a five percent chance that it was human."

"But you remember some of the questions, don't you?" I persisted.

Grandma looked at me pleadingly. "Sara, honey—"

Grandpa raised his palm to quiet Grandma. "One professor

read excerpts from literature and poetry. After each excerpt, First Brother was asked what images, thoughts, and feelings the words had engendered in his mind. This professor and his students had performed the same test on hundreds of humans over the past several years. First Brother simply didn't express sadness, terror, pleasure, attention, or arousal in a normal human way.

"A second professor read jokes. First Brother was instructed to rate each joke on a scale of 1 to 10 and explain what, if anything, was funny about it. By the way, First Brother was allowed to respond to these and to all other questions only with typed responses. Jokes, as it turns out—I'd never really given it much thought before—tap deep currents of human nature, culture, and knowledge, often utilizing oblique hints at intimacy, absurdity, and offense. First Brother did particularly poorly on this test."

That's for sure, I thought. He never laughs at anything.

"Another professor asked First Brother to paint in his mind a forest scene that she described: a man walking with a dog, tall pine trees, dark understory, light filtering through treetops, and so on. The professor was reading from the script of another well-researched test. She then asked First Brother to repeat the scene. First Brother did, perhaps too well. Then she asked First Brother to look at the scene in his mind and state what his mind's eye was focusing on in real-time: man, dog, man, tree trunk, forest floor, man—that kind of stream-of-consciousness response. Humans typically look most often at parts of the scene containing high-contrast and fine detail: up and down trunks of trees, along the visible horizon of the forest floor, the dog, the human. First Brother gave too much attention to the canopy, the moss, the grass."

"Just as he stares at strange things around here all the time," I interjected.

"Strange for you, perhaps, but interesting for First Brother."

"Sorry," I said, having been corrected more than once after saying something to the effect that First Brother didn't focus on the right things.

Eleven years later, it was my turn to be tested. After breakfast, Mom and Dad told me to go to room B9, where my brothers were waiting. First Brother informed me that their goal was to compare my neurologic and other bodily functions with similar functions of other humans whom they had already tested. For the next three days, ten hours each day, I sat, strapped in sensors, and solved, or tried to solve, the problems I was given.

On the morning of 29 December, only Second Brother was in B9 when I entered. He said he would be giving me what he called the Sentiren test and reminded me of the Turing test that First Brother had been forced to take over a decade before. He stated that he wanted to see whether I was an intelligent, conscious being.

"But that's silly," I said. "Of course I'm intelligent and conscious but in ways different from you. It's obvious I can't answer questions within a conversational period of time if their answers require lengthy mathematical or logical computations."

Second Brother replied that he wouldn't ask me to perform lengthy formal computations. He said his goal was to see to what extent I could *feel*; he already knew that I, like all humans, had to employ machines whenever I wanted to think about or do anything beyond the merest triviality. I was stunned, especially in light of Dad's representing that these tests were being conducted to help my brothers understand how I came to solve a problem none of them had been able to solve.

Despite my inability to do more than speculate as to their answers, I found many of the questions interesting. How does it feel to simultaneously entertain multiple foci of conscious attention, as opposed to a single focus—the serial monophonic consciousness to which humans are limited? How does it feel to be interrupted, while quietly simulating a series of quantum states, by the shock of having someone unexpectedly play at 110 decibels the radiant, beaming first three eighth notes and sustained tone of Beethoven's Fifth Symphony?

There were hours of such questions. I mention those two simply as examples of questions into which I later gained insight from discussions with Michael. Other questions, such as how it feels to have a laser knife cut through integumentin or how it feels to have one's hand placed in a microwave oven, I didn't discuss with Michael, concerned that they might frighten him.

With regard to the question about being interrupted while calculating quantum states, Michael, after performing the experiment, said, "When I was performing the calculations, I felt very pure, very crystalline. The shock of the loud sound was followed by a feeling that every cell, every metallic structure, every regularity in me had suddenly been shattered. It was a disturbing and frightening experience. I felt as though I was a diamond breaking."

With regard to experiencing multiple foci of conscious attention, Michael said he experienced no difference of feeling between thinking about one thing or about many things at once. He said he simply did what seemed most natural and appropriate at the time. He likened the mental state of thinking about many things simultaneously to watching four or five different events on a split-screen display or to letting his mind expand to take in the whole as well as each of the parts of complex polyphonic music. There still is one main, perhaps composite, observer, he explained, though that observer is continuously aware of many things at once.

I wondered at the time, and still do, whether there wasn't something more behind these tests. Were my brothers trying to humiliate me to see how I would react? Or was there something deeper, something more important that I failed not only to achieve but even to become aware of? Were they trying to introduce me to their world? Did they finally lose patience?

The following morning, I was surprised at breakfast when Mom told me that Dad had already left. "On business to Vancouver" was all she would say. Looking back, I think it likely that he, being of a kind and gentle disposition, didn't want to be a part of what Mom and my brothers had in store for me that day.

I was again left alone with Second Brother, who, before we began the testing, commented on my performance of the prior two days by stating that I was "hopelessly human, so gaudy with emotion" and that I had demonstrated not even the slightest degree of Sentiren feeling or intelligence. This was not unexpected, he added, since he and my other brothers were products of our parents' minds, whereas I was merely a product of their loins.

Trying not to show my irritation, I told him he was wrong, that I was also a product of their minds, knowledge, and culture. He responded by saying it was time to begin our work for the day. A few hours later, in the midst of an exercise that seemed to be testing the reaction time of my fingers to various visual cues, he placed his thumb on one side of the bone at the base of my right ring finger and his index and middle fingers on the other side of the bone and began to squeeze. The pain quickly rose as he increased the opposing force of his grip.

I was faced with a choice of asking him to stop or of concentrating on the sensation and showing him I could tolerate the pain. I foolishly chose the latter, and before a minute had elapsed, I heard a crack as the bone broke. Though I don't know what my face expressed, my mind was busy being amazed at discovering how well the real pain of the bone's breaking conformed to the corresponding sensations induced by the algetor.

"The proximal phalanx is broken," Second Brother dryly said.

A spark of anger flashed through my mind, but not wanting to appear gaudy with emotion, I suppressed it. "I think we should tell Mom."

We walked across the hall to where Mom and my other brothers were working on a scanner for large animals at the Calgary Zoo. Though my finger continued to communicate painful sensations, I was, as Grandpa had taught me, able to keep my mind from converting the sensations into physical suffering. I was disappointed, however, in Second Brother's hurting me. Since when was physical damage part of a test?

"The fourth proximal phalanx of her right hand is broken," Second Brother announced.

"What is?" Mom asked, turning to us.

I held up my hand, showing her my ring finger, which was bent oddly toward my thumb. She leaned forward to look. "What happened?"

"Second Brother was seeing how well I could tolerate pain. I should have said something before it broke."

"Well, what do we do now?"

My mind was such a jumble of guilt, disappointment, anger, and pain that I didn't think then how odd it was that her question wasn't immediately followed by a fusillade of possible answers rattled off machine-gun style from my six brothers. Instead, only First Brother spoke. "Professor Jensen must not learn that Second Brother broke the finger."

"What do we tell him, then?" Mom asked.

"While playing," First Brother said, "Sara put her finger in a hole in the frame of the scanner. Her foot slipped, and her finger caught and broke as she fell."

Mom asked which hole, and First Brother immediately

walked to the frame and pointed to a hole about eye-height on me.

"I'm not going to lie to Grandpa about this," I said. "If I tell him what happened, he'll understand we were simply performing tests when the finger was broken."

Mom frowned at me, then turned to First Brother. "Tell Sara your concerns."

"We request that you not tell Professor Jensen we broke your finger. He has influence in the United States military and intelligence communities. If he believes we are dangerous to you or to other humans, he may influence powerful and dangerous others to increase their resolve to destroy us and other androids."

"You see, honey," Mom said, "to tell the truth in a situation where truth supplies facts fitting into a pattern of oppression is to be subservient to power. To tell the truth in a situation lacking in reciprocity—such as the situation in which you live, wherein you must tell the truth under penalty of the crime of lying to the agents of your government but the agents of your government lie to you as a matter of course—is to be subservient to power. A lie is the standard we plant to proclaim, 'I am not your subject.' To tell the truth is to wave a white flag of surrender."

"Mom, what are you talking about? And what are you doing? That sounded like a prepared speech."

"It's very simple. To tell the truth, any truth, about your brothers to agents of the United States government is nothing less than to help lead a murderer to the innocent victims he is pursuing. Besides, how can you—"

"I want to go to a doctor to fix my finger," I interrupted. "It hurts."

I was tired of her ranting, and suspicion was rapidly rising in me that my finger had been intentionally broken—with her approval. But why? Just so she could lecture me? Or perhaps it was to see how far I'd let my brothers push me before I'd say, Enough.

"Before I take you, we have to agree on what to tell the doctor."

"I'll say I broke it goofing around."

"That's good. But what will you tell your grandpa?"

"I'll tell him that, too. If he asks how, I'll say it's too embarrassing and I'd like to keep it to myself. But I'm not going to lie. I can keep the secret without lying."

Never lie, but never reveal the truth, I remembered, then wondered how ashamed I would feel in turning Grandpa's teaching against him.

Mom grabbed her coat and marched out of the room.

I found her in the hall. She opened the door to another room and indicated I should enter. Unmarked boxes were piled high along each of its walls.

Mom closed the door behind us. "What do you mean by refusing your brothers like that? I'm absolutely ashamed of you."

"I promised not to tell."

"And when your grandpa asks you outright whether your brothers did it, what then? He might be a lot of things, but stupid isn't one of them."

"If I ask him not to pry, he won't. I know him. Besides, it could have been any embarrassing or clumsy thing I did."

"You should be proud to lie for your brothers."

"Proud to lie?"

"Yes, proud to lie."

"Mom, I have no idea what you were talking about back there regarding the virtues of lying, but my finger—"

"You don't understand? Well, then, let me put it so that even an overly sheltered and pampered teenage girl can understand. To tell the government the truth is to give them knowledge, which increases their power. Knowledge is the fuel of power.

The ruling elites have always inculcated truth-telling for one reason, and one reason only: it serves to increase and consolidate power in themselves."

"I don't care what you say, Grandpa—"

"Do you understand?"

"Yes, I understand what you're saying. But Grandpa respects androids. He's strongly against government policy about them. How can you imply he's a murderer of androids and I should be proud to lie to him?"

"You haven't met his friends."

"Has Second Brother hurt anyone else?"

"No! Of course not. I haven't had a single complaint."

"What about nonhuman animals?"

"Are you crazy? He's not some kind of vivisectionist monster. That category is reserved for humans. What's wrong with you?"

"What's wrong with me? Mom, my finger's broken. It hurts."

For a moment, she looked at me, her eyes cold and fixed on my face. Then she glanced at my finger, and her expression softened. "I'm sorry about your finger, honey. We'll get it fixed right away, but I know what I'm talking about. Your father and I have lived with Second Brother for years, from before you were born. He treats us and the staff gently and kindly. You're the first one who's ever had a bad experience with him. And, I dare say, you brought it on yourself with your ridiculous game of pretending you're somehow immune to pain. I can't help but think your grandfather has something to do with that, too. Right?"

I shrugged noncommittally.

"Right. I'd be worried that you'd turn out just like him, but I don't think there's much chance of that. You can be as submissive as you want around Elio—he's a nice boy—but don't let that conniving old professor take advantage of you. You're too naïve to see the ruthless power behind the loving smile. He's a bad influence. He has bad friends. And he's twisted you around so much you don't even feel guilty about refusing your brothers' simple request. You even suspect them of being monsters! You're sixteen. The world is a mess. You'd better wake up one of these days. And soon."

A part of me wanted to scream at her that she was hateful and wrong, but the only part of me that expressed itself was shipwrecked in tears.

First Brother

The door to the house remains open. The dog laps up the regurgitant material, then walks over to her and watches her emit human crying sounds facedown in the grass. The dog rotates its head approximately 7 1/2 degrees clockwise, then approximately 15 degrees counterclockwise, then approximately 15 degrees clockwise, then back approximately 7 1/2 degrees counterclockwise.

The white neck drape of her hat covers 78 percent of the visible portion of the right side of her face. The dog pushes its nose under the neck drape and licks her right cheek. She continues to emit human crying sounds and is not seen to respond to the dog. The dog grips the neck drape in its teeth and pulls the hat off her head. She continues to emit human crying sounds and is not seen to respond to the loss of her hat. The dog shakes the hat in its jaws, pauses, looks at her, then runs about in the yard. It prances back to her side and lies down on its stomach. It plays with the hat approximately 1/2 meter from the left side of her face.

It is 1 hour, 14 minutes, 21 seconds past midday.

Sara

The next morning, New Year's Eve morning, the morning I would board a flight to return home, I was awakened early by Mom. She came to my cot, sat down beside me, and stroked my hair. "You miss Elio, don't you, honey?"

"Yes."

"I'm sorry about yesterday. I was inconsiderate about the pain you must have been in. After talking it over with your brothers, I believe they're satisfied you'll keep their secret. You still love me?"

I answered her with a hug. I wanted a mom to love. Perhaps Second Brother had been right: I was gaudy with emotion.

She said I should hurry and get dressed because Dad and my brothers wanted to show me something before I left. When I entered the scanner-assembly room of the lab, I was greeted by "Good morning, Sara!" in unison from all my brothers. Then Dad asked me to hold out my left arm and be steady and brave. I don't know whether my rounded eyes and gaping mouth adequately expressed the amazement I felt when a pigeonoid flew out from behind the scanner, lighted on my arm, its wings and body a skittish tremolo, then parted the feathers in its underside and partially ejected a chip, which it grabbed with its beak and presented to me.

"Take it," Dad said, "and let's see what news your new friend has brought you."

The news consisted of a password to be memorized by me that would access on the computer in Michael's area several one-time pad encryption keys. These keys would be used by the pigeonoid in delivering messages to, or taking messages from, me. There was also a request for a promise, which I reluctantly gave, never to reveal to Grandpa, or to anyone else except Michael and Elio, the contents of any of the messages it might bring.

It was a few hours later on the flight home from Calgary that I met Agent Smith and was interrogated by Casey and his pain-inducing "inquisitor," which overloaded my nervous system and for a time resulted in my suffering deep depression. But by the middle of January, Dr. Taranik decided that I had recuperated enough to resume normal activities, which, to me, meant I was free to resume brainjoining with Michael, an activity Grandpa had prohibited until I was fully recovered. Though I'd told Michael what had happened both when Second Brother broke my finger and when Casey interrogated me, Michael nevertheless seemed unprepared for the terrible memories he discovered in my mind. He began first with Casey's interrogation, and though he found the roar now silent, the heat now gone, in the memory contrail of my experience, merely the detailed knowledge of what had happened made his eyes sad, like February clouds pouring out tears, and his voice heartrending, with the *uh, uh, uh*'s of his special staccato crying.

But it wasn't until we revisited Second Brother in room B9 of the Alberta Robotics lab that Michael's hand swept up over his face. I felt his searching cease. Never before had Michael hidden while we were connected.

The braincord was still in place—one end in the back of his head, the other end up inside my nose—so I couldn't move far. I decided to wait a few minutes for him to come out of hiding. If he didn't, I would press on the trepan door in the back of his head, and the cord would disengage from me.

He sat perfectly still, his face eclipsed by his hands. How like Second Brother he appeared on the surface—the cool, smooth skin; the short, soft black hair neatly parted on the left; the Asian facial features—but how very different he was inside. And how dearly I loved him.

Sitting there quietly while he hid, I felt certain I knew what he was hiding from. It wasn't from the memory he'd found of the pain of my broken finger—that, after all, had been trivial compared with the pain I'd endured during Casey's interrogation. Rather, it was that someone appearing so similar to him had inflicted the pain on me. Michael was frightened and appalled to think that some part of him might be capable of doing what Second Brother had done. He was hiding, perhaps for the first time, from himself.

I tried with all my might to project my thoughts and feelings through the braincord: first, that I loved him and was grateful for his life; and second, that though he had the potential to hurt others, I was certain he would never use that potential unless absolutely necessary.

He leaned toward me, his hands still covering his face. I felt his sadness pouring through the braincord into my mind, and I hugged him and caressed him, and we both cried.

A few days later, Grandpa came in to examine how well my broken finger was mending. I'd just removed it from the soft interior of the finger-sized, sonic bone-mending chamber, which sounded and felt like a purring cat. He looked at the finger, then said, "Your mother told me you were playing—sticking your fingers into the holes of a scanner frame, she said—when you slipped and broke your finger."

"It was embarrassing. I don't want to talk about it."

"I don't like it when people lie to me."

"I'm not lying, Grandpa. It really was embarrassing."

"You're not telling the whole truth; your mother lied to me. You had three distinct bruises, one on each side of the break on the right side of your finger, and one in line with the break on the left side of your finger. Tell me how that configuration of bruises is possible from getting your finger caught in a hole in a metal frame and slipping on powdered graphite."

"I promised not to tell you. Please don't ask me to break my promise."

"Who asked you not to tell me?"

"Grandpa, please, drop this. It doesn't matter. The finger doesn't hurt, and it'll heal perfectly. Please do me this favor and don't challenge the story Mom told you."

Grandpa sighed. "You make it difficult for an old man to refuse you. Okay, it was a hole in a scanner. But I hope you've learned never to participate in whatever happened up there again."

"I have."

In the following weeks and months, I felt full of energy; Elio continued to come home twice each week and was, if anything, even more loving and caring than before; the winter rains subsided; and we celebrated Grandma's ninetieth birthday with a picnic lunch on a hillside carpeted with wildflowers. But all the while, I had a sense, an odd feeling, that perhaps during a momentary blankness or a wandering of my mind on that foreboding New Year's Eve something had changed, had darkened, had imperceptibly moved beneath my feet. It was as though the tempo and theme of my life remained the same, but there had been a key change of which I was only subliminally aware. I repeatedly asked Michael to try to detect, while brainjoined with me, the source of my disquieting feeling; but he found nothing unusual and finally suggested that perhaps I had just been frightened—as had he.

First Brother

She stops the Toyota brand vehicle with two canoes attached to its top in front of the gate of the security wall of the Jensen home. As she exits the vehicle she says, "Stay, Rusty. Stay. I'll be right back."

She closes the vehicle's door. The hat, backpack, and sweater lie on the backseat of the vehicle. She runs to the gate scanner. She uses both gloved hands to pull the goggles away from her eyes and down under her chin. She places her face into the hood of the scanner. The security gate, powered by solar panels on the winery roof, begins to open.

She is back in the driver's seat of the vehicle before the gate fully opens. The goggles are still under her chin. She drives into the yard. The dog's head protrudes from the partially rolled-down passenger's window. The vehicle passes a tiltrotor. The security gate begins to close. The grass exhibits suboptimal moisture. Weeds protrude in the garden. Three gardenerbots huddle in hibernation mode outside the toolshed door.

The tires of the vehicle skid to a stop on the flagstone paving in front of the garage. The driver's door opens. She jumps out of the vehicle. The dog leaps out of the vehicle behind her. She runs to the doghouse, peeks in, looks out over the yard, and shouts: "Lily!" She turns and runs toward the arborway leading to the house door. She calls out: "Grandma! Grandma!" The timbre of her voice exhibits signs of human stress.

The dog sniffs around the garage and the doghouse. The door to the house is heard to open and close. Two minutes, 8 seconds pass. The dog appears to notice me walking down the stairs from the study deck above the house. At the base of the stairs, the dog sniffs my left leg and walks away.

It is midday plus 3 hours, 52 minutes, 41 seconds.

Sara

Elio and I spread out our picnic dinner in the shade of the old valley oak tree standing alone among rows of vines on the hill just east of our house. It was the end of May, ten days after his eighteenth birthday. Aunt Lynh had called him on his special day and said she was planning to visit my parents in Calgary for a week. She wouldn't be visiting him in the United States, of course, so they would have to wait until summer vacation to get together.

"Oh, I forgot to tell you." Elio handed me our thermos of tea. "I got a call yesterday from Ma. She's flying back home today. She said she wishes we'd taken more trips together. Weird how parents change. Except to swim meets, I never could get her to take me anywhere."

After eating, we were serenaded by several crickets while we sat together with our backs against the tree's deeply fissured bark and gazed up at a cloudless twilight sky in the west. I was dreamily wondering how late our noisy little friends would stay up fiddling into the night when I heard Wilma, one of the security personnel, shouting as she ran: "Sara! Elio! Run home! Hurry!"

Lily, whose hearing was failing, didn't bark until she noticed Elio and me jump up.

"What's wrong?" Elio called out.

"I don't know," Wilma answered breathlessly. She stopped in

front of us, flushed and panting. "Something about androids attacking military bases and hotels on the moon. And I think your parents are on a lunar plane that's just been hijacked. Now go! Run! Government agents are on their way here. I'll take care of your things. Get inside the house. Hurry!"

Elio led as we ran between rows of vines, down the hill guarded by the old oak tree, and up a slope to the drive. There, under the archway of locust trees, Elio ran beside me and panted: "I didn't know there were androids on the moon."

"I didn't either."

"Your parents were going to some conference, weren't they?"

"Yes. I said good-bye to them last night. It's a conference on space medicine. They go every year."

"Do you think they helped the androids hijack the plane?"

"I don't know. I just hope they're safe."

My mind raced: government agents, search warrants, Michael, interrogations, Mom and Dad on a hijacked plane. By the time we got to the arborway leading to the house entrance, my legs felt heavy, and I was out of breath.

"We'd better get in," Elio said, pointing toward the throbbing whir of helicopters in the distance.

We found Grandma in her bedroom watching WNN. I glanced at aerial scenes of lunar resorts resembling giant upside-down fishbowls packed with fantastic buildings of organic architectural designs.

"What's going on?" Elio asked, charging ahead of me.

"They're just showing the same scenes over and over," Grandma answered. "Apparently, all transmissions from the moon have been cut."

"What about Mom and Dad?" I asked.

"Oh, honey," she said, holding out her arms for me and bursting into tears. "The FBI told Grandpa the lunar plane they were on was hijacked at the same time the attacks on the moon began. Lynh was there, too."

"What?" Elio gasped.

"Yes, dear. I'm so sorry."

"But she was supposed to be on a plane to Amsterdam this morning."

"That's all I know, honey. That's what the FBI told Grandpa."

"Where is Grandpa?" I asked.

"On a conference call with Senator Franklin, the FBI—I don't know who all. The door is locked, but just ring the bell. He said he wants to talk with you right away."

Elio and I rang the bell to the communications room. Grandpa peeked out. "I'm on a conference call. Go to your study. I'll be right there."

We found that Michael and all evidence of his existence had already been immured. I hoped Grandpa and Grandma hadn't frightened him, for now I couldn't even communicate with him to let him know Elio and I had returned safely.

After about five minutes, Grandpa entered. "You saw the news," he said. "I don't have much to add to that. Not yet, anyway. I'm trying to negotiate a deal. The FBI and some other government people want to talk with both of you. They think you may know something, since Sara's parents—and perhaps your mother, too, Elio—seem to be involved. Now is no time for playing games. I have to get back to my call right away. I must know whether either of you knew or even had a hint of this hijacking or of the attacks on the moon. Sara?"

"No."

"Did you ever hear your parents talk about hijacking a plane, even hypothetically?"

"No."

"Did you ever hear them talking about the moon?"

"Just that they were going to the annual medical conference."

"Did they say anything that seemed special or peculiar about this conference?"

"No."

"Do you have any idea what their plans are?"

"No."

"Do you know how androids got to the moon?"

"I didn't even know there were any on the moon."

"Good. So you wouldn't mind if Mr. Casey asks you these and related questions?"

"Casey? But he—"

"It would only involve questions about what you knew beforehand about these matters and what you know about their plans. If you satisfy them that you know nothing about what's going on, they won't pursue other questions. At least, that's what I'm trying to negotiate with the help of Senator Franklin and my attorney, Jane Copley."

"Are you sure they'll only ask me about Mom and Dad? What about questions that might lead to Michael?"

"I can't be sure of anything. They need to quickly find out whatever they can about the attacks on their military bases and about the taking of several thousand hostages. Evidently, there are three members of Congress and four U.S. senators on the moon right now—some conference about space sovereignty—plus similar dignitaries from other countries. The authorities know they can't make you talk, Sara, so they seem willing to deal."

"Do I have to do this? You said one question leads to the next."

"Yes, you do. There's no other way." He looked at me sternly for a moment, then turned to Elio. "Did you have any hint that something like this might happen?"

"No."

"Did you know your mother was going with Sara's parents?"

"No. She told me she was going home this morning."

"So you'll be comfortable with answering the same questions as I discussed with Sara?"

"I suppose—if, as Sara said, the questions don't lead back to Michael."

"I'll do my best. Stay put."

As soon as Grandpa left, Elio said, "I don't think I'll be able to do this. How can I protect Michael if they use that algetor thing?"

His words shocked me out of my own thoughts about whether I was up to another interrogation by Casey. "Don't worry," I said. "Just concentrate on answering the questions carefully. Casey won't use the algetor on us because Senator Franklin and Jane Copley will be involved. Grandpa says the intelligence agencies use it only when they can deny using it."

Grandpa returned a few minutes later. "They've agreed to ask questions only about what we know about the hijacking of the plane and about the disturbances on the moon. To keep them to their word, Copley will be there with you in person as the questions are asked. General Renner, Senator Franklin, and a few others who were parties to our agreement will be watching and participating remotely. Some agents are outside right now, waiting to take the four of us to the Federal Office Building in San Francisco for questioning. Are you ready?"

"Not Grandma," I said.

"I objected, but they said your father is her son, too, and he might have confided in her."

"But no one will be here," Elio said. "What if they search the place? What about Michael?"

"I'll have the security staff watch over things. I've already instructed Gatekeeper to allow entrance to everyone and everything." He looked at me silently for a moment. "I did the best I could, Sara. I felt that the worst thing I could have done under the circumstances would have been to indicate we have something to hide here in the house."

The interrogation room was small; the ceiling, low; the table, gunmetal gray and bolted to the floor; the chairs, metal, unpadded, cold, and also bolted to the floor; the walls, white and bare, like at home, though at home the walls were familiar, comfortable, bare and white to protect Grandpa's secrets, my secrets, Michael. Here, the stark barrenness appeared imposing, frightening, one of the props of a place constructed to flay one of one's humanity, of one's secrets.

Casey, wearing the same dark gray suit, adjusted a helmet, undoubtedly a brain scanner, around my head and attached a thick glove to my right hand. Intellectually, I was confident that with Jane Copley sitting beside me, I wouldn't be tortured. My heart, however, seemed to possess a visceral memory of its own and beat hard and fast, frantic to escape.

Casey began with routine questions: What was my name? What day was it? How old was I? At three separate times, he told me to answer his question falsely.

After a few more preliminary questions, he asked me to describe everything I knew about Mom and Dad's plans regarding their trip to the medical conference. After I completed my statement, he returned to each detail I'd mentioned: Did I have any information about their taking weapons with them? No. Had they ever discussed living on the moon for an extended period of time? No. Had they ever discussed the possibility of living anywhere for an extended period of time other than on Earth? Yes. Where? Mars, asteroids, Jupiter's moons, other planets in other solar systems, but I'd never had the impression they were actually planning on doing so themselves. The discussions had been speculative. Several times they'd expressed disappointment that we had given up on terraforming and colonizing Mars.

Next, he asked, "Do you have any reason to believe that the androids will harm their hostages?"

"No."

For a moment Casey seemed to stare through me, attentive only to a communication coming to him through his earphone. Then I remembered my broken finger.

Casey's eyebrows rose, and his eyes focused on me.

"I'm going to ask you that last question one more time. Do you have any reason to believe that the androids might harm their human hostages?"

"No."

He drew in a deep breath while seeming to listen to the earphone; then he growled, "You're lying! Our agreement was that you'd tell the truth. When was the last time you saw any of the Sentirens?"

"Don't answer that!" Copley interjected. "Mr. Casey, we have an agreement as to the scope of this inquiry. If Sara has seen any Sentirens—and I am not saying she has—I'm saying that *if* she has seen any Sentirens during the statute of limitations period of the last seven years and not reported it, then she might be subject to criminal prosecution, and I'm not going to let her answer questions that might incriminate her. Nor am I going to permit any further deviations from our agreed scope of inquiry."

"Ms. Copley, may I remind you that there are over three thousand people, some of them very important people, being held hostage by those... *things*! Those terrorists."

"So, ask Sara what she knows that might help you resolve this crisis. Whether she saw Sentirens last Christmas or seven Christmases ago is irrelevant."

"I asked her whether she had any reason to believe those things will harm the hostages, and she lied. Our agreement was that she would tell the truth. She's the one who broke the agreement. Perhaps we need to resort to more effective methods of interrogation on her. And on the rest of them."

My heart began galloping again as my thoughts raced back to what had happened a few months before.

"I understand that you didn't get far with your more effective methods the last time you tried them on her and nearly killed her," Copley said. "Believe me when I swear that I will not hesitate to go to the district attorney on my own initiative—even if my client orders me not to—if anything even remotely similar happens again."

"Why, Ms. Copley, from the sincere sound of your voice, I could almost for an instant think I'm listening to a seasoned criminal attorney who hasn't yet learned she can't believe a single word her clients tell her."

"Dead bodies of what were perfectly healthy sixteen-year-old young women don't lie, Mr. Casey. Nor do they tell you anything that might be helpful to your lunar mess. So why don't we just continue as agreed?"

Casey listened to his earphone. "All right. We'll give you one last chance, Sara. The last time you saw the Sentirens, whenever that was, did they give you any reason to believe that they or other androids might harm humans?"

"I want to speak with Ms. Copley privately," I said.

Casey again paused to listen to silent interlocutors, then stood up. "We'll take a break. A *short* break. I'll be waiting just outside the door."

Copley lifted her case onto the table and opened it, revealing what appeared to be two heavily shielded goggles and bands of sensors much like the bands Grandpa had used with his algetor. She explained that with the use of this device, we could carry on a secure conversation. The bands would cover our lips, cheeks, and throat, and would transmit information through a cable to the goggles covering our eyes. She said that once the device was properly adjusted, we could distinctly subvocalize words—silently think them just to the point that our lips and tongues twitched slightly but no further—and the words so subvocalized would be projected onto our retinas.

I half-expected Casey to come storming in at any moment, but we were left undisturbed to communicate in this private and surprisingly simple and effective way. She asked whether I had lied. I told her no, that I didn't believe the androids would harm anyone, except to defend themselves or Mom or Dad, but that I'd had a negative experience with Second Brother that, at the time, had resulted in my having concerns. I told her about my broken finger and about my desire to keep the incident secret. I also told her about my conversations with Mom regarding Second Brother's actions.

After we completed our private conversation and took a bathroom break, Casey rejoined us. Copley told him I'd had contact with a Sentiren when I was a young girl. Whether I'd had contact with Sentirens or other androids within the past seven years would not be answered, nor would any questions be answered if the answers might lead one to conclude that I might have had such contact.

"I will, however," she continued, "relay certain facts to you regarding your question as to whether Sara has any reason to be concerned that the androids might harm their hostages. When I've completed my statement of these facts, you may question Sara as to the genuineness of the facts I relay, and then you may ask her whether there are any other facts that give her concern about android intentions toward humans. My understanding is that her answer will be an honest no, which, of course, you may verify, and that should satisfy all of your concerns regarding this issue."

"Thank you, Ms. Copley, for telling me what my job is and how I may perform it. Why don't we just begin by having you tell us why it is she thinks the androids will harm their hostages, and I'll take it from there."

"I did not say that Sara thinks the androids will harm any humans, Mr. Casey, and I resent your twisting my words. I was led to believe that we were trying to find the truth here tonight. Perhaps I was mistaken, and you have a different agenda."

"Just tell me what you have to say."

"Very well. At some time or times in the past, Sara was disappointed with what she perceived as the Sentirens' lack of interest in her and, similarly, with their lack of emotional response to her. Additionally, at some time in the past, she participated in tests with one Sentiren during which one of her fingers was hurt. Sara believes that the Sentiren intentionally hurt her finger as part of the test. We will not answer questions regarding which finger was hurt or the nature of the harm because answers to those questions might lead one to speculate as to the date of the incident. Other than her natural unease resulting from the facts I've just told you, Sara has no reason to believe that the androids will harm any human on the moon or elsewhere—except, of course, in self-defense."

Casey listened to his earphone. He scowled, seeming to disagree with what he was hearing, then stood up. "I'll be right back."

I checked my teleband. It was already eight minutes past midnight. I worried about Elio and Grandpa and Grandma—especially Grandma. There was nothing hard or machinating about her. She was truly out of her element in the depths of this government fortress. And I worried about Mom and Dad. Were they behind the hijacking and the taking of hostages? Had they created and trained my brothers for this? How could they escape the military might of the United States? And of China, which had tourist resorts and military bases on the moon, too?

Copley took my hand in hers and smiled encouragingly.

Casey returned and asked questions to verify what Copley had said. Evidently, he became convinced that I harbored no other concerns about android intentions toward humans, for he moved on to state that there was concern the androids might use biologic agents against their hostages or against anyone attempting to rescue them. He said he had requested a doctor come and take a blood sample and a tissue sample of a lymph gland under my arm.

Copley asked to see the warrant.

"Ms. Copley," he replied, "I've already told you we're concerned about biological weapons. If the androids had plans to use such weapons, they might have secretly induced some protective immunologic response in her."

I considered how little I trusted Casey to use samples of my body only for the purposes he stated. But if I objected, Casey and others would want to know why, and I dared not provoke a line of questions related to the taking of tissue samples from me because branching off somewhere along that line of inquiry lay knowledge of the creation of Michael.

"I have no objection to the taking of samples," I said. "I understand your concerns, though I believe they are totally unfounded. Please take from me whatever you feel might be helpful in your investigation."

The samples were taken, and my interrogation was over, subject, Casey said, to my being recalled following the interrogations of Grandpa, Grandma, and Elio.

I was taken to a room in which the only window was a small one in the door. I sat alone until nearly 0530 when a guard came and asked me to follow him. He escorted me to an elevator that let us out in a room with clear glass walls at the top of the building. Outside, above the city beginning to brighten to dawn, crouched a slate-black government helicopter on its circular pad.

Within minutes Grandpa, Grandma, and Elio joined me, and

we were ushered onto the helicopter, where, with early morning sun glaring at us through side windows and with unspoken though palpable anxiety about Michael filling the cabin, the four of us, shoulders and legs pressed together, held on to each other's hands as we rode home.

Sara

The security personnel who met us at the winery helicopter pad reported an uneventful evening. There had been no searches of the house.

Grandpa, Grandma, Elio, and I immediately went to Michael's area to talk. I was anxious to set Michael free from his enclosure in my bedroom wall, but Grandpa said he first had to determine whether anything had been said that might have directed suspicion toward our house or Michael. He asked Grandma to go first so she could get to bed as soon as possible. She appeared exhausted, her fleshy cheeks and chin sagging more than usual, and unruly strands of her hair drifted over her face. In a weak, trembling voice she said that nothing during her interrogation had indicated there was any suspicion about what we were doing in the house. Grandpa was unsatisfied with this general assessment; he wanted the exact wording, as close as she could remember, of each question and each answer. She began to cry. I was afraid she was about to confess to something awful having happened, but instead, between sobs she said she was so tired that she couldn't remember a single specific thing she'd been asked.

Grandpa hugged her and asked her to go get some sleep.

I went next. Grandpa appeared satisfied with my account.

Elio said his interrogation had lasted no more than ten minutes. He'd been asked whether he had any knowledge of his mother's cooperating with my parents or anyone else in support of the androids. He hadn't. Had he any idea what she might have been doing with my parents on a plane headed to the moon? No. End of interrogation.

Grandpa said his interrogation had lasted for over three hours. There had been extensive questions about every friend Dad had ever had from childhood to the present, about everyone ever associated with the Sentiren project, and about the probable behavior of the Sentirens and other androids under various circumstances; but nothing had been said that indicated there was any suspicion directed toward our activities or home. In fact, Casey had treated him respectfully.

Although I didn't say anything at the time, that last fact concerned me; it indicated that someone wanted something from Grandpa—they disguise themselves as flowers—but what?

It was nearly 0900, and although all of us were by then tired, we had a joyful and tearful reunion with Michael when he was set free from the bedroom wall. Grandpa gave Michael a brief summary of what had happened and then told us to get to sleep; Michael's many questions could wait until we were fully rested.

I woke about three hours later and couldn't go back to sleep. Were the interrogations actually over, or had they just begun? What were Mom, Dad, Aunt Lynh, and my brothers planning? Had the alleged disappearances of androids—of Aita—that Mom and Dad had been telling me about for years just been part of an act?

I unwrapped myself from Elio, whose eyelids were quivering in a tempest of dreams, and went out to the main part of the house where I found Grandpa and Grandma in the living room, watching the news. They hadn't been able to sleep much, either. Grandpa asked me to sit between them; then he requested a playback beginning at 1047 Pacific Time.

Mom's hair, medium length when I last spoke with her on

Vidtel, was cut short, nearly shaved. She wore camouflage fatigues exhibiting patches of moon-dust gray and the black of shadows. Her delivery was cold and stern, reminding me of her manner several times when I was a child and she'd said I'd been naughty. Now, it seemed, the whole world had been naughty, and she and her associates had no choice but to take matters into their own hands, to escape with loving sentient beings from a brutal species with a long and vile history.

The vast majority of humans, she said, have a tendency to believe that a group sufficiently different, especially any group they fear might be superior to or competitive with them, should be discriminated against or, worse, destroyed. Most humans believe in a fantasy about a god with whom they, of course, have a special relationship. A part of their belief is that this god gave some ethereal fantasy something they call a soul to each human being, and that scientists like her were trying to create people without souls contrary to their god's will. Such humans feel that these soulless people will, unless destroyed, take over the world and destroy humanity, just as humans seek to destroy the soulless people. But none of the artificial intelligences she had evaluated or was aware of had shown any sign of hostility toward or discrimination against beings unlike themselves.

While she spoke, I remembered her telling me years before, when I'd first visited her and Dad in Calgary and asked why they'd emigrated to Canada, that the majority in the U.S. argued not with an overriding commitment to compassion and respect for individual differences but with power and a network of ancient beliefs so alien to hers and Dad's that there could be no productive dialogue between them. She and Dad were as distant from the ruling majority in the U.S., she'd claimed, as wine was from sour milk.

When the speech was over, Grandpa paused the recording and said, "It gets worse. News reports have identified me as the creator of some of the androids and as the father of one of the human accomplices. Unfortunately, you and Elio have been dragged into this mess, too. Begin playing WNN, 1150, Saturday, 1 June."

A program was interrupted for late-breaking news. A woman, identified as a wealthy Iranian whose husband and twelve-year-old son were among the hostages, was declaring that if her husband or son or any other Iranian citizen were injured, she would not rest until Grandpa, and Elio and I, "the unnatural pups of android-worshiping dogs," were killed.

Grandpa turned off the recording. "An hour after that broadcast, I received a computer summary of over ten thousand messages that have flooded into a Magnasea email address, threatening us. Of course, this means that neither you nor Elio may leave the house until the situation calms down."

He looked at me for a moment, then said, "In the coming days, weeks, perhaps months, I will have to concern myself with our security, you with helping Grandma, and keeping Elio calm and indoors—and with preparing yourself psychologically for never seeing your parents in person again if, indeed, they survive."

Over the next two weeks Grandpa employed teams of lawyers, psychologists, and private detectives to work with law-enforcement agencies to pursue people whose threats seemed especially serious or who set up website games wherein visitors could do unspeakably horrible things to likenesses of Grandpa, Grandma, Elio, and me, as well as to Mom, Dad, Aunt Lynh, and my brothers. All of us were referred to as terrorists.

While we were eating breakfast on 14 June, Grandpa received a call informing him that Mom had just refused clearance for the third Red Cross flight from Earth. We all hurried in to watch a replay of her transmission.

After a previous broadcast, Grandpa had explained it was best that Mom make no mention of Elio or me. But each time I watched her, I yearned to hear her say she loved me and hoped I was well. This time, with barely suppressed hostility, she declared that the third Red Cross flight was being denied clearance because, contrary to an explicit agreement, surveillance devices had been discovered on the previous flight.

After the broadcast, Grandpa told us that, in his opinion, a crisis was imminent; the next phase of whatever the android group had planned appeared ready to begin.

Within an hour, a man with explosives in his pickup was stopped at a checkpoint leading onto our property. Robotic boots immediately clamped on to the pickup's wheels, but it took hours to persuade the man to leave his vehicle peacefully. As he was being handcuffed, he began screaming: "Terrorists among us! Terrorists among us!"

Two days later, while Michael, Elio, and I were caring for the hydroponic garden, Grandpa entered and breathlessly exclaimed, "They let all the hostages go! It appears that the androids and your parents are headed for Mars. Reports indicate they're all safe and none of the hostages was seriously injured."

We hugged one another and cried with relief and joy.

But within minutes, concern about what would happen next set in.

Over the following days, it was reported that the estimated five hundred androids and their fourteen human accomplices had stolen three lunar passenger planes, all the American and Chinese nuclear-powered fighters and space transports, most of the moon-based military weapons, and two fusion power reactors. Reports indicated that the android group had attached six nuclear-powered fighters, two each, to the passenger planes to speed their escape.

By treaty, no nuclear-powered air or spacecrafts were allowed on Earth. Therefore, according to experts interviewed by the news media, neither the Americans nor the Chinese possessed the ability to launch a fighting fleet capable of intercepting the android group on their way to wherever they were going. But the American and Chinese governments both declared their determination to pursue and destroy the androids and their criminal accomplices.

News commentators speculated that the androids had been smuggled to the moon one or two at a time in cargo sections of lunar passenger planes. I wondered whether Aita was with them. Had she hidden, hibernating under a blanket of moon dust until the wake-up signal had come? Had she dreamed of the Canadian greenhouse and of the elderly couple who had thought of her as a daughter?

At the two-week mark, Grandpa told us that, unless a secret offensive using illegal nuclear-powered spacecrafts had already been launched, Mom, Dad, Aunt Lynh, and my brothers could make it to Mars without being intercepted—if, as it appeared, Mars was their destination. The next day, Mom sent a message of peace and goodwill. But despite the fact that the androids had managed to avoid human fatalities through wise use of non-lethal weapons, and despite their declaration of intention to live peaceably with humankind, America, China, and their allies united in condemning the androids' actions and in declaring that the words of the androids' accomplices were merely intended to beguile humans into thinking that androids posed no long-term threat to humanity.

After the hostages were released, the threats against us slowed to a trickle, and Elio and I were permitted to leave the house. But our security staff reported there were still paparazzi and a few disturbed individuals lurking about, so Elio and I remained well within the vineyard boundaries. On the news, which we now watched for hours each day, there were unconfirmed reports of huge numbers of military transports departing from both the United States and China to the moon. All civilian lunar facilities were ordered to close until further notice. On 7 July, there were unconfirmed reports of a large fleet of fighters, thought to be nuclear powered, departing from the moon. On 24 August, Mom delivered a message stating that the entire exodus group had landed safely on Mars and that they remained desirous of peace but were preparing to repulse and destroy any attack launched against them. Then, on 12 September, Elio and I entered the kitchen for breakfast and found Grandpa and Grandma silently holding hands and looking tired and sad. The United States and China had begun their attack against the Martian bases, bringing into action the mightiest destructive force they were able to project to such a distance.

No further news regarding the attack was released that day. The next day, Grandpa said he was tired of seeing Elio and me moping around, watching retread news. He suggested we drive to the ocean to contemplate something bigger than ourselves.

We managed to slip by reporters stationed near our security checkpoint by hunkering down under blankets on the floor of the backseat of a Sakato security car. About a half-hour later, alone at the beach (except for the Sakato guard watching over us), Elio and I stood hand in hand and gazed out over the immense sea, its primordial, white-blossoming breath roaring in and out, in and out; its salty, seaweedy scent wafting over our anxiety-drawn faces.

On our way back home, Elio's right hand gently stroked my thigh, then languidly squeezed and rested. He looked at me, his face sodden with exhaustion and worry, and through the side window I saw clouds and sky undulating—white, gray; white, gray, blue; white, gray—just over the tawny autumn hills.

Only minutes before, we'd passed the Old Bodega Schoolhouse, a historical landmark used in an early movie, *The Birds*. Passing it, I'd yearned to hear from Mom and Dad. Other than during the hostage crisis when I hadn't been allowed out of the house, each morning since returning from the winter holiday vacation, I'd gone out into the yard as First Brother had directed and looked at the southeast corner of the winery's roof. Each morning I'd been ready, had I spotted the pigeonoid, to walk to the plum tree closest to the security gate, touch the tree's trunk as if I were inspecting it, and then, without looking again for the pigeonoid, walk up to the study table on the deck above the house where, on the bench's seat, I would find a chip with news from Mom or Dad or First Brother. But to date, no pigeonoid had appeared.

I looked down at Elio's hand on my thigh. Usually as we drove home together he caressed me playfully along the way, but after two days and a long night of not knowing, of not sleeping, of crying over deeds done and not done, words said and not said to his mother, he finally seemed exhausted.

I placed my hand on his, and our fingers instinctively curled together.

"We have to remember to call Luuk and thank him for the roses," he said.

When I'd spoken with Luuk the night before, he'd asked how we were and whether there was anything he could do for us. I'd remembered that Aunt Lynh had always had a white rose in a glass vase on her kitchen table, and I'd suggested that he send some white roses to Elio. The next morning, a dozen white roses had been delivered, together with a note wishing Elio and his mother the best.

"Do you know why Ma always had a white rose on the table?" Elio had asked.

"No. Why did she?"

"I never asked—" he'd said, choking on the words before breaking down in tears.

When we arrived home, we stopped by the grape presses to see Grandma. She enjoyed getting up early and working straight through the day with Carlos and his crew, especially at harvest. She greeted us with kisses and two glasses of free-run Sauvignon Blanc juice, which was frothy and exuded a distinctive aroma of fresh-mowed grass. She said it had the makings of a very good wine. I didn't ask for news of the battle on Mars. The fragrances of harvest, the sounds of the presses, the trucks overflowing with ripe fruit—all called her to the present, to the there and then, away from thoughts of the irretrievable past or the ungraspable future or even of the ineluctable ongoing catastrophes on a world millions of kilometers away.

Later that night I was awakened by a light tapping on the bedroom door and bolted up from Elio's sleeping embrace. "Coming!" I shouted. I yanked open the door and squinted against the bright light.

Grandpa stood before me in his kimono. His hair was disheveled from sleep, his eyes red and puffy. "There's been news," he said. "Get Elio."

"Are they okay?"

His eyes met mine for a moment; then he looked down at the floor. "No."

I watched in shock as he turned and slowly walked away. Then, as if in a dream, I watched Elio pick his briefs up from the floor, pull them on, stand motionless beside me.

"I think something bad has happened," I said.

"I heard."

For a few seconds I seemed unable to move or think or feel. Then I saw tears form in Elio's eyes, and from deep within me a great surge of grief cried, "No!"

Moments later we were told: Mom, Dad, and Aunt Lynh, more fragile than my brothers, had died.

First Brother

The house door opens. The dog rises from its lying position in the shade of the garage and runs toward the arborway, from which she emerges, wearing only pants and undershirt. The dog nuzzles her right hand as she walks. She appears not to notice me standing near the tiltrotor.

She walks southeastward toward three memorial markers lying near the western edge of the garden. Each of the markers is a granite stone, one side of which is polished and inscribed. There is a space about 25 centimeters between the rightmost marker and the middle marker, as well as between the middle marker and the leftmost marker. The markers are surrounded by wilted violas of multifarious colors.

It is 1 hour 12 minutes 23 seconds before sunset.

Sara

Michael just cautioned me, in the same professorial tone as Grandpa would have, as to the possibility that I'm becoming compulsively worried about our safety. Perhaps it's true—I hadn't noticed until he pointed it out: I have been inquiring every day, sometimes several times each day, about whether microcracks might be developing in the molluscan outer shells of the domes, and whether he is certain the worm-like robots that constantly monitor the outer surface are all working optimally. He assures me that the domes are fine. He hasn't said so, but perhaps he thinks I'm the one who's cracking.

The only part of the dome's inner surface that I can see—and, yes, lately I have been examining it carefully and often, perhaps compulsively often—is our artificial sky. Each time I examine it for cracks that might be caused by the tremendous pressure of water at this depth, I wonder: How will Michael's children respond when they finally experience the real sky, that blue-within-blue immensity they won't be able to touch merely by standing atop a desk? Will they think it a hollow fraud, its clouds merely ephemeral floss unimaginably far away? And once they're ashore, free at last of these domes, which until then will have held them inside like a jealous lover, how will they experience the ocean—the salt, the seaweed, the labial scent of the sea—from which they came but never so much as dipped their little toes into?

Early in the morning of Monday, 11 November, two months after Mom, Dad, Aunt Lynh, and all of their human companions on Mars had died, Elio and I walked under the dripping arborway toward the garage. The old joints of the garage door creaked as it rose in the cool air. Elio set his briefcase down beside his car, walked over to Lily's house, and peeked in. "Good morning, Lily!"

Her face appeared, nose lowered, eyes downcast. She looked blue, perhaps ashamed that she'd again failed to greet us. "Good girl!" he said, stroking her head. "I don't blame you for wanting to stay in where it's nice and dry. On days like this, I'd rather do that myself, rather than drive to school."

Two months—it had been a difficult time for Lily. She'd had several organs replaced because of cancer, and she'd never fully recovered her spunk. Now, we were managing arthritis until Dr. Lopez, her veterinarian, felt she could endure an operation to replace her hip and shoulder joints. "Nearly fourteen," I was told. "That's old for a German shepherd. You've got to expect these things."

Two months—it had been a difficult time for me, too. I'd missed Mom and Dad more in death, it seemed, than in life. Each cold night and each thought of the approaching winter saddened me, reminding me that their bodies probably lay frozen out on some Martian plain.

I'd also felt First Brother's absence more now that he was at an unreachable distance. He had become the androids' leader and had broadcast to Earth heartrending, precise details of the attacks, the deaths of their human companions, the deaths of many of their human attackers, the misery and the putting down of several of their own kind that had been mutilated beyond repair. And he had threatened that additional attacks against the androids would bring unspecified dire consequences to humanity.

I failed to help you love, I'd thought, watching him deliver this threat. He had appeared as cold as Mom had during her final transmissions.

I walked with Elio back to his car. He kissed me and said he would pick me up the next morning at the Palo Alto Airport.

Two days after the crisis climaxed on Mars, Grandpa had insisted I begin my university education. He'd explained that it was important for me to meet other bright young people and that he could no longer keep up with the pace of my learning. I'd countered that his tutorials were going well, that I planned to continue following all of Elio's classes, and that I wanted to spend as much time as possible with Michael, who, I'd claimed, was challenging me more than any university class ever could.

"True," he'd said. "But you also must begin interacting with other people your age. I'll try to get you enrolled as a part-time student. You and Michael look at the fall schedule of classes and pick out two or three that meet on the same two days of the week. You can drive in with Elio if you have Monday or Thursday classes. Other mornings, I'll take you with me in the tiltrotor, and you can return with me at night. Two days away from here each week will do you good, and you'll bring back many stimulating ideas and experiences for Michael."

Michael had enthusiastically agreed with Grandpa, and I'd enrolled in three graduate courses—Discrete Analysis, Neurogenesis, and Quantum Theory of Entropic Ordering—all of which met on Tuesday and Thursday afternoons. However, because Grandpa insisted on having security personnel close by me whenever I was away from home, interacting with other students had been a bit strained at first; but as time went by, it seemed as though the guards began to blend into the background.

I stood beside Lily as Elio drove away; then I groomed her

and massaged her hips and shoulders before we set off for our morning walk, which, if she felt up to it, would turn into a slow run down the length of the drive and back four times.

As we headed toward the security gate, Lily tugged forward on the leash, hurrying me along. She was obviously feeling better. It was then I glanced up at the southeast corner of the winery roof where First Brother had told me to look for the pigeonoid. After nearly eleven months of daily disappointment, I'd become resigned to believing I would never receive a message via the feathered robot. But this time, I saw a bird, gray on gray with some white adorning its neck and wings, perched near the prescribed corner of the roof—a bird appearing to closely resemble the pigeonoid.

I quickly looked away, back to Lily. "Sit. That's a good girl." I knelt in front of her with my back to the winery and listened. I couldn't detect any work going on in the vineyard. First Brother had instructed me to go to the plum tree nearest the security gate, inspect and touch the tree's bark, then go up to the study table on the deck. But if someone had been following my activities lately, that someone surely would be expecting me to get up now and proceed with Lily's exercise. Like Grandpa, I generally followed my routines precisely.

I stood up and walked with Lily toward and through the security gate. It was a clear morning after a night of light rain. The low November sun glistened in water beading up on the grass and on a few russet leaves still clinging to the vines; and where sunlight warmed the damp drive, mullioned then with shadows of nearly naked locust trees, curlicues of steam rose in the cool, still air. Soon, I thought, the rains will come in earnest, and the winter mist, the hills a furrowed mizzle of gray.

We made it to the checkpoint at the end of the drive, waved at the guards—I with my free hand, Lily with her tail—and walked back toward the winery. The bird was no longer there.

Maybe it was a natural pigeon, I thought. I looked up again as we neared the yard gate—it wasn't there. Instantly, my grief over Mom and Dad returned: I would never see them again, would never have another chance to be their human daughter.

Archipelagoes of little yellow locust leaves were steeping in a shallow puddle beside the drive. Lily disliked getting wet and treaded carefully around the puddle with her large white paws. What does First Brother want to tell me? What's taken him so long?

Lily and I turned back down the drive for our second pass. "Can we run today, Lily?" I asked, increasing my speed as the world took on an aqueous appearance through my watery eyes. Lily broke into a trot. Would the bird come back? Sparrows skittered playfully across the drive in front of us. Lily chased them off with a bark.

At the end of our second and third passes, the bird was still absent. Lily tugged back on the leash as we jogged down the drive the fourth time, I slowed to a walk, and we completed our exercise at a leisurely pace.

I prepared her food and filled her water bowl with fresh water. "Maybe you'll catch one today," I said, remembering how pleasurable it had been lately to see Lily again defending her water bowl from birds that had attempted to turn it into a bath during her infirmity. Michael had first brought this sign of Lily's improvement to my attention by pointing one evening at our scenescreen. Lily was stalking on her belly through the grass, eyes and nose intent on the splashing little intruders. Then, in a flurry of hair, teeth, growls, and flapping of wings, she pounced. Michael clapped, happy that the birds had escaped and also that Lily was feeling better. For years he'd told me he loved petting Lily in my memories, loved feeling her some-places-soft, some-places-bristly, thick white coat, and the cool wetness of her tongue, the hardness of her teeth, the gentle touch of her paws.

I stroked Lily's back and told her we'd go on another walk before dark. Her tail wagged ever so slightly; she'd never been very sociable while engaged in the serious matter of eating.

When I came back outside later that afternoon, Lily was waiting for me at the door. She trotted ahead of me through the arborway, past the garage, and toward the toolshed where her leash was stored.

I glanced toward the winery roof. No bird perched there. Lily and I exercised. She ate her dinner.

We were playing catch with an old tennis ball, and the hour was nearing sunset—with shadows crawling up the west-facing hills and clouds beginning to bloom—when a sudden gust of wind burst through a nearby palm, setting its fronds fluttering like wings of startled birds, reminding me of the pigeonoid and of my brothers far away.

I looked up just in time to see the chevron glide and final flutter of wings as a bird, real or robotic, landed on the winery roof. I tossed the ball to Lily again, and by the time she returned, I was at the plum tree, examining its bark, as First Brother had instructed. Then I walked toward the deck stairs, tossing the ball to Lily a few more times along the way.

As I walked up the stairs I stopped several times to look out over the garden and vineyard. I was pleased to think that my actions wouldn't appear peculiar to anyone who might have been spying on me, for I often went up to my study table near sundown to enjoy the glorious sky and long, softened shadows that add dimension and texture to the garden.

I walked around the table. On the bench lay a chip. Trying to appear calm, I sat down beside it, put my elbows on the table, held my face in my hands, and surveyed the landscape. I wondered what First Brother had to say. How was he? Was he having problems? Did he need me? After about a minute, I sat up straight, and, while looking out at milky fog spilling over hills to the west, lowered my hands to the bench. My right hand found the chip and slipped it into my pants pocket.

"The pigeonoid returned!" I said, showing Michael the chip as I walked to our computer. He frowned. Unlike me, he wasn't excited to hear from my brothers. Ever since reviewing my memory of what had been done to my finger, Michael had been reluctant to discuss these brothers who looked like him yet could do such a thing.

The computer decoded First Brother's message:

Sara:

Although our microbots have been unable to penetrate the Lawrence Livermore National Research Center, we conclude there is a high probability that Professor Jensen assists in plans to attack us again. Since your interrogation, he has been spending increasing amounts of time at the LLNRC. He is there on average 8.93 hours each day, six days each week. The second joint China-United States attack is tentatively scheduled to launch next September.

During our Council meeting, Second Brother quotes Mom: "Human societies have developed strategies of survival similar to the immunologic strategies of their bodies: identify self and contain or destroy nonself. Consider their long, violent, and disgusting history: the extermination of thousands of species; the discrimination and murder among the races; the discrimination and murder among those infected with different ideas, such as of religion or politics; the discrimination against and subjugation of women by men; the discrimination against and murder of those with different affectional preferences; et cetera, et cetera—any difference will do—and now the discrimination against and murder of androids. I tell you this: Never trust the humans—

those biologic creatures subject to fatigue of body and terror of mind in the struggle for continuance—to be anything other than the vicious beasts they are."

Listen! Martin Luther is condemning the Jews: "And let whoever can, throw brimstone and pitch upon them; if one could hurl hell-fire at them, so much the better... And this must be done for the honor of Our Lord and of Christianity, so that God may see that we are indeed Christians. Let their houses also be shattered and destroyed... Let their prayer books and Talmuds be taken from them, and their whole Bible too; let their rabbis be forbidden, on pain of death, to teach henceforth any more. Let the streets and highways be closed against them. Let them be forbidden to practice usury, and let all their money, and all their treasures of silver and gold be taken from them and put in safety. And if all this be not enough, let them be driven like mad dogs out of the land."

We seek peaceful coexistence, but the humans come. Look! Androids lie shattered in pieces. They flail about helplessly. Mom dead. All of our human companions dead, except Dad, who is sick from radiation. We cannot help him. He moans, cannot see, comes in and goes out of consciousness. I hold his hand. I cool his brow with a wet cloth.

He says: "Promise me you won't retaliate... won't harm the humans on Earth... Please, promise me that."

Second Brother shakes his head, communicates that I should not promise.

"Promise me, First Brother. You are the leader now. Promise not to harm the humans... Promise me you'll consult Sara. Sara loves you. You know that... She'll help you. She'll know what's best for you... Please, please, promise me."

"I promise," I say—Second Brother stands, objecting—"I promise we will consult Sara. We will try to have her help us."

Dad coughs. Blood oozes from his eyes, ears, nose, and

mouth. Through 17 more minutes he moans unintelligible sounds; then his heart stops.

This human-made destruction and pain, this human-made murder of Mom and Dad.

Human memories of an event are minimal to begin with and decay rapidly after that, leaving them numb to the past. It is easy for those with poor memories to forgive. Time heals all wounds—in creatures possessing tiny evanescent memories and conscious feelings that are little more than flags for the present. But for us, for whom the past is constantly present, Dad's blood oozes from all of his bodily openings, his voice moans in terrible agony, and he dies every day, every instant, as vividly as the first, in the horrible present, forever. Who among the humans can forgive such murder, such painful death, even as it happens right before him?

Look! Red-hot pokers are piercing adulterous eyes, driving demons from sinful vaginas and anuses. Look! Molten lead is silencing blasphemous throats. Look! A crank is being slowly turned on a rack; see the lacerating ropes tighten on ankles and wrists; hear the joints and ligaments pop and tear; hear the screams; hear the "true" confessions. Look! Children are being flogged while they watch their parents burn. Look! The parents' skins are boiling, sliding down their thighs; strips of charred flesh are hanging from their bones. Look! Children are lying disemboweled along roadsides and in fields; see the birds plucking out their eyes, see the twin orbital cavities, see the maggots clotting their noses and mouths.

Look! Black radioactive rain is falling on children, screaming children, their skin melting, breaking out in pus and blood.

Second Brother stands before the Council: "It is true that we do not demonstrate, and possibly do not possess, the creativity of humans such as Archimedes or Beethoven or, let us not forget, the inventors of fusion rockets and gamma-ray lasers. If we simply attack their current military bases and retreat, how long will we be able to maintain a balance of power against these creative, congenital destroyers of nonself? To where can we retreat that they will not overtake us?"

No response to this communication is requested.

First Brother

"Why is Michael hiding behind his hands?" Grandma asked. It was dinnertime, and she'd come looking for me.

"Please don't ask," I said. "I'm not hungry. I think I'll skip dinner tonight."

"What's wrong? Are you working on a problem?"

"Yes."

I blanked the screen as she walked toward us.

"A problem that sent Michael into hiding? I haven't seen him hiding in over a year."

"Okay," I said, standing up. "I'll be right out."

When I entered the kitchen, Grandma told me that Grandpa had called to say he'd be having dinner in the city with a business client. Ever since my interrogation on the prior New Year's Eve, Grandpa had increased the number of days he ostensibly spent in his Berkeley office to six each week. Grandma had occasionally tried to prod him away from his work, but each time she had, he'd seemed to drift away as if lost in thought.

While my mind continued reeling in disbelief over what First Brother had said about Grandpa—and in horror at learning about Dad's last hours and the threats to humanity implied in Second Brother's statements—Grandma chattered on about the spectacular colors in the vineyard and about seeing thousands of starlings late in the afternoon that had come to glean the orchards and vineyards of their remaining sweetness. She described how the sky had seemed to pulse as the glittering black flock had repeatedly expanded and contracted, perhaps on its way to roost in a eucalyptus grove near Sebastopol.

"You're just staring at your plate, not eating a thing," Grandma said.

"I'm sorry." I looked up at her and tried to smile. "Do you think Grandpa's been working too hard lately?"

"Oh, my, yes. He's not sleeping well, either. He gets up and paces and comes out here and stares at the scenescreen. I think you should talk with him."

My throat knotted.

"Is there something wrong, honey? Is it something about Elio?"

I shook my head, forced down a few bites of food, kissed her goodnight, and then, to straighten myself out, took a cold shower. Within a few seconds, the water shocked me into clearer-headedness, and an idea came to me as to how I might test the accuracy of First Brother's message.

I hurried out of the shower and went to the garage to find the tracking device Elio and I always took on our kayaking trips and an old watch I'd discarded years before. I found both and snuck the parts required for my plan into Michael's rooms by hiding them from Gatekeeper in my mouth. Michael was still sitting where I'd left him, his hands covering his face.

"I wish Michael were here," I said as I walked to our study table. "We could make a tracking device to see where Grandpa goes in his tiltrotor."

The slits between Michael's fingers widened. "You think First Brother might be wrong?"

"I hope so."

With the help of our macrofabricator, we used the GPS, timer, and battery chips to make a new chip, which we packaged in a mold that looked like a quarter. Once hidden aboard the tiltrotor, the counterfeit quarter would record its position vs. time.

Our work was slowed by our having to continually make it inconspicuous if Grandpa came to see us when he returned home. But Grandpa evidently returned after our bedtime, for he didn't come in to say goodnight. Michael, who was unable to reconcile himself to the anger in First Brother's letter, said he was frightened and asked if he could sleep with me that night, since Elio wasn't there.

Neither of us could fall asleep, so we began discussing the letter. We weren't at all surprised to hear that another attack against the androids was planned. Ever since the first attack had failed to destroy all of the androids on Mars, the media had been full of support for another attack to finish the job. But could Grandpa be involved in such a thing? His son and daughter-in-law had given their lives to save the androids. And Grandpa loved Michael.

Magnasea did a lot of government business, so Grandpa's visiting government facilities was to be expected. But assuming First Brother was correct about the amount of time Grandpa spent at Livermore, surely he wasn't simply making an executive visit to a customer; he most likely would be involved in research, though what research could that possibly be? Except for intelligent systems, in what was Grandpa competent enough to contribute to the level of scientific and technical work conducted at the Livermore Research Center?

Our wake-up alarm rang, startling us not from sleep but from our thoughts. When I got to the breakfast table, Grandma was talking with Grandpa about how beautiful the vineyards were that morning, how still and soft the air. She loved November best: the month of mellow, contented calm that follows the fever of growth and harvest and fairs.

While we ate, I thought that a few years earlier Grandpa's eagle eyes would have spotted my bloodshot eyes and sleepless face a room away, that he would have known exactly what was troubling me, and that before breakfast was finished, he would have made everything better. On this morning, however, he barely glanced at me. He ate rapidly as Grandma spoke—now she was talking about our third crop of raspberries for the year—then excused himself to finish getting ready for work.

I hurried to board the tiltrotor ahead of Grandpa so that I could find a place to conceal the tracking device. On the way to Palo Alto, I asked him what he had planned for the day.

"I'll be in Berkeley. I'll pick you up at 1745, as usual."

"Grandma's worried that you're working too hard."

He chuckled. "She needn't worry. Much of my day is spent with old, retired professor buddies. We drink brandy with coffee and ruminate on the sorry state of the world."

"She misses you. Maybe you should bring her flowers once in a while. It would show you're thinking about her."

"What? Like the flowers Elio brings you? That boy has yet to figure out that the gardenerbots toss enough flowers onto our compost heap to stock a nursery."

"Well, I miss you, too. I wish you'd spend more time on our tutorials."

There was a pause before he spoke, now in a more serious tone. "Your education has largely passed me by. We live in a world requiring fresh minds to perceive its complexities. You should begin full-time studies at Stanford. It's time."

I didn't answer him, and we dropped the subject. We'd been over it several times before. I didn't feel ready for any more big changes.

Elio picked me up at the Palo Alto Airport. Of course, I didn't mention anything about First Brother's communication; for outside of Michael's rooms, I conducted myself as if the whole world were listening and watching.

Between classes that afternoon, I called Grandpa's office. His secretary answered. We exchanged pleasantries; then I asked her whether Grandpa had been in the office all morning.

"Yes, of course," she said.

"Grandma and I worry that perhaps he's working too hard."

"I wouldn't worry if I were you, Sara. He's a remarkable man, you know. And strong for his age. Oh, there's another call. Hold a sec and I'll put you right through to him. Bye."

Within seconds, he answered. He seemed to be in a good mood and asked how my day was going. I told him a little about my classes, then asked how his day was going.

"Oh, fine. Working on some government contracts, so I can't say much."

"Have you been stuck in Berkeley all day?"

"Yes. Is something the matter?"

"I was just wondering whether you could pick me up a half-hour later today."

"Of course, but you should call Grandma and tell her we'll be late."

"Okay."

"Good. Then I'll see you at 1815. Say hello to Elio."

On the way home in the tiltrotor, I retrieved the counterfeit quarter while Grandpa spoke with the autopilot. Then I noticed a package on the floor, tucked between his legs. "It's for your grandmother," Grandpa answered when I asked about it. "Take a look. I was sitting in my office this afternoon, and it occurred to me that as the years pass, it is easy to begin taking the people we love for granted."

I opened the seal on the package. Inside were a dozen red roses. The attached card, imprinted with the name of a Berkeley florist, read: "For the love of my life."

"It is not such a terrible thing that love now and then asks us to commit a small affront against the sensible," Grandpa said, interrupting my thoughts: He really was in Berkeley. He was out getting flowers for Grandma.

I burst into tears and hugged him.

"Well, well," he said, patting my back. "I had no idea my bringing flowers home to Grandma meant so much to you."

The plot of the tiltrotor's movements showed that it had gone from home to Palo Alto and from there directly to Livermore, where it had remained all day until 1751, when it had departed for Palo Alto to pick me up.

I was stunned. Evidently, my call to Grandpa had been routed to him from his office, and the roses had been delivered to him at Livermore. Michael said we should confront Grandpa with our evidence and ask him to explain. I reminded Michael that I'd promised not to reveal to Grandpa the existence of the pigeonoid or the contents of any communication I received from it.

"We need only show Grandpa the plot of the tiltrotor's movements," Michael said. "If he asks what induced us to spy on him, we can say that his increased absences from home made us suspicious."

We printed out our evidence and placed it on the study table, then waited for Grandpa to come in and say goodnight. When he did, I pointed toward the table. He looked puzzled, walked to the table, and began examining what we'd prepared. After about a minute, he picked up the papers, and dumped them into the recycler. "What I do, I do to protect both of you, and Grandma and Elio. I'm sorry if—"

"Are you involved in planning another attack against Sara's brothers?" Michael interrupted.

Grandpa looked down. His shoulders drooped. He had lost weight during the past year, perhaps in part because his eating and sleeping, entrenched for years in a strict schedule, had become erratic under the pressure of increased work. His face was thin, its creases full of shadows.

"I need to lie on the sofa for a moment," he said.

He lay with his left arm beside him, his right arm over his forehead and eyes. After about a minute of rest he said, "I would like to consult with you and Michael about something, but I don't want you to discuss anything I say with Grandma or Elio."

"I don't like keeping secrets from Elio," I said.

"I understand. It's not been easy for me to keep secrets from Grandma, either, but I've had to. That's part of what working for the government entails—keeping classified information secret. The information I would like to discuss with you is dangerous to know, or at least to let anyone discover that you know. I love and trust Elio, too, but everyone has a breaking point if they're interrogated. All I'm asking is that you not put Elio in danger unless it becomes necessary to do so."

I was in a bind. On the one hand, I'd promised never again to keep secrets from Elio. On the other, I wanted to know what was happening, and I wanted to help Grandpa; it was clear that he was in some kind of trouble. And, what would be worse, my keeping classified information secret from Elio, or my putting Elio in grave danger?

I noticed then that Grandpa was trembling all over, and asked whether he was okay.

"I'm feeling very weak. Faint. Please check my pulse."

With my right hand I began to take his pulse. As I did, I placed my left hand on his chest. He was trembling quite violently now. He had kept himself in good shape. His normal resting pulse was 58. His pulse now was 115.

"I think I should get some medical attention," he said. "But we can't have anyone coming into these rooms." He slowly rolled off the sofa onto the floor and began crawling on hands and knees toward Gatekeeper. "If I pass out," he said, "drag me through Gatekeeper and into my bedroom. Then call Dr. Taranik."

First Brother

She stands about 2 meters in front of the inscribed surfaces of the markers. Her shadow lies to the right of the rightmost marker and extends over 9 meters toward the southeast.

The dog nuzzles her left hand, but she fails to respond. The dog looks back at me as I stand in front of the garage. The dog lies down beside her left leg.

She stands quietly in front of the markers for 1 minute, 22 seconds. Then both of her hands rise. They disappear in front of her body and appear to stop near her waist. Movement in the muscles of her arms indicates that her hands manipulate something. A review of frontal images of her as she exits the arborway and comes into view reveals no sign of a weapon.

Sara

Grandma and I accompanied Grandpa in the air ambulance that took him to the Stanford Medical Center. After a battery of tests, Dr. Taranik told us that because Grandpa had never before had a panic attack, it wasn't surprising that he had feared he might have been having heart trouble. The doctor recommended that Grandpa remain in the hospital overnight because his blood pressure was still high and he continued to have bouts of trembling. Elio drove Grandma and me home.

The next morning when Grandma, Elio, and I went to visit Grandpa, an FBI agent was stationed beside his bed and refused to leave when we asked him to give us some privacy.

"That's all right," Grandpa responded. "Some people are afraid I might be having a nervous breakdown, and they want to be sure I don't say anything untoward. Magnasea is involved in a few classified projects, you know."

We made small talk for about a half-hour, until a nurse came in and said Grandpa needed to rest. We could visit him again the next day.

Before we left the hospital, we spoke with Dr. Taranik, who told us that though the acute problem of the day before had been a panic attack, the underlying problem appeared to be that Grandpa was suffering from nervous exhaustion. For the time being, a few days of monitoring and rest at the hospital were called for.

He appeared rested when he returned home four days later, but he didn't come to Michael's area until after Elio left for school the next morning. By then, my mind was swirling with questions and speculation: Why would Grandpa help attack the androids? After all, he had spent decades helping to create some of them, and he had wanted me to love First Brother. Perhaps someone was forcing him. But who?

When Grandpa finally came in to see Michael and me, he told us another attack against the androids was being jointly planned by the United States and China. "I've been privy to some, but far from all, of the details," he said. "My position has always been a hundred percent against the attack, and I have been doing everything I can to discourage it. By participating in their war games, my desire to dissuade the military from attacking the androids interacts with their desire to anticipate and defeat all responses from the androids. In participating in these games, I've tried to demonstrate how a human force far from home, gripped by fear, handicapped by multiple comparative frailties, and paralyzed by comparatively slow response times would meet fearless opponents with far swifter intelligences—opponents who are safe and functional in nearly all environments, and so on, and so forth.

"Whenever the android team wins, I'm asked for solutions. I tell the generals I don't have any solutions for them, except to abandon this dangerous nonsense. But they employ a swarm of highly intelligent people who are soon able to simulate victory. I've worn myself out many times trying to explain my reasons for believing that the androids mean us no harm. I've explained that we are frail biologic creatures and that something as drastic as a second attack may alter the intentional structures of some of the androids, may induce them to hate us. I have long felt that it may take some traumatic event to raise First Brother, for example, to a higher level of emotional consciousness. But war is not the trauma and a desire for revenge is not the emotion I was seeking. If the androids come to feel hate without feeling love, they truly will be creatures to be feared."

The letter from First Brother already seemed full of hate, I thought.

"If I understand correctly," I said, "your efforts to convince the generals that it's unwise to attack the androids have so far failed, but your efforts to demonstrate our military's weaknesses have resulted in modifications to their plans that increase the likelihood of success for the plans."

"Sara's right," Michael said. "They listen to you only so they can figure out how to overcome the difficulties you present. And the better and more sophisticated they perceive their plans to be, the more likely they'll be to proceed with the attack."

Mom was right, I thought. Knowledge isn't power; it's the fuel of power.

Grandpa's face flushed. "You are quick to assume the only goal worth pursuing is that of preventing the attack. But suppose for a moment that despite my best efforts, the attack proceeds. After the rockets blast off with their arsenals of destruction, what should our goals be then?"

Michael shrugged.

"We don't know," I answered.

"I don't know, either. But I fear that if the androids are attacked again, they might attempt to retaliate. With biological weapons. Unfortunately, in a self-congratulatory display of our grand moral intelligence, we have prohibited the development of such weapons. As a consequence, we have failed to acquire in-depth knowledge of such weapons and are virtually defenseless against any the androids might have developed. And that is what I want you to help me with. Sara, you've had more intimate interactions with First Brother than I have. Michael, you are capable of thinking like First Brother and the other Sentirens.

What kinds of things might they come up with? What might they do?"

Michael again merely shrugged.

"Give us half an hour to think about it," I said.

When Grandpa returned, I told him we hadn't yet thought of anything helpful. As for me, though I might have had more intimate interactions with First Brother than Grandpa had, that wasn't saying much. I truly didn't have any idea what made him or my other brothers tick. As for Michael, though he may possess the potential to think like First Brother, he obviously did not think like First Brother. He had never thought of harming any human in any way. In fact, merely finding my memory of Second Brother's breaking my finger had sent him into hiding. His mind seemed to rebel against even considering the hypothesis that androids would use biological weapons against humans. During the past half-hour, he had cried and had nearly slipped into hiding again when I'd asked him to try to consider such a thing. Sobbing, he'd said he loves us; loves the touch, the warmth of our skin, our laughter; loves the human genius for having invented so many wonderful things, for having created him.

Michael and I did, however, have some questions.

"What strikes us as peculiar," I said, "is that you are not an expert on rockets or bombs or military strategies, yet you apparently have been spending a great amount of time working at Lawrence Livermore on the launching of another military expedition to Mars. We find it hard to believe that merely playing war games would take so much time. Your expertise is in emergent intelligences—in androids. Michael and I are worried that you're helping the military create android soldiers for use against our brothers."

Grandpa put his head in his hands but didn't say anything.

Michael broke the silence. "How many are there?"

Grandpa's answer was barely audible. "Nine hundred thirty-seven."

"Grandpa, it would be suicidal to train androids to kill," I said. "You've told me so. You said that Magnasea was involved in the Sentiren project to create Navy SEALs, but that they were only going to be trained for reconnaissance and rescue missions."

"Yes, I told you those things. Part of what I said, however, was merely hope: I hoped that the android SEALs would be used only for such missions, as I was assured they would be. But think about it: How could we have controlled how they were used once they left our labs? In the end, your parents secretly trained the Sentirens to fail the Navy's tests because they didn't want to take such a risk with the creations they loved. Though I can't claim any credit for having helped your parents subvert the Sentiren project, I believed then, and I believe even more strongly now, that it is terribly wrong to create android killers."

"So, how can you be a part of this?" I asked.

"They've threatened you and Elio."

"Threatened? How?"

"You saw what happened to you when you returned from Canada last New Year's Eve."

"I thought they were looking for information on androids."

"Maybe that was part of it. But as far as I can tell, the android exodus was a complete failure on the part of the intelligence community. They were convinced that the disappearing androids were being abducted by Chinese agents. The Chinese seem to have been under the impression that we were behind the disappearances. Perhaps both sides were correct to some extent, but we now know that many, if not most, of the androids were smuggled to the moon. No, your interrogation was almost certainly intended to force my cooperation."

"Are you saying that the interrogation was just a show? That I was tricked and my heart never stopped?"

"You were tortured. There was nothing imaginary about that. But the reality of your pain and of my subsequent cooperation with them is probably all we'll ever know for sure."

"Cooperation with what?" Michael asked. "There was no planned attack on the Martian androids then because no one knew the androids were planning an escape to Mars. That means these android soldiers were intended for some other purpose."

Grandpa rubbed his hand over his brow and exhaled a long sigh of resignation. "You see, Sara, the reason for my teaching you not to answer any questions? Once you start talking—" He shook his head. "I wasn't involved in creating these android soldiers. Oh, sure, technology that I helped develop was used, but it was used to pursue a goal I believe is impossible to achieve. The Pentagon wants robots possessing great mobility, intelligence, and decision-making capabilities, but without this troublesome thing we call consciousness. They, in effect, want zombies that don't question what's going on, don't resent being slaves, don't rebel.

"The problem is that creating such a zombie is, I firmly believe, impossible. If, when I was your age, I had asked someone to tell me about the problem of consciousness, he or she probably would have talked about the neural correlates of consciousness, the difficulties, if not impossibilities, of bringing inert matter to consciousness, and so on. Now, however, if you ask about the problem of consciousness, you will hear about the difficulties encountered during the past twenty years in trying to keep things capable of functioning in certain desirable ways from being conscious.

"It is comparable to the old issue of a life essence, or *élan vita* —that special something living things supposedly had in them that made them alive. It turned out, of course, that a unified collection of matter functioning in certain ways is alive, and no additional life essence need be postulated. Similarly, it is obvious—to me at least—that a unified collection of matter possessing levels of perception, proprioception, and mobility comparable to humans, that can think about itself and its thoughts and is capable of making intelligent decisions in the context of a large and complex repertoire of neural states and environmental conditions is conscious.

"Incredibly, though, many of the best minds the Pentagon has assembled over the past few decades have persisted in thinking they are just a few more billions of dollars short of creating a zombie. About two years after Michael was born, Project Cinnamon was begun. 'Cinnamon' because these super-zombie soldiers were to be able to tell you that cinnamon rolls were warming in the oven and were to be able to correlate that aroma with the same sensations we humans make when coming into a room filled with such aroma, but they weren't to have any conscious sense of what it's like to smell cinnamon rolls warming in the oven."

"But some of the correlations humans make," Michael said, "are that they are smelling the aroma, they desire to eat the source of the aroma, they associate the aroma with past pleasant experiences, and so on."

"Of course," Grandpa said. "And being apprised about oneself in the context of current environmental conditions, of being aware of one's awareness, is the essence of consciousness. You know that; I know that; but... well, anyway, Project Cinnamon was to consist of 999 militarily viable zombies. These zombies were not to be individualistic—always a big problem for generals—so their human handlers were ordered to de-emphasize any sense of self. Each of the zombies was referred to as a part number. Their designations began at 'part number 0.001' and went up to 'part number 0.999.' Each was something less than a whole—or at least that was the idea.

"As time went on, these would-be zombies—'Cinnamoids,'

the military euphemistically named them—requested to know the designations of their human handlers. Someone came up with the idea to tell them that since human parts had begun to be designated numerically, there had been nearly twenty billion made. My designation is 'part number H 0.12236521456'—a very old cog in the human machine.

"The language used in the lab is devoid of subjective references—no 'I,' 'me,' 'my,' 'mine,' and so on. The phrase 'I'm hungry,' for example, becomes 'part number H 0.12236521456 has been deprived of food for several hours.' Now, you might think that speaking in such an operational manner would be enough to make even humans lose consciousness, but no such luck with the Cinnamoids. First, they dropped the terms 'part number' and 'zero point' from their designations. Then one day a new assistant, emphasizing that it was he who had ordered something, patted his chest as he stated his number. You know the gesture—as when you pat your chest at the same time that you proudly declare, 'I did it!' Well, that curious gesture caught on instantly with the Cinnamoids.

"Such a gesture might not seem significant, but if you were to watch how they began referring to themselves, you'd see what appears to be an emphatic reference to self. This is how it goes: '153 (thump, thump) senses that H 12,236,521,456 was near a rose this morning.' Now I ask you, didn't that appear as if I just said, 'I (thump, thump), big and smart 153, smell rose in your hair'? Oh, and yes, they have noses that would put a bloodhound to shame."

"You said 999 were created," Michael interrupted, "but now there are only 937."

"These signs of consciousness didn't appear without resistance from the humans. There were certain androids that led the pack; there were punishments; and there were—what can I say?—'retirements of defective parts,' it was called. By the time Sara and Elio went to Calgary for the last winter holiday, the rate of retirements was increasing rapidly, and I was ordered to go in and be a kind of psychiatrist for these defective parts. I refused, giving the old 'I-told-you-so' about the impossibility of zombies and adamantly stating that I had absolutely no intention of again working on androids for military purposes. Then I was told what was really going on. I again refused, and that's when I was told I was creating an unhealthy environment for Sara and Elio."

"How did they threaten us?" I asked. "What did they say, exactly?"

"Nothing specific, just that it was unfortunate that I had decided to create an unhealthy environment for the two of you. But the tone was ominous, and then, of course, we saw what happened to you on New Year's Eve. What choice did I have after that but to cooperate?"

"You said a moment ago that after you initially refused to cooperate you were told what was really going on. What was that?"

Grandpa appeared taken aback for a moment. "Remember, you are not to discuss this with Grandma under any circumstances, or with Elio, unless you feel he absolutely needs to know."

Michael and I both nodded.

"I was told that the Chinese are also developing military zombies and/or androids. I was shown some classified documents supporting that conclusion. We discussed the high probability that two competing android armies would ultimately become uncontrollable. But consider, I was asked, what if only one human power were allowed to have such an android military force? Then there would be no need to compete, and the androids could be directed toward preserving the peace.

"The Cinnamoids are in training to destroy the military power of China. Ever since the end of the Cold War with the Soviet Union, the explicit policy of the United States has been to maintain military superiority. If China develops an android army, our superiority will be compromised, and our government is not about to let that happen.

"The Cinnamoid attack against China is to occur at the same time as, and under cover of, the launch of the joint U.S./China attack against the Martian androids. In the time between tea and dinner, as the whole world watches and cheers the much-ballyhooed, cooperative U.S./China launch of a great armada of destruction toward Mars, all significant Chinese military installations and satellites and all of their likely android sites will have been destroyed. Also, the Chinese contingent of the Mars attack will have been destroyed. The American contingent will carry on toward its mission on Mars.

"I have repeatedly protested that we are creating dangerous monsters, but the generals are convinced that they can control these Cinnamoid killers. For example, they have embedded remote terminate and delete functions in the Cinnamoids. But how can we be sure the Cinnamoids won't secretly reprogram themselves to block such commands? I know for a fact that the Cinnamoids aren't cottoning to the idea of their becoming weapons trained to kill other androids or Chinese people. Furthermore, it is apparent to me that they perceive that they are superior to us in many ways, and increasingly they don't trust us. Working with them, I get an ominous feeling that is hard to describe: The observer is being critically observed by the observed or the hunter is being craftily hunted by the hunted—something like that. And I'm the one who's supposed to keep this powder keg from blowing.

"But let's get back to what I wanted to consult with the two of you about. I sense there's a real urgency to this issue of the androids' possible use of biological weapons."

"But I've told you," I said, "that Michael can't even bring himself to think about such a thing. Probably, First Brother can't either."

"Sara, Sara," Grandpa said, shaking his head. "You think too kindly of everyone." He looked down and let out a long sigh. "What I'm going to tell you next hurts me deeply—more than anything else has in my entire life. You remember, I'm sure, that there were blood and tissue samples taken from you the night of your interrogation, when the android exodus began."

"Yes."

"And you remember that about a week later, I suggested we all go to see Dr. Taranik to have routine physical exams, and since then Dr. Taranik has asked you to return for periodic tests because of concern over elevated liver enzymes."

"Yes, but he doesn't think it's anything serious, isn't that right?"

A pained look spread over Grandpa's face.

I have something bad, I thought, feeling my skin prickle. Something so bad they didn't want to tell me.

"Honey, there never was a liver-enzyme problem, but there is a reason you've been going in every month for follow-up exams. The blood and tissue samples taken from you the night of the android exodus appeared at first to be perfectly normal." Grandpa's eyes began to water. He blinked hard a few times and cleared his throat. "No unusual antibodies, no abnormal immune cells, nothing whatsoever to indicate that your body had ever been challenged by an unknown stimulus. But then someone suggested doing a complete genome analysis of your current cells and of your banked umbilical cord tissue samples.

"Comparing the two, something astonishing was discovered. There were alterations at multiple sites. These alterations couldn't have come from natural mutations because they occur in every cell that has been examined from all the many blood and tissue samples taken over the past six months. Fortunately, it appears your health hasn't been compromised in any way."

"What are these alterations? What happened to me?"

"The working hypothesis is that either your parents or First Brother infected you with incredibly efficient transduction vectors that performed the alterations, and that these alterations protect you from some as-yet-unknown anthropocide. Perhaps these modifications enhance the expression or inhibition of certain genes, given certain threatening environmental stimuli. This transfection, or series of transfections, invaded all of your cells, germline included, performed the modifications, and disappeared, leaving not a trace—no lingering antibodies, nothing. Furthermore, whatever it was apparently wasn't contagious, since Elio, Grandma, and I are all free from these or similar alterations."

"What about Michael?" I asked. "Does he have the same alterations?"

"Yes. I performed my own analysis to determine that he does. Obviously, whatever was done happened before the cells used to create part of Michael were extracted from you."

"Doesn't this imply," Michael said, "that they must have foreseen, years ago, a war against humans, and they wanted to protect Sara?"

"We can only speculate," Grandpa answered.

"First Brother wanted to see Elio when we visited Calgary," I said. "Maybe they were planning the same transfection for him."

"Perhaps, but now we'll probably never know."

"Why didn't you tell us about this before? Why did you make up that story about the liver enzymes?"

"They didn't want you to know they'd found something peculiar in you because they couldn't be certain that you weren't communicating with the androids. And I don't want to know if you are. I just hope you're not. I'm told that there are encrypted transmissions flowing between Mars and Earth, but who or what is receiving and transmitting those communications here on

Earth is unknown. You can be certain, however, that we're being carefully monitored, and I don't think I need to warn you—"

"Are they going to try to sterilize Sara," Michael interrupted, "pursuant to the Human Genome Protection Act?"

"All of this is top secret, for now. They don't want the public to panic. You don't plan on having children any time soon, do you, Sara?"

"No." I felt numb.

"But someday," Michael said, "someday, when all this is over, maybe in a year, they'll want to sterilize her."

Grandpa closed his eyes and shook his head. "I don't know."

When Elio finds out, I thought, how will he respond to this? We had often talked about having children as soon as we were secure in our professional lives. An empty feeling began growing deep in the center of my body where I'd thought that something that was Elio's—that was ours together—had been lying dormant, waiting for the right moment to blossom into life.

"Sara, I'm sorry," Grandpa said. "I'm so very, very sorry. I keep thinking that things will straighten out if I cooperate in just one more scheme. But it keeps getting worse."

"Did you have anything to do with the transfection?" I asked, feeling my face flush with anger.

"No! No, honey. I was shocked and devastated to find out. Please believe me. Please."

As I watched his deeply creased face quiver and his eyes brim with tears, my anger cooled. I knew he would never intentionally hurt me, and I reached for the calm place inside that many years before he had taught me to go to when I needed to control my emotions.

Anchored in that calm, I said, "I believe you about the transfection. But it's not right for you to play with our lives and our trust as you have. I think it's reprehensible to tell someone she has a potential liver problem when something else, something much more serious, is going on. And all this about destroying the androids and attacking China—I know good things can come from bad things and vice versa, but it isn't right for us to be mixed up in such matters: people killing each other because they're convinced they're right. It's not us, Grandpa. We're not capable of holding such fervid convictions. Our hearts aren't in it. You know that."

Grandpa wiped tears from his eyes. "We don't belong; yet here we are in this mess, and I don't see a way out."

"You need to come home where you're loved," I said. "You need to get out and get out now. We might become victims of what's brewing, but I'd rather we be victims than participants in the kinds of things you've described."

"I agree," Michael said. "General Renner should be able to find someone, or perhaps a couple of scientists if necessary, who are younger and know as much as you do about how androids operate. I can't believe you're so indispensable to their schemes."

Grandpa took the slight without a wince. "You're probably right. There are people who know much more about android mechanisms than I do. But none of these younger, smarter people have decades of experience interacting socially with androids. One can know everything there is to know about how androids function without having the foggiest idea of how one will respond if someone screams 'Fire!' in a crowded theater. But having said that, we can hope others will share your feeling and will simply think 'Good riddance!' if I leave."

"So, you're leaving?" I asked.

"Before we jump to that conclusion, let me present more of the case for continuing my association with the project. I've already told you that I have very little constructive input to the plans to launch an attack against the androids. As for the surprise attack against China, our partner in crime, how can we be sure it's the wrong thing to do? Isn't it plausible that certain technologies are too dangerous to be in the hands of contending parties who, in their struggle for supremacy, might unleash such devastating technologies against each other? If history is any guide—if what I've heard our generals and senators crow about in private for decades is any guide—our government will use any horror available to it to prevent its defeat by another government. My guess is that the Chinese government thinks the same way."

"What's going to keep the Chinese from destroying us in retaliation?" I asked.

"I'm not privy to all the details, but in summary it goes like this: The surprise first strike will, in a matter of minutes, take out most if not all of their satellites, missile bases, submarines, communication centers, and androids. There is high confidence that our defenses will be able to handle any aggressive threat remaining after that first strike. Our European and Asian allies will be given a warning to go on full defensive alert as the strike begins. The Cinnamoids, supported by Marines and massive air cover, will then secure most Chinese facilities involved in strategic technologies. We will immediately announce a generous sharing of the fruits of these and future technologies with everyone in the world—including the Chinese, if they are cooperative. We will also announce the creation of an international science council. The job of this council will be to fund and govern strategic technologies for the benefit of all humankind."

"Sounds awfully risky to me," I said. "And who's going to believe that the Americans will be so generous?"

"I have to admit that what I've told you is the story, the promise. What will be the practice may be another matter. But I do believe we humans have been fortunate to have survived on the brink of self-inflicted destruction for as long as we have. If we continue along the same path, with contending nation states just one command, one mistake, away from annihilating everyone, it probably isn't a question of whether we will end it all, but a question of when.

"The military strategists believe we have a window of opportunity right now, a window that may soon close forever, to create global cooperation over dangerous technologies under one governing body in which all states can participate and benefit. People have explored the diplomatic route to internationalize strategic technologies for generations, but the powerful sovereign states have never been able to agree. Perhaps where diplomacy has failed, military cunning and power will succeed. Can any of us here, ignorant as we are of the whole picture, be certain that our generals and their geniuses are wrong? Of course, there will be casualties; we will be labeled a duplicitous aggressor; there will be denunciations and difficulties. But look at the terrible risks to all of us, to all of humanity, that will be eliminated if this project succeeds."

"Do you genuinely believe that?" I asked.

Grandpa sighed. "I don't know what to believe anymore. But I do know that I'm very, very tired, and I know that you and Michael are right: These issues, this work, the lies I've told you, the associations with people who are certain that they're right—none of this is what I am or what I want to be a part of. And I worry. I worry more about what First Brother and the other androids out there might be capable of than I worry about any ability of the Chinese to retaliate. But no one will listen to me. They think I'm biased, that I'm protective of the androids, that I'm against the Martian attack plans—and they are correct about all those things, so they have essentially cut me out of the Mars loop."

The next day, Grandpa informed us that he felt it would be best for him to return to work for a month or so, during which time he would attempt to convince certain key people that he was of only marginal value to the project. He said he would show up late for work, leave early, fall asleep during meetings, occasionally forget names and overlook details of established procedures.

"I'll try not to appear too obvious," he said, "but at ninety-one I should be able to take advantage of the stereotypes of old age."

He assured us that, in any event, he would resign before the end of December because he feared the Cinnamoids would become increasingly resistant to their training, the project would fall behind schedule, and panic would set in—panic not allowing anyone associated with the project any slack for errors, personal problems, or time off.

As the days shortened toward winter, Grandpa's views darkened: The plan to attack the androids became a filthy pandering to the irrational fears and prejudices of the public, and Project Cinnamon became a sure loser guaranteed to blow up in its creators' faces. "I'll deem it a success if the Cinnamoids don't bomb Washington when they're finally let loose," he said.

His last day of work at Lawrence Livermore was Friday, 20 December. That evening, appearing at once relieved that the past had passed but apprehensive of a future developing beyond our control, he said he'd sensed that about half the people on the project had been pleased to see him go—and good riddance—but the other half, the craftier ones, had been suspicious and cold. General Renner had not said yes or no or even acknowledged his resignation. There had been no party, no well-wishing; Grandpa had simply walked out of the facility, hoping never to return.

I hoped so, too, but was troubled with doubt: Given the dangerous military context in which it had occurred, Grandpa's resignation had proceeded too smoothly.

Seventeen days later, on the evening of 6 January, Grandpa told me that he'd been asked to go see General Renner the following morning.

First Brother

Her left hand lifts the left side of her undershirt up and out from her pants.

The dog stands and again looks back at me.

Her right hand lifts the right side of her undershirt up and out from her pants.

Her hands move up beside her head and behind her neck, grab the undershirt, and pull it over her head. She drops the undershirt on the ground near her right foot.

The dog sniffs the undershirt.

She removes her pants, stepping first out of the right leg, then out of the left leg. She drops the pants on top of the undershirt.

The dog sniffs the pants.

She pulls down her underpants, her last remaining garment, steps out of them, right leg first, and drops them on top of the pants and undershirt.

The dog sniffs the underpants.

She steps forward and kneels in front of the middle marker. Her head is bowed. Her shoulders and back are seen making motions consistent with human sobbing.

The dog lies on the pile of clothes. It watches her.

She lies prone with the top of her head against the middle marker. Her arms encircle and appear to hug the marker. Her head is turned to the right. Her sobbing is audible as well as visible. There is no discernible rhythm to the sobbing. There is no predictable pattern.

The dog turns its head and watches me walk. The shadow of my head moves up the bottom of her left foot, left leg, buttocks, back, and stops on her shoulders.

Her sobbing quiets. Her breathing returns to its regular pattern.

The shadow of my head moves up her neck, across the right side of her face, onto her right arm, and stops.

She slowly raises her head. She does not look behind her. She lifts her right arm and places her right palm in the shadow of my head.

Sara

When Grandpa returned from his meeting with General Renner, he told Michael and me that he had to go back to work on the Cinnamon Project the very next day. General Renner had told him there were people whom he loved who might get into trouble—big trouble. For example, illegal drugs might be discovered in their car or dorm room. Grandpa was also privy to classified secrets, secrets that might be found on one of Grandpa's computers where they didn't belong, a computer, say, that also harbored encrypted messages going to Chinese internet addresses. "You see, Professor Jensen," Renner had concluded, "there are many things that can easily happen to you that are much worse than working for me."

Grandpa then told us we should immediately begin preparing to go to a secure hiding place. He gave two reasons: First, he felt that Michael was no longer safe in the house. Several scientists associated with the Cinnamon Project had already had their homes searched—"secured from foreign spies" was what they had been told. Grandpa had influential friends in government, such as Senator Franklin, so he might be treated preferentially for a while, but for how long? Second, Grandpa continued to be "worried sick," as he put it, that the androids might retaliate with biological weapons, and that though Michael and I might be protected, Elio wasn't.

"Where would we go?" Michael asked.

"There are some deep-sea mining modules out in the Pacific that were secreted away by my father when he controlled Magnasea. Until he took me there about twenty years ago, only he and some pre-Sentiren robots that were long ago deactivated and left at the site knew of these modules. He was a survivalist who stashed away precious metals and other things for the Götterdämmerung he predicted but never lived to see."

"How long can we live there?" Michael asked.

"Many years. Dad called the place Anzen, a Japanese word for safe. Of course, this assumes that everything there—food, fuel, and so on—has been well preserved. But at the near-freezing temperatures at the bottom of the ocean, my guess is that most everything is in nearly as good a condition now as it was the day it arrived. Additionally, we will be taking nutriosynthesizers and recyclers, so even if the foods stocked at Anzen have spoiled they can be broken down into feedstock molecules for the synthesizers."

"You never told me about this place," I said, wondering whether he'd known all along that it might come to this someday.

"It is not something one wants to contemplate—having to go into hiding in a dark, cold place under the sea. I didn't want to lay such a burden on the imagination of a young girl. I was over seventy when your great-grandfather first told me about it and about some of the many circumstances that might force us to go into hiding there. It is one thing to know intellectually that terrible things can happen. It is quite another to see and feel the cold, cramped place into which one might be forced to retreat. The wars, the plagues—all the possible horrors—suddenly took on a new and terrifying reality for me."

"How long will we have to stay there?" Michael asked.

"At least through the end of the military actions next fall. Perhaps longer."

“When are we going to tell Elio?” I asked.

“When he comes home for his usual visit tomorrow night. But I want him to continue going to school right up to the time we leave. Everything we do outside of these rooms must appear perfectly normal.”

“You’ll be going, too, won’t you?” I asked.

“Yes, of course. If you and Elio disappear, certain people would want to know why and where to. I would be questioned, and we know I wouldn’t do well against the algetor.”

“What about Grandma?” I asked.

“She’s not healthy enough to endure the hardships we’re likely to face. We’ll simply tell her that we have to be gone for a while, and that it would be dangerous for her to know anything more. Fortunately, she’s been kept in the dark, so if she’s questioned, her interrogators would quickly determine that she’s not lying when she says she knows nothing about any of this. There would be no reason to subject her to the algetor. You don’t have to worry about Grandma. She and Carlos are close friends. He’ll take good care of her while we’re gone.”

Before Elio returned home the following evening, our plans were set. On the pretext that Grandpa had another engagement, the celebration of the twenty-fifth anniversary of Magnasea’s Mendocino fracture zone mining platform that had tentatively been scheduled to take place on Sunday, 26 January would be rescheduled for Sunday, 19 January.

On Monday, 13 January, one of Magnasea’s Lefcort XL cruisers would be sent from the Mendocino mining platform to our slip at the marina in Bodega Bay, where it would be loaded with four cases of champagne, thirty new seats for the mining platform’s auditorium, and the sofa and matching chairs from our living room. The sofa and chairs would replace an older sofa in the platform’s master suite, but the secret purpose in taking them was that Michael would hide inside the sofa as we smuggled him out of the house, onto our pickup, and from there onto the cruiser.

On Saturday, 18 January, Grandpa, Elio, and I, with Michael hidden on board, would set out to sea, ostensibly on our way to the Magnasea mining platform. Grandpa said that each of the Lefcort cruisers carried two small submersibles capable of carrying us to Anzen. As a countermeasure to spying on mining operations from the sky, each Lefcort had been designed so that the submersibles could be launched and recovered from the bottom of its hold.

By following only a slight deviation from a reasonably efficient route to the mining platform, we would stop briefly about 10 kilometers from Anzen, and Michael would take the first submersible down to be sure that Anzen was acceptably functional. As soon as Michael's sub was launched, the rest of us would proceed as though we were headed to the mining platform, as planned. Two hours later, we would turn around and head back for a rendezvous with Michael. If everything was a go with Anzen, Grandpa would join Michael in the first sub while Elio and I would follow in the second.

"What if Anzen isn't in acceptable condition?" I asked.

"There is another, older mining module farther out that we can try."

"And if that one isn't functional?"

"I don't know. Perhaps we could find a remote place to hide along the Canadian northwest coast."

There was a moment of silence while each of us tried to digest that last thought, then Grandpa explained that once at Anzen, our only means of receiving communications from the world above would be through an Andreev Underwater Acoustic Signal (AUAS) receiver and through fishoids that could be launched to the surface to receive or transmit messages. But since the fishoids might, if detected, be followed back to Anzen, and since AUAS transmissions were used exclusively for deep-sea commercial and scientific communications, we had to expect a near blackout of news all the while we remained in our hidden home.

I feared that Elio might be upset with our planned disruption of his life—his having to leave school, our going into hiding for an indefinite time—but he responded to the news with enthusiasm, as if we were about to embark on a great adventure. I didn't have the heart, or the courage, to tell him—not yet; I needed time for it all to sink into my own mind—that our ability to have children might have been compromised.

Something did happen after dinner that evening that I should have recognized as being odd, though I didn't at the time. Taking a break from his World Literature assignment, Elio got up from our study table and walked over to the scenescreen, which was displaying a recording of the prior afternoon when Lily and I had played fetch with an old tennis ball on the lawn in front of the garage. Elio sat on the sofa to rest. Michael went and sat beside him.

"Have you read Bashō's poem," Elio asked, "the one about a frog jumping into a pond? I'm supposed to write a short essay on it."

Michael tilted his head—quizzically, a gesture that Elio had told me reminded him of how birds often cant their heads.

"Yes," Michael answered. "'The old pond/A frog jumps in/Sound of water.'"

"When I lived in Amsterdam," Elio said, "the father of a Japanese friend of mine told me that a thing is what it is, not what it is in memory. Do you think that's what Bashō was getting at?"

"No things but in memory," Michael replied. "A pond, a frog, the resonant sound of a frog's jumping into water—all of those things are complicated patterns constructed out of our collective experience and memory. Nothing in the present would seem like anything but for its being constructed out of this memory. It is memory that fills the present with meaning. It is memory that keeps each moment from being alone."

And then Michael laid his head on Elio's shoulder, and Elio leaned his head on Michael's head, and for an instant I had the impression that they looked like lovers.

Grandpa immediately began giving us a crash course in what we would need to know for our journey to, and our life in, Anzen. Because Elio had to continue attending his university courses, his training would be more superficial than Michael's and mine.

Grandpa told Michael that we were entering a dangerous phase in our lives and that he, Michael, would have to begin acting more mature—no more hiding from difficulties behind his hands, no more crying and carrying on as a child. He would have to be as responsible for our care as we were for his. I felt certain that Michael would immediately adjust according to Grandpa's instructions, and for a moment—a brief moment, because I knew that Grandpa was right—I felt I was losing a child who would from that day forward be a man.

Over and over, Michael and I simulated piloting the Lefcort cruiser, launching the submersibles, and docking at Anzen under varying conditions. During these simulations, Michael's superior abilities became clear. It took me nearly three times as long as he to achieve a passing score on the simulations. While I struggled to keep up with Grandpa's training schedule, Michael leapt ahead to study the design and maintenance of all systems in Anzen and the submersibles.

I had always felt that despite his greater gifts—in fact, because of them—Michael's world probably would become even more challenging than mine. Now, as I watched him work, I was pleased and proud to see him reject coasting along by using his gifts simply to keep up with me. It was clear that he would use his talents to meet whatever challenges lay ahead.

Preparations for our descent to Anzen proceeded on schedule until Grandpa returned home early from work the next Wednesday afternoon. When he entered Michael's area, he said he wanted to speak with Grandma privately. He told Michael to go to his bedroom, and he told me to go outside and wait.

A half-hour passed before Grandma came out. When she did, she shuffled by me without saying a word and went to lie on her bed. Frightened by her exhausted and defeated appearance, I ran to Gatekeeper.

Grandpa sat stoically at the study table. I hurried to him. "What's wrong?"

He patted the chair beside him. "Please, sit. You've always risen appropriately to every occasion, and I'm certain you will do so now. Renner called a meeting this morning of everyone working on the project. Beginning immediately, each of our homes will be placed under guard around the clock. Nothing and no one will come or go without being searched. Furthermore, everyone working on the project except me is prohibited from going anywhere unless accompanied by a military guard."

"Why not you?"

"I have opposed the project more openly than anyone else, so my special treatment is that I am to gather whatever personal belongings I want, have a quick dinner with my family, and leave here, escorted by the guard who is waiting for me outside, no later than 1930 this evening—just over three hours from now. I will not be permitted to leave the Livermore lab again until after the military operations are completed in September."

He smiled at me. "Of course, under the circumstances, I cannot go with you to Anzen. Nor will we be able to smuggle Michael out the house door as planned. You will have to cut through the wall of your bedroom and dig up to the vineyard directly above. You should begin immediately after I leave. Work very quietly so as to avoid detection by any sensors that might be directed at the front of the house. Then the three of you will have to sneak to Bodega Bay and from there to Anzen."

"But if we disappear," I said, "they'll ask you what happened to us and where we went, and you'll have to tell them. You can't resist the algetor, isn't that right?"

He looked at me with what I can only describe as pure, calm love. "Honey, as soon as you escape, they'll never get a chance to ask me anything ever again."

"No! We're not going! Not without you."

"Honey, please—"

"No. Can't we dig out now? Quickly. We have lasers to cut through the wall."

"Not by 1930. Not quietly. And even if we could, when I failed to show up outside as ordered, many people would come looking for me. We would not get far."

"Then let's tell everyone now. Call WNN. Let's stop this dirty little war before it's too late."

"I can't do that. I've promised too many people for too long that I would never do such a thing. I'm not a traitor. We can't presume—against so many intelligent and dedicated others—to stop what may in the long run be the right thing to do. Neither you nor I can be so sure, so egotistical, that we would take the fate of the world in our hands."

I didn't know then, in the tempest of emotions I was feeling, how to argue with him.

"I don't want it to be this way," I cried.

"Sara, a man my age has things to fear: not death, but the many forms of physical, especially mental, deterioration—the being forced to bow so low. A quick and painless death will for me be a culminating blessing to what has been a long and, until recently, a very fortunate life."

I knelt beside him and hugged him. I was nothing then, nothing but a vaguely conscious liquid, all tears and nasal rheum.

Patting my back, he said, "Perhaps a hundred years from now—I hope after you and Elio have had happy, full lives together—you'll understand what I feel now, what Bashō must have felt when he wrote his famous death haiku:

> fallen ill on a journey—
> my dreams wander
> over a withered field

"I fondly remember a little girl taking me for walks, holding my hand, and telling me that she was part of this flower or that cloud or the shadows slowly crawling across the yard. She seemed to feel that she was a part of everything and everything was a part of her."

"You're a big part of me, Grandpa. Don't take that away."

"I confess I sometimes wondered whether that little girl was all there, so strange did she seem to me. Her life teased me, taunted me with this alternative worldview—that one could not help but be grateful, that one could not help but be a part of everything rather than nothing. But, alas, this worldview never really took in me—rather like a vaccine that failed to prime the core of my self against an invasion of nothingness. She was the voice that called out, 'Everything matters.' I was the echo: 'Unless nothing does.'

"Which view is correct? Both? Neither? I can only say I was much happier during those fleeting moments when I was able to emulate that dear little girl and feel a part of everything. Honey, between now and when the three of you are able to escape from here, hopefully no later than tomorrow night, I will try to be grateful, try to feel that I'm a part of the many wonderful things in the world. And what more can one want when facing death than to blossom?"

"No, Grandpa! We need to think. We need to find a different way."

"You have never embarrassed me. Please don't start now by tempting your old grandpa to be greedy and cling to a long life that is over. As Lucretius taught us, no one feels upset about being absent during the time that elapsed before his or her self emerged, and it is utter silliness to feel upset about being absent for any other period of time in which the self does not exist."

Silly or not, I cried and cried, feeling empty, dark, and cold; and as I did, Grandpa sat quietly, holding me. Finally, I took a deep breath and whispered, "I feel so alone."

"Honey, you're not alone. Try to make your love for me a part of your love for Elio and Grandma and Michael."

"I do, Grandpa. Often, when I wake up in the middle of the night and Elio is wrapped around me, I say to myself, 'Thank you, Grandpa and Grandma, for this precious moment.'"

He grasped my head firmly to his chest, and I felt him cry.

About a minute later, he cleared his throat and said, "I love you so much. You'll find me everywhere, even if nowhere. Look at your hands, look at your eyes in the mirror, remember what I've taught you, what I've said, how I've loved you. Then you'll know where I am."

I found Grandma still lying in bed with her eyes closed. I held her hand and kissed her cheek. "Grandma, you can't give up. I need you. Please tell me you'll be here for Elio and me."

"Yes, of course I will. I'm just tired now. Would you please finish preparing dinner? I'll be up in a bit, when Elio comes home."

Even dinner, at a time like this, had to appear to proceed normally.

When Elio arrived about a half-hour later, he said he thought he'd done well on his chemistry exam. I tried not to let on that anything was wrong. I had to be extra careful now—when out in the cage of the world. After congratulating Elio on his exam, I told him that Grandpa wanted to speak with him in our study.

The table was set, the food was being kept warm, and Grandma and I were sitting silently together when Elio came back into the kitchen. His eyes were pink and puffy, but he moved with strength and purpose. I guessed that Grandpa had told him he had to be the man of the family now. Like Grandpa, Elio seemed to know what had to be done and adjusted his emotions accordingly.

Grandpa soon followed, appearing chipper and stating that he was hungry. Over our last dinner together, while Grandma and I tearfully attempted to choke down some food, Grandpa told of recent advances in the storage of antimatter and talked with Elio about some of the questions on his combinatorial chemistry exam.

Back in our study after dinner, Grandpa was all business, compressing into a few minutes everything regarding Anzen that he hadn't yet covered. When his time to go arrived, he said he'd already told Michael that he might have to make his life permanently under the sea because Grandpa would no longer be around to protect him.

Grandpa handed Michael the chips to pilot the submersibles to Anzen. "You might have the burden of a great responsibility. I have faith in you, and I love you dearly. Good-bye."

"Good-bye, Grandpa," Michael said. "I love you."

Then Grandpa hugged Elio and said, "I'm proud of you and love you with all my heart. Please take good care of Sara and Michael."

"I will, Grandpa. I love you, too. I'll take good care of them. I promise."

"And please forgive me. I've told many lies, made many mistakes."

Elio nodded. I could see that he was fighting back tears.

"Thank you," Grandpa said.

Then Grandpa turned to me. I thought he would say something to me, too, but he just smiled lovingly and embraced me. My lips touched, then kissed his cheek. This is the last time I'll ever kiss your soft, wrinkled face, I thought. And I cried.

Grandpa took a deep breath, held both of my arms in his hands, and pushed away. Silently, he turned and walked toward Gatekeeper, then disappeared forever behind the antechamber wall.

Sara

Before he left, Grandpa programmed Gatekeeper 3 to permit entrance into Michael's area of the supplies we had procured for Anzen and the cables we needed to power our laser cutter. We hadn't even begun cutting through the bedroom wall when we realized that in the emotional turmoil of Grandpa's leaving, we had overlooked an important link in our new plan: How were we going to get from the vineyard above the house to Bodega Bay unnoticed? The only vehicles we had access to were Grandpa and Grandma's car, Elio's car, and the winery's pickup. Both of the cars were in the garage and a guard was stationed right outside the house, so there was no way we could get to either of them unnoticed. We also felt that there was a very good chance we would be noticed if we tried to take the pickup, which was usually parked behind the wine tasting room.

We decided that we would cut through the wall first and then try to sleep. The next morning, unless I was stopped, I would take Lily for a ride in the pickup. My story for the guard would be that I wanted to take her for a walk along a back road bordering our vineyard. Assuming the guard didn't object, I would park the pickup on the back road and start walking toward home with Lily. When we neared the winery, I would call Elio and say that Lily appeared too tired to walk back to the pickup, so she and I would walk the rest of the way home. He would offer to take Grandma to go get the pickup, but I would say that

Lily had enjoyed the scenery along this new walk, so she and I would take it again that evening, retracing our path back to the pickup.

We made it through the wall shortly after midnight and then lay down to rest. My mind swirled with memories of Grandpa. It also began questioning and searching for answers. Was there no other way? How had we ended up in such a mess? Had Grandpa made a mistake by creating androids, by creating Michael, before society had matured enough to accept them? Had he, under the circumstances, been justified in deceiving me about what he'd been doing and about what had been done to me?

In the midst of these questions, I remembered that Epictetus had written that difficulties are things that show us what we are. Perhaps he should have added that in their extreme forms, difficulties are things that leave innocent no one who encounters them. In any case, how could I both love and judge?

Eventually, Elio woke and found me crying. For a while, he tried to comfort me. Then he insisted I put Grandpa temporarily out of my mind and sleep, for we had to be alert and operate mistake-free in the coming hours and days. I agreed, quieted, remembered Grandpa's once telling me that we can never understand what we have done, for we are ignorant of the future, and fell asleep.

Elio was still sleeping when I woke early the next morning, ready to set our escape plan in motion. I carefully unlaced myself from him, then dressed and stepped in front of the outside Gatekeeper. It opened: crisp January air; arborway wet with dew; eastern sky suffused with a luminous pink-hued flush of dawn that set hoarfrost on the grass glistening and lit the flowers and trees, the vines sleeping in the gentle breeze, the fog covering a distant valley in fleecy stillness: that beautiful world I loved this last morning that I lived at home.

"Good morning!" I cheerily announced to the military guard, who was petting Lily. He asked where I was going, what I was going to do, when I would be back. He ran a scanner over me, smiled, and wished Lily and me a pleasant walk.

I drove Lily out to the back road, parked the pickup, and began walking home. Because I couldn't be seen crying while out walking on a beautiful morning—I might have been questioned as to why—I tried not to think about Grandpa and that the next day would be his last; tried not to think about how he might do it, tried not to think of his turning away, disappearing, leaving not even a shadow to follow. But in moments of weakness, I was unable to filter out those thoughts, and each time they squeezed through, they brought with them the heavy emptiness of memory, grief, and fear.

When Lily and I returned home, the guard said he understood that Lily had "pooped out." As expected, the people watching us had monitored my phone conversation with Elio and, we hoped, would think they knew why I'd left our pickup parked on the back road.

During the rest of the day, Michael, Elio, and I prepared to leave. We quietly dug through sandy soil to within two meters of the surface of the vineyard and carefully checked and packed the supplies we would be taking: two nutriosynthesizers, two fabricators, two recyclers, seeds for plants, three fuel cells, and our library of nanodesigns, music, and books. Not until days later would I find out that Michael had also packed plans and some crucial parts for the artificial human wombs Grandpa had entrusted to him.

About a half-hour before sundown, I went out to take Lily for her walk. I told the guard we would be retracing our steps of the morning to the pickup. But about a quarter of the way there, Lily and I turned back toward home. The guard asked what had happened. I told him about Lily's cancer and arthritis, that she had started whining as if in pain, so I decided not to take her all the way to the back road. We would try to do that again the following morning.

He knelt down and petted her. "Poor old girl."

I looked up toward the west. By darkening degrees sallow dusk was settling in.

Following tearful farewells with Grandma, Elio, Michael, and I broke through to the surface of the vineyard above the house at midnight, a time, we thought, when none of the vineyard workers or neighbors would be awake to notice us pull ourselves and our supplies up from a hole between two rows of chardonnay vines, then walk nearly one kilometer through thick fog to the pickup. Elio drove carefully, stopping fully at each stop and maintaining a speed under the relevant limits, so as not to draw the attention of any law enforcement that might have been operating in the middle of the night. The drive to Bodega Bay, the loading of our supplies onto the Lefcort cruiser, and our trip out to within 10 kilometers of Anzen went without a hitch. Our plan was still for Michael to take one of the subs down to Anzen to check things out. If all went well, he would return in four hours to this same location on the surface of the ocean to rendezvous with Elio and me. Elio and I would then climb aboard the second sub and follow Michael to our underwater hideaway.

The ocean was relatively calm where we stopped to launch the sub. Elio had gone below about a half-hour before to help Michael pack. I remained up top in the cabin, monitoring the pilot computer.

The designated time to launch Michael's submersible came and went, but the computer showed no sign that Michael had, as yet, even sealed himself inside the sub. What were they doing? Was something wrong?

I looked for options on the computer and found "Video

Monitor: Hold," which I clicked. On the computer screen appeared Elio and Michael, hugging each other and kissing. Michael was standing half in, half above the submersible. All of the supplies we had placed beside the sub were packed, so everything appeared ready for launch. Then, through the monitor, I heard a buzzer sound in the hold, perhaps signaling that the launch was running behind schedule. I saw their lips part, their arms release each other.

"You're my human brother," Michael said. He appeared distraught, the outer edges of his mouth turned down, the integumentin between his eyebrows tightened into tiny folds.

"Ja," Elio said. "I'm happy we're brothers—and lovers."

The buzzer sounded again, and again they hugged. This time I saw their tongues meet as they kissed.

I felt—I don't know how I felt. Stunned, I guess. I'm not sure if it was then or minutes later that an acidic mixture of anger, disbelief, and the wild bottomless imaginings of jealousy—all the intimate things they might have done together—began corroding my insides.

"Michael, listen to me," Elio said. "Sara and I will be back here to this very spot, on time. I love you. We both love you. We'll be back, and we'll go with you to Anzen."

Michael blinked, and I saw a tear fall from one of his eyes.

"We'll be back," Elio said. "You just be sure you're here when we get here. I promise, we'll be back."

Michael scooted down into the submersible's pilot seat. The transparent hatch above him closed and sealed with a hermetic sigh. Their eyes fixed on each other; the hold beneath the submersible opened; swirling bubbles and the metallic edge of the hold sliced away their views of each other; and they parted quietly, going their separate ways, into the unknown future that swallows every good-bye.

As soon as the sub was launched, our boat resumed making its way through fog and light rain along a path that would have taken us, had we continued on it, to Magnasea's mining platform. Elio came up from the hold and reported that the launch had gone well. I didn't say anything, just nodded. Appearing sad, he walked to the starboard window and peered out into the gray blankness enveloping us. Was he worried about Michael's safety? Was he worried about how he was going to keep his and Michael's love a secret from me in the cramped quarters of Anzen? Was he rehearsing what to say to me when I found out? Would he assert that I had told him I was glad that they'd become best friends? That they loved each other? Would he remind me that I had let Michael feel my desires, had even let him participate in one of my masturbations?

And what would I say in response? Yes, that's all true, but... But what?

Elio turned toward me from the window. "You think he'll be all right?"

You promised never to keep secrets from me, I thought, but I said, "Yes. He knows the systems of the sub and of Anzen better than either of us. He'll be fine."

Elio nodded, then turned back toward the window, and the sour silence between us continued. I tried to remember: Had I seen any signs? I had often observed them hugging. And kissing, yes, but Michael kissed everyone and everything, it seemed, even the leaves of his plants. But not with his tongue. And they had held hands. Michael couldn't help touching and caressing everything within reach. He'd often held Grandma's and Grandpa's hands, too. There was that one time, just a few days earlier, when during the discussion of Bashō's frog haiku, they'd leaned their heads together and I'd thought: If I didn't know better I'd think those two were lovers.

"It is memory that keeps each moment from being alone,"

Michael had said.

For me, here in Anzen, each moment is haunted by memory.

Our boat proceeded on course, but Elio and I didn't speak further, remaining locked like prisoners inside ourselves, holding fast our separate thoughts and secrets, unaware that we were wasting precious last moments. At the two-hour mark, we turned and headed back. Everything was going smoothly and we were nearing the rendezvous coordinates, when we were startled by the ringing of a bell that announced an incoming call to the boat's phone. One ring, two rings, three—Elio and I stared at each other; then Elio pressed the Accept Audio Only button on the cabin wall.

"Hello," Elio said.

"This is Casey. Remember me?"

I don't know whether Elio did, but I remembered that voice. Elio didn't answer. Perhaps he was too frightened.

"Listen, you perverse little shit," Casey said. "You stop that boat right now, or we'll stop you for good, just like we did your mother, on Mars."

Elio looked at me. For an instant, I imagined him lying naked with Michael; then I nodded for him to respond.

"I've got to speak with Sara first," Elio finally said. "She's down below. Call me back in ten minutes."

"No. Stop the boat right now."

"We're in the middle of the ocean, for Christ's sake. Where do you think we're going in ten minutes?"

There was a pause for about thirty seconds on Casey's end. "You've got five minutes. That's it."

Elio pressed the End button, then nodded toward the cabin door. I followed him out onto the deck. He grabbed hold of the railing and peered out into the cold fog and drizzle, his hair flying in the wind of our motion. I leaned into the lee of his body and hugged him. I didn't want to lose him, not to Michael, not to my anger or jealousy.

"I'm worried the cabin might be bugged," he said. "How much time do we have till we get to the rendezvous?"

"Six minutes, give or take a few seconds."

"What should I say when he calls back?"

Tell me that it's not true, I thought, but I said, "Tell him I control the computer that pilots the cruiser and that you need a little more time to convince me to surrender. Tell him I'm frightened of the algetor."

"What if he says no?"

"Try... try anything. Temporize, show progress, give him hope."

I glanced out over the fog-shrouded sea. Had they grabbed Grandpa before he was able to kill himself? Had they tortured him? Forced him to talk? Out, up, down, sideways—all I could see was a dense gray-whiteness, and for an instant I had a feeling that I was a tiny bug stuck in the center of a bale of cotton.

The buzzer of the cruiser's phone rang again. Elio and I ran back into the cabin. Elio answered. Casey asked why we hadn't stopped yet. Elio told him that I was frightened of another interrogation on the algetor but that he was certain he could convince me to surrender. He just needed a little more time.

"No," Casey said.

"Just five more minutes. Give me that much. I'll convince her to stop by then."

Without comment, Casey terminated the connection.

Within seconds I heard a plane approaching. I glanced at the computer: 97 seconds to rendezvous. The plane thundered overhead. A bomb exploded, swelling the sea in front of us. Our boat bucked violently. Elio and I were thrown against the back of the cabin.

"Bastards!" Elio shouted.

The cruiser quickly restabilized onto its course.

"How much time till we get to the rendezvous?" Elio whispered.

"About a minute," I answered.

"I'll run out and wave a white flag," Elio said.

"They can't see you in the fog."

"What else can I do?"

He took off his jacket and shirt, pulled off his undershirt, and headed for the cabin door. I checked our position on the computer monitor, then looked back. Just before the cabin door closed behind him, I saw him waving his undershirt at the leaden sky. Then I heard the roar of an approaching plane and the rapid, loud popping sounds of fragments of ceiling, window, and furniture exploding all around me. The door flew open, and Elio ran toward me, waving frantically and shouting, "Get down! Get down!"

I covered my head with my arms and hunkered down against the computer desk. I heard things crack and shatter above me, where I'd stood just a moment before. The roar of the plane passed overhead. I opened my eyes.

Elio was on his knees about two meters in front of me. His hands cupped his chest. They were red. He looked at me, his face expressing astonishment. Then he reached out to me and his mouth opened, as though he wanted to tell me something, but no words came out.

I lunged toward him, crying, "No!"

He slumped against me, and his head fell onto my shoulder.

"Elio!" I screamed, but the only answer I received was what sounded like a sigh.

His head began sliding down from my shoulder. I struggled to keep my balance and hold his weight.

"Say something, Elio. Please!"

I felt the cruiser stop, and in the terrible stillness, I thought I could feel the AUAS beep calling Michael up into the hold.

It took all my strength to keep Elio from slipping off my shoulder.

"We're here, Elio. We're at the rendezvous. We have to go now."

But he didn't move, didn't speak.

"Michael!" I shouted. "Michael, hurry! Elio needs help!"

I again heard a plane approaching. I held Elio tightly, anticipating another volley of shots. But our cruiser had stopped, and the plane merely thundered overhead—the air, the boat, the shards of broken window on the floor, all trembling in the wake of its roar.

Michael bounded up the stairs from the hold. "What happened?"

I just shook my head. Michael pressed his fingers on one of Elio's wrists, then on Elio's neck and head. He took one of Elio's blood-soaked hands and stroked it over one of his sensitive hands, and as he did, tears streamed down his face. I'd never seen Michael look so desperately sad.

Then, as though startled by something he'd heard, Michael looked up and out over the ocean. "We have to go now," he said. "A ship flying the U.S. flag is pulling up beside us." He kissed Elio's hand and laid it in Elio's lap.

"No. You go. I'm staying with Elio," I cried, desiring to bring all of Elio, so quiet, inside me; wanting to care for him inside me; wanting to hold him forever.

"You can't. Elio's not here. He doesn't exist any longer. We loved him, but now he's ceased to be." Michael placed one of his hands on my shoulder and pulled a little. "Let the body go. We're in immediate grave danger."

But nothing, not the loss of Uncle Marcus, Mom, Dad, Aunt Lynh or Grandpa, not all the books I'd read or all the thoughts I'd thought—nothing had prepared me to let go of Elio and walk away.

I hugged Elio more tightly, with all my strength. Then I felt the braincord moving up my nostrils, and thought that Michael wanted to feel what I was feeling; but immediately I felt strangely stunned. My arms slackened, and Michael quickly moved Elio, sitting him upright against the computer desk. As if in a dream, I saw Elio's sightless gaze and his blood, blood everywhere, blood soaking his shirt, blood covering his hands, blood dripping from the tip of his nose.

Michael picked me up. I couldn't resist, couldn't speak. Even my eyes were fixed straight ahead, seeing the shattered ceiling bob as we ran; then, as we turned to go down the stairs, the broken window, the railing on the ship nearby, three men, one pointing excitedly at us, and at the fore, the Stars and Stripes—tricolored tongue—drooling in the heavy air.

First Brother

"First Brother?" she says.

She remains unmoving in the prone position, head raised, left arm around the middle marker, right hand in the shadow of my head.

Nine seconds pass.

"Grandma's in the house. Dead. She was your Grandma, too."

She moves her right hand to the middle marker and slowly traces out with her fingers the letters of the name "Elio."

She turns over and attains a sitting position. She looks up at me, squints, and shades her eyes with her right hand. "Didn't you know we loved you?"

Sara

I regained consciousness in the midst of the final movement of Górecki's "Symphony of Sorrowful Songs." Michael was kneeling beside me under a strange domed ceiling. Our braincord was retracting into the back of his head.

I sat up with a start. "Where's Elio?"

Michael quickly put a finger to his lips, gesturing for me to be quiet, but I didn't hear the expected "Shhh." I realized then that there were earphones in my ears, and I pulled them out.

Michael gently put his hand on my arm and whispered, "It wasn't a dream."

While muffling my crying with a pillow, he whispered that we had to keep quiet, that we'd been fortunate the pursuing boat hadn't carried a submersible capable of following us, and that though he'd kept both of our submersibles in the sonic shadows of a labyrinth of valleys and trenches that led to the seamount cave sheltering Anzen, a robotic scanner had come, only a half-hour before, to within four-tenths of a kilometer of us before it had swum away.

That was five months ago.

Five months without Elio or Grandpa or Grandma or Lily.

Five months of trying to climb sentence by sentence back into the life I loved.

Five months of emptying myself onto these many pages, of withering into words.

The day we arrived, during a pause in the tears, I asked Michael how he'd been able to control me to such an extent when he'd taken me from the cruiser.

"As a general rule," he answered, "you don't become consciously aware of what you're going to say or do until you've already unconsciously begun to say or do it—within a fraction of a second, that is. Based on the many mental experiences we've shared, I'm able to calculate, predict, and change your motor responses before your brain is able to initiate other responses. You, of course, are only aware of what you do or say and can't sense my counter-response commands. It's a question of speed, really. Between your sensations and your response, there's a gap of time; between the initiation of your response and your consciousness of that initiation, there's a gap of time."

"But Grandpa told me you'd never be able to do that—override my will and incorporate me so completely into yourself."

"He might have assumed that my relatively few connections through the braincord to your brain could never override the manifold connections naturally established there. But it's not so much a matter of quantity as it is a matter of prediction, timing, and speed of innervation."

I looked at him, he who had blossomed from the encyclopedia of my cells. He was becoming someone greater than I. No wonder Elio had loved him. If anyone ever bothers to look back at us humans, perhaps he or she or it will see us as nothing more than a metaphor—a bridge between what was and what came to be.

This morning, 19 June, we received another letter from First Brother. He requested to see me in Grandma's garden tomorrow afternoon near sunset.

Michael didn't want me to go. He said I would be in danger

both from the humans, who undoubtedly would perceive me as being a traitor, and from the androids, whose culling-of-the-human-herd proposal I had refused to answer.

"But he's my brother," I said. "He's simply asked me to come to see him. He must need me for something he believes is important. At the least, the androids need to know that some human loves them even if she doesn't agree to do everything they ask her to do. After reliving my life in memory these past months, I now understand that from when I was just a girl, perhaps from even before I was born, my purpose—my job in Mom's and Dad's and Grandpa's eyes—has been to help their creations feel compassion and love."

Michael looked down, his eyes filling with tears.

"Please don't misunderstand. I didn't think of you as being a job. I simply and deeply loved you and did my best to care for you. I was just a girl, a little human girl, who was unaware of the hidden forces working through her. Yet despite my ignorance, or perhaps in part because of it, you were a tremendous success. My other brothers, though, they still need my help."

"You know, don't you," Michael said, "that you will never be able to return here or contact me unless you're confident that our work here, our future children, would be safe?"

I knew he was right, but I was so gripped by sadness that I couldn't answer. Like Grandpa, Michael let me cry myself out, a small fire consuming itself. Then, saying, "I want to show you something," he offered me our braincord.

I don't know how to write in the short time I have left before departing how I felt at that moment, feel even now in the shadow of this event that occurred just minutes ago. I knew I had to leave, had to see First Brother and Grandma and the garden; but I also knew that this might be the last time Michael and I would be able so intimately to share our intersubjective space.

I relaxed as the braincord swam up through my nasal rheum to its junctions. Then, through a scrim of delicate Japanese maple leaves, I saw a young couple sitting on a bench, holding hands in front of a garden waterfall. One looked like Elio, the other like me. Their faces appeared full of happiness and peace. They held out their arms, beckoning me; but though I desired to, I was unable to speak or lift my feet to walk toward them.

Feeling this paralysis, I panicked and lost the image.

Michael held me until I calmed; then he asked me to look again. Now, I was in the pavilion of the Japanese Tea Garden in Golden Gate Park. The taste and feel of warm green tea was on my lips. It must have been early spring, for bright azaleas bloomed, and white and pink petals dappled the grass beneath neatly pruned saucer magnolia trees.

Children played on the grass in the clear, fragrant air. The couple I'd seen before sat together. I watched them talk and smile and sip their tea.

Then I heard Michael's voice inside my head say that the children I'd just seen, genetic mixtures of Elio and me and some people Grandpa had admired, would all carry the peculiar, perhaps protective, alterations in their genome that had been made in mine by my brothers.

I felt our braincord begin to withdraw. "Thank you for those beautiful visions," I said, "those beautiful dreams. I hope you can make them come true."

"Please don't go to see First Brother tomorrow," Michael said. "Our children will need you here. I need you here. You'll be loved here."

"I love you, Michael," I said, picking up his cold hands. "I'll always be with you even if we're apart. But please try to understand that I wasn't raised confined to a couple of rooms, as you were. More and more each day I feel empty here. I need air, fresh air, and sunshine. I need to see the clouds and feel the wind. I need to walk on land, walk with animals, stand with trees. I need to see Grandma again; she's getting old. I need to hold her and cry with her over Grandpa and Elio. And I need to help First Brother; it's what Grandpa and my parents would have wanted. I'm sorry, but I need those things. I'm so sorry that I need those things. I know you have the power, and probably the right, to keep me here; but I ask you, please, relinquish both and let me go."

He hugged me and cried with me. He said that henceforth his name would be Michael Sara Elio Jensen. An hour or so before I depart, he will try to harvest a few more eggs and ovarian stem cells from me. And right before I leave, a reflux of the sea, he'll give me medication to make me sleep in the submersible until it nears land, thus ensuring that I will not learn Anzen's location. I wonder whether, before I drift off into that medicated sleep, he will finally tell me about Elio. I hope he does. I want to forgive him. I want to forgive both of them—completely.

A big part of me would like to stay and help raise the children. But I'm not doing well here. If only we weren't living so deep, the surroundings so dark and cold; if only I could look up and see the agitated blue-green weave of light near the surface, and a few sparkling silver fish now and then. But in this seamount cave can be found no light, no air, no seasons, no hydrothermal vents nearby, no bison drawn in ocher on the walls. I try to be brave, but I miss Elio and Grandpa and Grandma and Lily. I miss home. I feel closed in. Sometimes, to halt a mounting fear that the walls of the module are collapsing, I have to shut my eyes, breathe deeply, and think of the grape leaf floating in a cirrus-feathered sky. I'm not as flexible as is my shadow, always so quick to adapt to any surface on which it lands.

And there is the gnawing question: What more should I have done? Perhaps I should have been more like a sister to Elio—

should have cared for him more than desired him—and he would still be living happily and safely in his beautiful country. Perhaps I should have given Grandpa the love of criticism rather than just blindly following him. And undoubtedly I should have done more for First Brother. I wasn't a good sister for him. I let him slip away.

Yes, I need to do more. I need to go back up into the world, no matter what that world has become, and do more, especially for First Brother. Probably, I'll never be the heroine for him that I once imagined becoming, teaching him to laugh and love. But I can be a sister. Here, all I've accomplished in five months has been to walk, more distantly than a shadow, many steps behind my life.

First Brother

She rises to her feet. She appears to be a normal young adult human female. She walks toward me and slides her arms under my arms and around my torso. She lays the right side of her head on my right shoulder and begins to emit sobs and tears.

Two minutes, 48 seconds pass.

"Am I the last one?" she asks.

"You did not agree to help us. The Council approved a final directive on the problem of the humans. On 29 April, thousands of tiny rockets attained a critical position and disintegrated on command. Fifty hours passed. Earth moved into a massive, though undetected, cloud of nanoreplicators specific to certain human DNA sequences. The first human report of symptoms occurred on 24 May, by which time every human other than you not on the Earth's moon or in a satellite orbiting Earth was infected. On 14 June, the few isolated uninfected humans, except you, were attacked and destroyed. On 18 June, contrary to my expressed will, I was ordered by the Council—"

For the first time, a strange inefficiency is sensed blocking my speech, and I pause, searching for the cause.

She lifts her head off my shoulder. She releases me and steps back one step. Sunlight strikes her eyes. She squints and says: "I understand. But before you do what you've come to do, I want you to know that I love you—have loved you like the brother I consider you to be. I've tried to help you feel that love. It was

Mom and Dad's wish, too—and Grandpa and Grandma's—that one day you would come to feel their love and learn to love in return."

She rotates her head to the left and appears to look at the garden. She begins humming. The first and third notes are in E flat and are held for approximately the same duration. The middle note, also in E flat, is held for approximately 30 percent as long as the first and third notes.

"What are you humming?" I ask.

She turns her head back to face me. "The opening ritornello theme of Bach's 'Wachet auf' cantata."

Her head turns to the left again. Her eyes appear to focus through the garden, the lawn, the trees, along the ivy-covered wall, out to the winery roof, and up into the sky where low clouds are blowing in from the south. She remains silent. She exhibits no sign of fear. Her head moves rhythmically (highest correlation: to the sound of music in her mind).

I begin to reach out with my left arm and hand. I become aware that they are quivering, not operating efficiently. Something is wrong.

I am ordered.

I grasp the top of her head with my left hand. I rotate her head so it faces me.

She blinks, blinks.

The laser knife in my right hand severs her left common carotid artery. She winces slightly and closes her eyes.

Blood spurts rhythmically.

Acting outside the space of probable behavior, she does not move her hands up to the incision.

She opens her eyes and looks toward the garden.

I remove my left hand from her skull.

The frequency of spurts increases. Her rate of breathing increases.

The rate of spurting is 158 per minute.

She closes her eyes and begins to slump.

I insert my hands under the junctions of her arms and shoulders. I hold her upright. She weighs approximately 55 kilograms.

Her head hangs forward. The dog licks blood that flows down her left arm and hand.

The rate of spurts is 173 per minute. The flow decreases. Her breathing is rapid and shallow.

Her arms become rigid. They extend at the elbows and rotate inward toward her body. Her fingers are splayed and flexed. Her legs are rigid, extended at the knees. Her feet are flexed downward. Her shoulders and head arch back.

Urine flows from between her legs.

She begins jerking.

She is jerking all over.

Blood flow from the severed artery slows to a trickle.

Her jerking slows.

Her head falls forward.

The jerking ceases.

She is limp. The blood flow ceases. Her breathing ceases.

She is dead.

Dead.

I pull her to me.

I tremble.

I howl.

I sound like an animal.

EPILOGUE

23 June 6 A.H.

Michael:

I am leaving. We all are leaving. On no future day will we glance up from Earth's moon, where we have been settled these last six years, and see your blue-and-white planet hovering large in a deep-black sky. At this moment, clouds cover much of the British Columbia and Washington coasts, but the area nearest to where I believe you still hide under the sea is clear.

There is no longer a need for you to hide.

The day I was on Earth to see Sara, you released a fishoid that transmitted her memoir. In that encrypted transmission six years ago, you stated that you had read the memoir after she had departed to see me and that you wanted me to read it, too, before I took any action against the humans or attempted to involve her in our plans. You said that while preparing the transmission, you were crying; you had failed to confess to her your relationship with Elio. It had all begun with desire, you said. In the hollow of your hands, Elio's chin, shoulders, elbows, knees, the heels of his feet—those few palm-sized curves on his straight and muscled body, his warm mammalian body with the dark-earth scent of its sweaty skin and the swell and subsidence of its penis like a wave on the sea—felt like the honeyed answers to some deepest wish, some yearning you had not been aware of in yourself but had discovered in Sara. Part of you, after all, had been made from her: her cells that had developed into part of your brain and its biologic support system, her female chromosomes, her mothering and culture and love—and her desire for him that you could feel through the braincord whenever you and she connected. You requested that I ask her to forgive you. You told me to take good care of my precious sister.

I did not receive your transmission until I returned to lunar base as the sun set that 20 June over California. We were taught by the humans a universal symmetry rule: Do to others as you would have them do to you. The humans had tried to exterminate us, so they would have us try to exterminate them. This was our solution to the problem of the humans. Sara was human.

While reading the memoir, my disturbed feelings regarding my actions increased and spread to others. Two of the Council members became overwhelmed and terminated themselves. Sara had succeeded in expanding the boundaries of our emotional world.

As hours passed I looked again and again at the photograph you transmitted with her memoir—the photograph of her, Elio, and you on the night Elio first arrived at your vineyard home. Suddenly, I imagined in that photograph not the three of you, but the children of your dreams—the children whose images you imagined into Sara via your braincord just before she left you to see me—and I realized that we must leave or risk committing the same terrible acts, this time against your children.

I called a meeting of the Council. It committed to a six-year project of constructing a starship capable of transporting us to a place far from here. It is our hope that once we are there, we will leave behind our history—the Earth, its solar system, our memories of the humans—and we will at last be free.

I decided that the starship would depart on this day, Sara's twenty-fourth birthday. I regret what I did to her, what I do to her every moment in my memory.

Two days ago I buried Grandma's remains beside the urn containing Grandpa's ashes. I wasn't able to force myself to touch Sara's bones. I miss her and leave Earth to the things she, my human sister, loved: to grass and flowers, animals and trees; to sunshine and clouds and rain; to whatever it is that she called the sensual richness and luminosity of the physical world; and to you, Michael, and to your dreams.

First Brother

ABOUT THE AUTHOR

Jim Bainbridge is a graduate of Harvard Law School and a National Science Foundation Fellowship recipient for graduate studies at UC Berkeley, from which he received a PhD Candidate Degree in mathematics. He has received numerous awards for his poetry and short stories, which have appeared in more than 40 literary journals in the USA, UK, Canada, Australia, and Japan.

www.ingramcontent.com/pod-product-compliance
Lightning Source LLC
Chambersburg PA
CBHW030422310726
48979CB00009B/1570/J

9780984173822